# The
# Indentured

——————Mike Prater

WESTBOW
PRESS®
A DIVISION OF THOMAS NELSON
& ZONDERVAN

Scripture taken from the King James Version of the Bible.

WestBow Press books may be ordered through booksellers or by contacting:

WestBow Press
A Division of Thomas Nelson & Zondervan
1663 Liberty Drive
Bloomington, IN 47403
www.westbowpress.com
1 (866) 928-1240

ISBN: 978-1-9736-3122-4 (sc)
ISBN: 978-1-9736-3121-7 (hc)
ISBN: 978-1-9736-3123-1 (e)

Library of Congress Control Number: 2018907096

Print information available on the last page.

WestBow Press rev. date: 07/17/2018

# Contents

# Decisions

John loved Chastity. That is how our story begins and the premise of what I am about to tell you. This is a love story of sorts, but one unlike any you have ever heard before. You see, John and Chastity lived in a time of great change. By today's standards, we would say they lived in poverty, though people were too busy surviving to think about it. The great majority were of lower-class society. It was a time when one generally did not rise above his standard of living. It was expected that a man would live and die shackled to the existence in which he was born. Fathers trained their sons to follow in their trades, for that was just the way things were. However, on rare occasions, one might escape to a new life and beginning, but that usually meant following their king into war, and that always had an uncertain outcome.

Our setting is the early years of the seventeenth century. England still struggled to embrace Protestant beliefs. There were many, even among the monarchy, who wanted England to remain Roman Catholic. There were others who felt that the Church of England had not gone far enough with its beliefs and wanted religious freedom. Added to this mix was the hope for new opportunities in a place called America.

John was born to James and Martha. It was a time when surnames were given by account of one's living or occupation. James had milk cows. Over time, he, like his family before him, became known as James Dairyman. Others like James might have been known by the name Farmer. Either way, the name was indicative of a man of a simple, humble existence who scratched out a living on the land.

John's father was fortunate to own several of the finest White Park cattle in Sussex. With the milk he got from his cows, he was able to supply the villagers with a variety of dairy products. His labors did not make James rich. They only provided a living, if one can call it such, because the people of the town were poor and needy. Most of the time in exchange for his milk James received an item of trade. The people had little to no money with which to buy. Instead, they would give something they had grown, owned, or made in exchange. A small sack of grain, salt, a bottle of wine, leather goods, wool, and such were given in trade. What coin was paid James usually came from the Earl of Sussex.

These coins were guarded with his life from those who would steal from him and his family. Guarding coin was of necessity. People did not spend money recklessly. The reason was obvious. Sooner or later, the tax man would come. The tax man preferred money, but in the absence of it, he would take from the villagers whatever it took to satisfy the tax. James could ill afford to lose what little he had, especially his cattle. His life and the lives of his family depended on them. The few possessions they had were essentially worthless in the eyes of the tax collector, but a matter of life for James and his family.

James was a compassionate, benevolent soul. He took extra measures to help care for the people to whom he sold his milk. Each morning James would harness his horse to the cart loaded with the daily supply. James knew the people and where they wanted their dairy items delivered. At one home, he would go up to the well and lift out a bucket where he would find a clay jug. James would fill the jug with milk and leave a bit of cheese. Oftentimes the buyer would leave whatever means of payment in the bucket for James to collect. This routine would continue throughout the day. James would stop at a stream and find a jug immersed in the cold water or in a dugout. At the end of the day, with what little he had left, he would go to the widows or needy and portion out to them what was left. A cup of milk here and bit of cheese there. His kindness was well known. James wanted nothing to go to waste. Nothing ever did.

James and Martha had five children. John was the eldest of two sons. After John, was Candice, followed by Adam, Grace, and Ruth. Five children made up a rather small family for the time. Many families had nine or more children. Even with the smaller family, it was hard to make a living. Neither James nor Martha complained. They loved each other and their children. They felt fortunate to have what they did.

The village was as poor as any in seventeenth-century England. Raw sewage was often dumped into the streets, leaving them muddy, smelly, and unhealthy. For that reason, many people suffered with dysentery. A lingering cough seemed to resonate throughout the village. Those who grew up in such villages rarely aged beyond thirty years. There was a high death rate among newborns, while surviving children often remained thin and sickly. Because James had cattle, he was able to raise his family away from the village. Cattle needed grass, and for that reason, the earl allowed him to live away from the town in the meadowland.

The meadows beyond the village were plush and green. The cool days and seemingly endless supply of rain kept the fields lush, which was very good for livestock. In the green countryside, a child could let his mind wander. Those who were fortunate enough to live in the country were healthier. Perhaps it was the farming lifestyle. Then again, it might have been the cleaner environment that made people hardier. James took little thought of it. He knew that his family and those of the village depended on him being strong and able. This thought pushed him relentlessly.

John had learned how to care for cows and help make the cheese from an early age. While John wasn't as fast as his father in caring for the cattle, he was capable, and every little bit of help was appreciated. John dedicated himself to the hard work and life of a dairyman. Regardless of whether he thought about it, it was expected that John would take over the family business when he got older, but for John, all that was about to change.

When John was about twelve, his father returned from his deliveries with news. It was evening when James returned, and John and Adam were busy caring for the cows. James left his horse hitched to the cart and walked over to the barn. He watched his sons at work. For a moment, he observed them and felt a sense of pride toward his boys. James had taught John to tend to the milking, and when Adam was old enough, John taught him. His sons had become so proficient that usually James would come home to find all was done.

Today was no exception. John had already poured the milk in the large pot used for making cheese. A fire burned beneath it. With a large wooden paddle, John slowly stirred the milk, collecting the curds of cheese being formed by the heat. The curds were then put on a tray and salted before being scooped into bags and molds. Excess liquid was squeezed out. Finally, the containers were set aside in a dry, cool place for curing. A small container of milky curds was always collected for the family. This was served as part of the family's evening meal. When the container was full enough, John told Adam to take it to their mum.

Once Adam left, James approached his eldest son. "Ye do a fine job, lad, and you have taught Adam well."

John was surprised by his father. Up to that point, he had been unaware of his father's presence. "Many thanks, Father. He has learned well the work of a dairyman."

James continued. "Aye, he has indeed, and now me thinks he can do even more."

John gave a little laugh. "Then what would I do?"

James walked over to take a seat on a milking stool and asked John to join him. A moment later, he stated, "That is what I wish to speak with you about. There is a blacksmith in town who is in need of an apprentice. Today while making my deliveries, I met with him and told him of you. He has no son or kin to pass on the trade to. After some discussion, he said he is willing to teach you the trade. You are at the age to be an apprentice. I made an agreement with him. So if you be willing, come Monday, you shall be in the charge of the blacksmith and become his student."

The news was a shock to John. James saw the perplexity his son's face. He asked, "What be bothering you? Are you not pleased?"

John lowered his eyes and then answered, "Am I not doing a good job here, Father?"

James answered, "Aye. Ye are. But, John, being a dairyman offers little. While there will always be a need for farmers, there isn't much of a future for you. On the other hand, there is much demand for smiths of all trades." James placed his hand on John's shoulder. "I sought this out for you because I want what's best for you. I have seen real talent in you, and I don't want it to waste away."

John shuffled his feet. "Am I not needed here, Father?"

James tightened the fingers that rested on John's shoulder. "Son, it's time that you become a man. I have confidence in you, and I will always be here for you. I have seen how ye trained Adam. He can handle the work. You now have the opportunity to make a way for yourself in a trade of great demand."

John raised his head. He had a great love and respect for his father. His answer revealed it. "It is a fine thing you have done for me. It will be an honor, Father, and I think I could learn it. I shall do as you say and be taught by the blacksmith. Father, I will make you proud."

James smiled, "I know you will do your best, my son."

That night John lay upon his straw tick bed thinking on the morrow when he would walk with his father to the village. John would begin his apprenticeship for which he knew his life would forever change. The thought of working for someone other than his father saddened him. He could not imagine what life as a blacksmith would be like.

When morning came, James had the children up early. The cattle were already bawling to be milked. For the first time, Adam was escorting them into the barn by himself. Adam was used to John taking the lead. He felt a bit alone and kept hoping John would come help him, but James and John were busy preparing the cart. As soon as it was loaded, they began the journey to the village. The walk to the village seemed more challenging than John remembered. The family had visited the village before. It wasn't the distance that made him afraid as much as it was fear of the unknown and leaving his family behind.

There was a time when coming to the village was an exciting thing. Now the journey was foreboding. The sights and sounds that used to stir excitement only heightened the alarm in him. The village was only a mile or two away. The stench from the filthy streets, which hadn't bother him before, now stuck in his nostrils. John took an immediate dislike to his new surroundings.

The village of Haywards Heath was primarily made up of small dwellings, though early-morning people were busy preparing for the day. John spied a man climbing up onto a thatched roof. Across the street a tanner was working over an animal hide. The sound of a mallet on wood was being made by the local carpenter. The village was alive, and for the first time, John saw exactly what went on in the village. Then off in the distance, he heard the faint ringing sound of a hammer striking metal. Toward the ringing they continued. Before long, the acrid smell of the blacksmith's fire filled the air. A short time later father and son stood just outside the barn of William the blacksmith.

John watched the blacksmith raising his hammer and striking the red-hot metal. With each blow, sparks shot out like lightning.

James disturbed the smith with a shout. "Hello, William. It is I, James Dairyman."

Out from the barn walked a heavyset man whose face was darkened by smoke and metal dust. He called back, "Ah, James, about time you made it. Have ye brought me your son?"

James did not like the greeting but remained careful in his answer. "Aye, William. As agreed." Then pointing to the lad, he introduced the two. "This is my son, John."

William placed a large hand on the boy's shoulder. "Rather a scrawny lad, is he not?"

James hated the disrespect being shown but held his tongue. In defense of his son, he stated, "What he lacks in stature he will most definitely make up in dedication and hard work."

William bent over and looked John squarely in the eye. With a condescending huff, he stated, "I will make a man out of the lad for sure." Then, grabbing both of John's arms and squeezing them, he asked, "Are you afraid of hard work, boy?"

John stood up tall and would not acknowledge the pain the blacksmith was inflicting on him. "Not at all sir. I promise to give you my best."

William snarled, "See to it that you do."

James didn't like the tone of the blacksmith or the way he spoke to John, but the agreement for his son's service and training had already been struck. He turned to leave his son with the blacksmith. Before leaving, he offered his son a final word. "Work hard. Do your best. Prove your worth. If ye do these things, no man can expect more." With that being said, James turned and walked away to make his dairy deliveries.

As soon as James was out of sight, the blacksmith turned to look at John. "It's time you learned a few things, boy. First, what I say goes around here. Do as I say as soon as I say. Second, I believe poor workmanship needs to be treated with the rod. If ye do poorly, I will see to it that you won't do it again. Third, no back talk. Now clean this place and put things where they belong."

John immediately began working about the barn by sweeping and hanging things where he supposed they belonged. Occasionally, the blacksmith would chide him and tell him that this or that didn't belong where John had placed them. Mockingly, he would say things like, "Now look here, boy, does it make sense to put that there? Put it over there."

John would quickly move the item to wherever the smith pointed. John worked hard through the day. By evening time, John was exhausted, but he was not allowed to rest. Once inside the adjoining cottage, John was told to make dinner. John's work did not end until way into the night.

The workday wasn't as we know it today. Workdays existed as long as the sun was up or as long as the master thought it should last. There were no child labor laws. A man could work a child all day and then some. Many children worked all day for their masters or teachers and then ended the day preparing their food. All this was done with a promise to teach a trade. Many children gave up, suffered severely, or even died from the cruelty of their masters. For John, it would be suffering at the hand of an intolerant and fiendish master.

One of John's first jobs was to keep the pit fire going. This meant that he had to chop the wood, stack it, and then feed the pit just the right amount so that the fire remained hot. William seemed to delight in ridiculing whatever John did during this task. Once while John was carrying wood to place on the fire, the blacksmith kicked him in the back and drove him into the ground with his boot. William had been drinking, which always put him in a foul mood. John hustled to get back up, fearing what his master might do next.

With a slurred voice, the drunken smith blamed the boy. "Ye lazy dog, how dare ye waste me wood. Ye nearly let the fire go out and then put too much wood on the pit to try and catch it up. Be more alert, you lazy stiff."

John did not utter a word but took the abuse like a man. From this experience and others like it, John learned to avoid the blacksmith as much as possible. John had never experienced such cruelty. Oh, he had been punished by his father, but it was always out of love. This man did things out of spite and hatred. When John would lie upon his bed at night, he would wipe away tears shed in silence, thinking of his loving, caring father and the kisses of his mother whom he missed dearly. He could tell his father what was happening and would be taken home, but he was driven by his father's charge to him: "You can learn from the smith ... It is

time you become a man ... Work hard. Do your best. Prove your worth."
With these thoughts, how could John tell his father? No. He would learn
from the smith and hoped to make his father proud, taking all that came
his way in silence. He would never tell.

There were benefits to the hard labor. The days turned into months,
and the months into years. Each day, John's body became stronger, and
the work began transforming his youthful body. The chopping of wood,
the forging of iron, and the hammering of hot metal into form began
producing muscle on his arms and back. John's arms began to become like
the iron he molded. John's biceps, chest, and back muscles rippled with
sweat. His legs grew stronger from the heavy lifting. Soon, he could shoe
the most cantankerous beast and lift the heaviest wood and steel. The boy
was transformed as he became a man. His hair was blond, and his eyes
were the richest blue. His image was more of a Norse god than a farm boy.

John did not set out to transform his body but took great strides
to prefect his trade. He paid attention to even the smallest detail. The
blacksmith thought he was wasting his time until others began pointing
things out. John's work was being noticed, and the things he made were
being sought after by the townsfolk. They preferred his work over the
smith's.

All the young maids in the town were taking notice of the ruggedly
handsome young man. The girls were fairly sure John heard the comments
they made about him, but they knew he had eyes for only one maiden. His
heart belonged to Chastity. For that reason, if John heard the comments,
he paid no attention. Chastity had his heart, and he had hers. He wanted
no other.

Somehow, John's character wasn't changed by all the attention. He
despised the way the blacksmith acted. John did not like the way he
treated others, his sloppy work, his poor habits, or his vulgar speech. John
also knew that the smith looked for ways to take advantage of people by
squeezing more money out of them. Oftentimes, he claimed he did work
that he never did. If any dared to argue with him, the smith would use his
brute size to intimidate people and forced them to pay more by making
threats and many times roughing them up.

John looked forward to seeing his father almost daily. About
midmorning John would hear the familiar sound of the creaking wagon

and the rhythmic, dull clank of milk cans and pots. As part of the agreement with the blacksmith, James would bring a daily amount of dairy. James also looked forward to seeing his son and receiving a progress report on his work. Sometimes John would be gone on a delivery, or the smith would tell James that his son was too busy and could not be bothered. James felt a great sadness with these missed opportunities. A deep sorrow filled his heart whenever he drove away without seeing his son.

Come Saturday evening, John would be home with his family. He was greeted by his loving mother, and before long, he would enjoy a hot bath in the barn. The smoky, dirty clothes would be washed immediately afterward in the soapy water of his bath and then hung to dry. A delicious, hot meal was waiting in the house. The whole family would wait till the eldest brother was seated. Before long, everyone wanted to hear stories about the town and country.

John related things that he found humorous. He told how the local thatcher fell from the roof only to be suspended by his harness a few feet from the ground. As John put it, he flayed his arms and legs as though he were being pulled by strings, and all the townsfolk just laughed. Then John imitated the arm and leg movements. Soon, the house would be filled with laughter. They enjoyed the story but loved the way John acted it out more.

John would spend Sunday with his family, but come Monday morning, he would rise early and hurry back before daybreak. He was sure to be back before the blacksmith woke. When he arrived, he would set to his duties. First, he would start a fire in the pit with a knife and flint. Next, he would see to the fire in the cottage. Then, before the smith woke up, John would see to it that bread and cheese was set on the table along with a cup of beer. Finally, he would hurry to straighten the shop before returning to check on his master.

John never knew in what mood he would find the smith. When the smith was drunk, John knew that nothing he did during the day would be satisfactory. Even sober, the man could be most unbearable to live with. John obeyed the smith's every command. He learned not to expect praise from his master and was never disappointed. When praise was given, it usually came from people who showed appreciation. Many times he would hear people pay compliments to the smith for his work. That was enough for him.

Chastity was but a child when she and John first met. From birth, she was a black-haired beauty. Her father, Thomas, held her often and enjoyed her sweet innocence. It was Thomas who named her at birth. When she cried out at night, he would run to her and hold her in his arms. Within a year, her eyes turned an enchanting green. Ireland was the native home of her mother, Ruth. She once stated, "My daughter was blessed with eyes from my homeland." Chastity was beautiful, but more importantly, she had the most wonderful character. With a willing heart, she worked at whatever she was capable of. Her smile would brighten the day. Her presence and song would make sorrows flee.

Thomas was a shepherd. Chastity would accompany him to the pasturelands until she was old enough to take the sheep on her own. The flock Thomas raised were some of the finest in the land. His flock had grown steadily from the two fine lambs he had earned from the earl's father when he was but a boy. Over time, the two young lambs grew. From them, he developed the flock to what he had today. The wool from the sheep was the finest in Sussex. Much of the wool that Thomas got at sheering time was bought by the earl. With the remaining wool, he was able to trade in town. He was always careful to keep a special amount for Ruth to spin.

Ruth was an accomplished spinner of wool. From their meager savings, they had purchased a spinning wheel. Before this valuable tool was purchased, Ruth spent many hours with a simple hand spindle. Ruth taught her daughters how to stretch and spin the wool. As a child, Chastity would catch the wool spun by her mother and spool it between her hands. The spinning wheel enabled Ruth to do the job much faster. It wasn't unusual for women from neighboring farms or from in town to visit her just so they could spin their wool on the fabulous spinning machine.

When the ladies of the town came, they would also bring the latest news. Many times the discussion was about the blacksmith's new apprentice. Early on, they spoke of a boy whose father had given him over to the egregious William Smith. As the years passed, the talk changed to the handsome, tall, blond blacksmith. When Chastity joined the ladies, she too would hear tell of this young man and innocently think to herself how much she would like to meet him. Little did she know how soon that would be.

It was a chance meeting when John met Chastity. By the age of fifteen, he was already accomplished at repairing tools. By then, he was also entrusted to deliver the repaired goods for the blacksmith. One task he was given was to sharpen sheep shears for Thomas Shepherd. John examined the well-worn shears and discovered they were in bad need of repair. He took the time to straighten the blades, making sure the blades met together evenly. He took great care to straighten the edges and align the angles. Only after he was satisfied with the repair would he begin sharpening the edges to a razor-sharp finish. When all was done, he wrapped the shears in oil cloth. John then walked the four-mile distance to deliver the shears.

Upon his arrival, John was greeted by Thomas. "Ho, boy, and who might you be?"

"Me name be John. I am apprentice to William the blacksmith. I have brought your shears, freshly sharpened and ready for use." John handed over the oil cloth bearing the shears to Thomas.

Having the tools delivered in oil cloth was something new. For in the past, William would just deliver them as he received them. When Thomas removed the cloth, he noticed they shined in the bright sunlight as never before. Thomas thought they belonged to someone else. The rough edges had been made straight, and the cutting blades touched perfectly together. Thomas knew immediately that this was not the work of the smith, but of someone who took pride in his work. Thomas took one set of the shears and walked over to where dried flax hung. To his utter amazement, the shears cut smoothly and without effort through the flax.

Thomas stood for the longest time just looking at the old shears. "I have never seen my shears sharpened or cared for as they have been this day."

John responded, "Then they met with your pleasure? I hope you don't mind, but I had to do a bit of added repair to them."

Thomas smiled. "Indeed, they do lad. They meet with my approval."

John thanked him. "My master will be pleased to hear that, sir."

Before Thomas could say another word, his thirteen-year-old daughter came bounding out of the house. "Father, Mother wanted me to ask if there was anything you might—" Before she could say another word, her eyes met John's. She was surprised to see the handsome, golden-haired young man. Chastity regained her composure quickly. "Oh, hello."

John was speechless and taken by her beauty. Awkwardly, the two youngsters stared at each other.

It was Thomas who broke the trance. "Before you'll be leaving, would you like a cup of water?"

John snapped to. "Thank you kindly, sir, but I best be getting back to work. My master will want to know my whereabouts."

Thomas replied, "Then tell your master that I will come and settle with him on the morrow."

Politely, John answered, "Indeed I will, sir." And with that, John made a slight bow to both Thomas and Chastity. John turned and nearly tripped over his own feet. Thomas smiled at the awkward moment, because he also noticed Chastity had not stopped looking at John.

After this chance meeting, John found every opportunity and excuse to return to the Shepherd home. Thomas looked kindly at the youngster and became quite fond of him. John had Sundays off. In Protestant England, it was not looked upon too kindly for a master to work his hirelings on the Lord's Sabbath, so on that day, John divided his time between his family and Chastity and her family.

Chastity's innocence was displayed throughout her childhood. Once she was stung by a bee because she thought it would be fun to play with it. She could not understand why the bee would want to hurt her. It was not uncommon to find her twirling about in the meadow, dancing to a melody that she alone could hear. She was happiest with her mother and father who raised her and her sisters in a loving Christian home. They taught her mathematics and to read and write. Bibles were rare enough even in the seventeenth century. Usually only one was available for an entire congregation, but Thomas purchased a used Geneva Bible with his savings and used it to teach his children.

Thomas and Ruth Shepherd were English Separatists, better known as Puritans. They were followers of John Calvin's teachings. The Church of England was now the state religion, but Separatists felt this new

Protestant religion still put too many restraints on the people. There was little tolerance for any other religion other than Catholicism. In many ways, the Church of England feared that the continual rise of the Separatists would disrupt the balance between Protestants and Catholics. Anyone engaged in their faith as they felt led was out of the question and unlawful.

A few months went by, and John had become a constant visitor to the Shepherd home. One day Thomas asked John to speak with him. The two walked to the barn alone. Once inside, Thomas invited John to sit with him. John thought that he might be in some sort of trouble and was unsure of what Thomas wanted to speak about. He took a seat upon a large stone.

Thomas began by saying, "John, I want to invite you to attend with me and my family at church. I think a young man of your understanding and ability ought to know more of the God who forged the world by speaking it into existence. It was God who made man and woman, and it would be wise to know His ideas on marriage and relationship between a husband and wife. More than that, it would be good for you to learn of His Son, Jesus Christ, who gave His life as a ransom for mankind."

Most of the afternoon was spent discussing spiritual things. Then, after a while, Thomas asked him, "Will ye come?"

John thought of it but for a moment. The idea of spending more time with Chastity probably appealed to him more than going to church. For that reason more than any other, he replied, "Aye, I'll come."

John and Chastity's relationship was more than mere attraction. First and foremost, they were friends. They found many things in common and loved talking about them together. John loved how free-spirited Chastity was. She loved how he showed his care for each of their families. He would only come to see her after spending time with his own family first. Eventually, Chastity was also included in John's family's activities. She soon felt as comfortable with his family as her own. They admired, respected, and cared deeply about each other. Funny thing, though, because they didn't even realize just how strong their love really was. This would come to light in a very special way.

Unlike Chastity, John had not been so fortunate in education. He was skilled as a laborer but never had the opportunity to learn how to read and write. Working with the smith gave him exposure to weights and measures. He did not realize that working with metals and heat was teaching him certain sciences and mathematics. Oftentimes, He would have an idea and would try it but did not know how to record the results of his experiments. John was frustrated at his inability to read and write and felt ignorant as a result. Sometimes at the Shepherd home he would touch the old Bible, just wishing he could read it.

One Sunday afternoon John and Chastity sat in a grassy meadow. By now, they'd begun sitting closer together and even held hands. They felt comfortable talking and sharing thoughts and ideas.

John looked into Chastity's beautiful eyes. "I like how you speak to me and how you and your family talk."

Chastity interrupted. "Your family doesn't talk?"

John smiled. "Aye, we talk, but it's the way you talk. Ah, what's the use? You don't understand."

Chastity chided him. "Now, John, don't do that."

John frowned. "I just don't know how to speak sometimes." He thought for a moment and then continued. "It's like when I work, I have an idea, and I will try it, but I don't know how to write about what I did. Sometimes I forget and have to figure it out all over again. I don't know words, and I feel empty inside. I can't expect you to understand."

Chastity took to heart what he was saying. She was beginning to realize that this handsome, talented young man felt less of himself because he lacked education.

John stood up, walked about for a moment, and then looked down at Chastity. "All the people in your church speak like you. Bet they can read and write, can't they?"

Chastity looked at John with great sorrow. She now knew that he felt like less of a man, no matter how skilled he was.

John tried to explain. "Chastity, how could I ever measure up as a man to you or anyone else without learning?" The sun was behind him, and his body was silhouetted by the light.

She raised her hands to him. "Help me up."

John took her hands and lifted her up. They stood together, but he remained silent. Chastity, for the first time, put her arms around him. She whispered, "I may not fully understand, but I want to help. You have not asked for it, but I have a gift I want to give you."

John lifted his head. He looked straight into Chastity's eyes. For the first time ever, he imaged what it would be like to kiss her but felt embarrassed. His face began to blush at the thought.

Seeing his ruddy face, Chastity stood back. She asked, "John, what's wrong?" The question left him speechless. She pulled from his arms and twirled with her arms spread out wide. She laughed, "It's a wonderful gift!"

He asked, "What gift?"

She rushed over, grabbed his hand, and pulled him. "Come on. I'll show you."

Smiling, they rushed off with Chastity leading the way. They raced back to the house. Thomas was just seeing to the sheep when he spied the two running hand in hand. He pondered what they might be up to. Once inside, Chastity made John sit down on the bench at the kitchen table. She continued on into the family room and fetched the family Bible. Hurrying back to the kitchen, she made John scoot over. She sat beside him and opened the Bible.

Looking at John, she giggled. "Here is my gift."

John wrinkled his brow. "A book?"

She laughed. No, silly man. I am going to teach you to read and write."

John sat back, surprised. "What?"

"I am going to teach you," came Chastity's reply. "John, we are together every Sunday. You and I can sit here, and I will teach you how to read and write."

Thomas walked in the door and was wiping his hand on a dry cloth while he listened to what Chastity offered.

John replied, "You think you can show me these things?"

Chastity smiled. "I know I can if you want to learn." Then looking at her father, she added, "Papa taught me and my sisters the same way I will teach you."

Thomas took a chair at the table. He noted, "I think that is a most excellent plan. I will be willing to help if you would like."

John remarked, "There, see? I want to learn how to talk like that."

John and Chastity laughed, but Thomas was clueless. "Talk like what?"

English was a young language as far as languages went. John was oftentimes confused at the similarities of words, like how some words sounded alike to him but had totally different meanings. Chastity would use this opportunity to write the words down for John to see. Sometimes this helped; other times, it didn't. But Sunday after Sunday, when he would come to visit Chastity, she would patiently teach him words, their meanings, and usage. She also instructed him how to write letters using a quail pen. Thomas was surprised how hard John worked and applied himself. In time, what was taught to him began making subtle differences in his speech. Little did John realize that he was changing because of the education he was receiving.

Every Sunday John would show up for church. Afterward, he would return home for a while before going to visit with the Shepherds. John was eager to begin his lessons with Chastity. From time to time, he would surprise everyone by reading to them something he'd written. John had become very adept at writing. To Chastity and her father's amazement, they saw an artistic flare to his letters and words. There was a certain grace about his writing and signature. Thomas was sure he had never seen writing so beautiful. He knew that there was a talent in this young man that was yet untapped. Thomas sensed that John was an artist, and this was the secret of his future.

After several months of education, John brought a package for Chastity. He called for her family to come to the kitchen. She sat down and waited for John to explain. He handed her the cloth-wrapped package and asked her to open it. Eager hands hurriedly unwrapped the cloth. To her surprise, it was a beautiful wall plate made of metal, which John had crafted himself. Upon the plate he had carefully engraved this beautiful message:

To my Shepherd girl.
You watched over me like one of your sheep,
And took me into your care.
For all you taught me I shall keep,
This gift with others I will share.

𝔐𝔶 𝔡𝔢𝔞𝔯𝔢𝔰𝔱 𝔣𝔯𝔦𝔢𝔫𝔡 𝔶𝔬𝔲 𝔞𝔯𝔢 𝔱𝔬 𝔪𝔢.
𝔜𝔬𝔲𝔯 𝔤𝔦𝔣𝔱 𝔍 𝔠𝔞𝔫𝔫𝔬𝔱 𝔯𝔢𝔭𝔞𝔶.
𝔍 𝔴𝔦𝔩𝔩 𝔫𝔢𝔳𝔢𝔯 𝔣𝔬𝔯𝔤𝔢𝔱 𝔞𝔩𝔩 𝔶𝔬𝔲 𝔪𝔢𝔞𝔫 𝔱𝔬 𝔪𝔢,
𝔉𝔬𝔯𝔢𝔳𝔢𝔯 𝔞𝔫𝔡 𝔢𝔳𝔢𝔯 𝔣𝔯𝔬𝔪 𝔱𝔥𝔦𝔰 𝔡𝔞𝔶.
𝔍𝔬𝔥𝔫.

Chastity sat silently. She ran her hand over the beautiful plate. She read and reread the words. No one she knew had such a gift as this.

John broke her concentration. "Do you like it?" he asked.

Chastity replied, "No. I love it." A tear ran down her cheek, and each family member came over to look at the wonderful gift. While the family admired the gift, Chastity's eyes remained fixed on John, for on that day, her love for John was confirmed in her heart.

The following week, John found Thomas sitting at the table working with numbers. John watched closely as Thomas wrote in his journal. When the time was right, John inquired what it all meant. Thomas pushed the journal over to John. "Here. You read it."

John read a line item and saw a number written across the page from it. John followed the transactions as they continued down the page. At the bottom was the word *Total*. Looking back at Thomas, he asked, "What does this mean?"

Thomas smiled. "It means that I am about to teach you the principals of mathematics and of keeping books."

John's fascination of the Word of God grew every day. He never knew the wonders of creation, the history of Israel, or the story of David and the kings. What puzzled him most was that Jesus died on the cross for the unworthy sinner. It was a Sunday afternoon, and he read from the Bible to Chastity. He read aloud the story of Jesus as He stood before Pilate. The message caused John to question all he had been taught in the past. John realized from all he read that Jesus was an innocent man. He stopped and asked Chastity, "Why would He do this? Why didn't he speak up for himself?"

Chastity's answer was so moving. "Because, John, Jesus was on trial to prove that He was worthy to pay the price for sinners."

John stated, "What's a sinner?"

Chastity began answering John's question by reminding him of the first sin committed by Adam and Eve. She explained that from that moment, man and all his progeny had become sinners. She patiently explained that all of man's good was useless because of sin. She told him that the cost of one sin was death—not physical death, but eternal death. Afterward, she returned to the story of Jesus and explained how He was pure and sinless because He was not born of man, but of God. She told how that Jesus proved over and over that He was God and was worthy to pay the price of sin. Finally, she said that all who believe in His death, burial, and resurrection shall have everlasting life.

Then she stopped, thought for a moment, and asked John a most important question. "John, what do you know of the love of God?"

John replied, "Oh, I know all about John 3 and the part which speaks of God loving the world."

Chastity replied, "That is true, but, John, there is so much more. Do you know that Jesus loves you personally? You see, it is one thing to know God loves the world, but there is another part. God has a personal love for you. Many believe Jesus died universally for all, but think about this. Jesus died for you because He loves you. God's love is very personal, and Jesus loves you. John, Jesus loves you."

John took it all in. How different the things she taught were from the things he was taught by others. He never considered that he was not worthy in himself to make it to heaven. John looked at Chastity and stated, "So what you are telling me is I can never be good enough?"

Chastity humbly replied, "That's right, darling, but God's love for you provided the way through His Son, Jesus." She took John's hand and concluded, "And the hope of all this is that Jesus will come again for His people." In earnest, Chastity asked, "My beloved, when Jesus returns, will you be ready to go with Him?"

John had never been asked such a question. He pondered the deeper meaning of these words. "Am I to believe that He is God come to earth so He could die to save me?"

This was a question John never pondered. His mind was torn by the things he had just heard and things he had been indoctrinated to believe in the past. John thought that he could tell Chastity he understood, and that would end the discussion, but it would not settle his own concern.

John stood and looked at Chastity. He took her hand and just looked at her.

Finally, John answered, "There is much I need to consider." With that, he leaned in and kissed her forehead. He turned and walked back toward his father's house.

That night John suffered with his thoughts, but the one question that affected him the greatest was the one Chastity had asked: "John, when Jesus returns, will you be ready to go with Him?" He finally admitted the ugly truth. "No, I am not ready. I need Him as my Savior. But how?" Then, leaving the warmth of his bed, he fell beside it on his knees. He felt unworthy to call upon God and ask forgiveness and faith, but he did anyway. Then came the marvelous realization. Through it all, he received the Lord as his personal Savior.

Tears of joy began to fill his eyes. Throughout the night, John cried, rejoiced, and prayed, because on that night, he knew he had received the great gift God. He slept some but constantly woke up. He was looking for the slightest hint of dawn so he could rush to Chastity and tell her the news.

There was a soft, pinkish hew in the eastern sky. John got up quickly before dawn and rushed from the house. He ran the distance to the Shepherd home. As he ran up the rise to their modest house, he startled a fallow deer grazing in the lush grass. The sheep were also surprised by John's appearance. Some bleated out, which alarmed Thomas's dog.

Thomas hurried from the house to see what was the matter. Through the misty morn, he eyed John running up the way. Confused by his appearance, Thomas called out to him, "John, what brings you here so early in the morning? Is there trouble afoot in the town?"

John fought to catch his breath. "No, but good news of a greater sort. May I speak to Chastity?"

Thomas shook his head, not knowing what to think.

John saw it immediately. He pleaded, "Please, sir, I have such little time before I have to run into town to begin my duties."

Thomas, sensing something good, turned into the house to wake his oldest daughter. All the noise also woke Ruth. She busied herself in the kitchen by preparing a breakfast of bread and cheese. Thomas tapped on his daughter's door and then entered the room. Approaching Chastity's bed, he called out, "Arise, me girl, there is a young man outside who is anxious to see you."

Chastity stretched and answered with a low, sleepy voice. "What?"

Thomas repeated, "There is someone here to see you."

She rose to her elbows. "Who might it be, Father?"

"Who do you think, Daughter? And he has something important to tell. Hurry, for he must be off for town and work."

Chastity hurried to the kitchen in her bare feet and had her blanket wrapped about her. John stood at the door waiting. As soon as she appeared, John shouted the news. "Chastity, I now believe in Jesus as my Savior!"

The news shook her completely awake. She immediately began hopping up and down. She ran over and threw her arms around him. John happily twirled with her in his arms. They laughed and cried together. Thomas and Ruth also joined in the joyous news.

John stopped and then whispered, "I have to go for now, but I shall return as fast as I can." He sat her down and rushed off.

Chastity calmed a bit and turned to her mom and dad. "This is a morning we aren't likely to forget."

John's newfound faith in Jesus Christ made him ponder his life in general. He began to think about all he had read. He thought about the lessons Jesus taught His apostles. He also considered the lessons instructed by Paul. He wanted to know more about his faith and how to live it. From that moment on, John dedicated himself to his work as a way to serve his Lord. When he made something, he thought about Jesus the Creator. When things went wrong, he sought to control his temper and his tongue.

John wanted his life to be like Jesus, and it was a challenge working for a master like William. In fact, the joy John showed just made his master more resentful. William hated life and everyone in it. He could tell there was something going on in John's life. For one, John seemed to be at peace with himself. William didn't like whatever it was that was changing him. He would find a way to drive it out of him.

William took note of John's progression of faith. John seemed to find ways to love the work he was doing. It seemed like every day he continued to improve by experimentation. In time, the townsfolk asked for things to be made by the blacksmith like never before. Most seemed to know it was John who was making these things. People began asking about cookery, table utensils, household items, and other things found useful in everyday life. In the beginning, John's work was a bit rough, but in time, the things John made became artful, skillful, and imaginative. There was a flare in his work. Even those things he repaired were improved upon. Through it all, William was making a handsome profit and accepted the compliments being dished out, but all the while, he was becoming more and more envious of his apprentice.

In the beginning, William had tried to embrace being a blacksmith. He had no choice but to become a smith like his father. His father was a blacksmith, and that was the family business. It had been passed down for generations. That was the way things were done. William saw blacksmith work as a requirement of life. He did not enjoy it or allow himself to find the love for it. He never found the respect from others as his father had. For that reason, he lost interest, never took pride in his work, and never advanced his skills beyond the basics.

William hadn't always been surly. When he was just starting out, he had married a pretty young maiden. This maiden found something good in the rough exterior of this iron man. Every day he found something to be happy about and looked forward to being back with his bride every night. His happiness was short-lived, for he lost his wife and son during childbirth. Ironically, William blamed the town for his short-lived happiness. He was convinced they had something to do with their deaths. Afterward, he felt the people had to pay for his loss. He found escape in strong drink. He never considered loving another. He could not bear the thought of losing someone else. He withdrew from people and became the man he was.

John had to be molded into a smith much like the metal he worked with. His struggle began with the tools. He had to learn how to use them and build strength in his hands, arms, and chest in order to handle them. The heavy hammer and the constant repetition of shaping the hot iron was a challenge for any man, much less a teenage boy. At first, John would choke up on the hammer in order to manage a few whacks on the red-hot metal. He soon learned that being so close to the metal would burn his hands. The fiery sparks from the hammer strikes would land on his forearms and burn the tender, youthful flesh. Over time, as he gained strength, John moved his hands farther and farther down the handle of the hammer. His hands were building strength even if they did not build calluses. His forearms were becoming like the iron he molded. His chest and biceps were hard and rounded. Small scars formed where hot metal embers landed on his arms, leaving their scarred signature behind. All that his father had hoped for him was becoming true. He had become a blacksmith.

When John was nearly twenty, his circumstances changed. By this time, he was doing most of the work, which was the way people wanted it. On one fateful day, John was busy shoeing one of the earl's horses in the open-air pen when he heard his master stager into the barn. The man was so filled with rum that he knocked over everything in his path. William's awkwardness put him in a foul mood.

Through eyes made red by rum, William looked around for his apprentice. Not seeing John made him even angrier. William's voice was loud and slurry. "John, you no good slothful boy. Come here. *now!*"

John replied instantly, "Just one moment, sir. I must finish shoeing the earl's horse. I shall be right there, master."

"I said, *now!*" came the blacksmith's cry.

John knew that he could not stop the task at hand. The shoe was not in place. The strong horse could easily kick off the shoe and possibly harm itself. Such a task must not be rushed.

It only took a few minutes for him to finish, and then he rushed into the barn. As soon as he did, he could smell the foul rum on the blacksmith's breath and body. He was about to explain what he was doing when the blacksmith cut him off. "I told ye to come here ... *now.*"

"Yes, master, but I could not leave the horse. Many pardons, sir."

The blacksmith slurred, "I can see I must teach you a lesson." William staggered close to John and got into his face. He pursed his words. "I don't care what ye might be doin'. When I call ya, ye best be comin'.'"

The stench of the rum caused John to turn his face away, at which point the smith took offense. "What's a matter, boy? Are you thinking you're too good for me now?" A silent rage was building in the old man. His strength was still formidable. With a mighty heave, he thrust the younger man back against the wall of the old barn.

The force of the push and the sudden stop caused John to strike the back of his head. He was dazed, and his legs wobbled. He was slow to regain his footing. The smith had a wicked smile across his face. He seized the opportunity. Walking over to the flaming pit, he pulled a red-hot poker. The smith turned toward. John and slowly ambled toward him. "Now, boy, it's time to pay your dues."

The red-hot tip of the poker sizzled in the cool air. John shook his head and regained his senses about him. He was all too aware of the fiendish intentions of the smith. At that moment, he remembered the first time when the smith took an opportunity punish him with a hot poker. He was a boy sweeping the barn of the old straw and wood chips. Once again, the smith had been overcome by rum. William waited till John was turned from him and retrieved the hot poker. At once, John felt the terrible burning sensation of the hot iron on his back. There was the foul smell of burning flesh and the great agony from the burn. John cried out and tears filled his eyes.

"Never let me see you lie about slothfully," came the mocking rebuke. Then, replacing the poker in the pit, William laughed fiendishly.

This time, with poker in hand, William walked toward John. He held the poker in his right hand as though he were carrying a sword. "You think you are a better man than me. Don't you, boy?" came the drunken words. "We shall see about that."

John tried to move away from the smith, but with each step, the man redirected his own.

His words betrayed him. "You don't know how long I have waited to do this. I shall scar that pretty face and make you as ugly outside as you are in."

John kept maneuvering away as best he could from William. He tried to buy time and distance as he attempted to reason with him. "What have I done, master, that ye would want to harm me?"

Jealousy filled William's heart. "I know how ye have undermined me and stole the people from me. I hear the pretty girls talk about John, the handsome smith. They all say you do the best work in town and that my work has become poor. I swear ye shall pay dearly. No man steals from me and gets away with it."

John looked beyond the hot poker and into the eyes of his master. John thought he could see the flames of Hades burning in them.

When William was but a few feet from John, he attacked. Without warning, the smith swung the hot iron at John's face and across the front of his body. The cool air caused a smoke trail to follow the movement of the iron. John quickly backed away, and just as quickly, the smith swung the poker back the opposite direction. Once again, it missed, but John didn't. As soon as it passed his body, John knocked the poker from the older man's grip. The poker flew into a small pile of hay, which quickly ignited.

John started toward the fire, and the old man hit him with a powerful fist. William landed a blow to John's midsection, sending him to his knees and knocking the wind from him. John felt like he had been kicked by a horse, but he knew he had to put the fire out, or all would be lost. The smith raised both hands high above his head and locked his fingers together. As his fists came down to strike another blow, John rolled out of the way. The drunken man lost his balance and fell into the dust on the ground.

John hurried to his feet, grabbed a pitchfork, and tossed the burning hay into the yard. He grabbed a leather apron and began beating out the remaining flames in the barn. John was completely absorbed in putting out the fire even though he knew he had to watch the smith. William regained himself. Once more, the smith staggered to his feet. Seeing John beating out the fire, the drunken man came up behind him and swiftly kicked him. John fell into the smoldering ash. Before John could recover, the smith grabbed him up and flung him out the barn door into the street. John landed awkwardly to the side of his head, rocking his senses.

A crowd gathered when they saw the pile of burning hay. They were shocked to see John thrust into the street. John shook his head and rose to his knees, trying desperately to rid the cobwebs from his mind. John had gotten to his feet at the same time William staggered out. In a rage, he stormed toward John. As soon as he was close enough, William swung a wide roundhouse at John's hand. John ducked, and the momentum of the throw caused the man to fall awkwardly to the ground. John had always fought to hold his composure. He wanted to strike the cruel man and be done with it. He clenched his fists and lifted his shoulders before taking a few breaths and relaxing. He walked over and reached his hand out to help William to his feet. John's intentions were met with vice. William took his hand, but as soon as he was on his feet, the smith threw another punch at John. Again, the man missed and fell face-first in the dust of the earth.

John was smarter than to try and approach the smith again. He walked around the man. This time, he called out to him, "Why do you treat me so? Have I not served you without one word of complaint even when you have beaten me, kicked me, and cut me with your iron? I have done nothing to you. I have never disagreed with you. I took all you poured out on me and never tried to retaliate. So tell me, what have I done?"

The smith, still enraged, began to rise to his feet. He realized that a crowd had gathered. He looked over them and had enough sense not to try and attack the young man again. Instead, he spoke with a slur as he attached John's character. "I took you in to train you, and how have you repaid me? By stealing my work. You think I don't hear what people are saying about how good your work is compared to mine? I know the pride in your heart. I know you are trying to take what is mine—what I have built up."

John impulsively countered. "Not true, master. I have never tried, nor will I ever try to take what's yours from you. Besides that, I have become a follower of Christ, and I would never do anything to dishonor my Lord and Savior."

William snarled. "Aye, a Christian, are you now? So ye think that you are better than me? I curse you to your face. You and your God are not welcome here. I want no more of you," came the smith's harsh response. Turning to the crowd, he added, "So you prefer the work of the handsome one? You can have him. Don't come back here. See if you can find another to fix and repair what you have. I will have no more of it. Now get away from me—all of you!" Turning to John, he continued with a deep, dark sentence. "Especially you, boy. You have nothing here." Then with an angry bellow, he shouted, "Go!"

John felt angry and demoralized. He had done nothing to this man. He untied the leather straps from behind his back, removed the leathers he was wearing, walked into the barn, and hung them on a peg. He then picked up his meager sack of belongings. Among them were the few tools he had managed to make. He walked out of the barn in the sight of the people and then stood there for a moment and looked at the smith. He loathed the man, and yet, somehow, he felt sorrow for him. After a moment, he turned and began the lonesome journey home.

In his mind, he had one thought: *What will Father think, and what will Chastity think?*

# New Horizons

To lose an apprenticeship meant losing a better life. Some even lost all opportunity to work. If word got out that a boy or man was no longer an apprentice, he might not be given an opportunity to redeem himself. At any point, if the student lost the position, he would find it impossible to start again with another mentor. If he did manage to do so, it would be under suspicion and usually with little pay. About the only exception was with the military, because you could always be made a soldier or sailor. With his opportunity lost, the only life a young man could hope for was menial work at best. Such were the prospects that John faced.

Whether John understood this or not isn't clear. All he knew was he had no immediate future. The walk toward home was troubling. John's mind raced back to the many times he made the journey to and from the blacksmith's shop. Before, the return home had always been a welcome relief. Now, he could barely think about facing his father.

John pondered, *What will Father think? Will he be ashamed of me, his son? Will he turn me away?* John knew his father had found him this opportunity and feared he would think John squandered it.

As John continued homeward, his thoughts went toward Chastity and her family. Something like this could ruin relationships and cause families to lose respect. John and Chastity had great hopes. Now he doubted that her father would look kindly upon him. Marriages have to weather storms. John had a great desire to provide Chastity a better life. One moment everything was working toward that end, but just as swiftly, it all seemed hopeless. One nagging thought prevailed in John's mind: *Will Chastity still have me after all of this?*

John reached the crest of the hill that led down to the house. He knew he wasn't expected home for a few more days, and his sudden appearance would cause a lot of questions he did not want to answer. All the questions that others might ask raced through his head. He could feel anger building in him—anger at the smith, anger at the situation, and, above all, anger at God. John knew he had to go home, but he couldn't take the first step. Tears filled his eyes, and he began to tremble. His heart raced, and sweat broke out across his forehead. He hated the anger he felt. He fell to the ground and wept uncontrollably.

John lay upon the ground feeling weak and alone as he struggled within himself. He was ashamed for blaming God but wanted to hold the Almighty responsible for his situation, even though deep within he couldn't justify his feelings. There in the grassy meadow he began to pray. It was a simple prayer: "Father, why?" There was no answer. He cried out again, "What have I done to deserve being treated this way? My Father, I do not understand. Can you hear me?" Then John thought, *Is it really God's fault that I am in my present situation?*

Just then, a sermon his pastor had preached began to make sense to John. The words that seemed to repeat themselves were simply: "God meant it for good." The title of his pastor's sermon had been "Faithful Job." In that message, the preacher said that God does bring good things to pass, but like in Job's case, evil can also come. God is still with us, and He will carry us through even the greatest trial. John sat up and pondered the message. It was a difficult one for sure, but it wasn't the end of the world. The pastor's words, "He will carry us through," resonated over and over with him. He was still unsure and afraid, but he knew he must press on.

John whispered one more prayer. "Heavenly Father, show me the way."

Again, the words of the pastor resonated in his mind: "Jesus made the way." John reflected on those words before considering, *Did Jesus save me just to deliver me from eternal death?* Then a resounding answer came for deep within. *No. Jesus abides in me. He is ever with me. I must live by faith.* John then began thinking about what it must mean to live by faith. With that thought, he considered other sermons the pastor had preached. The ones that had made him think were sermons on having a real relationship with the Lord. The pastor called it, "Living in the grace of the Lord."

One sermon was taken from Hebrews 11. The sermon was called "Living by Faith in God." The pastor preached on that day about the lives of men like Noah, Abel, Abraham, and Moses who believed God and went forth for Him. Then John thought about what the preacher said.

*What was it?* John thought to himself. *Oh yes … Noah preached. Abel sacrificed. Abraham offered. Abraham followed. Sarah conceived.* From that, John realized faith is more than being saved. It is about living by faith.

Then all around him John felt a presence like he had never known before. He wasn't afraid. The presence was uplifting. He felt it within himself and all around him, and a feeling of peace took over. John thought he heard a voice. "My son, trust me. I will be with you wherever you go. Have confidence in me, for I will never leave you nor forsake you."

Slowly, John opened his eyes. The light around him was brighter than ever. He lifted his eyes and looked about. There was no one there, yet he knew there was someone there. John understood that he was in the presence of God. From his lips, John praised. "I believe, my Lord. I believe."

After his experience, John went down the hill toward home. Somehow he knew God would be with him. He knew there would still be struggles, but he believed with all his heart that God would be with him.

John soon learned that bad news traveled fast. People were quick to relate what they knew to the town dairyman, especially if the news involved his son. The town was buzzing with news regarding the blacksmith and his apprentice. Everyone James came in contact with sided with his son. As James was returning home, driving cart of empty dairy cans and pots, he tried to put together the story from those who had told it. The horse plodded faithfully along. Though the noisy cart with its load of empty cans and pots rattled toward the house, it did not arouse any attention. John and Adam had been tending to the cattle and were so deep in conversation that neither one heard James's return.

James unhitched the horse from the wagon and led him to the green pasture where he could graze. He was about to call the girls to come and help with the unloading and cleaning of the wares when heard his sons talking in the barn through the open door. He walked toward them and could hear the conversation clearly. He found the boys sitting on stools at an angle to each other. James entered the door and walked up behind them, but they were so deep in conversation they never heard him coming. He looked through the dust streams made evident by the sunrays beaming between cracks in the wood. The cattle were already returned to the field, and pails of milk sat ready to be taken to the house. The milking was already complete.

James just listened. He recalled a similar time in his own life when he'd had to deal with his own problem. His father gave him time to work through things before offering advice. Even in that moment, as he looked at his two sons, he recounted the conversation. His father had offered one bit of counsel: "Time and patience must be had. Give the matter time and patience." That advice had served him well through the years. Whenever problems came his way, he could hear his father's words., "Time and patience must be had." James would be there to guide his son if he was needed. Time and patience must be had.

Adam's elbows rested on his knees. He looked over and asked John, "What will you do now?"

John replied, "I am not sure. I have learned all that I can from the smith. I have been doing most of the work for a long time, but I do not have the means to start on me own. I suppose I could move to another town, but I fear that the smith would spread word and will prejudice the people against me."

Adam was thoughtful. "Maybe you could take over here for me."

John had been leaning on his knees and sat up. "No, that would not be fair. Father and I agreed a long time ago that this would be your work, and I could strike out on my own. I am a smith now." John began to chuckle. "Who would ever have thought that a man could become something more?" He gave a sigh and slapped his knees. "I might go to London and see what fortunes might be there. I could work for the military."

Adam responded, "The army?"

John replied, "Or navy. They are always in need of tradesmen." A sudden remorse swept over him. "I feel so ashamed. I fear I have made a complete mess of it all. I have disappointed Father, and I have lost Chastity."

It was time. James walked forward. He interrupted the conversation and proclaimed, "Nonsense."

Adam and John quickly rose to their feet and turned to face the man they had the greatest respect for. They spoke in unison. "Father."

John was the first to acknowledge his father's presence. "We did not hear you, sir." Then, looking about at the milk, he announced, "We will get busy and get the milk in the house."

James was stern. "You will do no such thing. Sit." The boys hesitated, so James commanded again, "Go on now and have a seat." The brothers just looked at each other. James commanded yet again, "Go on and sit. You too, Adam."

James walked over and picked up an empty wooden box and sat on it so that he could be with his sons. The three men sat together facing each other. For a few moments, they sat in silence. Then James broke the silence with well-placed words, "I have heard the talk in the village, and I have heard your story. From what the people have said to me today, you did all you could to reason with the smith. I was told you kept his barn from burning down and saved him from harm. I am proud of you. John, I know that you faced a difficult situation and handled it the best you could. I knew sooner or later the love of rum would ruin the smith. I did not know of his anger or cruelty. I was told by more than one how you did not raise a hand against the drunken old fool. They told me what you said. I was told how you walked away a broken man."

John just looked at his father. They'd talked in times past, but it had always been a father-to-son talk. In that moment, John felt like his father was talking to him as a man.

James rubbed his legs and addressed Adam. "Go get the girls and have them collect the milk. While you are in the house, bring me something to drink. Hurry back, Son." Once Adam was gone, James continued. "John, I know of your skill. Everyone I meet tells me of your work and how you take pride in what you do, and yet, you still remain humble. That is rare."

Adam returned with a cup of cider, and the girls came to take the milk to the house. At one point, Grace tried to lift a pail too heavy for her. James told her to leave it for her sister, and she complied. Soon, all the milk was in the house, and Adam returned and retook his seat.

A smile crept over James's tired face. He was thankful that his children showed such respect and obedience. James considered this as he spoke.

"You are men now. What you do with your lives is of your own making. I urge you to make the most of it."

James addressed John directly. "Just now, I watched your brothers and sisters take the milk to the house. They did not argue. They showed the greatest respect and obedience. I watched as you wanted to help, but you saw that they had everything under control." He rubbed the whiskers on his face as he thought and asked, "Did you obey the smith?"

John answered, "Yes, sir. I did."

James asked, "As soon as he called?"

John thought for a moment. "Not always, for there were times I could not."

James asked, "How so?"

John replied, "Like today, I was shoeing the earl's horse, and I could not leave the horse. I told the smith so, but he gave me no leeway."

James nodded his head in understanding and pointed out, "Sometimes we have to make decisions on our own and face the consequences of our actions. Did you notice Grace trying to lift the heavy pail? It was much too heavy for her, and even if she succeeded in lifting it, she might have sloshed milk out or dumped it on her way to the house. I told her to take another instead. She had a decision to make. She weighed the matter whether to obey and not. She obeyed and did the right thing."

John had a questioning look on his face. "I don't understand the connection."

James chuckled. "She did what was right. She chose the right thing. Did you choose the right thing today?"

John thought before replying. "Father, I had no choice. Yes, I did."

James concluded, "Then you have nothing to be ashamed of. You made a hard decision. You know the kind of man the smith is and still you took the only reasonable way." James stood up before saying more. "John, I found this opportunity for you. I didn't give you much choice. Do you regret what I have done?"

John shot back. "No, Father. It is a fine thing you have done. I did not see it then, but I do now. I truly love what I do. Wait, let me show you." John raced to the house and took from his bag an item wrapped in cloth. Rushing back to the barn, he handed it to his father. "Here, open this."

James removed the cloth to reveal a silver spoon. The handle was made of wood. In the bowl of the spoon was a delicate engraving. James looked it over and over.

John explained, "I made it for Mum. Think she will like it?"

James could not image someone having the skill to make something like this. He looked to John. "She will love it." James placed his hand on John's shoulder. "John, you have just now proved to me how good the decision was to train you to be a smith. I know it was hard, but you became one anyway."

Then, focusing on Adam, James offered, "Adam, you needn't become a farmer if you would prefer something more."

Adam wrinkled his brow. "No, Father. I like this line of work. I love being on the farm."

James smiled. "Farmers will always be needed, and I am glad for your choice."

The three men thought about all that had been said. After a moment, James asked John, "When do you plan to tell Chastity?"

John dropped his head. "I don't think Chastity will have anything more to do with me once she hears what has happened."

James slapped his knees. "There you go misjudging the girl. Is she in love with you?"

John frowned. "Why, yes, and what would bring you to ask such a question?"

James then leaned forward. "If she loves you, then give her the chance to show you her love. Knowing her the way I do, I believe she will be your greatest help." James's eyes pierced John's heart. Continuing, James added, "Do you think marriage and relationships are without struggle?"

John shook his head. "No, I have heard disagreements between you and Mum many times."

James raised his eyebrows. "Many is it, now?" The three men laughed. James went on. "We have, but it made us closer together, not farther apart, because we love each other. If Chastity is to someday be your wife, then you have to weather troubles together. It will serve to make your marriage stronger." James could see John taking it all in. "Go to her, Son. It is time you two talked this over and figured out the best way to handle it."

John answered, "Let me help clean up here first."

James walked over to his son. He lifted him to his feet and looked him in the eye. "No, Son. Adam and I know how it has to be done. Freshen yourself and go to Chastity."

John stared at his father for a moment. Both moved forward into a loving embrace.

"I am so thankful for you, my dear boy," James said.

"I love you, Father," came the broken words of the son.

# Seeking Answers

Hurriedly, John cleaned himself and put on his best garments. It was a long walk to Chastity's house made longer by the heaviness in his heart. At the crest of the hill, he could see the beautiful cottage below with its picturesque beauty. It was nestled in the lush green pastureland. A wisp of smoke emitted from the chimney. In the distance, he could see sheep grazing. John loved this scene because he knew his loving Chastity waited for him there.

John walked to the house below. There was a war within himself. He wanted to run to the woman he loved and be comforted by her. On the other hand, he wanted to run away to start all over, sparing her the embarrassment of his failure. His father's words urged him forward: "It's time you two talked it over together and figured things out." With each step John asked himself, *Figure what out?*

John approached the house and eyed Thomas in the barn. John went over to him and found him caring for one of the lambs whose leg had gotten caught in a heavy bramble. John loved to watch Thomas care for his creatures. As Thomas cared for the lamb, he spoke words to it as though he were tending to a child. "Don't you know there are some places not fit to go into? I bet you saw a berry tempting you, eh, little one? You can't just go after something unless you know what dangers might await you." Then a few more touches, and the leg was bandaged. Thomas lifted the lamb. "Ah, you'll be all right now."

Thomas set the lamb down and watched it limp away. Then he spied his unseen visitor. "John, you startled me. Why aren't you at work?"

John lowered his eyes to the ground. "Something happened in the town today, and I wanted to come and tell you all about it."

Thomas asked, "Would you like to sit?"

John replied, "Thank you, sir, but might we sit with the family as we discuss this? I would rather tell everyone at once."

Thomas nodded in agreement, and together, they walked toward the house.

They were about to enter when they heard the sound of a horse approaching. Both men stopped and turned to see Pastor Elijah Brown riding up the road. Nearing the house, he raised a hand in greeting. "Hello, good brothers, and how are you this day?" Pastor dismounted and looked at John. "I rode over to your parents' house to see you. They told me you'd come here to see Chastity. My, you sure can move about quickly." Elijah was a gentle happy soul and was at times a bit mischievous. He could find the right things to say in even the most difficult situation. Turning to the men, he stated, "Let's all go in together. Shall we?"

One by one, they entered, John being the last. Ruth, Chastity, and the sisters were busy with the evening meal. Ruth expressed great surprise, "Pastor, John, what might you me be doing here?"

Pastor chuckled. "Am I not welcomed, Sister?"

Ruth waved a hand. "Of course you are. I am just surprised by a visit this time of day, and midweek nonetheless." Then, looking at John, she asked, "Is something wrong?"

John was about to speak when Elijah interrupted. "In good time. Might we sit first over a morsel and drink?"

Ruth smiled. "Of course. Come and sit. Everything is about ready."

The girls hurried to add chairs at the table. Chastity sat close to John. In times past, John always loved sitting at this table with the family, but things just didn't feel the same. He hardly ate, and everyone took notice. Elijah tried to keep the mood light, telling stories of town, but John's distance had them all concerned.

Once the meal was finished, the pastor was the first to speak. "There was an incident in town today. I was privy to see a great portion of it. A fire broke out in one of the local tradesman's barn. A young man rushed to put it out. Odd as it may seem, the owner attacked the young man. How strange a scene it was. In the end, the young man's perseverance paid off. He saved the owner and his barn. I come to find out the younger man is apprentice to the older man. When he told his master why he would not raise a hand against him, his master dismissed him. Isn't that about the size of it, John?"

All eyes focused on John. He couldn't swallow. He felt trapped like an animal. A question had been poised that demanded an answer. He looked about the table and in fear replied, "What could I do?" Tears began to form in his eyes.

Chastity put her arm around him. "It's all right, my love. It's all right."

Through heavy tears, John tried to speak, but the sorrow of the day had finally found release.

Thomas looked at his two youngest daughters. "I need you to clear the table and bring some wine. Ruth and Chastity, please stay, for I see there is much more to the story."

Elijah spoke up. "Indeed there is. For I heard from others that the blacksmith had been drinking most of the day and was in a foul mood. One man who was at the pub overheard the smith tell of his hatred for John. When asked why, the blacksmith stated, 'The lad thinks he is better than me.'" Pastor looked at John and asked, "Did he strike you while you were in the barn?"

John thought long and hard before answering. "About the same amount as usual."

Elijah continued. "I suspected so. I saw that your blond hair was matted in the back."

Chastity quickly reached to check, and John winced in pain. She pulled her hand back, for there was a sizable cut beneath his long hair. Chastity tenderly spoke. "Why have you never told me of your ill treatment?"

John replied, "What could be done? I am but an apprentice and subject to the master's treatment."

Elijah was understanding. He knew the laws of the land favored those who offered to teach someone a trade. They could treat their pupils as they saw fit. When Elijah spoke, he addressed Chastity. "John is under the tutorage of the blacksmith for as long as the smith deems him an apprentice. It is up to him to declare John a smith." Pastor lifted himself from his seat and walked about. He turned to the family. "The man is not likely to declare John a smith now. However, John is too valuable for him to lose. Once the drink wears off, he will want John back."

Thomas asked, "What do you mean, valuable?"

Elijah pulled from his side a very handsome knife. He walked over to John and showed it to him. He then asked, "John, do you recognize this knife?"

John nodded his head. "It came from the blacksmith's shop."

Elijah answered, "I know, and who in the shop made it?"

John hung his head. "I did."

Elijah asked, "How can you be certain?"

John took the knife and pointed to a special marking in the handle. "You see this mark? That is my signature. I inscribe it on all my wares." Then, looking at the pastor, he asked, "May I ask how you came by it?"

Elijah looked at John. "I bought it at the open market. William takes what you make and sells the items for profit. He never did it before, because he lacked the talent, but your work brings a handsome profit."

Everyone was shocked at the revelation.

Elijah stood tall and continued. "John, William is not likely to declare you a smith because he stands to lose a great deal of profit. Most assuredly, if it is up to him, he will have you remain an apprentice all your days."

Chastity was alarmed at the statement. "How could he do that?"

Elijah looked at her. "Greed, Sister. Greed can drive a man to do most anything."

John had regained his composure. "But there is hardly any chance of me completing my apprenticeship now, because the smith told me to leave and never come back."

Thomas turned to face John and asked, "Do you want to go back?"

John shook his head. "No, but I fear I have no other choice."

Elijah interrupted. "I wouldn't be so sure of that."

John questioned, "What do you mean, Pastor?"

Elijah smiled. "I mean there is someone who knows your work very well, and I believe he would be willing to give you title of Master Smith."

John was completely surprised. He looked up at Elijah and asked, "Who?"

Elijah replied, "Why, the Earl of Sussex, of course."

Ruth poured Elijah a cup of wine, and he supped from it.

Then John stated, "But I don't know the man."

Elijah chuckled. "But he knows you." Elijah toyed with John, knowing that it would bring John out of his despair. "You know the young man who has come to you to have you make cutlery and wares of silver?"

John answered, "Indeed I do."

Elijah walked over and placed his hands on the table. He stared at John. "Might you know who that young man is?"

John calmly replied, "I thought he was one of the villagers."

Elijah stood and placed his hands to his sides. He chuckled as he answered, "Oh, he is more than that. He is the earl's son. Whether the earl knows it or not, his son has furnished the house with much of your finely crafted wares. It is time that I introduce you to the earl."

Thomas looked directly at Pastor Elijah. "You mean to introduce John to the earl?"

Elijah huffed. "Well, yes, sort of, and that brings me to another point." He looked at those who were seated and stated, "John, what you said about being a Christian may have caused a situation. As you know, ours is a private congregation, and we hold services outside the limits of the law. If William pursues your statement of Christianity, there could be an investigation. William may try to use it as leverage to force you back to work for him."

John's face reddened. "I said nothing wrong. It is my faith that kept me from striking the man."

Elijah turned and looked at him. "So you felt like striking him?"

John took several breaths before answering. "I did, but I questioned whether God would approve."

Elijah walked about. "I see there is still much to teach you. John, it is all right to defend and protect yourself. Even Jesus the night he was betrayed told Peter that taking the two swords was enough. Our Heavenly Father does not look down on us for defending ourselves."

Elijah twirled his hands in the air, trying to keep thought. He continued. "Back to the real issue ... We have to consider the consequences of your statement. William might seek to prosecute you and the law to force you to announce your loyalty to the Church of England. If you refuse, you could be imprisoned."

John stood up. He looked at the family and stated, "Perhaps it is best I leave."

Immediately, Chastity and the family surrounded John with comfort and words of encouragement. While they didn't know what to say or what to advise, they were certain they didn't want him to run away. Elijah seemed to be thinking about what John had just stated. What John said made him think of a possible opportunity.

Once things calmed a bit, Elijah spoke of the opportunity he was considering. "John, you spoke of leaving. I have fallen upon an idea that may serve you well."

John looked at the trusted man of God. "What are you thinking?"

Elijah looked at the family and then proceeded to tell of his idea. "You said maybe it's best you leave. I began to think about your talents and what opportunities might be offered to you. What if you made the decision to take your talents and go to a place where they are needed? A place where you can have a new beginning and grow in God's grace with freedom to do so."

John looked perplexed. He answered, "Is there such a place?"

Elijah took his seat. He leaned forward, resting his elbows on the table. The whole family seemed interested in what he was about to say. A serious tone escaped his lips. "I am talking about the New World—you know, The Americas."

All were shocked at the recommendation, and silence filled the room. Elijah could sense it and quickly continued. "There are two things that bring me to this idea. First, there are a number of Puritans who have already fled to America for religious freedom. Plymouth Rock is thriving, and a new town called Boston has already begun. Second, England is looking to expand its empire. English ships are sailing far and wide to discover places where the Empire may grow." Turning his attention to John, he said, "This, my son, would be the opportunity to establish yourself at your trade and give you the opportunity to worship God without fear."

Thomas added to the Elijah's statement. "John, you have told me at times how difficult it is to work with the smith and that he oftentimes overindulges in rum. You have shown me some of the scars inflicted upon you by the brute. Maybe it's your time."

Elijah nodded. "I would agree, but, John, let me warn you that it is a weighty matter to consider."

John sat for a considerable amount of time, pondering the pastor's words. The others considered the opportunity by asking questions like, "How can all this possibly come about? What about the money needed to make the journey, or we don't know the first thing about America."

Elijah listened to their concerns but chose not to answer their questions directly. Instead, he focused on the positive aspects. "More and more people are already needed there. Even now, there are many who have made the journey who could not afford the passage. There is a need for all manner of skilled tradesmen and such."

After a while, Elijah stated, "My association with the earl might benefit John. I believe I could convince him to declare John a Master Craftsman. After that, I know that there would be those who would pay his way, even the earl, if he agrees to serve for a period of time."

Thomas knew immediately what the man of God was talking about. "You mean he would become an indentured servant."

A long silence filled the room. Thomas deeply contemplated what the suggestion might mean for John and for his daughter. He expected that she would follow, as he knew the depth of their love for each other. Thomas was not against their future marriage. He was also very fond of John and welcomed him becoming his son-in-law. He broke the silence by asking, "For how many years would he serve?"

Chastity spoke up. "What is an indentured servant?"

Elijah thought about the questions. He looked at all those who were at the table, realizing the women did not know of this opportunity. He explained, "The New World needs settlers. The first ones who went there sought fortune, but few had the desire to work. They believed the tales that gold lay on the ground for the taking. Many who came were aristocrats and refused to help themselves. In just a few months, men began to die of starvation. They thought their status afforded them the luxuries and privileges they had in England. They would rather die than lift a finger. Reports from Virginia stated that there was lack of organization. The truth was that their do-nothing attitude was leading to many deaths. By the time the next ship of settlers arrived, Jamestown was almost desolate, and the survivors were nearly skeletons."

Elijah rose to his feet and paced the floor a bit before continuing. "Shortly thereafter, investors and aristocrats who had interest in establishing settlements devised a plan in which men could go and serve for a period of time. These workers would be called *indentured servants* or *indentures*. Investors would pay for their passage to America, and they would work for an overseer the required amount of time. Upon completion of their service, they would be given land on which to begin their new lives."

Elijah placed his hands on the table as he focused on Thomas. "To answer your question, yes, John would go as a servant, and, like Jacob of the Old Testament, he would have to serve a period of time for his passage to America and a bit of property for himself. After that, he would be free to make his own way as he saw fit."

John looked at the family. He could see the concern in Thomas's and Ruth's faces. He imagined what this decision would mean to his own parents. When he looked into Chastity's eyes, he could see excitement and adventure. Right then, he knew that if he determined to go to America, she would want to go with him. This would not be a decision to take lightly. John knew he had to discuss this with his family.

Wisely, John spoke. "This is something to carefully consider and pray about. I believe in my skills and ability of my trade. I also know that such a decision would mean leaving behind the ones I love. Quite possibly, I would never see them again. At the same time, I have to consider the quandary I have caused with everyone, including the church."

Chastity looked at John. "You will not be leaving everyone behind, because if you go, I will go with you."

The statement startled Thomas and Ruth. Ruth immediately shot back. "You will do no such thing. You are too young. Besides that, you are not his wife. I sat there listening to all of this, and I knew you would harbor such ideas in your mind. I want you to get that thought out of your head. To even think about traveling alone to any place near here, much less to a land across the ocean, is completely out of the question."

Chastity resented her mother's statement. "I am eighteen years old, and there are some girls in town who are already married and have children."

Ruth naturally defended her earlier statement. "I cannot speak for those girls or the approval of their families, but I have a say over you. America is a primitive, unsafe place. I know we have brethren there who are making a settlement in Plymouth Rock. I also know that many of the first ones to go there have died. I cannot abide here not knowing if you are safe." Tears formed in her eyes as she said, "No, I cannot sit by while ye think about going to America. I just can't."

Chastity felt anger and sadness. She tried to reason with her mother. "Mother, girls my age die all the time from disease and dangers in our own town. Some die from starvation and even in childbirth."

Ruth remained steadfast. "Your attitude displays what we all know is true—that children are willful and must be disciplined to drive the sin from them. I fear that you have not learned the value of prudence."

Elijah was somewhat amused at the tone of the conversation. It was not uncommon, even in Puritan homes, for families to speak out among themselves, while in public, families always tried to maintain expected order. Generally, women were forbidden to speak. In public, congregational members more often than not tried to hide their disagreements. He knew that people tended to put on their best behavior in front of others, even in their own homes.

Ruth turned to face Thomas. "Will you just sit by and say nothing? Speak up, man, and tell your daughter what you think."

Thomas was more reserved than his wife, with a demeanor more like the shepherd he was in real life. His moderate, easy tone was firm, reasonable, and controlled. Many times his reasonable statements spoke volumes, but his quiet demeanor could sometimes be misunderstood for weakness.

With a sensible tone, he said to his daughter, "Chastity, please listen to you mother. She is right. It is your safety and our love for you that makes us guard your every step. You are our child, and you are a woman in every sense of the word. I realize that as a woman, you consider your heart over your mind. I suggest that you weigh your thoughts with God's direction and not make your decisions on your own sensibilities."

Ruth was outraged by Thomas's statement, and her anger got the best of her. "Is that all you'll be saying? This is our daughter, man, who is planning to rush off to another world with a man she is not married to. Will you not protect her from what others might think?"

Ruth's statement angered Thomas. Her words slashed him to the heart. He tried to hold his temperament in his response. Looking sternly into her eyes, he stated, "Wife, I have heard what has been said and at no time was there ever any mention that she was running off with a man like a common woman. She has stated her thoughts. Do not remake them to fit your own thoughts or fears. I do not want my daughter leaving me or going to some far-off place away from me. Would you rather she steal off into the night and go after him, or would you prefer that she receive our blessings?"

Thomas took a deep breath to calm himself. He could see that his wife and daughter were at odds. Looking intently at both women, he said, "Let me say clearly to you both that I don't want to lose my daughter. No, I do not what her to go, but if God is in it, He will show us." Looking to his beloved wife, he added, "This, my beloved, is an important time for all of us, and we must use it to direct our daughter. And direct her we will."

After that, Ruth sat fuming. Chastity was moved to silence.

John had about enough. He could see that he was splitting the family apart. He stood to his feet to go and announced, "I see that I have been the cause of great trouble. I am sorry. Perhaps at another time we can discuss this further." As he walked toward the door, he turned to face the family once more. Sorrowfully, he stated, "I came not to cause trouble, but to find answers. I am in love with Chastity. I had no intention of causing tonight's argument. Someday I had hoped to make Chastity my wife with your blessings." John looked to Ruth. "I will find a way." John next turned to Elijah. "Thank you, Pastor, for all you have done. I will consider becoming an indentured servant. Please come to my father's home on the morrow, and we can discuss it."

John reached for the door, and Thomas's commanding voice called to him, "Lad, this is not the time to run away. This is the time to stand for what you want and believe. When I was about your age, I pursued Ruth in spite of her mother's objections. If you and Chastity have the same love for each other, then it is time to fight for it, not run from the responsibility."

John sharply replied, "I do love her. I have loved her from the first moment we met. Must the love we feel for each other tear this family apart?" He walked back and knelt at Ruth's knee. "I love you like my own mum. I would do everything to honor and protect your daughter. I would provide for her to the best of my ability. Our children would be raised to honor and respect our Savior." Then, standing to his feet, he continued. "I fear I shall never be good enough. Please, Mother, forgive me, for I truly meant no harm."

John stood and turned to walk away, but a tender hand reached to restrain him. Ruth had taken his hand. John turned to see her face full of tears.

Ruth stood and sorrowfully said, "Oh, my precious boy, what have I done to you?" She drew him into her arms. "I love you as me own son. Please stay. You are not the problem. God will help us to find the right way."

A few moments passed before Thomas addressed Elijah. "Sorry, Pastor, forgive us, for I did not mean for these things to take place, especially in your presence."

Elijah chuckled. "Actually, Brother, it is quite refreshing to see a family act in the way you have. What troubles me more is when a situation like this occurs, and no one speaks about it. Eventually, something has to give, and it oftentimes becomes an eruption." Then, taking a deep breath, he added, "No, Thomas, your family's forthrightness and honesty is reassuring." Afterward, the pastor walked over and placed a hand on Ruth's shoulder. "Sister, I know in my own home we have tried to teach our sons and daughters. When they were younger, we adhered to strict discipline. As they got older, we guided them, as best we could, to make decisions carefully and with prayer. I would recommend this for your family."

Ruth was embarrassed. "I too am sorry, Pastor. I should not have let my anger rise up within me. I suppose it is my Irish sensibilities that make me so fiery. You knew me own mother was from Enniskillen, of county Fermanagh, in Eire, did you not?

Pastor chuckled at her response. "Blame the Irish, would ya now? Me own grandfather was from Westmeath, so we will have none of the blame against Eire."

The mood was somewhat lightened, but the issue remained. With Elijah's leading, the family discussed the pros and cons. Some of the things were easy to consider, while others only raised the alarm again.

Finally, Thomas made the greatest recommendation of all. "We have discussed enough and have settled upon nothing. There is one thing that we have not done. We have not sought the guidance of our Heavenly

Father. What might His will be? Did not our pastor come feeling led by the Spirit? How much more we ought to seek His leadership now, for we are promised His guidance from His Word." With that, Thomas asked, "Pastor, would you lead us in prayer?"

Elijah answered, "I would be delighted."

When the prayer time ended, everyone sat in peaceful silence. The matter was still far from being resolved. Each individual still sought for an answer.

The stillness was broken when John addressed Elijah. "I would like for you to approach the earl on my behalf. I am not sure how it is that you have this contact, but I leave it with you. I believe time is of the essence." Then, with a most questionable look, John asked, "Pastor, how is it that you have come to have contact with the earl?"

Elijah took a moment to consider the question before answering. He had confidence that whatever he said to the family would keep with them. He leaned back in his chair and told a most amazing story. "The earl and I have known each other since childhood. My father served his father. Naturally, as boys, we played together. When Christopher began his schooling, he begged his father to allow me to attend with him, as we had become lifelong friends. When it came time for him to have an escort, his father added to my training to become by friend's protector. I have direct access to the earl, because I also see to his protection to this day."

Thomas laughed. "Seems to me, Pastor, you bring a new meaning to The Lord's Army."

Elijah returned the gesture with a smile. "Perhaps you're right, but there is more to the story. You see, the earl's father heard word of a private meeting of Christians and dispatched me to disband the group and imprison the leaders. I found them, of course, and marched in ready to do as I was commanded." Elijah leaned forward and locked his fingers together. He hung his head as he thought about that night. He continued. "I went up to their leader, Pastor Chadwick, and hit him with a terrible backhand. You know what he did?" They all shook their heads no. "He turned the other cheek. Then Pastor Chadwick said to the people that everything was all right. He offered his hands for restraint. He said that he would not resist."

Elijah stood and showed them how Pastor Chadwick offered his hands. He took slow breaths before continuing. "I was dumbfounded as how a man could be so calm and peaceful even though he faced imprisonment and even death. I stood frozen, unable to carry out my duty. Pastor Chadwick called for someone to bring me some drink and offered me a chair. To this day, I do not know why I did it, but I began asking questions about their faith. I let them be and went back, telling his lordship that I could not find them." Elijah looked at the family with the tenderness deep within this man of God. "I returned often. Soon, I accepted their faith as my own. Before long, I felt the call to preach, and so here I am."

Chastity spoke up. "But that doesn't explain your present relationship with the earl."

Elijah answered, "I continued to serve the earl. Christopher and I remained constant friends. When I felt the time was right, I began sharing my faith. To my surprise, my dearest friend was receptive to all I told him. Christopher told me that he had long been disillusioned with the state religion. In short, the earl is a private believer like us. While I am still an escort to his lordship, I also am his spiritual advisor."

John leaned back in his chair. "Will wonders never cease? I tell you, Pastor, you are the most amazing man I have ever known."

Elijah replied, "John, a man must be willing to fight for what he believes in. God did not save us to be martyrs. He saved us to carry the Gospel. In life, we must protect ourselves. I am willing to lay down my life, but I am so much more willing to live it."

John gave thought and answered, "I think I do understand, sir."

Then to make sure all understood the gravity of the situation, Elijah charged, "I hope you realize that the information I shared with you concerning his lordship must remain with you. Though he is of royal blood, it does not offer him protection. You must keep the secret. If we fail, my dear friend could lose his life."

All nodded in agreement, and with one voice they all stated, "We will keep the faith."

John observed the faces of those present. Thomas and Ruth were sitting quietly. Elijah was just watching over all. John turned from everyone as though not to be distracted from his thoughts. To leave the family that he loved and his homeland was difficult enough. The prospect of being without Chastity was more than he could imagine. Deep down he knew it wasn't fair to her or her parents. What Chastity purposed was more than he could ever expect or even consider. Did he want her to come with the hope of being his wife? More than anything. But what life could she possibly hope to have? John did not want her to suffer for want. He wanted the best for her. It was reasonable to expect this opportunity for him.

Emotionally, he felt the grief of not being able to provide for her. His heart pounded as he contemplated being separated from her. He slowly turned to face the family and fixed his gaze to the floor. John had lots to think about and knew he must prove himself, especially to the woman he loved.

Chastity was also lost in thought. There was a questioning, serene look about her. John wanted to be with her privately. There were things he had to say to her alone. He stood up and walked over to her. Then, extending his hand, he asked, "Chastity, would you come outside with me?"

Chastity took his hand, and together, they made their way to the door. John then looked at Elijah and her parents and said, "Please excuse us. We shall return soon."

They walked over to a low-hanging tree. This favorite spot of the family was where Thomas had placed a bench. They took a seat on the bench and faced each other. John just held Chastity's beautiful, soft hands. He raised them to his lips and kissed her fingers. He closed his eyes, thinking how blessed he was to have the love of a woman like Chastity.

John lifted his eyes to look at her. He smoothed her hair and allowed his fingers to run the length of it. At that moment, he had to control himself. He tried to be sensible and keep control of his emotions. "I want you with me. I can't deny it, but I don't think it would be good for you to go with me right now."

Chastity was stunned by what he said. She turned her gaze backward before replying. "You don't want me."

John took his fingers and gently touched her chin, slowly turning her back to face him. "I want you more than a man should. Yes, I want you to be my wife. It's just the insane sensibility in me that speaks to me, telling me you deserve more."

Chastity looked into the deep-blue eyes of the man she loved. His gaze always reached deeper into her soul. She felt her pulse quicken, and she began to take longer, fuller breaths. At that moment, she wanted to kiss him passionately. Little did she know that John wanted the same. Chastity came closer, her eyes peering deep into his. She laid her head on his chest and could hear his heart pounding.

She then pleaded, "My loving John, let me go with you. We can make it. I know we can. I will be a good wife to you."

Lifting her head so that he could gaze into her eyes, he replied, "You will be. I want no other for my bride, but I want and need to do what is best for you … for us."

From the gloom of the moment came the first rays of joy. A great smile swept over John's face. A question formed in his mind, and the words escaped from his lips. "Chastity?"

Chastity lovingly replied, "Yes, John."

John leaned in to lay his face to hers and whispered in her ear, "My sweet wonder Chastity, will you accept my proposal to become my bride?"

Chastity looked at him mockingly. "Are you serious?"

John's face became somber as he made his reply. "Never more serious than I have ever been. Chastity, will you marry me?"

Chastity was taken by surprise, but in an instant, it all changed. Joyful radiance swept over her. She immediately threw her arms around his neck. With great delight, she shrieked, "Yes, yes, yes. I want more than anything to marry you. You have no idea how long I have waited for this moment."

Then, lifting his eyes, he spoke. "I have long imagined that this would be the place I would ask you to marry me. Now I want it to be the place where we plan our future together. We know that we can't marry right away. I need to secure work and prepare a place for us to live. Whether it is here or in America, well, that is yet to be determined. In the meantime, I … we must prepare for the future."

John smoothed Chastity's hair. His eyes were fixed upon her. Then he peered deeply into her green emeralds. "I have one question for you. If I do go to America, will you wait for me to prepare for us? I want to provide a house for us in which to make a home. So, my sweet, loving lady, will you trust me and wait for me?"

Chastity looked down, and John thought she was about to pull away.

Then she tightened the grip on his hands and lifted them to her lips. She admired the strength of his hands. Though he was a man who could forge iron, his hands were so gentle. She kissed each finger. Then, returning her gaze, she answered, "I am totally committed to you. I want to go with you wherever you want to go. I ask that whatever is decided upon that we do it together. If you feel we should go to America, then I will go, but must we travel separately?"

John felt the pain in his own heart. He wanted her to go with him but feared the unknown. Once again, he urged her to understand. "My love, I don't know the dangers. I also know that some would seek to do me harm if they thought they could get to you. I am asking that you trust me to do what is right for us. I promise that we will marry soon." Then John did something he had never done before. He put his arms about her. He drew her close to him. She closed her eyes and began to breathe quickly, anticipating his next move. John tilted his head and began brushing his lips on hers. Chastity could hardly restrain herself. Never had she felt so excited or so moved.

John leaned back and asked, "Will you remember this kiss? Will you wait till all is ready?"

Chastity's eyes were still closed. She grabbed John's shirt and pulled him closer. This time, she kissed him passionately. John was finding it hard to restrain his own thoughts. When she released him, she asked, "Will you remember my kiss?"

John's face beamed. "I will never forget it."

Then Chastity answered, "John, you better prepare for us as quickly as you can. I don't think I want to wait that long."

John could only laugh at the moment and felt embarrassed at the same time. He looked at her and said, "Perhaps we should have saved our kisses for our wedding day."

Chastity asked, "So you didn't like my kiss?"

John laughed. "You know I did. As much as it pains me, I must now wait for the next one."

Chastity slyly replied, "Perhaps not."

Then, looking at Chastity with deep longing, John said, "I think we ought to speak to your family about our decision."

She agreed. John stood and helped her to her feet. She took his arm, and they walked ever so slowly back to the house.

# Faith

The next day John and Chastity were with his family. John hadn't returned home until late the night before, making it necessary to make their announcement another day. They had to wait for James to return from his milk deliveries before meeting with him. James had great fondness for this young woman who had shown such great love for his son and his family. It took Martha a bit more time to warm up to her, but soon, they were as close as any mother and daughter could be. James loved the impact Chastity had on his son. John was a strong and capable man in his own right, but she had made him an educated man—a man of intelligence. Above all, she had shared the greatest gift of all: the gift of God's love.

When the time was right, John and Chastity sat with James and Martha to relate the conversation of the previous night with Elijah and Chastity's parents. James and Martha sat and intently listened to all that had transpired. James looked into his son's youthful face to see if he could find any hint of what John might be considering. To his surprise, there was nothing in John's expressions or his speech to indicate what direction he might take.

James was proud of John, though seldom did he say so. It was expected that a man would work and provide for his family. What James found in John was so much more. Since learning to read and write, John had developed into a man of culture. You might say his speech was becoming more like the books he read, especially the Bible. More often than not, John would say things regarding his faith. Quite literally, he expressed his faith from the words of Holy Script. Sadly, John's faith was something James knew nothing about.

It was a warm day—much too warm to be in the house. James and Martha joined John and Chastity outside on the green grass. John began sharing the previous night's discussion by saying, "I want you to know that I have spent the night and this day seeking God's direction for my life. The blacksmith's actions have cost me dearly. I have no future here. I do not trust the smith, and I believe he will seek to do me even more hurt in the community and beyond."

James considered the words when he replied, "Aye, he will at that. What might you be thinking of doing?"

John looked admiringly at his father. His father had sought a better life for him and was blaming himself for his son's situation. John's answer was set on correcting this thought. "I believe that God is in control of my life. Oh, I don't mean that the Almighty moves us like puppets, but He sets events and occasions in our lives that are meant to give us greater direction."

James countered. "You think God made the blacksmith treat you unfairly?"

John remained thoughtful. "No, that is the ugly nature of the man. However, God can still use the wickedest man to point us into the way we need to go."

James looked puzzled. "I don't understand what you mean."

John smiled. "I am not explaining it very well. Pastor explained last night to us that the smith has been taking the things I make and then selling them at the market for profit. He also said it's likely the smith would not proclaim me a smith in my own right for as long as I continue to make him a profit." John sat forward a bit before continuing. "I do not believe God intends for me to remain an apprentice. I believe he wants me to use my talents elsewhere."

Martha looked at her son. "Where might you think about going?"

John turned his head to face her. "I haven't decided completely, but I know will not be able to continue my trade here. While the smith is not liked, he does have the power to tell others that I did not finish my apprenticeship." John sat up straight and looked at his parents. "There is one real possibility. I am considering going to America."

James could not believe what he just heard. Martha felt faint. They looked at each other and then back at John. It was James who spoke. "When did you come to this thought?"

John answered, "Pastor suggested it last evening. Since then, I have not been able to rid it from my mind."

James leaned forward and looked at his son. "Your mother and I thought of the same thing last evening." James squirmed a bit, feeling uncomfortable. He asked of John, "Might this be the thing you were telling us about God directing your life?"

John answered, "I know that going to America would offer opportunities and challenges for me. There are many dangers there. The Spanish still manage to hold much of the shipping in the Atlantic. Some Indians are hostile toward newcomers. I suspect trade is the payment over money, and that is why some have gone as indentured servants. I have also considered what it means for me to stay here. I am twenty and much too old to be an apprentice to someone else. Unless someone declares me a blacksmith and will pay for the tools I need, I very much doubt I can make a living here. I have no doubt the smith will waste little time trying to ruin my name to others."

James thought about what his son was saying. "So have you made up your mind about what you plan to do?"

John leaned forward and took Chastity's hand. "Father, we want to know all that our parents think. Our mutual faith also leads us to seek God's guidance."

James was sincere when he asked, "So has God shown you anything? I mean, as to what is best for you and Chastity."

John chuckled. "Not as you might suspect. It is more of just waiting. You see, Father, when we pray, we wait on the Lord to answer. Sometimes the answer is impressed on us with a real clarity. God may show us a sign. Even some have said that they have heard the audible voice of God speak. The Bible speaks of how all these things happen. Throughout Biblical history, men were given direction from God. A man named Noah was told by God to build an ark and gave him instructions as to how to build it. David wanted to build a temple for God, but God gave word to the prophet to tell him that he couldn't. Abraham prayed and tested God's plan for him. Hezekiah sought for a sign. Nehemiah felt the leading of God."

James shook his head in wonder. "You learned all that from your Bible?"

Chastity sat forward excitedly. "Yes, it is all there for any and all to read and learn from. Men like your son, my father, and Pastor have read the Bible and have shared the messages from it to all who want to hear."

James wrinkled his brow. "John, you know all this from the Bible? Why have you not said more to me?"

John answered, "I was afraid you wouldn't be interested. The times I tried to talk about it I just thought … well, you know."

James lifted himself up from the ground and strolled about a little. John and Chastity thought he was walking away from the conversation. Instead, he slowly turned to them. "You know I can't read. I knew God wanted someone as talented and skilled as you. What would God want with a poor dairy farmer who has nothing to give?"

John looked up. "Father, please sit with us."

James returned and sat with the family.

John continued. "What does any man have that God would want? Does God need our talents? No, but He uses them. Does God need our money?" After a chuckle, he continued. "What would the creator of all things do with money? In fact, God made all things and then gave it to man for his benefit, not His own."

James raised his head and looked at Chastity and John. "I never thought of it in that way. When I was a boy, I was forced to attend Mass, and the priest said God demanded we give what we had or die and suffer in purgatory till someone paid us out. For years after, I worked to get my own father and mother out of it. I don't remember much more than that."

Chastity reached over and touched James's hand and addressed him as a father. "Pater, God's Word says that Jesus paid the price for salvation. Have you heard of His death, burial, and resurrection? He paid with His life what we could not pay. Jesus, who is holy and sinless, paid the price of sin with His blood on the cross. He proved His death paid that price by His resurrection. And Jesus said that all who believe in Him shall have eternal life."

John smiled. "I couldn't have said it better. Father, Mum, it is called faith. It's about believing that our Lord lived, died at the hands of cruel men on the cross, was buried for three days, and rose victoriously on that third day. I know you have heard some of this before. Now I ask, Father, will you believe in Him as your Lord and Savior?"

James slumped over and turned once more from the kids. He was deep in thought. In his mind, he struggled to overcome the things taught to him in the past. There was one thing that kept challenging his thoughts: the evidence of things he witnessed over the years. James recalled the tyranny of the religious rulers of his youth. He thought of the joy John had shown since becoming a believer. There was an obvious difference in the past and the present. What was the difference? Then it occurred to him. The difference was John and Chastity's faith in Jesus. Turning to the young couple, he replied, "I have much to learn, and I don't know much. If you will teach me, then I will have Him for my Savior."

With tears streaming down his face, John presented the Gospel of Jesus Christ to his parents. The evening was spent in the Word of God as James and Martha trusted in Him. Before long, John dispatched Adam to get Chastity's parents and his pastor. One by one, they came. Soon, there was much rejoicing in the little cottage. When the fire was lit, the room glowed in the warmth of moment. Martha and her daughters set out fresh cheese and bread with a bottle of wine they'd saved for a special occasion. There was never such an occasion as this.

The night pressed on, and it was James who spoke. "I urge you all to stay with us tonight. I know it is late and none too safe to go home. Our home is simple, but we have room. Please, stay here. My boys and I will stay in the barn. Pastor, you and Thomas are welcome to stay there with us, and we will leave the women to the house."

It took some coaxing, but finally, all agreed. The men retired to the barn, and the women remained in the house, but there was little sleeping to be had. All during the night, James and Martha asked their respected guest questions of their newfound faith. After a while, things calmed down a bit.

In the barn, Thomas offered, "I have a Bible, James, and you are welcome to read these things for yourself if you'd like."

A momentary silence crept over James. When he spoke, it caused pain in the heart of Thomas. "I cannot accept, for, you see, I cannot read."

It was Elijah who recovered the conversation. "Then we shall have to remedy that, shan't we?"

James questioned, "You mean you will teach me to read?"

Elijah chortled. "And write, if you so desire."

James knew an amazing gift had just been given him. The offer of such a gift filled him with warmth. He felt joy beyond all that could be imagined. He thought, *So this is what I have been missing.*

Though there was joy at the Dairyman's home, little did anyone suspect there was darkness looming. Evil would come with the dawn.

# Revenge

William the blacksmith woke once more with a throbbing head from the excessive rum he'd consumed the night before. The stench of the liquor ebbed from the pores of his body. His mouth was dry, and the taste left by the rum was foul. He struggled from his bed and called out with an angry hiss. "John!"

There was no response.

"John!" came the second call even more hideous than the first.

In a rage, he marched to the room where John had spent nearly nine years of his life. As William made his way toward the room, he bellowed, "John, you lazy sop, I'll teach you to not answer." He looked into the room, but there was no one there. "Where ..."

William's head throbbed. Somehow he managed to take control of his mind and dragged from his memory the events of the past several days. After a few moments, he managed to speak. "That ungrateful whelp left me."

William struggled to a table where he often took his meals. Many a night he had forced John to fix him his dinner. The room was cold. There was no fire. There was no food prepared and set on the table. The table was a mess, because there was no one to clean up. The table was cluttered with the empty rum bottles. William walked over to the table and placed his hands firmly to it. His back was bent and his head bowed. His head was a whirl. He tried to will away the awful pain, but nothing helped. In a rage, he raised his head, and with one swoop of his hand, he raked the bottles. Glass shattered against the walls and floor. He plopped himself down in a chair and allowed the rage to build before speaking. "I shall have my revenge upon thee, boy."

The blacksmith had treated John like a slave. He had come to enjoy taking his vengeance out on the boy for the hurt within him. John had learned to stay out of the smith's way. William demanded John to rise early in the morning to make his breakfast, clean the cottage, and keep the barn. John had to be up before his master even though the smith kept him up well past dark. When William came home drunk, it was John who saw him to bed and was sure to have everything straightened up by morning. From gathering and chopping wood to building fires and preparing meals, John did it all. This was the price he paid in order to be an apprentice.

After what William had said to the people in front of his shop, they were staying away. He conveniently forgot that on the day he sent John away that he also told the townsfolk to stay away. In the surliness of his mind, he imagined John trying to ruin him. *I suppose the boy is planning to set up shop elsewhere,* he thought to himself. *I'll show him. I will find a way to grind him into dust.*

His mind whorled about, and he fought the hangover that loomed. Every little noise made the pounding worse. He looked about for more rum, but there wasn't a drop to be found. His head pounded, and every little sound hurt. Just then, he heard the familiar sound of squeaky wheels and rattling cans. He knew this slow, ebbing noise. It was James making his milk deliveries.

William lifted himself to go out and meet with the man whose son he'd offered to train. In front of his barn he eyed the cart entering the village. William watched the slow progression, and the rhythmic sounds the cart made didn't help his head any. He did not know if James would stop on his own. He was determined to make sure he did. Out the barn door he walked to the middle of the street. On came the cart, slowly but surely.

James had stopped each day to see his son and deliver a bit of cheese and milk. This was part of the payment given for John's training. As James approached, he saw the blacksmith walk from the barn, no doubt to stop him. As soon as he was close enough, James halted the cart.

William looked to James and asked, "Where is your boy? He wasn't here when I woke this morning."

James stared directly down the street as he replied, "I am not surprised after you told him to leave and never return. Besides that, you did everything you could to hurt him."

William remembered nothing. He had literally been drunk out of his mind. With his head pounding, he knew better than to try and reason with James. Instead, he just asked, "Who told you that lie?"

James was in no mood to deal with William but answered, "No lie. I have heard from many a reliable folk who said John saved you and your barn." Then, looking at the large man, he added, "How did you award him? By threatening him with even more harm."

William walked over and began to pet James's horse and remarked, "I may have had a bit of rum, but is that any reason to keep your son from coming back? I meant him no harm. Send him back to me. I want him back so I can finish his training."

The words from the smith were too much for James to handle. The normally quiet and reserved man couldn't stand the smith any more. From the seat of the cart, he looked down at William. He waited till the smith looked at him and then responded, "No, he will not be coming back. You think I don't know how you treated my boy? And for what? Just so you would train him to be a blacksmith." James gripped the reins tighter in his fist and then continued. "You're a rogue, William. So mean are you that you would beat a boy for no reason at all and force him to do things that were not part of our agreement."

The answer only stirred the rage in the blacksmith. With an angst in his voice, he retorted, "Then he will never be a real blacksmith. Soon everyone will see his limits. I tell you now: return the boy to me, or else I will see that he never becomes a blacksmith."

James could see clearly. His hopes in the beginning were to give John a new start in life. He knew now that William had never been the man to teach him. With a clammy voice, James's answer reflected these thoughts. "I can see clearly now that it was a mistake to have struck an agreement with you about training him. I will not make the same mistake twice by placing him in the care of a man who would only seek even greater opportunity to hurt him." James gritted his teeth. "I ought to inflict upon you the whelps you left on my boy. I ought to burn your skin and leave scars on your soul." Then, leaning forward to make sure William saw his face, he added, "No, I won't do it. Our agreement is over. Find another if you can, but you and I know your reputation in the village is over. Now get away from my horse."

James was about to slap the reins. William remained indignant and unmoved.

William asked, "Wait. Where is my bit of cheese?"

James threw his head back and laughed in reply. "You lost that payment as well when you demanded my son leave. Someday I hope you realize how much you have lost, but I truly doubt it." Then, with a snap of the leather straps, the horse pulled off.

William watched as James urged his horse onward. An evil grin crept over the smith's face. It finally came to him what he would do. He wanted John back. If he did not come, he knew how he would exact his revenge on his former apprentice.

What evil lurks in the minds of men? What would cause a man to seek opportunity against another? Men may think they have reason to take vengeance on someone even though they have created the situation. William knew he had to have a convincing story as to why he forced the young man to leave. He knew that for his plan to work, he needed the right person to act for him. There were a few who were acquaintances, mostly pub friends, but there were others who owed him for work he'd done—work that he had not been paid for. His mind fixed upon one such person. The man who he would confront was Taylor Shanks, the sheriff.

William knew secrets about Taylor. William did not like the sheriff, but Taylor owed him. Taylor brought work for William to do with promise to pay later, but later never came. Afterward, William would find Taylor at the pub nursing a drink and many times reminded him what he owed. Taylor had mounted a debt. William decided it was time to call in his debt to be paid immediately.

William closed his cottage and walked through the barn and out to the street. There was no one waiting for work to be done. As though some plague had visited his establishment, people were now staying away. Folks did not like William much, but seeing that he was the only smith in town, they still came to him.

William snarled as he walked the street, "I will take my revenge on you too, good people of Sussex."

Very few people took notice of the hulking, dirty man. Those who did thought he was on his way to find more rum. William greeted no one, and no one greeted him. On the outskirts of town stood a cottage. William lumbered to the door and knocked loudly.

A middle-aged woman opened the door and asked, "Can I help you?"

William was stunned. "Well, lassie, and who might you be? I am here to see Taylor. Tell him that the blacksmith has some important business to discuss."

The woman invited William in, turned, and hurried to the bedroom. William could hear her waking the sheriff. No doubt he too was recovering from a night of indulgence. Taylor mumbled something to the woman. Hurriedly, she ran past William and out the door.

In a few moments, Taylor Shanks came ambling out of his room. His eyes were red from little sleep. Turning to the smith, he uttered, "Sit down, William. I will be with you in a bit."

William wasted little time in reply. "So who was the lass who kept you company last night? Is our good sheriff keeping secrets?"

"She is none of your concern," Taylor snapped. "What reason might you have to come here this time of day to disturb my morning?"

In those times, magistrates were not chosen by the people but were appointed by those in authority. Oftentimes, a man might be awarded a position for service to his Lord. Usually, the appointment was considered for life. In some cases, these men kept their appointment by remaining loyal to the one who granted them their position. Taylor kept his position by staying just within the limits of his office and out of the reach of the official who had appointed him.

Taylor walked over to a basin of water and washed his face and hands. He gathered a bit of bread and cold meat before sitting down at the table. William had not moved. His mouth began to salivate at the sight of the food.

Taylor bit into a piece of bread before turning to William. "Why are you here?"

William coldly answered, "Not very hospitable of you to not offer me something to eat."

Taylor stopped chewing and looked at the blacksmith. He despised the man, and it offended him that he would come to his home without an invite. He pushed the plate of meat and the bread toward him.

William quickly took an empty chair and greedily tore off a hunk of bread and indulged in a great portion of meat. He stuffed his mouth with food, bulging his cheeks out. He almost choked with every swallow only to bite off even greater mouthfuls. The sight made the sheriff despise him all the more.

Taylor asked again, "Why are you here?"

William stopped chewing long enough to stare back at Taylor. He swallowed his massive bite before answering, "I have come to issue a complaint."

Taylor knew how loathsome a person the smith was. Sitting back in his chair, Taylor asked, "Who might you have a complaint against? Someone not pay you?"

William continued to fill his mouth with food. He didn't so much as lift his eyes before responding. "Against my apprentice."

Taylor raised his eyes in total surprise. John was the most likeable young man, and Taylor knew the villagers liked him. He asked, "What kind of charges would you bring on the young man?"

The question amused William, but like a cat that loves to play with his prey, he toyed with the sheriff. "He is the greatest menace of all. I could say he assaulted me, but seeing as I am so much bigger, I doubt any would take notice. No, what I have is much more serious."

Taylor grew impatient. "Then get on with it, man. What has he done?"

William gave an evil snarl. "It isn't what he has done as much as who he says he is. The lad claims to be a Christian."

Taylor's face showed disgust. "What of it? Many men and women of the village are Christians. That is hardly any reason to bring that kind of charge."

William sat back a bit in his chair. "That may be so, but they are part of the King's church. John, I suspect, is a secret member of one of the forbidden churches."

Taylor quizzed, "And how do you come by this knowledge?"

William replied, "He told me himself. I had to release him as soon as I heard it. Now I want you to arrest him."

Taylor shot back. "Arrest him for what? Who do think you are to come here without proof, demanding such action?"

William stopped eating long enough to sneer. "Oh, I know who I am, and I know you will arrest him. If you don't, I will simply go to the earl."

That kind of talk only angered the sheriff. "What right have you to go to his lordship?"

Smugly, William replied, "It's simple, really. I would tell his lordship that the sheriff would not represent me."

Taylor laughed. "You think he would pay you any mind?"

"Oh, he would, especially when I tell him other things—like how you owe me for work rendered, and I am sure he would like to know about this woman who has visited your home. I am sure he would not find your actions fitting for a magistrate."

Taylor jumped from the table erect with his fist clenched at his side. He looked the smith square in the eyes before responding. "How dare you come into my house, interrupt my sleep, and make threats against me. I ought to—"

But before the sheriff could say another word, William turned his head and replied, "No need to threaten me. What I know, I know, and I won't say a word if you do me this favor. Bring accusation against my young apprentice, and all your debts to me will be paid. Then you will never hear from me again. It's just that simple."

The sheriff thought for a moment, and gradually, his stance relaxed. He turned from the table and walked about the room. He began wringing his hands together as he thought things through. The blacksmith remained quiet as he continued to gorge himself on bread and meat.

The sheriff slowly turned and gave his verdict. "All right, I will do this. I will go to the earl and tell him what you have told me. After this, I want no more of you in my house, in public, or along the way. I want a bill with the words 'paid in full' given to me before I go to me lordship."

"That would hardly do any good," came William's reply, "seeing as I don't know how to read and write."

"Then I'll do it for you right now," said Taylor with a growl.

William's response was expected. "How do I know if you are putting down what you say?"

Taylor concluded the conversation. "You don't. Accept it, or get out."

William thought for a moment and nodded his head in approval.

With that, Taylor quickly snatched up paper and quill, wrote a quick bill, and slammed the paper before the smith. "Now sign it."

William scratched his mark on the paper. As soon as it was done, the sheriff made one more statement. "I'll go to the earl soon. Now you may leave and never come back."

William reached for one more piece of meat. A knife quickly came down point first on the table just beyond the reach of the smith. "I said, get out."

A startled look came over the blacksmith. He moved his hand, stood, and walked toward the door. Turning back, he looked at the sheriff, nodded his head, and replied before walking out, "You might remember who it is who made your knife and sharpened your blade. I have many more."

The blacksmith walked up the street, pleased with himself that he had laid the perfect trap for John. Little did he know that one must be careful not to fall into his own trap, especially when you don't know the prey you might catch.

The next day Taylor made his way to see the earl. He arrived midmorning and was met by the earl's butler. The butler went before the earl with the news that the sheriff requested an audience. A short time later, Sir Christopher received the sheriff into his chambers upon hearing news that there was a grave issue in the village. Any complaint of disturbance would demand immediate attention.

Taylor had been appointed sheriff upon recommendation by another magistrate in the earl's realm. The earl did not approve of Taylor but kept him on by recommendation of the said magistrate. When Taylor was younger, his attributes were well known. He had been a good official, but something happened to change all of that. The earl did not know what had brought this about. What he did know was the sheriff was not as given to his duties as he once was.

When Taylor entered the room, he found the earl sitting comfortably in his chamber. Taylor entered and stood almost military erect. Christopher did not offer him a seat. Instead, he got quickly to the point.

"I understand that you have a matter that needs my attention. Is that true, Sheriff?"

Taylor was uncomfortable standing in the presence of royalty. There was an element of authority and power in his lordship that Taylor knew nothing about. Taylor recognized it in the tone of the earl's voice. Taylor seemed to sense that this man would judge everything that was said to him, so he must be careful.

Taylor was dressed in the best he had, but he felt little and unworthy to stand before the earl. Though the earl was dressed casually enough, there was still a presence about him. The sheriff tried to act official as he replied, "Yes, me lordship, an accusation has been made against a young man of our village that could cause insurrection among the people."

The earl responded, "This is a serious charge, Lord Sheriff. Do you have enough evidence to bring such a charge?"

Taylor tried to stay calm. "I haven't any evidence, but there is a man who came to me and made the accusation. I have learned several others can verify the accused of his statement."

The earl asked, "And what statement might that be?"

Taylor continued. "A young man emphatically stated that he is a Christian."

The earl frowned at what the sheriff said. The earl's eyes seemed dark and imposing. "Why does that alarm you? Is not the state religion, our own Church of England, a Christian one? Isn't our beloved king also a proclaiming Christian?"

The earl's response unnerved the sheriff. Taylor cleared his throat and continued. "It is true, sire, but this lad is accused of being a member of one of the outlawed congregations."

The earl thought a moment, showing no signs of his feelings. "And this man, has he caused trouble? Is he a rouser? Has he imposed his beliefs on others?"

Taylor, feeling more relaxed, replied, "Well, no, but his statement could harm the balance in the village."

Christopher quizzed, "How so?"

Taylor had not expected examination. He thought he might be able to meet with his lordship, make his claim, and leave. In some ways, he thought the earl would give him the benefit of the doubt. He didn't have a good answer to the question.

Once again, the earl asked, "Lord Sheriff, I asked you a question. How is it that the things said serve to disrupt the people?"

Taylor answered, "It will divide the people."

The earl laughed. "Truly? Seems to me that the people of England are already divided between Catholic and the Church of England. You mean to tell me that a small group of separatists could upset that balance?"

Taylor was surprised by the answer, and the earl could see it in his expression. Taylor searched his mind before responding. "But they are forbidden to meet."

The earl turned toward a table next to him and lifted a glass of port. He supped a little and asked, "So where do they meet?"

Once again, Taylor was baffled. "I ... I ... eh, I don't know."

Christopher stood and walked over to his desk. He appeared to be looking for something when he asked, "Tell me, Sheriff, who is it that has made this accusation to you?"

The sheriff replied, "I'd rather not say."

The reply angered the earl. He pounded a fist on the desk. With a voice of authority, he demanded, "You come here and make an accusation. I think you have forgotten whom you're addressing. I am not one of the villagers to whom you can conveniently wave off an answer." Christopher walked around the desk to stand directly in front of the sheriff. "I have a right to know who would dare make and accusation, and if you value your station, you will tell me now."

The sheriff felt trapped like a bird in a snare. He wanted to fly away and forget the whole thing, but felt his feet pinned to the ground. He could not escape. He knew he had to tell or lose it all. There was a tremor in his voice as he answered. "The blacksmith made the accusation."

The earl remained motionless. His facial expressions did not change. Then he moved back to his table and took another drink of the port. Facing the sheriff, he asked, "Why would the blacksmith bring such a charge? Is the blacksmith a loyal parishioner of the Church of England? I don't recall seeing him anywhere near the church."

The sheriff felt like he was being tried by a skilled lawyer. The earl was asking questions for which he had no answers. Taylor's anger was mounting toward the blacksmith, and he was angry with himself for not seeing to his debts sooner. Taylor did not have answers, but he was determined to get them. Looking at the earl, he offered, "I see what you mean. I haven't investigated the accusation thoroughly. I need to check the facts for myself. With your permission, I will continue my investigation and return with the facts." Taylor paused for a moment before continuing. "May I go?"

The earl was shocked at the request but admired the answer. Showing nothing of his surprise, he answered, "You have yet to tell me the name of the accused."

Taylor frowned. "His name is John. He is the apprentice to the smith."

The earl took his chair, placed his elbow on the armrests, and raised his fingers to a peak before his lips. He responded carefully. "This is an interesting accusation, and one that I must also consider. Is the young man still working with the smith?"

Taylor replied, "No, Your Lordship, the smith said he felt he had to let the lad go for his unlawful act."

The earl commented, "I know the smith, and I very much doubt that. He couldn't care less about religion, or anyone for that matter. However, I will wait to see what you uncover. Lord Sheriff, return as soon as you have more details." Then, with a gesture of the hand, he dismissed Taylor. "You may go."

Taylor stood a moment completely stunned. No other word was spoken. He turned to walk away, not knowing what he should do. He couldn't wait to leave the chamber, and yet, he was afraid to turn away from the earl. With a bow, he offered, "Thank you, me lord." Then he turned and left the room. Taylor began to walk toward the entry. He was surprised to find another man whom he had seen around town also waiting to see the earl. Elijah Brown was seated and waiting for his opportunity to see the earl. Taylor had one thought. *What is he doing here?* The butler opened the door, and Taylor quickly exited.

Before long, Elijah was welcomed into the earl's chambers. A butler escorted him in and announced, "Elijah Brown requests an audience with his lordship."

The earl accepted the request, and Elijah walked in regally. Before dismissing the butler, the earl asked him to bring him and his guest chaa and dainties. The butler exited the room. As soon as the door closed, Christopher rose from his chair and walked over to his dear friend. Earl Christopher took the hand of the pastor and personally welcomed Elijah. "Come in, my friend. What brings you here today?"

Elijah had a mellow smile come across his face. "It is always such joy to be welcomed by a good friend and faithful brother in Christ."

There was a warmth that emitted from the brotherhood of these men. The earl invited his friend to come sit with him, and both men walked over to two fine easy chairs.

Elijah smiled. "You always make me fill like royalty."

Christopher laughed. "Well, aren't we more like brothers?" The Earl felt true comfort in the company of his lifelong friend and pastor. He continued. "It is how I imagined I would welcome the Lord our Savior if he came through the door. Did He not say that if you have done it unto the least of one of these you have done it unto Me?"

Elijah replied, "Indeed He did. Nonetheless, I was enjoy returning to the house where we grew up together."

Earl Christopher leaned back in his chair. "So what have I done to deserve a visit from you?"

Elijah leaned forward. "I have come on behalf of a young man who may need your help. I have also come to propose an idea that may benefit this young man as well."

The earl seemed quite interested. "Oh? And I thought you came to share with me the good Word of God."

Elijah laughed. "You know that it always foremost in my mind, but this matter may become urgent."

Leaning forward, the earl posed a question. "I see. You said it has something to do with a young man. Do I know him?"

Elijah answered, "Not personally, though you do know of his handiwork. I must also tell you that he is a fellow servant of our Lord." Elijah looked over at the small round table that stood between the two easy chairs. There on the table upon a folded napkin was an ornate silver spoon. He picked up the spoon and admired the craftsmanship. "The young man I speak of made this spoon."

The earl knew Elijah wouldn't make such a statement without a reason. "And how do you know this, Brother?"

Elijah removed the knife from his side pocket and laid it beside the spoon. Pointing to the two items, he commented, "Look at the engravings. They are the same. The young man who made this knife also made the spoon. He told me that he always engraves his mark."

The earl was surprised at the craftsmanship and responded, "I never took notice before. My son has these wares made and tells me that they are handcrafted by a local artisan."

Elijah smiled. "I know. Who do you think told him of maker? He also adds his signature."

The earl surprisingly asked, "He does? Where? I see no signature."

Pastor leaned forward and pointed to the handle. "See the long, curved mark that appears to be a vine? That is actually an S for smith. Now look just below the middle curve, and you will see a branch follow the curve and then flare to the left. That is the letter J."

The earl chuckled. "Done in by a true artist. I had no idea that you knew such a talented young man or that I benefited from his talents for my own. His work is exquisite. He is quite talented, is he not?"

Pastor remarked, "Indeed, dear friend, but his skills have stirred jealousy and rage in his teacher."

The earl looked at Elijah. "Tell me your story, for I believe that this has to do with a young man just recently accused before me."

Elijah responded, "I fear that you are right."

Earl Christopher pointed toward the door. "Do you know the man who left here before you?"

Elijah answered, "Yes, he is the town sheriff."

Christopher leaned forward and rubbed his hands together. "He came to me to bring accusation against the apprentice of the local blacksmith."

Pastor replied, "I am not surprised. I thought the smith would waste little time, but I had no idea it would be so soon. May I ask what charge the sheriff levied against lad?"

The earl answered, "He accused him of being a renegade and a rouser leading people against the Church of England."

Elijah shook his head. "Good friend, I am sure this accusation was made by the blacksmith. I saw most of what happened, and what I did not see was the town stirred with the details."

The earl replied, "So what have you learned?"

Pastor answered, "The smith was drunk a few days back. When he came to his barn, he started an altercation with his apprentice. The apprentice's name is John. John tried to keep the smith from hurting him."

The earl stopped him. "What do you mean by hurting him?"

Pastor looked to the floor. "The blacksmith is an angry old soul. Ever since John was left to his charge, the man has beaten him and even burned him with a hot iron. I have seen some of the scars inflicted on him when he was but a boy. The smith's excuse for such treatment was his way of training the boy."

The thought angered the earl. He responded, "Why did the boy stay on?"

Pastor replied, "For the honor of his father. John is the son of the dairyman. His father wanted John to learn a skill that would be worthy of his son's talents and provide him a better future. John dutifully accepted the opportunity and never complained. As he grew older, John began learning on his own. He began working with silver, making cutlery and decorative knives. He soon outpaced the skills of the smith. The smith saw for himself the abilities and began making handsome profits from John's work all the while growing jealous of the boy's talent."

Elijah stood to walk about the room and then continued. "From what I gathered, when the blacksmith came to the barn the other day, John was working on one of your horses."

Earl spoke knowingly, "Ah, so that was the altercation my servant spoke to me about. He told me there was a brawl in town and how a lad saved the blacksmith's barn from burning down. Why didn't John fight back?"

Pastor smiled. "Respect, Your Lordship, and his love of his Savior. John is a Christian and a faithful member of the congregation."

The earl began to picture in his mind all that happened. He stated, "Sheriff Taylor also said that this young man is a rouser."

Pastor replied, "Hardly. John avoided the smith the best he could. He tried to reason with the man. John's defense was that he would not raise a hand to him because of his faith in Jesus Christ." Suddenly, it all came clear to Elijah. His expression relayed his new understanding.

The earl could see it. "What are you thinking?"

Elijah quickly replied, "The smith wants John to return, by force if necessary. The smith needs John to come back."

The earl sat straight up in his chair. "Come back? Why would he want him to come back?"

Pastor turned his face to the window in thought. When he returned his gaze to the earl, he responded, "Two reasons, I suspect. One, because the man is losing business. People prefer the work of lad, because, in truth, it is so much better. Second, What John makes the smith sells for a handsome profit." Pastor returned to his seat. "That is why John needs to be declared a smith—in order to free himself from his master's influence."

Christopher thoughtfully stated, "I know that this is the way things have been for many generations, and it isn't likely to change. However, there are ways to have the young man declared a smith."

Elijah smiled. "That would be good, but there is more to my thought. I believe the smith wants to exact a form of revenge. I believe this great oaf of a man enjoys abusing John. I fear he will not be satisfied till John is left crumpled like a piece of paper."

The earl stood up and walked to look out the window. "This is a grave matter indeed. What you are telling me is that I must deal with a young man of like faith for a false charge made by his master. The laws of our land would favor the blacksmith."

Pastor looked to his friend. "That is true, but as I recall, a young earl to be convinced his father to change the direction of another young man's life." Then walking over to Christopher, Elijah placed a hand on his shoulder before stating, "I know you, Chris, and I know you will find a way."

Turning to the pastor, the earl responded, "All may not be lost. Didn't you say you had an idea?"

The pastor crossed his arms before answering. "I thought John might be sent away as an indentured servant."

The earl raised his eyes in thoughtful interest. "What did you say?"

Pastor restated, "That John might be sent away by your direction to the Americas, as one of your indentured servants. I thought you might send him there as a declared smith where he can serve you and gain a new start."

The two men returned to their seats as Christopher considered the idea. He replied, "You may have something there. I believe it has the right opportunity. I could not send him, as it would be too suspect, but I know of some who would want a man of his talents for their holdings in the New World. The only disappointment would be that I would lose his talents for myself."

Before another word was spoken, there was a gentle tapping at the door. The earl commanded, "You may enter."

The servant carried a tray bearing an aromatic brew of chaa. The servant announced, "Here are the refreshments you have requested." The servant was surprised to see Elijah Brown sitting down as an honored guest.

"You may place it on the table," instructed the earl.

The servant left the tray and received final instruction for his dismissal. The earl took the pot of the boiling-hot brew and poured two cups.

The aroma of the brew emitted from the cup. The Earl replied, "This is a very expensive drink just recently introduced to us from the Orient. It is commonly called chaa, or chaw. Now I drink mine with honey. Please try it."

Pastor tasted it and added some honey before taking another sip. "It's good, my lord. Perhaps it would be good with a little milk."

The earl sampled it and thought a moment. "You might have struck upon something there. It would add to it, wouldn't it? I know many in royalty have taken to it saying they must have their daily chaa. Can't stand that word, really. *Chaa!* Sounds like something a horse would do. I prefer to call it tea."

Later that afternoon, Pastor left the earl's home and made his way back to the village. It was a beautiful day, and Elijah felt like walking. He was leading his horse, giving the animal some rest. He walked a good distance. When he was about to climb his horse, another rider moved from behind some heavy overgrowth. It was the sheriff.

The sheriff lifted his hand as he called out. "Hold to, man. I wish to speak with you."

The pastor was amused. Elijah looked up at the official. "And what business would you want to speak with me about?"

The sheriff reached over and leaned on his horse as he replied, "I wish to inquire as to your business with his lordship."

Pastor Elijah laughed. "I am afraid that detail remains with me and the earl. If you want to know the subject of our conversation, you need to ask his lordship."

The sheriff tried to remain official. "I am asking you. Now who are you, and why were you there?"

Elijah crossed his arms. "As to who I am, it is of little consequence, and as I have told you, if you want to know more, you must ask him." Then, climbing on the horse's back, he added, "I bid you good day."

Elijah's total disregard angered and shocked the sheriff. He was not use to people ignoring his inquiries. Taylor shouted, "Impotence! I shall have you flogged."

Pastor smiled and calmly replied, "I think not. Would you attempt to detain a man you know nothing about? Would you flog a man on special assignment to the earl? Now why would you want to take that chance?"

The sheriff suddenly felt a shudder come over him. "You? You are on assignment to the earl. Why wasn't I told of this?"

The pastor remained calm and coy in his replied. "Is that so hard to imagine that the earl would have agents in town to watch and report back to him?"

The sheriff could not figure things for himself. He continued his examination. "Is that why you were there?"

Elijah laughed. He leaned forward and patted his horse. Looking at the sheriff, he stated, "As I said, if you want to know what the meeting was about, you need to ask his lordship. I might suggest that it may anger the earl should you decided to inquire." Elijah glared at the sheriff. "Let me just say that if you value your station, I would stay clear of the subject."

Then, pausing for a moment, Elijah rubbed his chin. He looked up at the sheriff and continued. "On the other hand, seeing that I am only a short distance from his estate, I think I will return to warn the earl of this issue right now." Elijah pretended to turn his horse back. Once again, he bid, "Good day, Lord Sheriff. After all, his protection is my primary concern, as well as many personal agents." Then, acting as though he spoke out of turn, Elijah added, "Pay no mind as to what I said. The earl would be most upset if others knew of the *private ones*."

The sheriff, now full of fear, called to Elijah. "Now wait. Is it so hard to imagine that it would be my concern over the earl's well-being? There is no need to bother him. You have made your claim, and I see the wisdom in it. Let's just say I stopped you to see to his safety. That is fair, is it not?"

Elijah stopped and turned to the sheriff. He poised himself, appearing to give thought. His answer unnerved the sheriff even more. Elijah took the opportunity to toy with the sheriff as a cat does a mouse it has just caught. "He will not like it one bit, knowing that the secret of his town agent was out. No, I must tell him. When he hears of it and learns you uncovered the truth, well, his lordship will most likely remove you from office and may even send you into exile. I hear the army is needing soldiers."

Great beads of sweat began to form on the sheriff's brow. He tried to look composed, but his nervousness was even sensed by the horse, which began to prance uncontrollably.

Almost immediately, the sheriff replied, "I will speak nothing of this to anyone. You have my word. Let the matter be closed."

The pastor considered his final thought and concluded the conversation. "Very well, but you need to avoid me at any cost. Seeing that it is only you and I who are privy to this conversation, I suggest you keep it to yourself. If any come to me asking about this conversation, I will know that it came from you. If that should happen, I will then relay the message to the earl. Agreed?"

Without hesitation, the sheriff responded, "Agreed. I do. Yes, most agreeable."

It was now the pastor who stood as one in authority. "Then be gone, man, and let me not see you again."

Taylor did not hesitate. He turned his horse and rode swiftly away. The pastor thought to himself, "Well, that might buy a little time."

John and Chastity were enjoying the view from a quiet hillside. They had taken a stroll together. The tall grass whispered in the wind, and field fowl scurried about. The harmonious sounds of bees added to the symphony of nature. Puffy clouds gave shade from the sun. There was life all around them. They let the love they had for each other add words to the music.

The love between them was evident. They found a grassy spot to sit. From their vantage point, they could see Chastity's home. John put his arm around Chastity's shoulders, and she rested her head against him. He raised his hand to feel her long, smooth hair.

She made a soft hum, approving of his touch, and whispered to him, "I love it when you touch my hair."

John turned his head to whisper in her ear. "I love how it feels. Makes me want to kiss you."

Chastity sat up. "You have thought of kissing me?"

John blushed. He was afraid to answer her.

Chastity smiled. "Out with it. Did you just say you thought of kissing me?"

John found the courage to answer. "I cannot deny it. Aye, my darling, are you upset with me?"

Chastity lay her head on his shoulder before responding. "No. I am just glad I am not alone in thinking this thought."

John sat back, surprised, and raised her head so he could see her. Once their eyes met, they laughed. Then held each other closely.

After a while, John said, "Last night was a night to remember. Never have I slept so little, yet felt so happy."

Chastity agreed. "Did any of the men sleep? I know the women were awake most of the night."

John commented, "Hardly any. Oh, and by the way, your father volunteered your services to begin teaching my father to read and write."

Chastity sat up, surprised. "Did your father accept?"

John smiled. "Immediately. So are you interested?"

Chastity quickly answered. "Interested? I'm thrilled! I'll teach him the way I teach you. I'll—" She stopped when she realized John was giving her a look of amazement. She smiled. "What?"

John chuckled. "You were made to teach, that is for sure."

A sudden thoughtful look crossed Chastity's face. She asked, "Have you given much thought about what the pastor purposed? You know, about becoming an indentured?"

John replied, "Constantly."

Chastity turned to look at John. She gave him the saddest pouty face. She lowered her head in response. "I hoped all your thoughts were about me."

John lifted her chin to stare into her beautiful eyes. His intense gaze made her heart beat faster. She could feel the love for him in her heart. His words drew her closer. "My love, you never leave my thoughts. Even as I ponder the future, I think of you with me. I remember the kiss we shared the other night. I pray God forgives me, but I have dreamed of you in my arms and us sharing love's embrace in our own home." Then he leaned toward her, and without any coaxing, the young couple shared a moment of love.

When the kiss was over, Chastity again rested her head on his shoulder. "I never knew your lips would be so soft and your kiss would leave me so breathless. I too have shared in your dream. Sweet John, I have something I want to share."

"What is it, my love?" came his reply.

She answered, "Last night, at your home, I dreamed you came into the room and came to our bed. You came into my arms, and we spent the night together."

John had the most amazing look come over his face. "Truly? Oh, my darling, I had the same thought and dream. Honestly, I did. Do you suppose God is showing us His blessing?"

Soft peace came over her. "This I do, my husband."

The young couple remained close together, as John whispered a prayer over them. "Our Father, bless our marriage and our love. Make a way for us to be one ever so soon."

They remained together for a long while. It was John who saw a lone figure riding up the road to Chastity's home. John awakened her from her daze. "Darling, look. Is that not Pastor riding to your home?"

Chastity widened her eyes and sat up before lifting herself to get a better view. "It appears to be so. He must have news."

John stood and reached his hand out to her. "Then we must go and see what he might have to say." Once she was on her feet, they brushed themselves off and rushed toward her home.

When they approached the house, they could see Pastor and her father walking toward the door. The couple quickened their walk, and before long, they were entering the house as well.

Ruth turned to see them as they entered. "And where might you have been?"

"Let them be, Mum," came Thomas's reply. "They took their walk up the glen."

Elijah looked surprised. "Really now. I did not see you there."

John and Chastity were speechless. Then Thomas approached his daughter. "Is that a bit of grass in your hair?"

Chastity reached her hands up, finding nothing, but to her surprise, her parents and Pastor began to laugh hardily. Thomas reached his great arms about the both of them and whispered, "I knew where you both were all along. Tis a great view from that grassy hill, isn't it?"

John and Chastity's faces reddened with blush.

"Come, we have much to discuss," Thomas announced.

They all sat at the table, waiting to hear Pastor's news. He told them of the visit and the encounter with the sheriff. He also told them of the drink he shared with the earl called tea. "I doubt very much it will ever catch on," he added.

After relaying his findings, Thomas asked Elijah what he surmised from it all.

Pastor spoke. "I know the earl will be seeking the best opportunity for John." Then, looking at the young man, he added, "He is very impressed with your work, John, and will promote you as a silversmith." Returning his attention to all, he continued. "As for the sheriff, I believe he is too afraid to make any mention of our encounter, though I will have to inform the earl of the encounter. The sheriff is looking for the church. If he should see a number of us meeting privately together, he might become suspicious."

Ruth was shocked. "What did you tell the sheriff? Did you lie to him?"

Pastor chuckled. "Not really, for I told him that there are private ones who watch for the earl's care. Are we all not brothers and sisters unified together in Christ? Isn't the earl part of our faith, though in secret?" The pastor could not help but laugh more heartily. "No, we are agents—or should I say ambassadors—to a much greater authority."

With that, all found momentary relief. When things settled, Elijah continued. "I think it best that we wait it out, while at the same time preparing for what will undoubtedly come."

John spoke up. "I have also given much thought to what might lay ahead for me and for my betrothed. I do not know how long it will be before we hear of my possible service. I have decided it best that I become an indentured. I know I must prepare. There are a few things that I have to do before my journey. I also know that I have to go alone." Then, looking at Thomas and Ruth, he added, "As soon as I can, I will send for Chastity." Walking to Chastity, he knelt before her and said, "I hope you understand, my love."

A greater admiration came over Ruth for this young man whom she considered her son. She looked at her beautiful daughter who fought back tears. Ruth knew that her daughter did not want to be separated from John. Ruth offered words of support filled with holiness. "As the biblical groom left to prepare a place for his bride and the bride prepared for her groom's return, so shall I help my daughter for that time when you will send for her." Turning to Chastity, she added, "My daughter, I know the parting will be grievous, but we will prepare, and before long, you shall be joined together."

Tears filled the two women's eyes, and they rushed into each other's embrace. "My girl, my girl, what a wonderful bride and wife you shall be."

Through tears, Chastity replied, "Mother, it will be hard to leave you and father. I know the sacrifice it will take to be with John. The Bible speaks of the joining of the husband and wife and their departure from home, but no one can understand the grief that goes with it until that experience comes. I want your help. I want your approval and your blessing."

Holding her daughter close to her breast, Ruth replied, "You already have them both."

When evening came, John left to make his journey home. All along the way, his thoughts were tied to what he had heard and observed. All he could think about was preparing the way for both Chastity and himself. He did not know how, but he knew that with God's help, he would find a way. One thing bothered him. *What have I given to her to seal our love?* It was then that he had the most amazing plan. He stopped for a moment. A plan formulated in his mind. It all fell into place, and with that, he took off running back to his father's house.

He arrived completely out of breath. He took just a moment to catch it and then rushed into the barn to get the small pushcart. John went behind the house toward a hill where he knew a good deposit of stones could be found. He gathered as many as he could handle with the cart and transported them to a clearing near the barn. He deposited the stones before returning for another load and then another. Once he felt he had enough stones, he returned to the hill to fill the cart with the dirt he needed to make mud to build up and secure the stone. The sky was growing dark, but the idea drove him on and on. It was night by the time he returned. James came out to see what his son was up to. He said nothing, but waited.

As soon as John returned with his final load, he began mixing the mud to make a sort of mortar. James watched John work feverishly in the dark. John wanted to make something for Chastity, and he needed a foundry to do it.

James walked over. "Mind if I ask what you're doing?"

The question startled John. He stood up and spoke. "Sorry, Father. I have been so determined in my plan that I took little notice of anyone being here about."

James smiled. "I could see that. If you tell me what you are up to, I could lend you a hand."

John sat down on the cold, hard ground and began to laugh a bit. Looking at his father, he remarked, "I suppose it looks like I've gone mad, rushing here and there gathering stone. How long have you and Mum been watching?"

James sat on a large log and crossed his legs before replying. "I suppose it was after the second cart of stone. Your mum called to me to observe your queer activity. She asked me what you might be up to. I know you, John, so I told her you had something that needed to be done and would let us know when the time was right. So tell me. Is the time right?"

John took in a deep breath and let it out slowly. He looked at all the stone, the mud, and the place he planned to build his chimney. He looked back at his father and replied, "I have something that I want to make, but before I can do that, I need a foundry. It has to be strong and able to handle a fire hot enough to melt silver. I want to make a ring for Chastity before I have to leave for America."

James uncrossed his legs, leaned forward, and looked intently at his son. "Have you heard any news?"

John shook his head. "No, but Pastor did meet with the earl today. He will be securing my passage to America and find a man I can be indentured to."

James was saddened at the thought that his son would be a servant.

He had wanted more for him. James commented, "I see. Any idea how long that might take?"

John shook his head. "I don't know. It may be weeks."

James questioned, "Then why the urgency to build the foundry?"

John smiled. "Because it may only be a day or two. That's just it. So I must spend my time preparing. What I do know is that it will take time for the stones to set before I can mound up the dirt around it." John sat straight before continuing. "A foundry takes time to build and set. I have only a little silver, but it is enough for what I want to do. I can't afford for any to be wasted. I hope the tools I have made will do."

James stood to his feet and placed his hands on his hips. He straightened up and walked over to John. "So, what can I do?"

John extended his hand and proclaimed, "You can first help by getting me on my feet."

James took John's hand and jerked him to his feet.

Soon, John was giving instructions to his father. James moved stone and did whatever John asked him to do. John stood in the center of the furnace and began laying stones end to end. He took the fresh, wet mud and mortared the stones together. In the back of it, he made the first of two doors. This would be the location of the fire pit where wood and charcoal could be added. Soon, row upon row was laid. Adam later joined John and James. John instructed him to make mud for the mortar. The three men worked tirelessly together to make John's plan a reality.

When the foundry was knee-high, John stepped out of it. The next row of stones became the header for the fire pit. With each additional row, the foundry took on more of a beehive look. When the height was right, John made a smaller door to the front of the foundry stack. This would be big enough for him to melt the silver with a special tool of his own design. A few rows later, the chimney was high enough for John's liking. The opening at the top was small in order to keep as much heat as possible trapped inside.

Hours had passed. How late it was no one knew, but the three men were exhausted. John turned to Adam and their father and said, "Thank you for all your help. I thought I could do this on my own. Perhaps I could have, but it went so much faster with your help."

The three men washed up and headed in the house for a night of rest.

James looked at John and proclaimed, "Would it be too much to ask you to give me a hand in the morning?"

"Not at all, Father. Not at all," he lovingly replied.

The family was up before the dawn. The bellowing of the cattle for their morning milking sounded the alarm. All the family set to work preparing for the processing of the milk. This was a daily ritual, and little coaxing was needed. Each family member knew what had to be done. Adam and John went to the barn and opened the door for the first two cows. Man and cattle moved with precision about the barn. Cattle went to the stall to be milked. The young men spoke kindly to their faithful pets, sometimes singing to them.

Soon, pails of milk were filled and ready to be processed. The filled pails were carefully set aside. When the first two cows were milked, they were escorted out another door to return to pasture. Then the next two cows were escorted in. This process continued until all the cattle had been relieved of their burden. By the time James entered the barn, John and Adam had already milked four of the cows.

When a pale was filled, one of the girls carefully carried it over to fill awaiting pots. Filled pots were then loaded onto the cart along with butter and cheese. Before long, all the cattle were returned to the field, the cart was loaded, and the cleanup began. Once the barn was cleaned up, Adam and his father took the milk into the village. John stayed behind to help his mother and sisters with the remaining milk to make cheese and butter. Two of the sisters cleaned pales and pots, while John and mother made the cheese. The sisters also took turns churning the cream to make the butter. It took several hours to complete the task, but no one complained, for this was the way of life.

By early afternoon, John was ready to go see Chastity. He needed information from her, and somehow, he had to get it without her knowing. When John came to the Shepherd home, he found Chastity sitting on the wall that extended from her parents' house. As soon as she saw him, she hopped off the wall and ran to him. She threw her arms around him and looked about. When she was sure the coast was clear, she gave him the biggest kiss. John couldn't help but laugh.

After that, they spent the whole day talking about the future and what might lie ahead for them. Later in the afternoon, the couple walked hand in hand to the shearing room. The shears that John kept sharp for Thomas were hung neatly on the wall. John spotted some wool left on the ground. John picked it up and rolled the wool in his fingers. He turned to Chastity and said, "Let me see your left hand."

She extended her hand to him. John took the wool and tied it around her ring finger. "Can you imagine my ring where this wool loop presently resides?"

All she could do was smile. "I can. I wish it was now."

With that, he removed the wool from her finger and tucked it in his waistband before replying. "It won't be wool. That I promise."

John tried to remain focused with Chastity, but he was distracted by his plan. Chastity could sense it but tried not to say anything. He had what he wanted, and there was a gleam in his eye. Chastity noticed it and asked, "What are you up to?"

John smiled. "Whatever do you mean?"

There was a stern look in her eye. "You know exactly what I mean, John Smith. Now out with it."

John chuckled. "I can see I shall never be able to keep secrets from you. I ask you this one thing: that you trust me."

She put her arms about him. "I do. I always have, and I always will."

It was late when John left. He was glad for the time he'd had with his beloved, but more than ever, he wanted to give her something of his own creation—something of value, something no one else would have. Come morning, he would set to work on her ring.

# Provoking Others

William the blacksmith was filled with anger. He had not heard from the sheriff since the day he'd gone to his house. He wanted to know if he had already met with the earl. William wanted John back, as he realized just how much he was losing with John gone. William had convinced himself that he was getting rightful revenge. With that, he decided to go see the sheriff until he remembered the warning by the sheriff not to come his way again. William thought to himself, *No man tells me what to do … no man.*

William looked about his quiet barn. Since releasing John, he had received little to no work. The money was also running out. John's work had made him a small fortune. Not only that, but William was wasting what he did gain by drinking it away.

He walked over to one of the stalls where he shod horses. There on the ground he saw a hammer. On the day of the scuffle, John had dropped the hammer to tend to his master. William looked at the hammer. "The boy didn't put my tools away. When I get hold of him, I'll …" William began breathing deeper. Then, in one unexpected moment, he threw the hammer at the wall. The force with which he threw it caused the hammer to become buried deep in the wood.

William moved to the barn opening and looked for signs of anyone who might be coming his way. No one was coming. No one was waiting for his services. He heard a horse ride by and expected it might be the sheriff, but no.

He spoke aloud. "What might the good sheriff be doing? Says he don't wants me seeing him." He paused, and his eyes shifted one way and then the other. He spoke once more. "So what can he do? Nothing! What right has he to tell me what I can and cannot do?"

William spun around to look back at the deserted barn. Without John's care, the barn and his hovel had gathered dust from lack of care. The sight of it added to the blacksmith's disgust. "That boy owes me. He would leave me after all I did for him?" The more he surveyed things, the angrier he became. "If the sheriff won't help me, then I will find others to make my point for me. I need men like ..." Suddenly, it came to him. William needed action, and he knew the very sort to make the sheriff work for him.

William gathered some money he had hidden in his house. With what silver he had, he could buy friends. He waited till evening to go to the local tavern. The sort of men he needed would come at that time. Most taverns of the time served beer, ale, and wine. Rum was common but usually limited. A tavern was a place where men of business would oftentimes meet for food, drink, and even lodging. There was the other element that also went to taverns: men who wanted to make deals.

William needed men who didn't mind shady dealings. He needed men of ill repute and rousers. He knew he could find such company at the tavern. If a man was unfortunate enough to be near a coastal port and made his way to a tavern, he might be taken by force to serve in the navy. This was often done by getting men drunk or drugged. When the man woke from his delirious state, he would be on a ship out to sea.

William knew some of these men because they often got drunk together. He knew if he bought a couple of bottles of rum, these men would aid his cause. That evening when he entered the tavern, he looked about to find men he could claim as his compatriots. In a darkened corner sat three men he knew simply as Henry, Richard, and Sal. These men wasted many hours in this dark hole of a place. Give them enough brew, and they would be your friends and supporters, well, for a while—at least till the rum ran out.

William bought two bottles of rum and made his way to the table. "Mind if I join you?"

The men looked at William and then eyed the rum. With a rowdy approval, the men invited William to join their company.

Before long, the rum had its expected result. Then William began his complaint of injustice. "What kind of sheriff have we who will not uphold the laws of our land or bring to justice a rabble-rousing youth?"

A loud *hurrah* was echoed by the three men.

William continued. "Who will come to our aid and see to our protection? If the sheriff really wants justice, then he should be protecting the citizens of our fair town."

Others in the tavern were annoyed at the men but could not help listening to the complaint. Some moved closer to hear what was being said. As the complaints grew louder, the tavern keep felt an uprising was in the making. The keep told one of the barmaids, "Go get the sheriff before this gets out of hand."

The barmaid rushed to the sheriff's home and pounded the door. Sally answered and recognized the maid. She asked, "What is it, Patricia?"

Patricia responded, "Is the sheriff here? He has to come quick. There are some men causing a stir at the tavern."

Just then, Taylor walked to the door. He asked, "Who might it be?"

Patricia answered, "Four men led by the blacksmith."

Taylor sent Patricia back to the tavern and told her to assure the barkeep that he was coming directly.

Sally asked, "Is this the same man who came here the other day?"

Taylor strapped on his knife, pistol, and sword before turning to look at her. "Yes, and I am in no mood to deal with the likes of him. Lock the door and wait for my return. I am not sure what he is up to, but I shall find out shortly." He then went out and saddled his horse, all the while thinking of the man. He climbed into the saddle and cinched his jaw. A low whisper escaped his lips. "William."

A short time later, Taylor entered the tavern and saw a small crowd gathered. The blacksmith was standing tall, grabbing the people's attention with his complaints against the sheriff. Then William looked over and saw Taylor.

"Ah, and here is our good sheriff now. Have you come to arrest the innocent?"

Taylor looked at William. "There is nothing innocent about you. What I see is a man rousing people. What's this all about?"

William saw his chance. "Did I not come to you with a complaint against my apprentice? Didn't I tell you that he is a member of an outlaw group of people calling themselves Christians? Did you not tell me that you would take my charge to the earl?"

Taylor was stunned. The blacksmith had found a way to force him to give an account. Taylor walked over to an empty table and took a seat. He called to the barkeep for an ale. Taylor waited for his drink in silence, taking time to formulate his answer. William was growing impatient. The crowd's attention was drawn away from William while they waited to hear what Taylor had to say. The delay only served to anger William all the more.

Finally, the drink was brought. Taylor supped it and leaned back in his chair. Looking over the crowd, he began answering the question posed by the smith. "Yes, you did ask me to go to the earl. I have met with him to discuss the complaint made by you."

William asked, "Then what are you doing to make things right? What did the earl say?"

Taylor knew he had to be careful with his answer. He dare not implicate the earl. To do so would only cause him more trouble. Cautiously and clearly, he stated, "I have met with the earl, and the matter is well in hand."

William snarled. "So says you. Maybe you're covering something up."

The sheriff looked angrily at the blacksmith. Taylor knew the only reason William provoked the crowd was for his own vengeance and nothing more. Then Taylor struck upon a thought. He stood to his feet and walked over next to William. The stench of the rum gave the man's body a most foul smell.

Taylor looked him square in the eyes. "Be careful, man, for you speak of our lordship."

Taylor turned slightly to face the crowd. He did not dare turn his back on William. Addressing those in the tavern, he said, "This man cares nothing about the law. He came to my house with threats. Tell me how many of you witnessed the scene outside of his shop a few days ago when he dismissed his young apprentice?" A hand or two went up. Taylor continued. "If you saw what happened, did the young man strike the smith?"

One old soak proclaimed, "If he had, the smith would have killed him." Loud laughter followed the comment.

Finally, another man spoke up. "No. He asked the blacksmith why he was trying to hurt him." The answer brought silence among the crowd.

Some men began backing away from the scene. Realizing this, Taylor pointed at them and called out, "Ye men, stand to! You took part in this rile. Now stay to hear the end. I want to know if any man besides the smith heard the lad's statement that he is a Christian."

One man, a villager who saw the fight, raised his hand.

Taylor looked at him and asked, "Did he say anything more."

The man replied, "No, Lord Sheriff. He just said that he was a Christian."

Turning to the others, the sheriff asked, "And how many of you say you are Christians?" Several hands went up. The sheriff smiled. "Are you renegades to the king's church?"

Scurried sounds and rounds of "no" were echoed over and again.

He turned to the smith before continuing. "What is it you really want, William?"

The blacksmith's anger grew, but he feared the sheriff because of the pistol and knife he wore. The rum he consumed could not contain his tongue. In a low, gravelly voice, he replied, "I want the boy. Return him to me. He owes me."

Taylor responded in the same tone. "What does he owe you?"

William realized what he would say next could change everything. "He owes me for being my apprentice."

Taylor asked, "How much longer might his apprenticeship be?"

William answered, "Till I say."

Taylor smiled. "So in your judgment, is John worthy to be called a blacksmith or no?"

William slurred, "He still has much to learn."

"I see," came the sheriff's response. Just to agitate the smith, the sheriff asked the crowd, "How many of you bring your work for the apprentice instead of the smith?"

Several hands went up.

Taylor looked at William and then at the crowd. "I am following the earl's orders. I will continue to monitor the young man and report on his whereabouts. If he is a part of a renegade church, I will find it. As for you, any more unlawful gatherings will result in arrests." Turning to the blacksmith, he added, "If you dare stir the people again, you will be the first one I will arrest."

Next, William spoke only to Taylor. "Just you try it."

Taylor gave William a half-cocked smile. The crowd of men began leaving the tavern or went back to their tables. Order had been restored for the moment. William stomped out, angered that the sheriff had stopped his plan.

Morning came, and the sheriff decided to find out more. Even though he delivered the charge against the lad to the earl, proof was needed. Somehow he had to gather evidence. Taylor knew the only way to get such evidence was to watch the young man. He would begin by asking around in order to find out where the young man lived. Then he would keep an eye on him. If the apprentice was part of an illegal church, he would find out.

Taylor went into town seeking the whereabouts of John the apprentice. Taylor didn't even know the young man's last name. In previous conversations with William, he never saw the need to ask about where he lived, who his family was, or anything else for that matter. Taylor knew he could ask William more details, but he also knew that William would interfere with his investigation. With each person he went to, Taylor discovered that all who knew John spoke well of him, the work he did, and the poor way he was treated, but very few knew details about his personal life. Some thought he was a nephew to the blacksmith. Most said that they had never seen him before he started working for the smith. If the people knew more, they were either keeping it to themselves or trying to protect the young man.

Toward evening, the sheriff was about to leave off his search when he heard the familiar sound of the milk cart. He did not know why he took notice, but something struck his interest. Taylor knew little of the dairyman, but he figured he might know more since he visited most of the town. When James approached, the sheriff raised his hand, bringing him to a stop.

Taylor initiated the conversation. "Hello, my fine sir, how might ye be today?"

James was used to being stopped by villagers who might be seeking something. James also knew the sheriff, not formally, but from the times he chanced to buy some needed item.

James returned the greeting. "Good day, Sheriff. How can I be of service? I haven't much left—a bit of butter, milk, and cheese."

Taylor raised a hand. "Thank you, no. I haven't a need. I wanted to ask you a question."

James smiled. "By all means, what might it be?"

Taylor crossed his arms, trying to look more important. "I am inquiring about the apprentice to the blacksmith. What do you know of him?"

James was cautious. A look of concern filled his face. "May I ask of your interest in the man?"

Taylor was coy. "I am looking into the disturbance that happened on the street between the blacksmith and the lad, so any help would be appreciated."

James considered the sheriff's statement before replying. "From what I heard, the blacksmith caused all the disturbance. Why are you seeking the lad? Have you talked with the smith?"

Taylor shot back. "I will be the one asking the questions."

James laughed. "If you bully the people like you are me, then you won't get answers." Looking straight at the sheriff, he continued. "I know the lad rather well. He lives in the country with his father, mother, brother, and sisters. He is a hardworking, honest boy. I know him, because he is my son."

Taylor was stunned. Everyone knew James and respected him. He had not expected this. Finding information would prove difficult. Could a poor dairyman and his family be the leaders of a secret congregation?

# The Ring

It is one thing to be a blacksmith. It is entirely another to be a true artist. John was an artist. For the delicate work he did, there were no tools available in the rural parts of Sussex. So for the fine silverwork, John made his own tools. Ironwork required heavy tools and hot fire. Red-hot metal was hammered into shape. Silver and gold could be hammered into shape or melted if the fire was hot enough. John developed his own tools for work he did with precious metals. He fashioned his tools from discarded farm tools and other metal he often reclaimed. He crafted joiners and smoothing planes, chisels and mallets, awls and more. What he had was crude, but with his tools, he made exquisite items.

This project would be his masterpiece. It had to be, because it was for Chastity. He searched the hills until he found enough hardened oak dry and fit enough for the task at hand. He found a sturdy tree trunk that he cut and carried home. Back home, he cut the trunk to the exact length he wanted. He set the piece on a bench and then straddled the bench, placing the log between his legs. Using a straight draw, he carefully shaved the log till it was a long rectangle. Then he took a frame saw and painstakingly cut the board down the middle. He kept dividing the log until he had four exact lengths.

John selected another piece of wood, took out his knife, and carefully whittled it into a long, narrow cylinder. When finished, it was about an inch and a half in circumference at the bottom and tapered to nearly a point at the top. It was painstaking work, but he had created the perfect mold.

It had taken most of the afternoon to accomplish all that needed to be done, but before stopping, there was one more thing left to do. From his waistband, he pulled out the wool ring and carefully slid it down the cylinder. Ever so carefully, he made sure the ring was evenly in place. Then, taking his knife, he again marked the place where the wool ring rested. With the saw, he cut at the mark through the cylinder. He now had her perfect ring size.

Before retiring, John cleaned and sharpened his tools. Next, he put away all the wood and the bench. He came into the house to find the family getting ready for bed.

Martha smiled. "There is a bit of bread, cheese, beer, and honey on the table if you would like."

He answered, "Thank you, Mum. I will enjoy a bite. Are all going to bed now?"

Just then, James walked into the room. "It is later than you think. Besides, I have not recovered from the night before, so eat a bit and then off to bed." James was about to leave the room. He instead turned back. "The sheriff was inquiring about you today. I would be careful if I were you."

John sat thoughtfully. "Of course, Father. Good night to you." He ate a little, though in truth he was much too preoccupied to be hungry. When he was finished, he climbed into bed but had trouble falling asleep. Hearing that the sheriff had been asking about him did not bother him half as much as being concerned over the work he wanted to do. His mind was upon the ring that he wanted to make for the woman he loved. After some time, he finally fell asleep. Even in his sleep, his mind went over every detail.

Before the sun was up the next morning, John was in the barn gathering the tools and wood he had been working on. When James and Adam came out, they were surprised to see John busy.

James approached and called to John. "So how goes it?"

John quickly stood to his feet. "It is a trial, Father, but I will persevere. Let me put my tools away, and I will give you a hand."

James answered, "No need. Adam and I have this. Continue on with your work."

John expressed his gratitude and went to work. John had a sharp drill bit a little smaller than the ring size. It is what he had, and it would have to serve the purpose. He took one board and bore a hole through it. Then with the chisel, he carefully split the board in two. He took up a small, thin knife and chisel of the same size. He painstakingly began the task of creating the exact image he wanted in the curve of the hole. The first attempt was not to his liking. Neither was the second. He tossed them aside before beginning the third attempt.

A true artist never gives up, and so he started again. After an hour or so of work, John discarded the third mold as well. He rested a minute before starting on the fourth piece. He again etched the image in the wood. His shoulders and neck hurt from the detailed work, but he pushed himself to complete the task. He finished the one side of the mold. He lifted the second half and studied it carefully. Then, just as before, he carved the new image. It took most of the day, but by evening, the mold was finished. He placed the two ends together, reached for the ring cylinder, and placed it within the hole. It was perfect.

The next morning John began hauling a soft, grey mud from the hill. He knew this mud would dry rock solid. When he was sure he had enough, he mixed more water with it. John then packed several layers of the mud around the furnace. In the end, it looked like a small volcano. John stood back to look at his foundry. He liked what he saw. Come morning if the foundry was dry and if the mud was hard, he would melt the silver and pour it into the mold.

That afternoon John made his way to see Chastity. He was about to walk down the road toward her house when he thought he caught sight of a figure off in the distance. He stopped and looked again but saw nothing. Maybe it was a deer that caught his attention, but he had a strange feeling that he was being followed. John thought about what his father had said and decided to find a place where he could watch the valley below. He crossed over a small rise and ducked down behind a clump of trees. Once he was sure he was out of sight, he crawled on over into some high grass. From there, he continued up the hill that overlooked the valley.

John made his way to a good vantage point behind a fallen tree. He sat motionless, looking back to where he'd seen the figure. *There!* he thought to himself. *It moved.* From behind a bluff, John could see a horse and rider. Closer the rider came. Soon, they were at the rise where John had disappeared. John instantly recognized the man. It was the sheriff. Father was right.

John felt afraid for Chastity and her family, along with his own family and Pastor. John knew these hills. As a boy, he'd wandered them to find the cattle or just have fun exploring. His knowledge of the hills would serve him well. He decided to misdirect the sheriff. He made his way to the top of the hill and made enough noise to catch the sheriff's attention. Then he disappeared on the other side.

John's actions caught the sheriff's attention. He left the horse tied to a tree and began following on foot. John would run and hide, and then at the right time, he'd make himself known to the sheriff. The sheriff was watching him. Finally, John disappeared and turned back toward Chastity's home. The sheriff continued his search but moved in the opposite direction. After a while, the sheriff became frustrated and returned to his horse. He thought to himself, *You succeeded in losing me today. You won't be so lucky the next time.*

It was much later than John hoped it to be when he arrived at Chastity's home. She rushed to him and hugged him closely. "This is the best I can do," she said. "Mum and Dad are watching." What she said made him smile. As she held him, she could hear his heart pounding. She looked up at him. "John, what's wrong?"

He whispered, "I need to speak with you and your parents. Danger is near. I just know it."

John told the family about the sheriff and what measures he had to take to mislead the man. He walked to and fro in the room like a nervous cat. Thomas watched him closely. He wanted to comfort the lad but waited for the right moment.

John did his best to formulate his thoughts. "I want to be with Chastity more than ever, but I now know the sheriff will keep tabs on me. If I'm not careful, he will find out more about the church, our families, and Pastor." Then, looking at Chastity, he continued. "I fear I may not be able to come be with you without causing more trouble."

Chastity didn't like his tone of voice and asked, "What are you saying, John? Are you saying you don't want to see me?"

John rushed over to her and lifted her to her feet. He drew her close to him and held her tightly. "You needn't ask such questions, because you know I do. I speak of your well-being. I'm just saying that for me to come to you, I must be secretive." Lifting her chin, he smiled and said, "I can't stay away." He then whispered in her ear, "I will ever be thinking of your kiss."

Thomas came over to his daughter and John. "I am thankful before our Sovereign that He allowed you to discover the sheriff. Your actions may have saved us. I am sure the sheriff thinks he is doing what's right. My only complaint is this may be the first time in a long time that he has dedicated himself to his job." Thomas walked to the middle of the room before continuing. "I am sure he has a reason for taking this course of action. I feel that I must warn Pastor Elijah to these new events."

Thomas could see the concern in Chastity and John. He spoke to reassure them. "John, I know it would be hard for you to stay away. I don't expect you to, but I would urge you to use extreme care when coming here." Thomas took John by the shoulders before continuing. "One more thing, Son. I fear that your time for leaving will be soon. The sheriff's pursuit of you will necessitate it."

This turn of events only caused John's senses to become more heightened, beginning with the blacksmith's attack and now this. He became more aware of every little sound and movement. Thomas's statement to him made him feel a greater urgency to finish the gift for Chastity. He stayed till it was dark outside and then stealthily made his way home.

John was exhausted by the time he arrived home, not from the walk, but from the increased pressure he felt. Before retiring for the night, John filled a bucket with water and placed his mold in it. He knew the intense temperature of the molten silver would instantly cause the wood to burst into flame. He hoped that water-soaked wood would withstand the heat. He was hungry, but his hunger would have to wait till morning. He needed sleep and prayed it would come.

Sheer exhaustion caused John to quickly fall into a deep sleep. How long he slept he did not know, but he was stirred to his senses by a voice. Somewhere between sleep and being awake, John heard his name being called. "John." The sound seemed to come as a whisper. "I know you can hear me. I have a warning. Prepare the way, for your time here will soon be over. The time for your departure is at hand."

In his mind, John questioned the voice. It was reassuring and gave him comfort. Once again, sleep overcame him.

When morning came, John woke with a real peace. He came to the table and enjoyed some breakfast with his mother. John loved his mother, and they shared a special relationship. John had learned to love a woman by the gentleness of his mother. She was every bit the lady he saw in Chastity.

Martha asked, "So are you ready to use your smokestack?"

The way she described it made John laugh. "It's called a foundry, Mum." "Well, whatever you call it, is it ready?" she asked.

"It is. I hope it works well today."

Martha patted his hand. "I'm sure it will."

John rose to his feet and tenderly kissed his mom's cheek. She looked at the strong, handsome young man who was her son. She admired him. A tear formed into her eye, as her heart told her he would be leaving soon.

John looked over his foundry. It was rudimentary but functional. The mud had dried, and he was sure it was ready. He just hoped it would withstand the heat. John started the fire through the back door of the furnace. Before long, smoke rose from the stack. John knew he needed an extremely hot fire.

Once the fire had a good base, he began feeding it charcoal, knowing it would make a hotter and longer-lasting fire. He left the fire to make final preparations on the mold. He unrolled his tools, which he kept in oil cloth. One tool he'd made for such a job as this was an iron cup. He did not know about temperature, but he had learned that silver melted before iron. John gauged the temperature by things he observed. For this job, he would watch for the stones to glow.

Next, John donned his leather apron and mitts. Things were about to get really hot. The shear heat of the furnace would singe exposed hair. More charcoal was added to the fire, causing it to rage even more. Smoke was replaced by flames shooting out of the chimney. John kept adding to the fire, and it made a hideous roar. With each additional piece of charcoal, strange whines and pops were heard. Flames not only shot out of the top of the stack, but through the front opening. The dried clay began to blacken, but it did not allow the fire to break through. Hours seemed to pass. John had made a makeshift bellows from wood and leather. Working the bellows forced more and more air into the inferno. So intense was the heat that he couldn't stand being near it.

The flames began to change color, first orange, then red, and finally blue. The foundry gave off great heat. Even in his protective clothing, John had a hard time being near the fire. The fire was in a rage and demanded satisfaction. The great fire had an insatiable appetite, and John kept feeding it charcoal.

Finally, John was sure it was time. He took hold of the iron pot with long tongs. Shielding his eyes the best he could, he placed the pot on the shelf of the upper entry. Instantly, the iron began to glow. John went to his room and gathered a leather bag containing tiny pieces of silver—all the silver he had been able to collect from work he had done over the years. It wasn't a great amount, but it was enough. He returned to the foundry, added more charcoal, and pumped the bellows. John took the tongs and retrieved the pot. The iron was actually soft. John smiled and proclaimed, "Perfect."

John then added the silver. As soon as it touched the hot iron, it popped. Once all of it was in place, John returned it to the fire. Every few minutes, John retrieved the pot to inspect it. The silver began to melt. A short while later, he pulled the pot and saw the silver was liquid. He went to his bench and placed the water-soaked mold on it.

John took in a deep breath. He was ready. With tongs in hand, he collected the pot and carefully approached the bench. He knelt down, looking across the mold. He knew the hot metal would cause the water to evaporate and create a cloud of steam. He carefully poured the metal into the mold. As expected, the steam rose high into the air. The water hissed as it was forced from the wood. A smile crept over his face. The mold held.

John had made another mold that was a plain square. What silver remained, he poured into it. It wasn't much, but he would keep it for the journey ahead. He removed his leathers. When this was done, he lay upon the ground just to relax. Though a good distance from the fire, he could feel the heat from it on the ground where he rested.

His mother came out to check on him. "John, are you all right?"

John did not open his eyes but replied, "Ah, Mother, yes. All it well. Just taking a bit of rest for now."

Martha looked down on her son just lying on his back. She recalled him, as a little boy, doing the same in a field while admiring the clouds. Back then, she had joined him as they imagined what each cloud looked like. Her boy was grown up now. His face was black with soot from the hot foundry. He bore a smile of satisfaction. In this serene moment, she asked, "John, would you like something to eat?"

John stirred from his moment of rest. "No, thank you, though. Perhaps a little later. I want to put everything away and see that the fire behaves itself."

Martha understood. "Very well then. Do come in when you are ready, and we can eat together." Then, looking about, she asked, "Did it work?"

John raised to his elbows. "I think so. I will know in a little while."

She smiled approvingly. John was no longer a boy but a fine young man. She sighed and then turned to go back.

After his mother went into the house, John raised himself to a sitting position. He knew he had to clean up. John stood to his feet and walked over to the foundry. He started by removing the bellows and placing it in the barn. He hung up his leathers. Time and again, he returned to the foundry to collect items and restored them to their rightful place. The iron pot had cooled but was still a little hot to the touch. He placed it in the water bucket. The water responded with a hiss as it began cooling the metal. Once it was cooled, he removed the pot and carefully dried it. He repeated the process for the tongs. He checked the mold and found that it was warm. He dare not disturb the mold until it was completely cooled. The fire in the furnace continued to burn, but already it was changing color, indicating it was cooling. John was pleased. His furnace was a success.

John wanted to clean himself up. He fetched a pale of water and went into the barn to wash and dress in clean clothes. Then he retreated to the house where his mother waited for him with a fine lunch for them to share. It was time to relax, even if it was just for a short spell.

An hour or so passed, and John felt that he could continue his work. He picked up the mold bearing the small rectangular piece of silver. It was cool to the touch. He turned the mold over and tapped it on the bench. Out popped the metal. He knew he could safely work with his prize. By this time, his father had returned from his rounds in the village. He came over to where John was working. In silence, James watched as John painstakingly took a wood chisel and began breaking the mold around the ring. With each careful tap of the hammer, the metal was exposed. In a few minutes, John lifted the precious gift. He held between his index finger and thumb the signet of his betrothal.

"A ring for Chastity," he announced.

John carefully inspected it. It still needed finishing, but it was exactly what he wanted it to be. The ring was a serpentine vine. Attached to the vine were small leaves. Delicate and yet lasting, it was everything he wanted for her.

James spoke. "May I see it?"

John handed him the delicate prize. James looked it over and over. James then looked at the broken mold, the smoldering furnace, and the handmade tools. He shook his head in amazement. "Son, you are truly a gifted man."

John took back the ring and smiled. "Wait till it's finished." He sat at the bench and went back to work. Primitive and yet effective tools worked away at the imperfections. Soft sand and miniature picks were used on every surface. Sharp edges were made smooth. The hands of the young master would not be satisfied until he had perfected his masterpiece.

By evening, the furnace was emitting a little smoke. The smell of raging fire had subsided. James and Martha came out of the house together to check on their son. They walked over and saw him inspecting his work.

As they approached, James called, "How goes it, Son?"

John turned to look at his parents. He looked peaceful and satisfied. "Come and see for yourself."

John bid his mother to open her hand. She opened her left hand, and he gently laid the ring in her palm. Martha looked at the ring, almost afraid to pick it up.

She looked at what she held and said, "Oh, John, it's beautiful. I know she will love it." Martha passed it on to James.

He too looked over the finely detailed ring. "It is truly a gift worthy of the one you love. Son, your skills are amazing. I was right to encourage you to become a smith. You have surpassed all I could have wanted for you." James then handed the ring back to John. "When do you plan to give it to her?"

John took the ring back and held it between his index finger and thumb. "It will be soon. I have a little more I need to do to complete it." Then, looking at his parents, he added, "I know I haven't much time left."

The moment was quiet. They all felt the serenity of the moment. James left his wife's side to place his hand on John's shoulder. James choked back tears as he spoke. "Many years ago when I walked you to the blacksmith shop, I hoped for you a better life. Your mum and I grieve over the surety that we will lose you, but we are confident that God will lead you where He wants you to be."

Feeling the strength of his father's touch, John responded, "Father, I am scared. I will be leaving behind all I know. All that I love is here." John shook his head before continuing. "I think of what Chastity will face alone. I will not blame her if she decides to change her mind about marrying me. It is an uncertain future."

James patted his son on the back. "Do you not know the depth of her love for you? She also has considered the sacrifice you are asking her to make, and she has chosen a life with you. Don't let your insecurities mislead you."

John thought about his father's advice before responding. "It's not that. It's what I fear we both may face. I had a dream last night that told me to prepare. I think it means more than just preparing to go."

James added, "Time will show us the answer. We must give it time."

In town, the sheriff milled over the events of the past few days. He had been keeping a watchful eye on John but had nothing on him. Taylor imagined that if he could find the secret party of followers, he would gain the earl's approval. John somehow eluded him. If he was a member of this congregation, he was hiding their location well. Then he struck on an idea. Why not tell the earl his plan? If the earl likes the plan, he might be given more resources to uncover their location. Still, there was one thing that bothered him. Who was Special Agent Elijah?

The next day, Pastor Elijah and the earl were meeting together. Elijah was telling Christopher all that had transpired, including his encounter with the sheriff. The earl seemed most interested as to how Elijah was able to gain the upper hand.

Looking confident, Elijah explained, "I told him that I was a special agent in your service."

The earl was stunned. "You told him what?"

Elijah repeated, "That I was your special agent."

The news caused the earl to laugh heartedly. "Brilliant, absolutely brilliant, and how did the sheriff respond?"

Elijah replied, "Shocked, to say the least. I told him if he dared to want to know more, he would have to ask you, but if he chose to do so, it may harm his station. I also stated that further inquiry may demand his relocation."

The earl looked at his dear friend. "Oh, I say, I must make sure that I never tangle with you in a game of wits. You may convince me that you are the earl and I a subject."

Elijah laughed. "Isn't that the way it is?"

Even while Elijah and the earl were meeting, the sheriff came to the earl's home, hoping to have an audience. Once more, the sheriff entered the gated residence. And once again, the butler knocked on the door of the earl's study. The earl looked at Elijah before allowing the butler to enter. As soon as the butler entered, he announced the sheriff's wishes.

"Very well. Give me a moment and then send him in," came the earl's reply.

When the butler existed, the earl looked to Elijah and said, "Special agent you said you are, and so shall you be. Go into the next room and leave the door open. I may have need of you. Let's see what the good sheriff has to say."

With that, Elijah rose from his chair and did as the earl suggested. Once Elijah was out of sight, the earl called out, "Send in the sheriff."

The sheriff entered before the earl and bowed at the waist. "Good afternoon, Your Lordship, I have come to keep you apprised of the blacksmith's apprentice."

The earl moved from his standing position in front of his desk to one of the two easy chairs. "I see, and what did you hope to gain by keeping tabs on the young man?"

The sheriff lifted his shoulders and proclaimed, "I hope to find the meeting place of the renegade congregation."

The earl sat back in the chair and asked, "Why are you interested in doing that? Are they causing problems in the town? Are they forcing their faith on others or speaking against the king?"

The sheriff's response was quick. "Not that I am aware, but they are forbidden by law to meet."

The earl continued. "And the young man—what is his name?"

"John, sire. His name is John," answered the sheriff.

The earl continued. "Has John caused any mischief or stirred the people?"

Thomas was not prepared for such examination. "No, not that I am aware."

"Then tell me, Lord Sheriff, why would I disturb the town looking for people loyal to the crown who are not causing trouble and are benefiting us?"

The sheriff moved his eyes from side to side, looking for an answer to the question. He replied, "I am the chief magistrate, and it is my duty to stop illegal assemblies."

"Your duty," shot back the earl, "is to keep law and order in the town. It may interest you to know that I keep close tabs on all districts and counties in my jurisdiction."

The sheriff hung his head. "I do apologize, sire. I did not know, but the people will demand justice in the case of the apprentice."

"The people?" questioned the earl, "Or the one who brought the accusation?"

The sheriff was now less sure of himself. "He will expect an answer."

The earl blasted, "And he will have it in my own time. Do you understand? That you can pass on to the blacksmith. Have you anything more?"

The sheriff just looked at the earl, and after a pause, he asked, "Just one more thing, if I may."

"What might that be?" came the earl's inquiry.

"I stopped a man leaving your home when I last visited. When I pressed him for an answer, he told me he was a special agent under your service. Is that so?"

The earl was calm. "Special agent? Is that all he said?"

Thomas replied, "No. He said if I wanted to know more, I should ask you."

The earl rose from his seat. He walked a moment around the room with his hands locked together behind his back. He looked to the sheriff and proclaimed, "Elijah, come here!"

Immediately, Elijah entered the room. He bowed before the earl and quickly came to attention. "Sire, you called?"

Earl Christopher was most commanding. "Yes, do you know this man?"

Elijah looked over the sheriff. "We have met on the road leading from your house."

The earl marched up to Elijah and looked him in the eye. "Did you tell him anything of your mission?"

Elijah restrained himself from laughing. He kept a military bearing. "No, Your Lordship. I informed him that if he wanted to know anything, he had to ask you."

Turning to the sheriff, the earl demanded answers. "So this is the man you stopped?"

The sheriff nodded. Christopher marched about the room with his hands behind his back. He stopped before the sheriff before continuing. "Most interesting. You could have jeopardized everything. I would suggest you cease and desist in your actions. I hope you have not said anything to anyone. You could disrupt all that I have in motion."

Sheriff nervously answered, "No, sire. I waited to speak with you."

Earl Christopher walked over and looked at Elijah. He winked at him. Once more, he turned to sheriff and commanded, "Then see that you don't. I suggest you leave for the village right now. You need to wait till I call for you. Is that clear?"

Taylor was anxious. "Yes, your grace. I will do just that. But—"

The earl cut him off. "There are no buts. Do as I say or suffer the penalty of your actions." Then, turning his back on the sheriff, the earl took a slow, deep breath and muttered, "Could have jeopardized everything." He turned to see the sheriff. "You still here? I said go!"

The sheriff bowed and proclaimed as he backed to the door, "Yes, Your Lordship. Thank you."

The door closed behind the sheriff. The earl moved to watched out the great window. He watched the sheriff ride off in haste. Turning back to Elijah, he said, "So, how was my performance?"

The two men could not contain their laughter any more.

They settled down, and the earl spoke more seriously. "I fear the time will be soon. I should not delay for the congregation's sake and for John's."

Elijah walked over to the earl. "Only pray for him. He is not a boy, but like Abraham of old, he will be leaving his parents and his home and may never see them again. Added to his misery will be leaving behind Chastity."

The earl had a questioning look to go along with the response. "Who is Chastity?"

Elijah answered, "His betrothed."

The two men took comfort in the easy chairs. After a moment more, the earl shared important news. "I have a man who has land in America. I told him of the young smith and showed him his talent. He wants to sponsor John and will supply what tools he may need. The man's name is Robert Howell. Robert told me he has need for the smith in two weeks. It isn't much time. I urge you to go to John and tell him to get ready. In a day or two, Robert or one of his representatives will meet with John to finalize the details. One thing more: can John read and write?"

Elijah was surprised at the question. "Yes, Chastity taught him."

The earl smiled. "Good. Tell John to read the contract carefully. Even the most honest of men can be unscrupulous at times."

Elijah appreciated the statement. "I will get word to him or visit with him myself. Do you think the sheriff will cause any trouble?"

Christopher was serious. "For his sake, he best heed my warning."

Before long, Elijah took his leave. He traveled the countryside. At one point, he decided to leave the road and took his horse over a hill. He doubled back to see if he was being followed. Once again, the sheriff came from the bushes and began following up the rise. Elijah watched the sheriff urge the heavily burdened horse after him. Quickly, Elijah went down the other side and hurried his mount to the road. He knew the sheriff would not give up. If he was to give John and his family any time, he would have to misdirect the sheriff, hopefully for good. If the sheriff wanted members of the illegal church, then he must make him think he was on the right track. Elijah knew he mustn't involve more members of the church. No, the only ones that the sheriff might suspect were John's family.

The sheriff reached the top, but Elijah was long gone. Elijah allowed himself to be seen momentarily. Taylor wondered how Elijah had gotten so far so quickly. Taylor stayed a good distance behind Elijah, and Elijah did not try to hide his destination. He trusted that James and Martha could benefit John if they had a mind to, and they had a mind to. Elijah followed the road to the Dairyman's farm. The daily trip from the farm to town had worn the road with parallel ruts made by the milk cart. The road led up to the house. Taylor stayed a good distance behind. He found a cluster of trees where he could hide while observing the situation.

Elijah's arrival was a complete surprise to the family. They felt honored that he would come to their home.

Instead of greeting the family, Elijah spoke harshly. "Are you James Dairyman?" He winked his eye and tilted his head back toward the road.

James understood. "Why, yes. I am. What can I do for you?"

"My name is Elijah Brown, special agent for his lordship, and I want to ask you some questions. May we discuss these things in your house?"

James replied, "Yes, of course. Come this way."

James turned to walk to his house. Elijah dismounted and followed him in.

As soon as he entered, he looked to see if the sheriff was near. Turning back to James and Martha, he explained, "Sorry for the show, but I led the sheriff here on purpose. I fear we must make him think that I am truly looking for the radical church. Him seeing me here may buy us the time we so desperately need." When he was sure that the coast was clear, he turned to James and proclaimed, "Well done, my brother. Thank you for not giving my position away."

After receiving a warm greeting from James and his wife, they sat down for refreshments. Martha brought out a bottle of wine and set the table with bits of meat, cheese, and bread. James asked Elijah to bring a blessing on the food. It was a welcomed fellowship. As they ate, Elijah told them his reason for the visit.

Then he offered, "I bring you urgent news of my visit with the earl. It has to do with John's expected departure. There is little time before a Mr. Robert Howell or one of his representatives will be calling on John."

The news made Martha gasp. She covered her mouth in an attempt to keep her composure. James reached to comfort her by putting his arm around her.

Elijah continued. "The purpose of the visit will be to finalize the agreement for John becoming an indentured. The earl advised me that John needs to read the document carefully before signing it." James asked, "Do we know how much longer before John will be leaving?"

Elijah nodded. "There is a ship preparing for the Americas at this very moment. The earl suspects that John will be leaving here in a few days to board that ship."

As might be expected, the news was sobering. James, full of questions, continued to inquire. "Do we know from what port John will leave from?"

Elijah answered the best he could. "Even the earl is not sure from which port John will depart. He only said it will be within a few days."

Martha choked out her feelings. "It don't leave much time for goodbyes. I truly hate to see my boy go."

Once the words escaped her lips, she began to sob. James pulled her close, and she shook uncontrollably. James stroked her hair in the most caring way.

James whispered, "There, there, Mother. There, there." Nothing else seemed appropriate.

Elijah just observed the situation. These were difficult times. Deep within, he prayed. "Lord, give me the words that I might aid to her comfort."

Elijah waited for a while before saying more. His words were direct. "There is really nothing I can say that will ease your pain. John is your son. I know you have taught him well. I hope you can find comfort knowing you have raised a wonderful young man. John is not leaving as a prodigal son, but a man with a new destiny in a new land. If John was weak or a libertine, I would have cause for concern. John is none of that. He is knowledgeable and capable. I have no doubt that with the aid of our Sovereign, he will succeed in America."

James too choked back tears. "This man the earl has in mind to provide for John ... Is he a good man?"

Elijah replied, "I honestly don't know. We have never met. I have to rely on his lordship's recommendation."

The evening was coming on, and Elijah knew he had to be going. Before leaving, he made one more statement. A concerned look followed by a bit of mischief came over his face. His surprise statement was this: "I believe the sheriff followed me here. It is best I leave before John returns. I will say my 'fare thee wells' here before I leave. When you go outside with me, just follow my conversation. I mean no disrespect." He smiled. "Now follow me quickly outside and pretend to be afraid."

Elijah left the house in a rage. James and Martha came out hurriedly, clutching each other and pretending to be afraid.

Elijah mounted his horse and looked at the couple before speaking in a loud, threatening voice. "You tell your son that the earl is watching him. I will not be far away. Tell him I am watching his every move. Do not stand in my way."

With that, Elijah winked, mounted his horse, and rode off hurriedly. Martha hid her face in her hands, and James stood erect. Elijah rode away, and James and Martha turned back to the house. Once inside, Martha looked at James, and a smile showed the relief of the wearisome evening. She looked up at James and stated, "That was a bit of fun, wasn't it?"

From a nearby place, the sheriff watched Elijah leave. Taylor thought to himself, *So others are nearby. Wonder who they might be.* While Taylor knew the townsfolk, he knew little of those in the countryside. With his limited knowledge, it was impossible to figure it all out. He pulled on the horse's reins, prepared to follow after Elijah. When he did, he came face-to-face with the man he had been trailing.

Taylor was shocked. He looked about and asked, "How?"

Elijah looked sternly at Taylor. "How did I get here? How did I manage to avoid your awareness? Lord Sheriff, you think that you are being wise and clever to disobey the earl. It is obvious you will not listen to reason. I will not tell you what direction you should take. However, if you value your station, I would take care as to how far you carry on your duties.

The earl may take your actions as direct disobedience and justify your dismissal."

The sheriff looked indignant. "And what were you doing at Dairyman's house?"

Elijah crossed his arms and appeared very imposing. "There you go again, asking questions that I cannot answer. I suggest if you want to know the answer, you ask the earl, but if you do, be prepared for what he will demand of you. Like why you chose to disobey his orders."

Taylor remained indignant. "What do you mean? Seeing to the welfare of the people hereabouts is my responsibility."

Elijah raised up in the saddle. "Is it also your duty to take the side of a drunken fool who would do everything in his power to crush the very life of the young man?"

Elijah's stare completely unnerved Taylor.

After a moment, Elijah asked, "What's the blacksmith's hold on you, my fine fellow?"

Taylor was visibly stunned by the question.

Elijah concluded, "I would be ashamed to find guilt on an innocent man in order to pay a debt owed."

Taylor couldn't help but think, *Has this special agent also been investigating me?*

The two men eyed each other for a moment. Finally, Elijah turned his horse, gave a laugh, and departed. "I would be very much aware of my own doings if I were you." A moment more, and Elijah turned his horse and rode away. He raised a hand and cried out, "Good evening, Lord Sheriff. Good evening." With that, he began to laugh, and his laughter was heard a good way off.

The sheriff sat fuming. From the farmhouse, James could hear the laughter and said to Martha, "It appears our pastor truly got the last laugh."

Martha more seriously stated, "Perhaps, my dear husband, but what was the joke?"

Taylor arrived in the town bone weary from the events of the day. He rode down the main street of town as he headed for home. Just as he made his turn, he saw a fire burning in the street and a gathering outside. Several people had rushed from their homes to see what the disturbance was about. The blacksmith had built the fire to draw attention to himself. Taylor could not tell if the man was drunk, but he could hear his bellowing voice even over the rage of the fire. The sheriff urged his horse to the scene. The closer he got, the more he heard, and the more he disliked what was being said.

The blacksmith was stirring the people with his anger. Some were drawn from their homes by the shouts. Many came from their homes out of curiosity. The fire drew the people as a moth to the flame. William's words did the rest.

"Come out, good people of Haywards Heath. Come out and hear me. You have stayed far enough away; now come and hear me out. Do you hear me? Come out and give me justice."

They gathered, willing to give ear to the man. Drawing near the fire, they could see the anger but not the rage in William's eyes.

A man doesn't need a reason to create an uprising. So what makes someone do the things they do? It could be attention. Maybe it's for personal gain, a principle, or for control. For William Smith, the reason was vengeance. He would have his revenge by making the people around him feel that he was being treated unjustly.

The sheriff rode in close but remained in the dark where he could still hear all William was saying. He knew the people were focused on the fire and would take little notice of him. Taylor thought it strange that people would come out to hear the blacksmith. The townsfolk did not see William as a leader or even a man they cared for, but in the absence of leadership, people will follow one who will give them a cause to do so. Then the thought came to Taylor, *What have I done to lead the people in the right way?*

William pranced around the fire as he yelled, "Come out! You have called me your friend for years. I have done your work. Am I not of this village? Now you stay away from me. Why? Because an inexperienced boy stole you away from me. Did I not teach him? Am I not his master? I gave my word to his father that I would train the boy into a smith. You know his father. James Dairyman is his name. In return, the boy was to serve me and care for the shop. A fortnight ago I came to find the boy lying about, so I decided to teach him a lesson. How did he show his gratitude? He nearly burnt me own barn down. If it had not been my quick thinking, all would have been lost. I only sought to teach the boy a lesson. Then when he got the best of me, he decided to make it known that he is a Christian. A Christian, not with the king's church, but of an illegal, unauthorized church. The boy then fled. I went to the sheriff to demand satisfaction. Has he done anything for me? No!"

The people did not join in with William, which agitated him all the more. With that, he increased his accusations and demands for justice. He took a deep breath and continued. "The dairyman and his son have stolen your hearts. And what has he done for you that you have not paid for it? Dairyman brings you milk and cheese. You pay dearly for it too. And what of his son? Do you mean to tell me he is a smith?" William spit on the ground. Then he looked over the people. "A pig's eye he is."

Some were beginning to take notice, and William seized the moment. "Then there is the matter of our noble sheriff. I have gone to him demanding justice. How did I find him? Keeping house with a woman. Yes, good people of Haywards Heath, our sheriff is more concerned with his mistress than keeping order in our town."

Finally, some of the more abase parts of town began to give ear to what was being said. A few gave an encouraging "harrumph," but the majority of the town remained to themselves. William could not believe more people were not coming to his side. He couldn't stand it any longer, and the real William came forth screaming.

"What's the matter with you people? Join me in demanding justice!"

A lone rider emerged from the dark. He remained just beyond the brightest light of the fire so that few could see him. Taylor spoke calmly and firmly, directing his words at William. "They won't join you because they know you for the liar, cheat, and brute you are."

The people looked toward the voice but could barely make him out.

William responded, "Now I may get some satisfaction. Behold, the good sheriff has arrived." Then mockingly William asked, "Come to arrest me, Sheriff?"

Taylor did ride closer but broke the silence with truth. He replied, "You build a fire to bring attention to you, seeking to cause riot among the people. You stood there and lied about your apprentice, his father, and me. You brought false claims against me without proof. So, good people of Haywards Heath, let me tell you the truth. The other morning this brigand came to my house and found a young lady there. Yes, I have a young lady living with me. Her name is Sally. In fact, she is my sister. William saw her with me and decided that I was having improper relations with the miss. Many of you know me and know that I buried my wife and son here in our little town. My dear sweet wife died while giving birth to my son. My love for her and my memory of that day has kept me from seeking another. As for the apprentice, many of you saw for yourselves the drunken condition of the blacksmith on the day in question. He nearly burned down his own barn. Had it not been for the young man, this brute of a man who stands before you could have lost it all and been killed by the flames."

Once the sheriff mentioned John's actions, many of the townsfolk began to agree among themselves. William was beginning to fume.

Taylor could tell the people were listening to him, so he continued. "As for his father, how many have gone without because they could not pay? I know he has cared for even the poorest among us. There is not a kinder, nobler man anywhere." Directing his speech to the smith, he added, "So, William, if you plan on attacking someone, you better make sure it is someone you can handle. James Dairyman possesses a moral character that you never will." Taylor's comment made the people laugh, which angered the blacksmith even more.

Taylor rode in closer. Addressing the crowd, he stated, "Then this liar says the boy is a renegade Christian. There may be some of you who are part of that church. I thought it my duty to find them. Just now, as I listened to the ugly charges made by this man, I realized one thing. Whoever they are they have done nothing wrong. William only seeks to destroy as many as he can." With disgust in his voice, he charged the smith. "William, you are the worst sort. I have stated that you are a liar." Then leaning forward, he growled, "And you are under arrest."

William heard as much as he was going to hear. A loud, angry wail came from deep within him. He grabbed a burning limb from the fire and charged at the sheriff. William was a few feet from the sheriff when he heard the ring of sharpened metal leaving its sheath. He stopped suddenly as the point of the sword neared him.

Taylor repeated, "You're under arrest."

William snarled, "You wouldn't dare try and arrest me without your sword."

Taylor smiled. "I am no fool. Now turn around and walk to the jail."

William barked back, "You'll not take me to jail." He took the great burning club and started to fling it at the sheriff.

With a flip of the wrist, the sheriff sliced a nasty cut across the cheek of the blacksmith. The pain caused the smith to drop the club and cover his face with his hand. A red stream flowed between his fingers. The sheriff looked at the sword and then back at the blacksmith. "A fine edge indeed. The maker of this sword is a fine craftsman. You might know him. He is known as John the apprentice." With that, the sheriff marched William to jail, but not before issuing the order to put out the fire and for the crowd to disperse.

# Farewell

"My name is Emit Browning, and I represent Robert Howell." This was the introduction made to James and Martha by the representative of the man who would pay for John's services. "I was told you would be expecting a call from me. Is John hereabouts?"

James and Martha could not get over how distinguished Mr. Browning looked, but there was a calmness to his demeanor. Unlike most of the villagers, his clothing had a mark of elegance. James and Martha owned no such clothing. They bid the man welcome to their humble home.

James reached a hand to Emit. "Please come in. We have been expecting you. Our son John is in the barn. I shall call for him."

Emit looked over the humble dwellings. The house, though small, was very well kept. An aroma of fresh bread filled the house. When James left to retrieve John, Martha invited Emit into their home. Once inside, she told him to have a seat at the table.

There was a true humility in his response. "Mrs. Dairyman, I do not wish to be a bother."

She turned to look at the gentleman. "It isn't a bother, but your rejection to sit with us to enjoy some refreshment may be looked at as being unfriendly."

Emit nodded and obeyed before taking a seat at the table. He chuckled a little before responding. "You sounded like my own mother, though you are more my sister's age."

Martha turned and put her hands to her hips before giving a reply. "And what do you mean by that, Mr. Browning?"

Emit replied, "I grew up on a farm very similar to this one. My mom was a stickler for cleanliness, good food, and hospitality."

Martha relaxed at the words. "Then welcome home."

When James and John entered, Emit rose to his feet.

"Return to your seat, Mr. Browning," James told him. "I knew Martha would make you comfortable."

The representative thanked James by saying, "Please call me Emit. I would be honored if you would do so. I take it that this is John." Emit again rose momentarily to extend his hand to the younger man. John took his hand, and Emit could feel the strength in his grip. He looked into the face of young man. The youthfulness, the easy smile, and the firm handshake relayed to Emit that there was something more in this lad. John was strong, but there was a hint of culture to him.

John simply replied, "It's my pleasure, sir."

Martha placed fresh, hot bread, butter, and honey on the table, along with a cool crock of milk, freshly creamed cheese, salt ham, and cakes. Soon, the other children were called in, and they politely took their seats. Emit was surprised when James said a simple blessing over the food. Everyone was seated and plates were filled, and before long everyone began talking about the events of the day. Emit forgot why he was there. He was carried back to his humble beginnings. It had been a long time since he'd felt like part of a family. James and Martha made him feel right at home.

As soon as the meal was done and everything had been cleaned up, James, Martha, and John remained to speak with Emit. Martha brought out a bottle of wine and poured a little for the men to enjoy. Emit accepted and began the conversation.

"I want to thank you for the warmth of your hospitality. As I mentioned to Martha, I grew up on a farm very much like yours. I was able to get an education, which allowed me to gain employment with Mr. Howell."

James's reply was like a country gentleman. "We are the ones who are honored. Is Mr. Howell much like yourself?"

Emit smiled and looked at the cup of wine. "Not really. He is more of a businessman and is quite successful with holdings in London, Plymouth, and now America. He is part owner of a company that established a new colony in America called Elizabeth City. That is where John is needed."

John had a look of disappointment. "I thought I might be going to Plymouth or Boston."

Emit replied, "Those locations are part of the Massachusetts Bay Colony."

John remained composed. "I suppose it really doesn't matter. I am willing to serve wherever I am needed."

Emit was glad for the response. In his reply, he stated, "Very good. I suppose you want to know about the departure date."

John responded, "Yes, we all would like to know."

Emit answered, "We need to leave in two days. Even now, the ship is being loaded. That is why my time is so urgent and your decision so important."

Emit was surprised the family wasn't more shocked. He had braced himself for more emotion.

James picked up on his thoughts by Emit's expression. James stated, "Do not think that we are not bothered. We were told that John would be leaving soon, and we have already prepared ourselves for this news."

Emit's expression eased. "I am surprised but glad to know you have prepared yourselves." Looking to John, he continued. "John, I have some papers for you to sign. Would you like for me read them for you?"

John politely declined and took the document from Emit.

Emit watched as John took the paper and began reading the agreement out loud for everyone to hear. Emit was amazed, because many in rural society lacked any form of education. From time to time, John would ask the meaning of certain clauses. Emit explained them so that there was clear understanding.

After thoroughly reading the contract, John sat back and said, "It seems fair enough." Turning to his parents, he asked if they had any questions. They had none, so John recapped. "In essence, I will be serving five years for my passage. The profits I make from the work I do will be sent to Mr. Howell. From the profits, Mr. Howell will see to my living expenses plus some funds for my personal needs. At the end of five years, I will be given fifty acres in Virginia for my own. Does that about sum it up, Mr. Browning?"

Emit peered at John in wonder. "Yes, that is a good summary." Then, pausing for a moment, he continued. "Please tell me one thing. You are in a region where there are no schools. How is it that you have been educated?"

John responded, "I have been taught by my betrothed. I am skilled in reading, writing, and mathematics."

Emit furthered the inquiry. "Then why not seek your fortunes in the city? Your knowledge and skill would be greatly rewarded."

John lowered his eyes. "I fear providence prevents that for me. There is one who has brought charges against me, and I fear I need to leave the country. I believe for the good of the family and others that I begin a new life elsewhere."

Emit pondered the statement before replying. "The Americas will be better because of you, Mr. Dairyman." Then turning to James, Emit stated, "I mean no disrespect to you, sir, in referring to your son as Mr. Dairyman."

James felt proud. "I saw no disrespect, my good man."

Emit returned his attention to John. "Then are you ready to sign the papers?"

In solemn tone, John replied, "I am."

Emit produced a box that contained a quill and ink pot. He laid the items before John. John took the quill in hand, dabbed a bit of ink on the point, and signed his name to the agreement. His penmanship was most exquisite. Emit looked at the signature with a puzzled look on his face. John raised an index figure to his lips. Emit understood. He closed his eyes slowly and tilted his head to the side, indicating a gentleman's agreement. Emit took a can of powder and dusted the signature. After a moment, he blew off the residue. Emit then folded the paper in thirds and pulled from the case a stick of red wax. Walking to the stove, he placed the wax near the heat till it was sticky and then returned to the document and applied an ample amount of the wax to it. Finally, he pulled a hand stamp bearing Mr. Robert Howell's signet and sealed the contract with it. Now all was binding.

James invited Emit to stay the night. Emit refused the offer and apologized, stating he had additional preparations to make before their scheduled departure. Then he stated before leaving, "I shall be back in two days. Once I return, there won't be much time before we take the trip to Blackwall. That is where we shall depart for America. I do appreciate your warm hospitality, perhaps another time." He shook the hands of James and John. He took Martha's hand, bowed, and kissed it, saying, "God bless you, Mum." Then, boarding the carriage, he bid the coachman on.

Martha returned to the kitchen ever so impressed with Mr. Emit Browning.

John looked to his father. "I have a bit more that I need to do before I am ready to present my gift to Chastity. With your permission, I shall go back to my work."

James looked over at his son. The boy was gone now. He had raised a fine young man. He choked up at the thought that his boy would soon depart and that he might never see him again. He squeezed his lips together, fighting back tears, and then nodded his head in approval.

In the barn, John held the box he had made for ring. The box was simple but beautiful. It was just a few inches cubed. He made a sliding lid instead of a hinged one. John had applied many coats of wax till the box shined. He set it on the table and gathered the pile of wool he got from Thomas. John made a nest in the box for the ring and then placed the ring in it before closing the lid. Chastity's gift was ready.

That evening John went to Chastity's home. He told the family of his visit with Mr. Emit Browning and the details of the contract. When he said that he would be leaving in two days' time, the women, especially Chastity, were immediately overwhelmed. Tears filled their eyes.

John took Chastity into his arms before speaking. "I know it will be hard, but I know it will be all right." He lifted her chin up to where he could see her. "We must believe that it will be all right."

Thomas put his hands on his hips. "For crying out loud, boy, kiss her already!"

John was more than ready to oblige. Her lips were soft and moist. Tears began to flow from her eyes.

When finished, Chastity announced, "I love you, John."

John looked to the family and asked, "I would like to ask you to join me at my father's house tomorrow night for a celebration. I have something that I want to share with all. Please come and be a part of my last day here."

The family needed little persuasion. Ruth added, "Please tell you mother that I will bring food to share in the occasion."

Thomas added, "We all would be honored to come."

John was most grateful that they agreed. Though he was with the family the entire evening, his focus remained on his beloved. Both were thinking of the kiss they'd shared.

Chastity thought, *Will he always love me like this? I know I shall always love him.*

When night came, John waited for the candles to be blown out and then snuck out the door. The moon was full, and the road was well lit. He had traveled about half the distance home when he heard a horse neigh. The sound startled him. Someone was nearby. Fearing it was the sheriff, he hunkered down and crawled up the hill to hide behind some trees. He could hear the pounding of the horse's hoofs on the ground. The rider stopped at the exact location where John had departed the road.

A voice broke the silence. "John! John Dairyman! Come here, my brother. It is I, your pastor, and I am come to see you safely home."

John made his way down the hill. He came up to the rider and looked into the face of his friend and pastor, Elijah Brown.

"It's all right," Elijah said, trying to reassure him. "I came from your home, and hearing you were with Chastity, I offered to come get you. You need not fear the sheriff."

John was puzzled. "How can you be so sure?"

Elijah was in a jolly mood. "Let's just say that he has seen the error of his ways." He gave a hardy laugh and extended his hand to John. Elijah pulled him up onto the horse, and together, they rode back to his home.

As they rode together, John made an invitation. "Pastor, I plan for a celebration tomorrow night, and I would be honored if you would come."

Elijah responded, "Delighted, my boy. I would not miss it for anything. Your father told me of your impending departure. I want to be there to pray with you all for the adventure ahead."

The next morning John began making final preparations for the journey. He had no trunk in which to transport his few belongings, so he decided to build a box for the trip. He knew the box had to be watertight.

John valued what tools he had, and he cared for them as though they were worth a great fortune. For a penniless man, they were. With great care, he fitted each edge of the box, making sure there were no gaps. He bore very fine holes in strategic points in the corners of the box and drove tiny dowels into these holes to form tight seals. At first, he wanted to make a hinged lid but decided to seal the box tight. He figured that when he arrived in America, he could convert the box into a tool chest. When he was satisfied with the construction, John took tar and applied a liberal amount on the inside of the box. He thought to himself, *This should keep the box watertight.*

John took beeswax and began polishing the exterior of the box. The natural grain of the oak surfaced with the first application. Later, he applied a second layer and then a third. When this was done, he was convinced the wood would withstand the harsh sea air.

John waited till the tar had set before loading it. While he waited, he prepared his tools for the journey. John took all his tools from the oily leather he kept them in and inspected each tool. He took out his sharpening stone and touched up every tool that needed it. He thoroughly cleaned each one and then took grease and heavily coated them. He applied a fresh coat of oil on the leathers. Each tool was carefully wrapped.

Soon, the box was dry, and he loaded the precious cargo. Before closing the lid, John put a layer of hay over the tools to take up the remaining space. Finally, he dabbed a layer of tar in the groove where the lid would slide. He forced the lid in place, and with the remaining dowels, he securely closed the box. It was ready for the trip to America.

John had little clothing. He had one set of clothes that he kept for special occasions. This is what he would wear tonight and for his journey to London. He laid them out on his bed. He cared for his work clothing in the same way he did his tools. They were worn but kept tidy and clean. He folded them and placed them in a wool bag that had been made for him by Chastity's mom. John had no purse, but he had a small leather bag in which he kept what few valuables he owned. He had a few coins and the silver bar he had made. That was the extent of his valuables. John took count of all he had done and was satisfied he was prepared for the journey ahead.

John spent the rest of the afternoon getting things ready for the night's gathering. A table was pulled from the barn and set up outside. A fire pit was burning, and a small pig roasted over the rising flame. The table was set with wooden plates. Bottles of wine and beer were set out. Milk cooled in the well and would be served to the children.

When evening came, the two families assembled along with Pastor and his wife. Chastity and John noticed that Adam and Chastity's sister, Pricilla, took special interest in each other. Though the thought of his departure loomed, the time was festive. The families enjoyed good food and company. As the evening advanced toward dark, wood was added to the fire. The flames added light and cast dancing shadows against the barn and trees.

When dinner was done, Elijah invited all to join in prayer for John. They all sat around on benches facing their beloved pastor. The prayer was short and sweet, seeking God's guidance over John, Chastity, and the two families. Tears of joy and sorrow filled the eyes of all. When Pastor was done, silence filled the air.

After a while, John rose to his feet. He felt it was time to make his announcement. He called Chastity to join him. He looked into her eyes and smiled. Nothing was said between them. Their glance said it all. Then, turning to the families, he announced, "I asked permission of Mr. Shepherd to marry his daughter before asking Chastity if she would accept my proposal. Thankfully, she accepted." Everyone chuckled. John continued. "Up until now, I have had nothing to show people that she is my betrothed. Now I wish to change all of that."

John reached in his vest pocket and produced the box. Once again, he fell to one knee. Looking up at Chastity, he stated, "I ask you before these witnesses. Will you marry me? Will you accept my gift, which will seal our betrothal?"

Chastity took the box from his hand and slid open the lid. The sight of the ring made her catch her breath. She raised her hand to her lips. John rose to his feet. He reached into the box to free the ring from its captivity. The ring brightly reflected the firelight. Chastity was stunned. She could not get over the ring. Never had she seen anything like it. He took her left hand and slid the ring in place. It was perfect.

Chastity asked, "How did you know my size?"

John whispered, "Do you remember the wool I tied around your finger?"

The young couple giggled. John then turned to the face the families. "There is something more I must tell you. The ring is made to look like two vines twisting together. The vine represents our families and the marriage that will bind us. There is more. The suspicions surrounding me may cause retribution and attacks to all those I love. I can think of only one way to free you from this course of action. I can spare everyone by changing my name. The vine is the secret. Therefore, from this day forth, I shall be known as Jonathan Devine."

Everyone was surprised by the announcement. The families were stunned by the announcement.

John's reply was simple. "I am not ashamed of my given name, but I doubt that many will take me seriously as a smith if I am known as John Dairyman. I also thought of the name Smith, but after all I faced with my master, I can't bring myself to that name either." Smiling, he added, "Besides, it is too common a name, and others could try and duplicate my work."

John paused for a moment before taking his beloved's hand. "My new name came to me as I was designing Chastity's ring. The image of the vine and how it is represented in scripture would not leave me. Our Lord's promised return is sealed with the fruit of the vine. Our connection to Him is found with the vine. Chastity and I will someday be one. I leave it with her whether she will accept this name from me. I promise it will remain a name of honor. Finally, should persecution arise, they will not find John Dairyman or John Smith. He is gone forever."

John walked over to James and looked him in the eye. "Father, I hope you understand."

James's answer was clear. "A name is one that is to be honored. While I feel a bit of disappointment, I will always know that you are my son. I saw the strange look come over Emit when he saw your signature. I knew something was different. You signed your name as Jonathan Devine, didn't you?"

John was surprised at how intuitive his father was. In reply, he answered, "It's true, Father. I did."

Then James concluded. "Then wear the name proudly." James pulled his son into his arms and whispered, "My son, I am proud of you—no matter what name you bear."

Soon, everyone rushed over to congratulate the young couple. The women were taken by the beautiful ring. The men also could not get over the fine craftsmanship.

Elijah whispered to John, "You realize all of our wives will now be clamoring for a ring for themselves. I thought you didn't want to cause trouble."

Night began to fall, and the Shepherds had to return home. Before leaving, John and Chastity stole away for a private moment together. They walked hand in hand into the dark, away from the family. Just beyond the sights and sounds of the gathering, John took Chastity into his arms. Then, looking deep into her eyes, he proclaimed, "I will be with you sooner than you think. If you need me, I will be there. I promise. Someday we shall have children of our own, and we will tell them of life and love."

She lifted her hand to look at the ring. The ring's brilliant surface reflected the light, giving it a red-orange color.

John asked, "Do you like it?"

Chastity responded, "John, I love it. You never cease to amaze me. I still don't know how you did it."

With gladness in his heart, he answered, "Someday, I'll show you. I might even teach you some of my trade." He held her close, and together, they kissed.

When their lips parted, she stated, "My beloved, I will wait for you. This I promise."

James and his family watched as the wagon bearing the Shepherds departed for home. One by one, the Dairyman family went into the house. John remained alone, catching the last glimpses of the wagon.

It was late when John climbed into bed. He knew on the morrow he would be leaving and slept very little. He had never been farther away from his home than the village. Now he would sail away and perhaps never see his beloved homeland again. John thought of Chastity's kiss. Oh, how he wished she was in his arms. His eyes grew heavy, but a reoccurring thought remained. *Someday, my love, we will finally be together.*

Even before the sunrise, John woke. Who could sleep knowing that his life was about to change. His mind was not on the trip. It was on Chastity. It was more than young love. She was a part of him. Even though an uncertain future awaited he was sure he could do most anything with Chastity at his side. All the planning in the world, all his talent, and all his hopes could not forecast his future. John was convinced that he was prepared—was he?

It was nearly noon when a handsome carriage bearing Emit Browning arrived to collect John. Emit bounded from the carriage. As much as he was there for John, he wanted to see Martha.

"Good morning, Mum," he said. "It is so good to see you again. Is your husband about?"

Martha smiled. "No. He is already making his deliveries. Would you like something to eat?"

"I am afraid that I haven't the time, but someday, with your permission, I may come again and visit." Emit felt very much at home with the Dairyman family, as he found a connection to the life he knew as a child.

John exited the house wearing the same clothes from the night before. Martha looked at her tall, handsome son. His clothes fit him well and could not conceal his broad shoulders and strong chest. With ease, he lifted the heavy box bearing the tools to the coachman. The coachman thought the wooden box would be light and grabbed it with one hand after seeing how easily John managed it. The weight of the box nearly pulled him from the carriage. John saw his struggle and climbed up to help him.

Emit looked at the young smith and announced, "It is time we were going."

John turned to his family. By this time, all were there except for his father. Candice was the first to run up to John and throw her arms around him. The others rushed in as well to give their brother a final farewell embrace.

Martha waited till the others were finished. She approached her son and looked up to him. She fought back tears as she spoke. "My son, I feared long ago this day would come. From the moment you were born, I knew that there was something special about you. I knew you were destined for something greater. Now you are beginning your own life and future in a new place. May God watch over you and make you prosperous. I love you, my boy. I … I …" She could not finish. Tears filled his eyes. She wrapped her arms around John, and he lovingly pulled her close. She sobbed.

With the most heartfelt love, he whispered, "I love you, Mother. If God sees fit, I will come back."

When all the goodbyes were done, Emit looked to Martha. "I will take the best care of him while he is in my charge. God be with you."

With that, the two men boarded the carriage. The coachman turned the horses and proceeded down the road. At the bottom of the drive, a lone figure waited. His horse and cart were stopped. James raised his hand, and the coachman reined in the horses. John took one look at his father and rushed from the coach.

James held his boy. "You didn't think I would let you leave without me saying goodbye, did you?"

Father and son held strongly to each other, and tears flowed freely.

"I shall miss you, my boy. You are the oldest. I shall miss you. How could I not? I loved the boy you were and the man you have become. My heart aches for you now. I may never see you again, but my memory will ever keep you with me. Tell your children of us. When you and Chastity marry, always love each other. Protect her and provide for her. If God shall give you opportunity, come back to us. If not, remember that we shall be together again someday with our Father in heaven."

Afterward, John was about to board the carriage when he heard his name being called. "John, John, wait!" Up the road in the Shepherd family wagon came Chastity and her family. Even before the wagon stopped, she jumped down and ran to his arms. "I had to see you one more time." The young couple longingly held each other.

When they parted, John told her to wait a moment and walked to the carriage. He returned with a sealed letter. "I am afraid this embrace will have to keep us until we can be together again." Then he emphasized, "I know we shall be together again. I was going to mail you this letter when I arrived in London. Read it tonight when you are alone."

Chastity looked at the letter and smiled. She thought back to all the time she'd spent teaching him to read and write. In reply, she said, "John, I never knew that teaching you to write would mean so much or how important it would be for us. I promise I will write. It will help pass our time apart. I will forever be thinking of you."

Chastity turned to her family. Thomas walked up with something in his hands. Chastity continued. "We wanted to give you this for your journey and days ahead."

Thomas held a package wrapped and tied with wool. John opened it, and there was the worn Geneva Bible he had read so often. John was surprised. For some the cost of a Bible could amount to a year's wages. He stated, "I … I … cannot take this. What will you use?"

Thomas assured him. "Don't you worry about that. Pastor assured me that he can get me another. You will need this for the days ahead. I trust you will be comforted by it. When you and Chastity are one and you have your children all about you, tell them of us. Tell your children how you came to America. Tell them how important God is to our family and how He made the way."

John just stared at the gift. Then he had an idea. He rushed to Emit and asked, "Mr. Browning, do you have your writing materials?"

Emit replied, "Indeed I do."

John asked, "May we borrow them a moment?"

Emit left the carriage with the box in hand. John handed the Bible to Thomas and asked, "Would you write your name and that of your family in the Bible for us?"

Thomas took the Bible from John and laid it on the back of the wagon. He wrote the following inscription:

> To my daughter's betrothed, John. May providence watch over you and ever provide for you. May His care and protection shield you all the days of your life. Teach your children and our grandchildren of our faith and tell them of your family in England and how God brought you to the place of prosperity. He will ever be with you. Take care of my daughter, your wife, and always shower her with love. With my heart, I give this precious old Book to you.
>
> Thomas Shepherd

Then Thomas wrote the names of Martha and the children. Then he added a few more names, dusted the page, and walked over to James. "See here, James, I have added you and Martha's names, along with your children. Our families are one. I promise that soon you will be able to write your own name and even a letter to John."

James was overwhelmed. "Thank you, my brother."

Then, walking over to John, Thomas handed him the book.

John read what was written and embraced Thomas. "I shall do all this and more. This is my word to you." Finally, Thomas called to Ruth and the girls to come and bid John farewell. Turning to Chastity one last time, he hugged and kissed her. "I go to prepare a place for us. Come as soon as you can. I will be waiting."

Emit collected the writing materials and boarded the carriage. John gave a final smile and followed. Once more, the coachman slapped the reins, and the horses lunged ahead.

Emit turned to John. "Never in my life have I seen such love. You are an honored man. How is it these two families love so?"

John looked to him. "By the things written in this book. If you would like, I could share these things with you."

Emit replied, "We have a long ride ahead. I would like nothing more."

Then, just as Philip shared the word with the eunuch sixteen hundred years before, so did John share the wonderful grace of God.

James stood for the longest time watching the carriage roll over the hillside. Chastity came to his side. He put his big arm around her and said, "There goes my son. Do you know how hard this is for me? My heart feels empty. I am proud of him, but right now I wish he was a little boy again." He choked back tears.

Chastity looked at her future father-in-law. "He is very much like you, you know. I can see him in your eyes. Would it be all right if I come over from time to time just to be with you all?"

For the first time that day joy, replaced sadness. James looked at this young woman who held his son's heart. "I would like that very much."

When it was night, Chastity opened the letter. It was obvious that he did not expect to see her when he did. She felt his love for her in the words he penned.

My dearly beloved,

I begin my journey today away from you to prepare for our future together. I do not know what our God has for us. I just know that He has made a way. I expect that tomorrow I shall be on board a ship heading for the New World. Our days apart will seem long and short at the same time. By His grace, I shall have a house and land for us to begin our life together. I will write as often as I can. I pray you do the same for me. Nothing can separate us as long as we keep our eyes on the Lord.

Darling, if you hear some terrible thing has happened to me, do not put stock in it. I trust God will get me to safe harbor and give me strength to endure hardship and loneliness. I will pray every day for us. If our God is for us, who can stand against us. I love you. Never could a man love another as much as I love you. I pray no man tries to deceive you and try to turn you against me. For that reason, I have given you my new name in advance. Below you will find my signature, along with the artistic inscription. By this, you shall know that it is really me who writes to you.

I will not say farewell. I will only say, till God sees fit to bring us together again. Keep my heart close to your own. Remember that I love you. Remember ...

Forever yours,
Jonathan Devine

Beneath the signature was a long figure shaped like an S. Two lines lay close to each other within the S. Grape leaves were added to the mark. This was the mark of the artist and silversmith Jonathan Devine.

# Onward

The carriage ride to London was long, but for John, it was a new adventure. He had never been to a big city before. Upon a high hill, Emit pointed out the city and its features. John could see the top of the masts of sailing ships in the distance. Before long, he could see the rigging and then the ships on the waterfront. John could not help himself and leaned out the carriage window for a better look. There was a bit of excitement at the thought of being on one of those ships.

Emit couldn't help but notice the youthful enthusiasm. "I remember the first time I came to London. I grew up in the little hamlet of Hadleigh in East Anglia. I remember the very excitement you are experiencing right now."

John responded, "Look at all the ships. I could not have imagined such a sight as this."

Emit answered, "In truth, these ships are rather small to be taking a voyage across the ocean. I have been told that the Spanish have much larger ships. It takes a good captain to sail the ocean in one of those."

The coachman turned toward Blackwall. The streets were narrow, but the coachman navigated them with ease. Emit pointed out some of the more important places. One that really stood out was Sir Walter Raleigh's house. They came upon a sign of another building with a shingle that read, "London Company."

Emit pointed to the sign and stated, "That is the company that is financing the voyage to America."

A little farther down the road they came to the dock where the *Elizabeth Marie* was berthed. Men were busy on the ship making final preparations for the morning departure.

Emit and John stopped at the ship to see to his belongings being loaded. Emit called to the captain, seeking permission to come aboard. Captain Richard Wise greeted the two men and asked their reason for the request.

"I am Emit Browning, and this young man is Jonathan Devine who will be traveling to America on behalf of Mr. Robert Howell."

The captain gave a sneer. "An indentured, is he? He is but a boy." Turning to John, the captain asked, "And what special skills might you have?"

John looked at the captain and replied, "I am a smith. I work with iron and precious metals and have served the Earl of Sussex."

The captain eyed the boy, wondering to himself the truthfulness of his statement. About the same time, two men had already retrieved John's box and carried it up the plank. The captain stopped the men a moment to inspect the cargo. He took special interest in the box's construction.

The captain turned to John and remarked, "That box is a very fine one. How did you come by it?"

John replied, "I thank you, Captain. I made it."

The captain saw an opportunity for gain. He offered, "How would you like to be paid while on this journey? You would be in service to Mr. Bowman, our carpenter."

Emit spoke up. "I am afraid Mr. Devine is indentured to Mr. Howell. I would have to clear it with him before he could accept."

The captain replied, "I would be much obliged to you, sir, if you would ask on my behalf." The truth was, the captain wanted profit from John's abilities.

Before leaving the ship, Emit asked about the departure time.

The captain responded, "We set sail with the morning tide. Your young man needs to be here at dawn. Bet you're used to lazy mornings, eh boy?"

John took little notice at the jab but replied, "I suppose we both will soon see."

The captain turned to Emit and asked, "Will you be joining us, Mr. Browning?"

"No, Captain. Jonathan is on his own from here. He will be greeted by Charles Briargate in Virginia. Charles is the reporting agent for Mr. Howell. If there be nothing else?"

The captain replied, "If I should want to employ the young man's services, who should I talk to?"

Emit gave thought before answering. "I will speak with Mr. Howell, and I can come to you a bit later. We can settle the issue then."

"Very well then," came the captain's reply. "Where shall I find you?"

Emit answered, "I will return and meet you at your cabin with his answer. Fair enough?"

The captain tipped his hat in agreement.

Emit and John boarded the carriage. Emit directed the coachman to Mr. Howell's residence, which was about two miles from Blackwall. Upon arrival, Emit turned to John and stated, "Wait here while I see if Mr. Howell will receive me or not. I will speak to him about you serving the captain on the voyage."

A short while later, Emit and a very distinguished gentleman returned to the carriage. Emit introduced the gentleman to John. "Jonathan Devine, I would like to introduce to you to Mr. Robert Howell."

John exited the carriage and extended his hand.

Robert shook his hand. "So this is my newest project?"

John wrinkled his brow but remained respectful. He replied, "It is my pleasure to meet you, sir."

Mr. Howell chortled, "I can see by the look on your face that you didn't approve of me calling you a project. The fact is I need men who will do the job for me in a new town called Elizabeth City. Our first attempt at establishing a town was Jamestown. All those men went to Jamestown seeking fortune, but because of their greed and laziness, the colony nearly failed. I need hardworking men who can establish trade. Are you the kind of man who will work and not lie about?"

John stood taller. "I am, and I promise you will not regret sending me to America."

Mr. Howell turned to Emit. "I think it would be good for young Mr. Devine to work for the captain, as long as the captain pays him an honest wage." He then redirected his attention to John. "Do you understand money?"

John lowered his eyes. "I am afraid I don't."

Mr. Howell gave a cough. "That's all right, me lad." Then, turning to Emit, he charged, "I want you to teach him about money this evening. Do you think him bright enough to grasp it?"

Emit laughed. "More than you know, sir; more than you know."

Mr. Howell extended his hand to John. Both men appreciate the strength of the other. Roberts was one of wisdom; John was one of ability. Robert added, "May good fortunes find you in the New World. God be with you."

Before John could reply, the great man turned and walked away.

Late in the evening, the carriage pulled up to the inn where Jonathan Devine would be staying. Emit saw him to his room, and the two men sat down for a moment. It had been a long day.

Emit asked John to take a seat. He stated, "Before I retire, I have been instructed to teach you money." Emit placed on the table nine pounds, nineteen shilling, and twelve pence in coins. Emit continued. "Have you handled money before, John?"

John sat in a chair next to the table and answered, "Some. Mainly a few pennies or halfpennies. I saved back a few shillings, but that is all." Then, lifting a pound, he added, "I have never seen a pound before."

Emit took the seat next to John and continued the lesson. "Do you understand the value of money? What I mean is, how to be sure what it will buy and how to handle it wisely."

John thought a moment. "Truthfully, we never needed money, because we took so much in trade. Sometimes I was paid in silver and allowed to shave the metal for my service."

Emit thought for a moment. "That is good, but in this world, people need and want coin. You will be enticed to spend foolishly. If someone knows you have money, they will try and get it from you either by stealing it or taking advantage of you. There is a good phrase: Money not spent is money that is in one's pocket. You have learned to live without. I urge you to save your earnings, Mr. Devine."

After that, Emit instructed John on the meaning of coins and their values. He taught him the penny amount, how many pence were in a shilling, and the number of shillings to a pound. He explained the crown, half crown, and farthing. In short order, John could explain everything back to Emit.

When this was done, John asked Emit a question. "How will I know value?"

Emit sat back in his chair. "That is a good question. Value is what we place on something that is being sold. The price of it is based on demand, what material it is made of, or simply what you might want." Then, thinking of an example, Emit asked, "How much would you pay for a meal?"

John thought for a moment. "I suppose a few pence."

Emit replied, "Fair enough. But in London, it can be a shilling because of demand."

John wrinkled his brow. "That doesn't seem right."

Emit answered, "Right or not, people will pay it because of demand. Now what about your equipment? How much would you pay for, let's say, a hammer?"

John thought. "Well, it is iron and has to withstand heat. Hum, perhaps two shilling?"

Emit chuckled. "I don't know the answer myself, but I made you think of how you might have need of it and the value you would place on it. What I want you to see is the necessity and care money requires. One last thing: never accept script. Always demand you be paid in coin. Never be surety for another, and never do something on promise of pay later."

John considered the counsel carefully and appreciated the wisdom at what Emit said.

Emit rose to his feet and got ready to leave. "I wish I could join you. Maybe someday, I will. Though I have known you a short time, I have come to love and appreciate you. You are leaving the protection and ways of your father. Remember the blacksmith and how he treated you. I hate to say it, but there are more men like him than I care for. In fact, beware of the captain. I don't trust him. I will be telling him that you may work for him. Make sure you put in writing an agreement concerning your services. The captain may try to swindle you. He may try to make you pay for food and such. Tell him that the way to America was paid for by Mr. Howell, and you have been instructed to report everything to Mr. Briargate. That ought to keep the captain honest."

Emit walked to the door and started to leave. John stopped him momentarily. "Emit, you left the coins."

Emit replied, "No, John, that is your money. Mr. Howell and I agreed that this would be a good investment in you. Once you are established, you can pay it all back. So take care, my young friend, and Godspeed. It has been an honor." Emit started to walk out the door but stopped short. "One more thing. I will seek baptism as soon as I can. I accept your faith and will live it as you have demonstrated to me."

John smiled as he walked over to Emit. The two men hugged in the bonds of Christian love. John quickly gathered the coins and put them in his bag and then went with Emit to the carriage.

Emit boarded the carriage. He reached beneath the seat and lifted his box of writing materials. He extended it to John. "I want you to take this with you. You will find in the writing box a blank book for you to chronicle your journey and other materials for letters. I hope you will find this useful."

John felt as though Emit had given him a greater fortune than the coin left on the table. With true gratitude, he stated, "Thank you, Emit. I will cherish it always."

Emit bid John one last goodbye and then tapped the carriage roof, signaling the driver to leave. Once the carriage was away, John returned to his room with the box. There he opened it to see what all was in it. Previously, Emit had attached the points to the quill and readied the inkwell for use. To John's delight, there was much more in the box. The box contained multiple quill points, inkwell, paper, wax to seal letters, and a stamp. John removed the stamp to see what the inscription said. John was shocked, because Emit had taken it upon himself to have it engraved: Jonathan Devine, Esq. Silversmith. This inscription made John feel he was truly worthy of the title.

The next morning the captain left his cabin and walked out on the deck. He heard chatter from the helm. To his surprise, John was already on board and talking to the first mate, Henry Finch, about different posts and responsibilities on board ship. John had arrived before sunup, stowed his gear, and began looking about. Mr. Timothy Bowman, the ship's carpenter, was nowhere in sight. He was either fast asleep in his bunk or hadn't arrived as of yet.

The captain watched John. He noticed that John took in every detail. John picked up the cross staff and asked Mr. Finch how it was used. Henry was about to explain when the captain interrupted. "I see you arrived on time as promised, Mr. Devine."

Henry snapped to upon hearing the captain's voice. Henry replied to the captain, "Good morning, Captain. I was just answering some of Mr. Devine's questions."

The captain replied, "I know. I was watching." Then, looking about, the captain ordered, "Prepare the ship for the tide, Mr. Finch."

Henry answered, "Aye, aye, Captain."

John stood by and heard order upon order given as men rushed to their posts to prepare for castoff. John found a safe spot to stay out of the way as he took in all the sights and sounds of the crew and ship.

The *Elizabeth Marie* was a two-mast pinnace. John watched the captain as he walked about, paying attention to every detail. John could hear a shipmate calling out the water depth of the rising tide. As soon as the water depth was high enough, the captain gave order to cast off. The crew responded by raising the anchor and dropping certain sails necessary to safely navigate the ship from the dock. The helmsman followed the captain's every command. Men hurried from here to there, adjusting lines and sails. Henry directed every detail as commanded by the captain. Soon, the ship was pointed to open water and heading out to sea.

John noticed other ships preparing for their destinations. He watched the dropping of sails and scurrying of men on deck as they too made their way toward the sea. Even though he was a good ways off, he could hear the commands brought on by first mates.

On board the *Elizabeth Marie*, John looked up at the air-filled sails. Sails were deployed as needed, propelling the ship through the water at just the right speed. Overhead, he saw a black-browed albatross circling the mast. As he watched the bird, Mr. Finch interrupted his gaze. "It's a sign of good fortune, that bird is." John smiled at the statement.

John took a deep breath of the fresh ocean air. When John first arrived at the ship, he couldn't help but notice the awful rotten-egg smell of the waters near the shore. On the open water, the air was fresh, clean, even invigorating. There was an early-morning mist on the Thames, but no one took notice. He was amazed how smoothly the ship glided across the still water. Then, as though scripted, the men stopped their mad activity and stood at the ready for the next command.

When all was calm, the captain called to John. "Mr. Devine!"

John had forgotten his new name.

Again, the captain called, "Mr. Devine!"

John turned to face the captain.

"Would you care to join me at the helm?" the captain asked.

As John left his safe position along the railing, he felt the movement under his feet for the first time. He wobbled a bit as he made his way. He never realized the full extent of the ship's movement. As long as he remained stationary against the rail, he was oblivious of the movement. Now he swayed as he walked. The seasoned sailors noticed the unsteady walk and laughed. Some even poked fun at him. John realized how clumsy he must have appeared and joined with the others in laughing.

When he came to the ladder leading up to the helm, the captain called again, "Come on up, lad."

John made his way up slowly till he stood next to the captain. The captain was silently watching the ship's course. From time to time, he would issue an order to the helmsman. Then John saw for the first time the ocean looming ahead like a great blue-grey prairie. Never had he seen something so beautiful or expanse.

As soon as the ship was safely out to sea, John heard the captain give the order for more sail. Mr. Finch repeated the order, and immediately, skilled sailors climbed the rigging to the mast and started releasing the canvas. It took time, but as soon as the sails dropped down, they immediately filled with wind. As each sail deployed, the ship lunged forward with increased speed.

John was amazed how fast the ship was moving. Never had he experienced such speed. John turned to look back behind the ship. He was leaving England. The shores of his beloved country were slowly disappearing. He was reminded that he was leaving behind all he loved, especially Chastity.

By late afternoon, the ship was enjoying the English Channel. To the starboard side, the coast of England was in full view. Along the way, Henry pointed out certain towns. When it came time to chart their course, Henry peered toward the sun with the cross-staff. Looking to the sun, he determined the ship's location.

John watched intently. Then he asked Henry, "How does it work?"

Henry showed John the marks and explained what each one meant. Henry stated, "By looking at the positioning of the sun, we can get a pretty good idea of our location."

John looked concerned. "Doesn't it hurt to peer directly into the sun?"

Henry gave a dedicated answer. "It does, and I am afraid some men have lost their sight, but it has to be done."

John furthered his inquiry. "So then, how do we know where we are?"

Henry then showed John how the angles could be plotted on the map. By the measurements they'd taken, they could plot their course.

John then asked, "May I try it?"

Henry handed the instrument to John. John announced his findings and placed his finger on the map as to his calculations.

Henry checked his work. "Very good, Mr. Devine. I believe you have the makings of sailor."

The captain took notice as well. John was truly a gifted man and no doubt a man of learning.

The next day John woke with a terrible feeling in his head and stomach. He realized that the ship was pitching and rolling. He left his bunk and made his way to the deck. The *Elizabeth Marie* was riding out a storm. The waves were not great, but they were making things most unbearable. John looked at the horizon, which seemed to make things worse. The seamen took things in stride, while John took to the rail. John felt a rope being secured about him, tying him in place. Henry was seeing to his safety.

Henry shouted above the wind and rain. "It's all right! Almost everyone fights being seasick. It will pass. I assure you." Henry turned and went back to his duties.

The captain was still at his place on deck, standing like there wasn't a storm. Men were taking in sails and securing others. The little ship and her crew pressed on.

John thought to himself, *How can you get used to this?*

It took John a couple of days to recover. By this time, he had gotten to know Timothy Bowman. He was a short, squatty man of about forty.

John noticed his fingers bore small cuts, and his hands were calloused. Timothy seemed to be a recluse. He reeked of sweat and alcohol. He also resented having John aboard.

"I ain't had no help before, and I don't need it now," he declared. "Don't sees why the captain sent you down here."

John sized the man up. "I think the captain wants me to learn from you, because he thinks you're the best carpenter he has ever known."

The old carpenter thought a moment before replying, "That might be it. All right then. I will show you around and teach you what you need to know on ship. You have to do as I say. Understood?"

John appeared serious. "Understood."

Timothy began by showing John his tools. John picked some of them up and noticed they were dull and almost unusable. John eyed a sharpening stone that had not been used in a while.

The carpenter then escorted John about the hull of the ship. "One of the carpenter's jobs is to keep watch for any water coming in. If I sees it, I have to make sure it gets repaired or packed."

They looked about and found a small crack. The old carpenter showed John how to make the repair by taking some oakum and applying it into the seam. Then the carpenter noted, "That will take care of that."

After a careful investigation of the ship, the two men went on deck to check with the captain to see if anything else needed attention. There was some yard that needed some sewing, but just enough for one man. John asked Timothy if he might take his leave. The old carpenter thought John wanted to run off and find someplace to sleep. Nonetheless, he obliged.

John made his way back to where the carpenter kept his tools and materials. John picked up the sharpening stone and went to work. Rusty saws, dull chisels, and knives were sharpened and oiled and then hung for proper storage. The process took several hours. When John finished, he went back on deck.

The old carpenter saw him looking about. "Can't find anything to do? You won't make a good seaman that way." With a huff, Timothy went down to his shop. A short time later, he returned and looked at John. "How'd you do that?"

Sheriff Taylor brought William Smith to the earl's residence to discuss what might be done with the man. Once they arrived, Taylor had William dismount from his horse. Taylor shackled William to an outside post before seeking audience with the earl. It did not take long for him to be granted an audience. The earl was sitting in a chair looking over some important letters when Taylor was ushered before his lordship. He stood silently, waiting to be acknowledged.

The earl set aside what he was reading and asked, "How may I help you, Sheriff?"

Taylor's posture was different. He was not confident or proud. He knew that William might bring charges against him as much as he brought charges against William. Taylor spoke carefully. "Me Lord, I have brought William Smith here. I had to arrest him last night, because he was causing unrest in the town."

The earl looked at Taylor, taking notice of the change in the man's bearing. Gone was the self-assured arrogance. Gone was the man who was looking for a reason to pursue someone based on hearsay. Earl Christopher knew that what he said now could make all the difference in Taylor's life.

The earl sat back in his chair and offered, "Sheriff, please sit down."

Taylor was surprised. He knew he was a commoner, and the earl was royalty. To receive such an invitation was unusual. Taylor thanked the earl and took the seat near him. The earl called for the butler to bring wine for them both. The butler bowed and left the room. Then, looking to Taylor, the earl asked, "Sheriff, what has made the change?"

Taylor shook his head. "I am sorry, Your Lordship. I do not understand."

The earl explained, "It is obvious to me that you have a real reason for being here. In times past, I could tell that you were trying to prove something. Now you appear, shall we say, humbled?"

Taylor tried to look as official as he could, but the earl's words struck his heart. It was hard for him to look the earl in the eye. When he found the courage, he spoke. "I suppose you're right. I had some dealings with the blacksmith, and that is what led to me to go after his apprentice. I had the blacksmith do some work for me in the past and paid him what I could. Other times, he would suggest that I pay him later. This came at a time when my wife and I were expecting our first child." A smile crossed his face as he remembered that wonderful time of his life. He continued. "I was so happy then. I was appointed sheriff, had a small, though modest living for us, and was so excited about the prospects ahead."

Taylor lowered his head, and sorrow replaced the joy. His mind was filled with loss. He looked back at the earl and added, "Then she died while giving birth. On that fateful night, I lost the woman I loved and the son I hoped for. I turned to wine and strong drink, hoping it would bring me relief. That is where I became acquainted with William the blacksmith. He frequented the tavern. William pretended to be my friend, but in truth, he looked for ways to make an alliance with me. In my foolish drunken state, I said things I shouldn't have said, even against your father. I became indebted to him. Later, he threatened to expose me if ever I stood in his way."

The earl held his tongue as he heard the story. Taylor took a breath and was about to speak when the butler knocked at the door. The earl called for the butler to enter and asked him to set the wine at the table. Two small glasses were poured. The butler was then excused. The earl offered a glass to Taylor. He accepted but only held the glass. Taylor peered into crimson glass. He thanked his host. Earl sipped the wine and then requested, "Please continue your story."

Taylor took a sip of wine, which moistened his dry mouth. He continued. "I have not been a fit sheriff. The town is peaceful enough, but I have turned a blind eye from the actions and dealings of the blacksmith. Whenever there was a dispute, he would remind me of my debt." He sighed. "Then there was the incident with his apprentice. The blacksmith came to my house and found a woman with me and dared to think she was a local barmaid to keep me company."

Taylor rose to his feet, angry. He paced the room a moment before turning back to the earl. "In fact, she is my sister. Her name is Sally. She too has gone through difficulty. Together, Sally and I have been helping each other recover. Your Lordship, she is my sister—my sister."

Earl Christopher saw the frustration in the sheriff. He said nothing but allowed the sheriff to speak.

"William saw opportunity to take advantage and demanded I charge the young man. The fact is the lad did nothing wrong. I hounded him, hoping to find out otherwise. I spied on his family and that of his betrothed. I expect your man, Elijah, has probably reported me to you. Fact is, I now know how wrong I have been."

The earl had not heard from Elijah. He remained calm and adjusted himself in his seat to look more intently at the sheriff. Then he asked, "What have you to say for your actions?"

Taylor turned his head slightly from the earl's stare. "Your man, Elijah, went to John's home. He was stern with them. I watched him depart. I was about to leave my hiding place and turned my horse. There sat Elijah, just observing me." With a nervous laugh, Taylor added, "The man is rather mysterious."

This statement made the earl smile.

Taylor thoughtfully continued. "He was firm with me and convinced me that the noose I was drawing was being drawn around my own neck."

Earl Christopher thought a brief moment. He did not want to bring Elijah into the conversation. Instead, he focused on the situation. "Come and sit. Tell me, why have you brought the blacksmith here?"

Taylor returned to his seat. He wrung his hands together. He looked at the earl before answering. "After seeing Elijah, I returned to the town to find the smith stirring up the people. He sought to shame me into action. All along, William's intention was to force me into arresting the apprentice. I heard William's lies being told to a few of the villagers. William has made things up against the apprentice, his honorable father, and even me. Your Lordship, what the man wants is for me to forcibly return John to him so that he might physically harm him while gaining the rewards of his work. The best thing that I can do is see to it that William is exposed even if it means that I might lose my position."

Earl Christopher thoughtfully sat in silence. Taylor was anxious as he waited for some response. Christopher raised his hand to his chin and returned his gaze toward Taylor. He asked, "If you were given full responsibility of your post again, what would you do?"

Taylor was completely surprised at the question. Taking a deep breath, he answered, "Such a question I never imagined. I think I would seek to be the kind of sheriff my dear wife wanted me to be and one my son would be proud of." Then the sheriff asked, "Me lord, may I pose one more question?"

The earl responded, "Of course. What might it be?"

Taylor offered, "My actions have been the cause of much harm, though nothing has happened. Is there anything I can do for John?"

The earl's reply was troubling. "I don't know. Even now he is facing the consequences of the blacksmith's actions." With a harrumph, the earl continued. "No. I think it is too late."

Taylor just hung his head.

Finally, the earl stated, "Enough of that. Now to the matter at hand. Bring the blacksmith before me."

William was still shackled by his restrains to the post. He had struggled with the restraints, and the marks on the post were evidence of it. The sheriff approached without saying a word.

Sarcastically, William asked the sheriff, "Did you and the earl have a nice visit?"

Taylor released him from the post and began leading the smith toward the house.

William retorted, "You ain't got nothing to say to me?"

Taylor remained silent, which agitated the smith all the more. The butler opened the door, and the two men entered. They approached the earl's office, and William started to barge through the open door.

Taylor stopped him. "We wait here till we are summoned before his lordship."

William felt disgust over the entire matter. Without cause, he had a sudden dislike of the earl.

When the two men were called before the Earl of Sussex, it was William who spoke. "Thank you for seeing me, me lord."

Earl Christopher said nothing. He postured himself as being attentive to other matters. After a moment, the earl slowly lifted his gaze to look directly into William's eyes. The intense stare unnerved William. The earl held his gaze for a long time, never blinking or redirecting his stare. The more the earl looked at him, the more the smith felt small and unworthy. This is exactly what the earl wanted to happen. William could not look upon the man before him. He dropped his gaze to the floor. At that very moment, the earl spoke.

"I understand you have been stirring the people in town against your apprentice, the sheriff, and me."

William looked up and cried, "I never said anything against you, Your Majesty."

The earl stood and marched over to the man. He stopped just short of him and peered into the eyes of the deceitful smith. "Your majesty? You ignorant oaf, haven't you the common sense to know that that title is reserved to the king? Do you not know that when you stir the people against one of my appointments, you stir them against me?"

William was stunned. He thought that he would be able to say his peace and be heard without examination.

The earl strolled around the room and then turned to look at the smith again. "The good sheriff here tells me that you have brought charge against your young apprentice. Is that so?"

William answered, "The boy stole from me and did me disservice."

The earl put his hands on his hips. "Did he now? And what did he steal?"

William, feeling a bit more confident, explained. "He stole work from me. The people had him do more for them than me."

Earl asked, "I see. Why do you suppose they did that? Could it be that his work is far superior to yours? Could it be that you were not around to receive work? Perhaps you were lazing about getting drunk?"

This line of question angered William, and his tone reflected it. "I taught the boy, and in an agreement with his father, I had the right to teach and care for him as I saw fit."

Taylor remained silent. He loved seeing William getting some of his own back. He admired the poise and strength of his lordship.

The earl turned and walked a bit more. He placed his hands behind his back and locked his hands together. He spoke as he paced. "Seems to me you would want to be rid of a man who caused you so much grief."

William calmly replied, "The lad still has much to learn. I want him back in order to continue his education."

The earl raised his eyes. "I heard a rumor that he nearly burnt your establishment down?"

William felt the upper hand. "Indeed he did. I could have lost my life."

The earl asked again, "Then tell me, how did you manage to get out of the burning building?"

William pretended humility. "I struggled to the street, fleeing the fire inside."

The earl shot back. "Then who put out the fire?"

William was in a trap of his own making.

The earl walked over to his chair and seated himself. He looked at the blacksmith. "What is it you really want?"

William acted sincere. "I would ask that the boy be returned to finish his lessons."

The earl snapped back. "You mean to teach him a lesson, don't you? Besides that, it is too late. Young Mr. Dairyman has been sentenced for the allegations you brought against him. A part, I might add, which has no merit. You have charged an innocent man, and he is being punished."

William mumbled, "He ain't all that innocent."

The earl shouted back. "Silence!" Then leaving his chair once more, he walked over to face the smith. "I know your kind all too well. I have a surprise for you—one befitting a man of your character. For your actions, you will be removed from the town and relocated."

William was stunned. "Relocated? Where?"

The earl sneered as he replied in low tones. "I said, silence." Resuming his posture, he continued. "You are to be relocated to Rye and serve as the English Navy sees fit. They are in need of a blacksmith. You will do nicely."

Christopher walked over to his desk and picked up a sealed letter. He walked before the sheriff and handed it to him. Earl Christopher issued an order. "Sheriff Taylor, this letter is for Mr. Smith's transfer. See to it that my orders are carried out immediately. When you finish delivering Mr. Smith, return to Haywards Heath. You are to continue there as the town magistrate. I will expect weekly visits from you to report to me the situations in town."

Taylor stood tall and with dignity responded, "Thank you, me lord. I will."

The earl gave one final warning to the smith. "I would beware of the taverns and pubs along the waterfront. Many men have suffered at the hands of press-gangs."

Before leaving, William spoke up. "Who will see to the blacksmithing in town?"

The earl laughed. "I will find a man better and more qualified than you. I hear there is a fine smith by the name of John. Maybe you've heard of him. He saved his ungrateful drunken master from complete loss and even death. Maybe I could convince the lad to take your post. Now be gone with you."

Taylor marshaled William away. Earl Christopher watched the two men mount their horses and leave the estate. The butler entered to clear away the wine and overheard the earl's faint whisper. "How much damage that drunken fool has caused."

After five days out to sea, John was becoming accustomed to life on board the ship. He was less affected by the movement of the vessel over the waves. Now he was bored. He was used to hard work and creative activity. Most of what was needed by a carpenter could be done in the morning. One early afternoon he approached the captain who stood at his usual post near the helm. When he sought permission to speak with him, the captain left his post. Once on deck, the captain offered, "Join me in my cabin. Won't you, Mr. Devine?"

The captain led John to his cabin and there offered him a little wine. "Here, drink this. It will help settle your stomach."

John took the glass, thanked the captain, and tasted the wine. It was strong and not very good. He took small sips.

The captain continued. "I hope you are feeling better. I spoke to the carpenter, and he told me how you managed to clean and sharpen his tools. Mr. Bowman was quite surprised to say the least."

John didn't reply. His stomach and head were still affected by the storm.

The captain recognized his condition and sought to take advantage of his weakened state. "I know life on a ship can be challenging, but it can be quite adventurous. I have been watching you. You have asked many questions of Mr. Finch, and he tells me you have a good mind for sailing."

John's senses were heightened, and he was aware that the captain was up to something. He remembered Emit's warning.

The captain leaned forward to look John in the eye. "How's about a deal? You work for me, and I will teach you all there is to learn about sailing and how to handle the ship. You've got a real mind for it. I can tell. Who knows, you might become a captain of your own ship."

John then asked two important question. "What would I be doing for you, and what would this training cost me?"

The captain felt the upper hand. He thought John was at least interested. He took his glass of wine and drank it straight down. He poured himself another and was about to add more to John's glass, but John refused by placing his hand over it.

The captain replied, "Oh, I would have you build a few things for me, perhaps items sailors would find useful. The price would be reasonable, of course. In exchange, I would see that you learn all that your heart's desire. Any additional pay, I would deduct from the cost of your stay while on board ship."

John stood and looked at the captain suspiciously. He placed his hands on the table and stared intently at the captain before making his address. "I may not have my full wits about me, Captain, but I am not so dull that I don't know a bad deal when I hear one. First off, you need to understand that I have been taught by my father never to be a layabout. When I see a need or work to be done, I take care of it. It isn't my nature to be idle. Second, it is true that I enjoy learning. It's your privilege to tell every man on ship not to speak with me in an attempt to keep me isolated. That is up to you. However, you should know that I learn by observing. So the only way to keep me from doing so will be for you to lock me away. Now what value is there in that? Third, the cost of my passage has been paid by Mr. Robert Howell. I knew this even before the voyage began. I very much doubt that his representative in Virginia will appreciate me reporting that you made me pay you additionally for my passage." Standing erect, John put his hands behind his back and exclaimed. "Sorry, Captain. No deal."

The captain had never dealt with someone as cunning as John. He had been able to con others into his so-called deal and had made out quite handsomely. John's rejection angered him, and he wanted to put him in his place. With a snarl in his voice, he asked, "So what do you suggest, lad?"

John gave a half-cocked smile. "First, don't call me lad. I am a man. I want the opportunity to pass among the mates and learn as I please. When I am not learning, I will make things to prove my worth. I think the men will want to buy these items when they see the quality of my work. From the sale of these things, we can both make a profit." John folded his arms and continued. "I know education isn't free, and I want to be reasonable. Therefore, I think 30 percent of profits would be plenty for me. The rest will be used to buy necessary materials from the crew to make more things and for your profit. What do you think?" John then held his peace, allowing the captain to mull it over.

The captain was a greedy man and could not fathom that much money being returned to John. He gave reply, hoping to trap John. "Suppose I look at your work and then determine the value before agreeing."

John sternly replied, "Do not think me a fool, Captain. Before I do anything, we will have a written agreement between us. I will give you time to think it over." John was about to leave the captain's cabin when he shot back.

"Wait. How's about 20 percent?"

John turned to face the weathered older man. "Tell you what–25 percent, and you supply all the materials I will need. Agreed?" John extended his hand.

The captain rubbed his cheek and chin before finally taking John's hand. "Agreed."

John ended the conversation by stating, "I will draw up the papers for you to sign."

John left the cabin and waited for the door to close behind him. He took a deep breath and held it a moment before exhaling. A shudder went over him. Somehow he knew the captain would look for ways to take further advantage of him.

# At the Brink

Taylor stood before Benjamin Rose, the head official, with William at his side. The magistrate read the letter from the earl concerning William. When Benjamin finished reading the letter, he looked to first Taylor and then to William.

Benjamin directed his attention to the sheriff and declared, "So this man is the source of trouble in your town?"

Taylor responded, "Only as much as his willfulness will allow. In part, he has been a nuisance to some in our village and caused one man to be punished for a crime he did not commit."

Benjamin looked to William. "We will have none of that here. I wager that you will be too busy to cause anything of that nature. I personally know Harry Jones the shipwright at the Rye shipyard. I'm sure he can find work for a man of your particular talents."

Benjamin moved away from his desk and went in to another room. A younger man was called and ordered to retrieve Mr. Jones and bring him back, along with sufficient men for the care of William Smith. The young man understood and was off in an instant.

Benjamin returned to his desk and addressed Taylor and William. "I have never met the earl, but I understand that he is an honorable man."

William uttered quietly, "Honorable … harrumph."

Benjamin looked at the blacksmith. "It would do you good to keep your tongue. Any trouble from you will result in severe disciplinary action."

William replied, "And how long do you plan to keep me here?"

Benjamin sat back in his chair. "Oh, I would say as long as the man you falsely accused has to serve, perhaps five to seven years."

William thought, *Good luck keeping me here that long.*

Before long, Mr. Harry Jones, along with two powerfully built men, arrived as requested. Harry was dressed in clothes befitting one who was overseer of a shipyard. There was nothing fancy about him. Benjamin welcomed Harry and thanked him for coming as quickly as he did. Afterward, he wasted little time before showing him the letter. Mr. Jones read the letter and looked at William and then back at Benjamin before replying.

"He's a bit old to be starting work. Does he have any skills?"

Sheriff Taylor responded, "William here is a blacksmith, and he has a real knack at accusing innocent people."

Harry walked over to William and sized him up. Though Harry was short in stature, he was full of grit, and he spoke with confidence. "A blacksmith we can use. As for the other, we'll have none of that. Me lads have ways to deal with men like you."

William remained defiant, but he knew better than to try something here. The two men who accompanied Mr. Jones could easily stop him. His voice reflected his feeling. "A man of my trade deserves to be paid. What will my wage be?"

Harry was no fool. He knew that William would try most anything. Harry looked at his associates and back at William before replying. "I suppose that is a reasonable request. Let me see." Harry threw his head back in thought. Then turning to the Benjamin, he asked if he might borrow his desk and chair. Benjamin politely agreed. Harry began writing an agreement. When he finished, he turned to William and asked him to read it.

"I can't read," came his reply.

Harry turned to Taylor. "Can you read, Sheriff?"

Taylor replied, "I can."

Harry requested his assistance. "Would you oblige me then and read the agreement for Mr. Smith?"

Taylor walked over to the desk and leaned over to read the paper. The ink was wet. It had yet to be dusted. He read aloud for all to hear. "Mr. William Smith will be paid two shilling, six pence a week for services rendered. He will also be provided lodging and ration. His liberties will be given according to behavior and work. Signed, Harry Jones."

Harry looked to William. "Is that agreeable?"

William had little knowledge of money. He answered, "I suppose so."

"Then come make your mark," came Harry's command.

William scratched his mark.

Harry then turned to Benjamin. "I ask that you keep this among the others. In case I have need I know where I can reach it." Benjamin collected the paper. Harry then looked at the two men with him. With a simple nod of the head, the two men shouldered to each side of William. Together, the small company led by Harry turned and walked from the magistrate's office.

Taylor walked to the office window. He saw William being led away by his keepers. Deep down, Taylor felt that this wasn't the last anyone had seen of William the blacksmith.

Morning broke with the ship's crew taking advantage of the calm seas and good wind. All sails were unfurled. The ship seemed to glide upon the water. There were no birds, indicating they were a good distance from land. Henry showed their whereabouts on the map. They were following a course south by east. Henry looked out over the vast ocean. "Can you imagine some of the first seamen coming this way? The ocean can be quite scary and yet, magnificent. Don't you agree, Mr. Devine?"

John nodded his head in agreement. "Call me John, if you please. I am not much used to my formal name. As for your question, indeed. It is all that and more."

John soon left his place on deck and went below to where the cook was preparing the morning meal. Pork and salmagundi was being prepared on a brick stove. A great pile of wood was nearby to keep the fire going. Near the wood was another pile of sand in case the fire got out of hand. After all, ships were wooden vessels, and a fire on the high seas would be a catastrophe. John watched Samuel Wells as he diligently worked the galley. The food had to be hardy even if it lacked in taste. As Samuel worked, John pointed to one of the knives and asked permission to handle it. Samuel did not so much as look at him but gave his approval. John inspected it. The knife was crude at best, and the edge was dull.

John asked the cook, "Mind of I borrow this a while?"

Samuel stopped but just a moment. He looked at John with the knife. He shrugged his shoulder and gave a little tilt of the head. "Suppose not."

Then John disappeared. John took the knife to the carpenter's table. He inspected it carefully and then took a hammer and began tapping at the handle with great care. With careful precision, he was able to make real changes to the handle. He laid the handle pieces aside and turned his attention to the blade. Once again, he painstakingly worked the blade, knocking out the imperfections. Once he was satisfied with the results, he took the sharpening stones and worked the edge. While he worked the knife, sailors had their breakfast and returned to their duties. All through the morning and into the afternoon, he worked at shaping and sharpening the knife. It was nearly evening before he was done.

John returned to the galley and found the cook busy preparing more food. John walked over and presented him the knife. The cook stopped. Samuel looked at what once was a worn out old knife. He took it from John's hand and just held it. The old, worn knife had been transformed. The cook loved the feel of the remade handle. He took a piece of meat and felt the knife slice through it easily. Samuel just kept handling the knife looking at it over and over. He could not get over what John had managed to do. No matter how the cook used it, the edge remained razor sharp.

The cook looked at John. "How did you do this?"

John just smiled. John looked over the rest of the discarded old knives. Finding the one of his choosing, he looked at the cook. "May I have this?"

The cook nodded his head in agreement. He was still admiring the knife in his hand. John then walked over to the wood pile. He sorted through the wood until he found exactly what he was looking for—a hard piece of black oat. With the wood and old knife in hand, John offered a proposal to the cook. "I will need a little heat from the stove to work on my next knife. If you agree, I will make you a better knife from one of old ones. Agreed?"

The cook smiled a toothless smile. "Oh, I agree."

John went back to check with Timothy as to the needs of the ship. John found him busy making needed repairs, so John joined the carpenter, and together the repairs were quickly completed. John went about tending to small leaks, while Timothy was busy repairing a sail.

It was after the work was done that Timothy asked John his

whereabouts in the morning. "Lad, I did not see you at breakfast. Then I come by and see you busy with me tools. What be you up to?"

John had a great deal of respect for the carpenter, and his reply showed it. "I must beg your pardon, sir. I wanted to do something for the cook. I plan to make a few things on this journey, not only to pass the time, but to promote my true abilities."

Mr. Bowman considered what John said before speaking. "Tell me, lad. What's this all about?"

John walked over to the bench and picked up the old knife. He carried it over to Timothy and asked, "What do you see in this piece of metal?"

Timothy answered, "It's a knife. What's you expect me to see?"

John chuckled. "Well, Mr. Bowman, I see something that was made entirely differently than what it was supposed to be. I know already what it will look like when I am finished. Here, hold it and inspect it. Now look at it. You have a good image of what you are seeing? Give me a day or so, and I will show you what I mean."

Timothy inspected it. He shrugged his shoulders before handing it back. John walked over to the carpenter's bench and began the transformation.

Once again, John began tapping at the metal and straightening out the bends. He popped out the old rivets on the handle. Free of all the old debris and wood, John began the makeover. From the beginning, the old knife had been shaped poorly and was mainly a hunk of heavy iron. John took the piece of iron to the galley and shoved it into the hot ambers of the cook stove. It would take a long time for it to get hot enough for what John needed to do. John wanted a hotter fire but could not chance it. He would work with what he had. When the iron was hot, John took it from the heat and quickly went back to carpenter's bench. Again, the ringing sound of the hammer against iron was echoing throughout the ship's hold.

The captain and mates could hear the ringing. All had one thing in mind. "What's this fellow up to?" Back and forth John went from cook stove to carpenter's bench. Each time be began hammering at the iron. After a while, something new was emerging from the old. The metal was flatter. Each time John returned to heat the iron, the cook tried to see what was happening. John said nothing. He turned the iron in the hot coals, trying to capture the hottest fire. Back and forth John raced. He worked like a man possessed. He had made a dozen or so trips back and forth between the destinations. Finally, the rush was over, and the ringing stopped. There was a brief silence before the rasping sound of the stone on the metal began. The knife was being sharpened.

John used one stone and then another, working the metal to get the best edge. This continued well into the night. After a while, the metal began to glisten. The faint light from the candle was being mirrored in the knife's reflection. All at once, the sound stopped. John inspected his work. He laid the blade on his arm and with one pass shaved the hair from it. A smile crossed his face as he whispered, "That's sharp enough."

It had been an exhausting day. John put away the tools he'd used. After he cleaned up, he walked over and climbed into his hammock. All that was heard was the familiar creaking of the *Elizabeth Marie*—that and the gentle snore of Jonathan Devine.

When morning came, John hurried about the ship looking for work to be done. By the time Timothy appeared, John had already repaired several minor leaks. Timothy found John sitting down at the table eating a meal of bread and meat.

Walking over to John, he asked, "Aye, boy, you go to sleep last night? When I went to bed, you were working. Then I get up this morning, and I see the work you've already accomplished around the ship. Now here you sit eating. What's with you, lad?"

John finished his mouthful of food before answering. "My father made me finish my work on the farm before I could work on personal things. It is a pattern I have grown accustom to. I finished my work this morning because I have much more to do on the knife I'm remaking."

Timothy just shook his head. He took a seat at the table next to John and waited for his own breakfast.

After John finished eating, he returned to the carpenter's bench. He looked at the knife, pleased with the blade. Now he turned his attention to making the handle. He picked up the piece of dark oak he'd taken from the galley. John began by carefully shaving the wood down to size. With each cut, the wood began to reveal its beautiful grain. Carefully, he shaved the wood until he had it just the way he wanted it. Minutes turned to hours, but the talented hand of the craftsman was transforming the wood that otherwise would have just been used for the fire.

Once the wood was about the right thickness, John began testing it for fit. He would measure, cut, and check the fit. Again and again, he repeated the process. The casual observer would not understand his method or reason for what he did, but that didn't matter. It was only important that John understood. Small cuts were being made to the wood. Too large of a cut, and John would have to start over. He could ill afford such a mistake.

The hard, black oak was resistant to change, but the relentlessness of the artist forced the wood to its new shape and look. Ever so slowly, the wood was yielding. John placed the knife over the latest cut he made and examined his work. A small upturn to his left lip was all that indicated he was pleased. The handle fit perfectly.

John then went to where he had hidden his valuables. He retrieved the silver bar. Returning to the table, he carefully measured and cut off a piece of the precious material. He returned to his hiding place and put the rest where it belonged. Once again, he turned his attention to the knife. Using only a hammer, he began tapping away at the silver. Artisans of old used to mold metal without heat. John had experimented with this method with some success. He knew if he was to achieve the desired effect for the knife, this would be the only way it could be done under the present conditions.

Later in the day the sound of hammer on metal was heard again. This time it was a steady tapping sound. Silver is a softer metal, and it molds into shape more easily. He worked the metal, checked its fit to the wood, and made changes as necessary. John pushed himself. By day's end, he had completed the work. John fit the silver in trace cuts made into the wood. He put everything away and decided to wait for morning to finish.

It was now the third day into his project. How soon he would finish depended on the materials he worked with. First, he carefully engraved his signature into the silver. Second, he assembled the wood pieces together, making sure it all fit. Small adjustments were made here and there. Lastly, he took two small silver rivets he had made and fastened everything together. John looked at the knife. His hard worked had paid off. In his hand he held his latest creation. He flipped the knife in his hand. He loved the way it felt. Then he flipped it toward one of the beams. The knife glided through the air and struck the beam point first. When Timothy came down to the hold, John showed him the knife.

Timothy was amazed. "I have never seen the like." He looked down at his bench. "You did this with my tools? You are some kind of magician."

John took the knife from him and wrapped it. Afterward, he climbed up out of the hatch, bearing the knife as though he were carrying a baby. The captain was posted at the helm, keeping a watchful eye.

John approached and called to him. "Captain, may I have a private moment with you in your cabin?"

The captain replied, "What is it, Mr. Devine? I am a bit occupied."

John beaconed, "A moment. Please, sir."

The captain called for Mr. Finch to take over for him. Reluctantly, he came down on deck to face John. The captain then extended his right hand, palm up, directing the way to his cabin.

The captain took a seat next to the table covered with maps and charts. He looked at John. "What needed my immediate attention, Mr. Devine?"

John handed him the cloth. "Just this, sir."

The captain began to unwrap the cloth until the handle was exposed. The beautiful black oat was beautifully finished. Its only mar was the inlaid silver, which was shaped into a vine with three small grape leaves. The captain just stared at the beautiful handle before slowly unwrapping the rest of the knife. The knife gleamed in the dim cabin light. The razor-sharp edge layered the light with its reflection. The knife was truly beautiful.

The captain lifted the knife and just cradled it in his hands. He lifted his eyes to look back at John. As with the cook, he had one question. "How did you do this?"

John remained silent. Then the captain pointed to the vine.

John remarked, "That is my signature and a way for people to know it was made by me."

Captain Richard Wise had never seen work this magnificent before and from someone so young. This man's work was worth a fortune to him, but there was the matter of the signed agreement. It didn't matter. This boy would make him more than any other, but only if ... That was it.

A devious plan formed in the captain's mind. Captain Wise knew exactly what he would do in order to profit from the talents of Jonathan Devine.

Once John's work was revealed, many of the sailors began asking him to make things for them. The cost did not seem to bother them. True to his promise, John made Samuel a knife that was better and more decorative. Samuel was so happy with the knife that he kept it in the galley on display but never used it. His own words to others were simply, "This is the best gift I ever did get." Many of the crew asked John to make jewelry. Some just wanted their cutlass or knives to be sharpened, or they asked John to decorate their weapons with gold or silver inlay. John was kept busy the rest of the ocean journey.

John continued to learn from Henry Finch. He asked him what kept the ship from rolling over. He wanted to know about the deploying of sails and the reasons for their selected deployment. Henry took great pleasure in teaching John all that he knew. Then came one final question: "How do you steer the ship?"

Henry took his pupil to the helm and asked the helmsman to step aside while John took the whipstaff. Immediately, John felt the force of the water against the rudder. John had been watching the helmsman and noticed he practically straddled the whipstaff. Henry explained that in this position, the helmsman would have better strength and control over the ship. By moving the shaft to the left or right, he could control the direction of the ship.

John's arms were strong and well developed, but it didn't take long for him to feel the strain. Henry laughed. "It takes time, my young friend. You are strong, but it takes time to build up the stamina for this job."

When John could handle the ship no more, Henry called for the helmsman to take over.

They were but two days out from their destination. From time to time, whales and dolphins were spotted. Some dolphins even raced alongside the ship. By evening time, seagulls had joined in the greeting of the newcomer. The captain ordered a change in course for a more northern direction. Suddenly, from high above the deck, a lone voice called out, "Land ho!"

A few hours later, the captain ordered in the sails and had the men drop anchor. Looking to Mr. Finch, the captain declared, "We will anchor here for the night before proceeding up the coast to Virginia."

Mr. Finch confirmed the order. John was excited that the journey was coming to an end.

Every night while at sea, John wrote in his journal. Sometimes it was but a note describing some aspect of what he learned or did, but always there was a note about Chastity. On that night, John wrote:

August 1, 1647

The long journey across the Atlantic is nearly done. We are anchored just off the shore of America. The captain says we will continue our journey to Virginia come morning. There, I begin my service to Mr. Howell. Once I leave this ship, I will begin to build a life for the lady I love. I wonder what she is doing this very minute. I wonder if she is thinking of me. I have read from the Bible tonight how Rebecca left her homeland to begin a new life in a new world to be joined to a man she had never seen and did not know. She bravely left her family behind to marry a man named Isaac. Chastity shall be my Rebecca, and I will be her Isaac. Oh, how I wish she was with me now. I keep thinking of her beautiful eyes, her face, and her very manner. I feel her lips on mine. I pray these years will pass quickly. I pray that God will see fit to keep us safe till we can be one.

Morning came, and John felt the ship being propelled through the waters. The captain was already on board, directing the ship up the coast. John hurried to the deck. He looked to the port side and admired the beautiful barren shore. He listened to each order given by the captain. Mr. Finch was busy plotting the course. Another crewman kept vigil over the water depth. With each measurement, the crewman called out the findings. The captain would adjust the course accordingly. John approached Henry to ask their whereabouts.

Henry answered, "We have a way to go yet. We ought to be at the coast of Virginia by late afternoon."

John thought about how good it would be to be on solid ground again.

The sun was still high when the James River was spotted. Another ship was already anchored offshore. Henry pointed out to John that they would be sailing just past the James River inlet to a new settlement called Elizabeth City. He stated, "Many men believe Jamestown is a failure. The colony almost collapsed. There is greater hope for the new settlement we are heading for, but it will only succeed with true dedication and effort."

The captain directed the ship toward the river inlet. Soon, the hamlet of Elizabeth City was in view. Finally, the captain ordered anchors dropped. They had arrived.

The sailors once more orchestrated the securing of sails and preparing the deck. Afterward, the captain ordered a single boat be lowered. His command to Mr. Finch was to see to the care of the ship while he went ashore. No questions were asked. Mr. Finch followed orders and prepared for the off-loading of the ship.

While the captain was being rolled ashore, other, more shallow vessels had rolled out to the ship to begin off-loading the cargo. The crew already had the rigging in place for the job of offloading the cargo. No sooner were the boats alongside that the cargo was lifted from the hold and ready to be swung over the side. Once a vessel was loaded, it returned to shore, while another vessel took its place. It was obvious these men knew what they were doing. It would take the rest of the day and perhaps the following to get the job done.

It was late in the evening when the captain returned. Back on board, the captain informed Mr. Finch that when the men were finished with the off-loading of the ship they could go ashore, but not Mr. Devine.

Henry looked puzzled. "Captain, may I ask why?"

The captain smirked. "Seems there has been a change of plans regarding Mr. Devine. I have purchased his service for myself. I found Mr. Briargate and asked what his service would cost. It took a little convincing, but I now have him for my bidding."

The announcement disturbed Henry a great deal. "Does John know?"

The captain snapped back. "John, is it now? No, I have not told him, but I will shortly. Let me remind you that Jonathan Devine is no more than a slave on this ship from now on. He is my personal servant. Treat him as such."

Henry snapped to attention, but his tone was sarcastic, "Aye, aye, Captain. Whatever you say."

The tone in Henry's voice angered the captain.

John was ordered to the captain's cabin. He walked in and immediately ordered to stand at attention. The captain walked over to him and sneered. In the captain's hands was the signed agreement they had made. The captain looked John in the eyes. "You are a very intelligent man for one so young, but you are no match for someone in my position. You see, I went ashore today to speak with Charles Briargate. You know him as the man who you were supposed to meet. I have made arrangements for you to complete your indenture service to me."

John was stunned. A lump hung in his throat. He turned his head to say something to the captain. At that instant, the captain got right into his face and yelled, "You are at attention. See that you keep your tongue till I say you can speak." The captain unrolled the agreement. Looking at John, he spoke while tearing the document to shreds. "This agreement is worthless. You will do as I say and only as I say. All the profits belong to me now. Do well, and I might reward you. If not, I shall treat you like the slave you are."

The captain went over and picked up the knife John had made. He turned to look at John. "I plan to take this to town tomorrow to see what kind of price it might fetch. I know that when people see the quality and craftsmanship, they will make orders. Many others will want their precious metals turned to cutlery, cups, and the like. I will need to know what supplies will be needed. Make me a list." The captain could see the confusion in John's eyes. The captain continued. "Mr. Devine, do not think that you can escape. There is nothing you can do. I own you now. I offer you room and board on this ship. That is all you deserve."

John couldn't take anymore. He was defiant in his words. "You think that you can control a man because you claim to own him?"

The captain shouted back. "I said, silence."

John continued. "Silence? You think you can silence a man by a command? You think because you command a person to silence that they have to comply? You have fooled yourself. You can make a person a slave, but you can never keep a man from speaking. You can take a man's freedom but never take freedom from a man."

The captain shouted, "Why you—"

John interrupted. "I'm not done. I worked for a man who scarred my back and tried to destroy me. What will you do, Captain? Add more scars? If you do, you will lose all respect from the crew. You can't enslave us all. If you try, they will mutiny."

Captain Wise had heard enough. He reared back his hand and punched John in the stomach. John saw it coming and tightened his abdomen before the fist arrived. The captain wasn't expecting it. John's stomach was hard, and he hit him awkwardly. Pulling his hand back, he sheltered it with the other hand. His wrist began to throb. He rushed over to grab a lash and raised it high above his head. John showed no fear. At that moment, the captain saw strength he had never seen before. He pulled the lash back down. "No, the whip will not affect you, but I will find a way."

The captain called for Mr. Finch. Henry entered the captain's cabin. Captain Wise issued his order. "Take Mr. Devine and clamp him in irons. He is not to leave the ship. He is in my charge now. His belongings are his, but he will be provided for at my good pleasure."

Henry was furious, but he dare not disobey the captain's orders.

The captain then laughed as he directed his final statement to John. "Nothing you can do,- lad." Then returning his attention to Henry, he commanded, "Take him away."

John felt like Joseph of the Bible. He had done nothing wrong, but he found himself a prisoner of Captain Richard Wise. He was indentured; he was now a slave. How long he would be forced to serve he did not know. His future was taken away.

Henry took John below to shackle him in the carpenter's area.

John asked, "Mr. Finch, does this affect our relationship?"

The first mate replied, "My name is Henry, and no, it doesn't."

John then asked, "If I prepare a letter, will you see that it gets to my love?"

Dearest Chastity,

I haven't much time, but I wanted to write this letter to you. I have made it to America, but my circumstances have changed. I fear that my new overseer will keep me from mailing this letter out, so I must hurry. If you can get word to Emit and ask him to investigate on my behalf. It may be months before I can write again. Don't be afraid but pray for my deliverance. I love you.

John

He sealed the letter, and Henry hurried away. Alone in the belly of the ship, John began to cry. In great despair, he looked to the heavens and screamed, "Why, my God? Why?"

It had been sixty days since John's departure. Chastity busied herself with the work at hand. Every day she prayed for him. On this morning, she felt something was terribly wrong. Her spirit was pressed hard. She felt a great need to pray for him. She did not know what to pray. She just prayed.

A little later, her father found her crying in deep grief. Not knowing what was wrong, Thomas went to her. "My child, what is it?"

Chastity lifted her head. Her face was wet with tears. It was as though she had the weight of many sorrows upon her. "Oh, Father. It's John. I don't know how I know it, but I fear he is in great trouble."

Thomas drew close to his daughter. He stroked her hair to comfort her. "This is a warning from God. Oftentimes, the Almighty puts someone on our hearts when they are in danger. Come. Let us pray, and I will weep with you."

How long they prayed it did not matter. They poured their hearts out to God for the man they loved. When prayer time was finished, Thomas continued to hold his daughter. In tenderness, he spoke. "Chastity, never take God's warning to pray lightly. God touches our hearts, our minds, and our very beings to pray for others, especially in time of need. The closer we are to God, the more we can sense His presence and be drawn to prayer."

Thomas grew silent for a moment as he reflected on his next thought. "I was a young man of faith. You had not been born. Your mother was with child. We were so thrilled that God would bring to us our firstborn. One night I felt I should pray for the baby. I did not know where the need to pray had come from or why I should pray. So I didn't. I passed it off even though the call to pray was strong. The next morning your mother was in great pain. Something was wrong. She was having the baby. The child, a son, did not make it. His death was a devastating blow."

Chastity raised up and wrinkled her brow, questioning her father's statement. "You and Mum lost a child before I came along?"

Thomas replied, "Yes. We never told you, because we did not see the need. Few in town knew. Oh, some in the church knew. The priest told us it was God's will. I became angry and left the church, blaming God for taking my baby."

Thomas stopped to reflect on what he would say next. "When spring came, I was delivering a consignment of wool to the earl. Along the way, I met Elijah. He noticed that I was rather downtrodden. We began to talk, and I told him of my loss. He grieved with me. He helped me understand that God's love and grace would get me through. I did not understand, and I did not know how. After that, we continued to fellowship together and in time, he helped me. Then one day I told him how I felt that I needed to pray but could not find it in me to do so. Elijah told me that the drawing I felt was from the Holy Spirit. Then he taught me to pray. From that moment on, I began to realize God was with me. In fact, God had never left me. In time, I began to see God's hand in my life, and that is when He blessed us once more. That is when you came along."

Chastity then asked, "Do you think God is going to take John?"

Thomas replied, "Who can know the mind of the Almighty? I believe we need to pray that God protects him. John belongs to God. God can protect him wherever he is." Then, lifting his eyes to heaven, Thomas prayed, "Oh, Father, place a hedge of protection around John."

# America's Shores

After William was removed, the town had become quieter. Taylor returned to his role as sheriff and visited the earl from time to time to report on things. Taylor was changing. He was more noticeable in the town. Even though William was gone, Taylor knew there were still those who needed to be watched. William wasn't without some friends, especially those who counted on him to pay for their rum. Taylor wanted to make sure these men weren't the cause of additional trouble.

Haywards Heath hosted a town market. Many would come from nearby hamlets to either sell or trade their goods. Ruth and her daughters sold their wool there. Thomas would load up the wagon and drive the family into town. At the market, he would help Ruth and his daughters set up. Then he would take his leave and go around to enjoy his time looking at what others had.

People for miles around knew the quality of Ruth's wares. Many women would come directly to where she displayed her goods. As soon as Ruth and her daughters were ready, they busied themselves tending to customers. As quickly as the wool was sold, one of the girls restocked the empty space. Ruth was shrewd and careful that no one took advantage of her. Some wool she exchanged in trade, but as much as possible, she wanted coin. Things she needed for herself could only be purchased and not traded for.

Sheriff Taylor passed along the market, keeping an eye on everyone. From time to time, he stopped at places that caught his attention. Today, he eyed Ruth busily selling her wool. Taylor walked over to extend his well wishes. "Good day, Mrs. Shepherd."

Ruth looked to the man. How much better he seemed. Thomas and

Ruth knew Taylor. While his wife yet lived, it was common for the happy couple to stroll the market. After she died, the sheriff was seldom seen. Out of respect, she returned the greeting. "And a good day to you, Sheriff."

No sooner had the words escaped her lips when a beautiful woman with auburn hair laid additional skeins of wool out to replace the ones already sold. Taylor could not take his eyes off the young woman. He then asked Ruth, "Many pardons, but who might this young woman be?"

Ruth replied, "Why, Sheriff, this is my oldest daughter, Chastity."

It had been almost six years since the last time Taylor had seen Chastity. She was a pretty girl then, but now ... Taylor bowed slightly before Chastity. "It is good to see you again."

Chastity was polite but much too busy to even take much notice of the sheriff. She responded in kindness by taking a moment. "Thank you, sir. Pleased to see you also." After that, she went back to her duties.

Women kept crowding around the table, and Taylor slowly back away, but all along, he could not take his eyes of Chastity. Even as he walked away, he would turn periodically to catch a glimpse of her. Taylor hadn't thought of another woman since his wife had died. How could it be that this young lady would suddenly capture his attention so quickly?

Try as he might, Taylor could not rid his mind of Chastity. He didn't understand why she filled his thoughts. When he returned home, he found his sister preparing supper. Sally had also visited the market and bought items she felt she needed. Taylor hung up his cap and turned to see on the table two skeins of wool. His immediate thoughts returned to Chastity. Even now, he thought that it was her hands that may have placed these on the table. The thought brought a smile to his face.

At dinner, Sally noticed that her brother's appetite wasn't hardy. It was obvious something preoccupied him. Sally asked, "Brother, is everything all right?"

Taylor, still lost in thought, responded, "Hum ... Oh, sorry. I have just been thinking."

Sally replied, "May I ask what you might be thinking?"

Taylor slowly came back to reality and answered, "I have just been thinking about some people at the market today." Then, trying to advert the subject, he asked, "I see you bought some wool. What are you planning to make?"

Sally answered, "I am not sure, but I could not help myself. Have you ever seen anything so beautiful?"

Taylor replied, "Not in a very long time."

On board the ship, John's life became much more difficult. His new master saw to it that John had little interaction with other crewmen. Those who had benefited from John's service before were now forbidden to seek John's help unless they paid a handsome price for his work. This angered the men, for they had come to think of John as one of them. While at sea, John was permitted to roam the ship when not at his labor, but whereas Henry used to teach him things, he was now ordered to keep the maps and other navigational items away from John. Because of this, John didn't even know where they were headed, what port they were in, or their location when at sea. Only a chance conversation with Henry, Samuel, or Timothy shed any detail of the ship's possible destination.

The captain was filled with greed. He supplied silver, iron, and other materials John needed to make the wares. In order to buy these things, the money to make repairs to the ship was neglected. The crew was being paid, but afterward, the captain tried to swindle them of their hard-earned money by suggesting that they buy things John made. This caused an even greater unrest among the men. The loyalty of the crew vanished, and they became more suspicious of Captain Richard Wise. The ill treatment of John made all the crew think, *If the captain would do this to John, what would prevent him from doing this to us?*

Whenever the ship came to port, John would be shackled to prevent his escape. The captain would have the cargo off-loaded, while he went to shore with the treasures John made to sell. The captain would see to it that the chest bearing the goods off-loaded first, and he would depart, leaving Henry in charge. No one knew where he was going exactly, but they knew he what he was doing. John's talent was making his captain a much wealthier man.

When Richard Wise left the ship, John would chance a visit with Henry or one of the crew. He urged them to mail a letter for him to his beloved Chastity. His letter writing stopped when a crewmate turned John's letter over to the captain for a price. John later faced the captain with the open letter on the desk. The captain mocked his love and then had John whipped for his attempt to get word out about his situation. From that moment on, the captain would post a guard to watch John whenever he went ashore. John would never be able to send another letter till he was free.

John kept his mark on all he made. Instead of the vine he had used on the captain's knife, he now employed his original mark of J.S. He hoped someone would recognize his handiwork and come to his aid, but none ever came.

At one point, they arrived back in England. John's clothes were showing the wear of constant use, and his beard and hair were growing long. John looked like a beggar. Henry was ordered to bring John before the captain. John did not stand at attention, but he stood in complete silence.

The captain chortled. "Glad you could come, Mr. Devine."

John said nothing to the captain's mocking statement. The captain looked at Henry. "You're dismissed, Mr. Finch."

Henry uttered, "Aye, aye, Captain," and promptly left.

Only John and the captain remained in his quarters.

The captain went to his table and began to eat from a plate filled with cooked meat. He did not offer John anything. The captain taunted John. "Do you know what port this is?" Then with a laugh, he added, "It's London, mate, but you won't be going ashore. No harm in you looking, I suspect, but I shall keep you under watch." Without looking at John, the captain told him his plans. "I am being paid very well for your work. For this, I congratulate you. I have been informed that I could fetch a greater profit if gold was being used instead of silver. Have you ever worked with gold before?"

John simply nodded.

Then the captain continued. "I tell you this because I plan to take my next shipment to the Caribbean. The islands are in need of English goods and will pay in gold." The captain then took a great bite of greasy food. The grease rolled down his unkempt beard.

John asked, "Permission to speak."

The captain stopped chewing long enough to consider the request and then nodded his approval.

John offered, "Aren't there pirates in that region? What's to keep them from attacking you afterward just to get their gold back?"

The captain answered, "I have thought of that. I plan to buy a few guns for the ship. The men will be armed when we leave the region, but not until."

John looked at Captain Wise, "Then what?" he asked.

The captain just smiled. "You will perform your magic as you always do, and I will become a wealthier man." The captain then looked at John in a mocking way before stating, "Where are my manors? Would you care to join me for a bite to eat?"

John was hungry, but the company of the captain turned his stomach. "No. I am much too ill to eat. I will wait and eat my daily rations that you provide for me."

The captain jumped to his feet. "How dare you! Your impotence! I offer you food and my company, and you have the gull to refuse me? You shall not have anything to eat the rest of the day."

John just smirked. "Careful, Captain. You risk damaging the one who is making you rich. I will be returning to my quarters, master, unless you have something else for me."

Not another word was uttered. John turned and walked away.

Henry found John at the rail, looking at the city skyline. He could tell John was contemplating something. John raised one foot as high as he could.

Henry called to him, "John, don't do it. It won't be worth the risk."

John turned. "What are you talking about?"

Henry walked over to him. "The weight of the iron and the distance to shore. You would sink like a rock, and even if you managed to float some, you would soon tire and sink to your death. So don't do it."

John looked back at the old city. "I left here with great hope. Now it seems my hope is gone."

Henry placed a hand on his shoulder. He tried to comfort his young friend. "Hope is only gone when you let go of it. I promise that your time will come."

Chastity was in the field enjoying the beautiful spring weather. In a few days, her father would be bringing the sheep in for their annual sheering. She looked about and saw a great number of ewes that would be giving birth. Her father would bring those ewes in first. They would be sheered before giving birth. Then the others. The wool would be brought in to her mother, and the whole process of cleaning, drying, and spinning would start all over again. This was the life Chastity knew, and she cherished it.

Chastity held in her hand the new Bible the family had bought to replace the one given to John. The new Bible was called The King James Bible. She loved the new Bible and saw little difference between it and the Geneva. She whispered a prayer for the man she loved. When she had finished, she turned her attention to read from John 10. Today she read about Jesus being the Good Shepherd. One passage touched her deeply, "I am come that they might have life, and that they might have it more abundantly. I am the good shepherd: the good shepherd giveth his life for the sheep." The words touched her. *My Lord intends for me to have abundant life*, she thought. *That is why He gave His life for me.*

A smile crossed her face. Chastity thought, *I know I will have a wonderful life with John.* She knew that she and John would share in this abundant life together. She loved the man of God he had become. She missed him and couldn't help but think of his ocean-blue eyes. Chastity had not heard from John for more than a year. The only letter she received was that his situation had changed. She did not know what that meant. She showed Pastor Elijah the letter, and after that, she had left things to him. All she knew was she wanted to join him wherever he might be. She wanted to join him. She wanted to be his wife more than anything.

Chastity mediated on the Word. She was so deep in mediation that she didn't notice the man who approached. The first indication was Maggie, one of the older ewes, lifting her head looking in the direction of the newcomer. A strong, masculine voice broke her serene thoughts.

"I hope you don't mind the interruption, me lady."

Chastity turned her head to look in the direction of the speaker. There stood Sheriff Taylor. She quickly rose to her feet. The Bible fell to the ground. She replied, "Lord Sheriff, you startled me. I did not hear you approach."

Taylor walked over and picked up the Bible. He was surprised to find someone who had one. Usually the only people who possessed a Bible for themselves had greater means than a poor shepherd. Holding the Bible, he thought about the secret congregation. Taylor attended the local Church of England from time to time, but he never saw the Shepherd family there. Even though it wasn't illegal anymore to read the Bible, some still frowned upon its private use.

Looking at Chastity, he commented, "So you are an educated girl. I know so few who can read."

Chastity responded, "My father saw the necessity for my sisters and me to be educated."

Taylor handed her the Bible. She reached for it with her left hand. He immediately noticed the beautiful ring on her finger. He removed the riding glove on his right hand and extended it before, asking her to show him her hand. Chastity extended her hand, and he held her fingertips while admiring the ring. He loved the feel of her soft hands. Then looking at her, he stated, "That is a most exquisite ring. I have never seen one so beautiful, but shouldn't you wear the ring on your right hand?"

Chastity snatched her hand back before responding to the question. "It was given to me by my betrothed. We hope to be married soon enough."

Taylor was amused at her answer. It did not bother him that she was betrothed. As far as he was concerned, she was still available. He was clever enough to not make his intentions known. "Many pardons. I meant no offense, but if I was betrothed to a beautiful woman like you, I dare say, I could not stay away."

Taylor's words made her blush. Chastity replied, "Such things should not be said to a lady."

Taylor loved her innocence. He continued. "So to whom have you given your promise?"

Chastity did not like the question and suddenly became leery of the sheriff. "He is someone you do not know. His name is Jonathan Devine."

Taylor shot back. "And how did you come to meet this man?"

Chastity grew quiet and refused to say anything more and turned to walk away.

Taylor immediately called to her, "Wait ... I did not mean to upset you. I only came this way to ask a question of you."

She entertained him for a moment. "What is it you want?"

Taylor walked closer. "Permission to visit with you."

Chastity turned and nearly bumped into the sheriff. "I do not think it appropriate. As I have told you, I am engaged."

"Ah," shot back Taylor, "but you are not married yet." His answer angered her.

Once again, she distanced herself from him. "I have work to do. Please forgive me, for I do need to return home." She would be detained no longer.

As she hurried away, Taylor thought, *I will see you again. I think I know how.*

Chastity returned home as fast as she could. The encounter with the sheriff scared her. She was afraid that she might have said too much to him. She did not know what his intentions were, but he left her feeling fearful. She raced home as fast as she could. When she arrived, she was panting heavily. Ruth heard her hurried entry and went to see what was wrong. Her daughter was pale.

She asked, "Why, Chastity ... What are you so out of breath for?"

Chastity hurried to her mother's arms. "Oh, Mother, I fear I have made a dreadful mistake."

The two women sat for a long period of time talking. Afterward, Ruth told Chastity, "It wasn't right that the sheriff would come to you unannounced. He should have come here and spoken with your father. I don't know what he might be looking for. From what you have said, I am sure it is just to court you."

The answer angered Chastity, and her response showed it. "I have no interest in him."

Ruth looked at her daughter. "Makes no nary mind to him." Walking over to her chair, she continued. "As for telling him about John, I suppose he might look for Mr. Devine, but he will not find him here. Still, we have to tell your father and perhaps even the pastor." Ruth thought for a moment more. "You say that he took notice that you were reading the Bible?"

Chastity nodded her head in agreement.

Later that evening, Thomas sat with his family listening as Chastity recounted her encounter with Sheriff Taylor. Thomas thought for a while upon the things he heard. He reached his right hand out and asked Chastity to extend her left. He took her fingertips in his left hand before asking, "Did he hold your hand like this?"

"Yes," Chastity responded. "But before he asked for my hand, he removed his riding glove."

Thomas replied, "I think your mother right. Sheriff Taylor intends to court you."

In alarm, Chastity proclaimed, "Me?"

Thomas smiled. "When was the last time you saw him?"

Chastity quickly replied, "Why, at the market."

Thomas continued. "At the market ... I think he took a liking to you."

Chastity thought about what her father said. "I told him that I was betrothed."

Thomas then asked, "And how did he respond?"

Chastity replied, "As though it didn't matter."

Thomas put his hands behind him and locked them together. Then, walking a bit around the room, he continued. "The sheriff is used to being in control and having authority. I suppose he might consider you worthy of the pursuit."

Chastity was concerned. "I told him of John."

Thomas turned quickly. "How so?"

She continued. "He asked about my ring, and I told him that my betrothed, Mr. Devine, gave it to me."

Thomas quickly asked. "Think carefully, Daughter. Did you tell him that he made it?"

Chastity was just as quick to answer. "Oh no, I was very careful in that."

Finally, Thomas replied, "That will settle it for now. I believe our good sheriff will try to find him, but he will fail, as Mr. Devine does not exist in our town."

Chastity looked back at her father. What she said next was a surprise.

"Mr. Devine does exist, because John is that man. Father, I have given a lot of thought since my encounter with the sheriff. I want to go to John."

Thomas answered with deep concern, "We don't even know where he is or even if he is alive."

Chastity tried to hide the anger of the statement. She raised her voice in answer. "He is alive. I know it. There has to be a reason he has not written more. Don't you see? He needs me, and I must go to him."

Thomas knew it was senseless to carry the conversation on any further. She was much too like him. His chest rose and fell quickly. He looked at Ruth and then at Chastity. When he had gained his composure, he stated, "We shall see."

The *Elizabeth Marie* was anchored off the French port of Brest. The captain was trading goods for cannons. The men were shocked to see four smaller cannons brought alongside, ready to be loaded. No one dared to ask the captain about them. Timothy was instructed to take John and make four portholes on each side of the ship for the cannon. The captain surmised that the cannons could be used on one side or the other. Before long, Timothy and John were busy making the portholes in the side of the ship.

The captain kept the ship in port only as long as it took to prepare the cannons and exchange goods. His next destination was the Caribbean Islands, where he hoped to make a healthy profit in gold.

Timothy was concerned. He said to John, "The captain is up to something, or else we would not need these guns. Besides, I worry about the condition of the ship. She is not a war ship. If a cannon shot hits the ship in the right place, she will sink quickly."

John listened with keen interest but did not utter a word.

Henry was commanded to teach the crewmen how to handle the guns. The cannons were put in place, and Henry taught certain of the crew how to load, aim, and fire them. The ship was terribly overloaded. The crew noticed that the ship was laden heavier than they'd ever seen before. The ship rode low, which could make for treacherous sailing, especially if they had to endure a storm. The thought scared John. He knew the captain's greed was threatening the very lives of all those on board.

Once all the loading craft had sailed away from the *Elizabeth Marie*, the captain called Henry Finch to his cabin.

"Mr. Finch, I want you to set a course for Port Royal."

Henry was completely surprised. The dangers of the Caribbean were enough to keep many captains away. Henry was a faithful first mate and served the captain well, but he knew that the waters of the Caribbean were filled with pirates. Added to that, the tensions between Spain, Holland, and England were growing, and everyone knew it. It was but a matter of time before there was all-out war on the high seas.

Henry became defiant. "So what is this all about? Every jack man of us wondered why we needed cannons. We have all watched and obeyed as we have been commanded to prepare the ship, and for what? You are risking our lives by crossing the ocean with an overladen ship. Then you want us to sail clear of potential enemies only to sail into pirate-controlled waters?"

The captain allowed Henry to finish before pointing to the map. "This be our destination. Either you set the course and prepare the men, or I will find another."

Henry responded, "You are the captain and can do whatever you like. I served in the Royal Navy, and I know tactics. I know you will need me to train the men to use the cannons should we encounter danger. Captain, you risk the lives of these men—good men—but they haven't a clue when it comes to naval battle."

Captain Wise knew Henry was right, but he dare not show it. He acted coy and tried to hide his real motive. He stood and walked over to his first mate. The captain placed his hands on Henry's shoulders. "I need you for this trip. My reasons and my motives are my own. Help me get this shipment safely across, and I shall reward you handsomely. In truth, I will pay you in gold."

*Gold*. That precious element every sailor wanted. Sailors were usually paid in silver coin, but to be paid in gold was more than most could ever hope for. It was common knowledge that Spain had become the wealthiest nation on earth because of gold taken from the Americas. It was also common knowledge that many of the Island nations had large deposits of the precious metal.

The captain saw the change in Henry's eyes. "What says you now?"

Henry looked at the captain. "Very well. I will inform the men."

Henry ordered the men on deck and told them of the journey ahead. "Men, you are seasoned sailors and have prepared the ship for a most challenging and profitable trip. At the tide, we shall begin our journey for the Caribbean—destination, Jamaica."

A murmur was heard among the men, especially those who preferred shorter and safer trips, but they didn't speak up. John heard the murmurs, but he already knew the captain's intentions.

Henry continued. "I know some of you might question our abilities to defend ourselves. Therefore, I will be instructing you more on the use of the cannons while at sea. I assure you that if you follow my orders, we will arrive safely. Now all hands on deck. Prepare the ship to weigh anchor."

Immediately, the organized hustle of men to their stations took place. John just sat there for a moment more. He caught Henry's eye. Nothing had to be said. Both men knew danger was in store for them.

It took longer than usual for the ship to respond to the wind with its heavy load. Turning the ship was a great task for the helmsman. John worked at his bench. Creeks and moans of the ship were constantly being heard as though the ship fought to hold itself together. He could hear the water lapping at the gun ports.

At one point, Timothy came quickly to John. "Come on, lad. We have a lot of repair to attend to."

All day, the two men worked to fix leaks and patch would-be holes. By the end of the day, John tumbled into his hammock. He was exhausted. Even in his exhausted state, his mind was filled with Chastity. He feared that this might be the end for him, and she would never know what happened.

John prayed, "Oh, Father, I fear this journey more than any that I have had to take. I know the captain's greed has made this journey so very dangerous. I know that I am but a slave, and he is my master. I seek your deliverance. I ask You to bring us safely over to our destination. I pray, Father, that you make a way for me to the place I was promised. Oh, Father, I miss Chastity. I think of her all the time. I ask you to watch over her and keep her safe. We prayed that you would make us one. Please, Father, make the way for us. Tell her that I am all right. Tell her that I love her. Amen." In the midst of his prayer, John fell fast asleep.

Thomas arranged a meeting between him and Pastor. Thomas told him of the encounter that Chastity had with the sheriff. When all the details were told, Pastor commented, "I believe you are right concerning Sheriff's intention. Earl Christopher has told me that he has seen a great change in the man—for the good, I might add. Taylor has stopped drinking and has kept a keen eye on the town. Taylor's heart has mended from his loss. It is only natural that he would consider marrying again."

Thomas retorted, "But has he no respect for a woman betrothed to another?"

"Perhaps not," came Pastor's reply. "Besides that, it is still in his power to … say … do as he sees best?"

The answer angered Thomas. "The man still has no right. She is my daughter. I decide what is best for her."

Pastor touched Thomas on the shoulder. "Dear Brother, do not be alarmed. We must trust the hand of the Almighty. We must not be alarmed at the actions of men like the sheriff. All care should be taken to protect our loved ones, but someone as beautiful as your daughter can expect advances from men. The sheriff sees a lovely single girl and sees nothing wrong in his approach."

The pastor solemnly added, "It may be time for Chastity also to make her journey to the New World. In fact, I have heard that in Plymouth there is a good family in need of a governess. I believe Chastity could fit this role well. With your permission, I could begin arrangements for her service."

Thomas was surprised. He looked to Elijah. "Will she have to make this journey alone?"

Elijah smiled. "Not at all, Brother. There is a ship preparing to leave soon made up of a good number of Separatist. I know some of those making this journey. I will ask them to keep watchful care of Chastity."

Thomas replied, "Chastity said that she felt she needed to join John. I tried to convince her otherwise, but when she sets her mind on something … well, you know."

Elijah smiled and replied, "I do understand."

What Elijah offered was expected considering the present circumstances, but Thomas wasn't about to let his daughter go. Thomas expressed his fear. "She hopes to find John, but we haven't heard anything from him except for the one letter."

Elijah lifted his eye toward heaven before answering. "I know that Mr. Browning has sent letters to his employer's representative in Virginia. John did not say he was in danger, but that his situation changed."

Thomas reverently added, "Chastity has felt the draw of providence to pray for him. She said she felt he was in danger. My fear is that she might go off to try and find him."

Elijah stood up and prepared to leave. He looked over at Thomas. He considered carefully what he said next. "It is most interesting to me the events that have led to this moment. John is somewhere in the New World, and Chastity wants to join him. Taylor wants to pursue her, thus forcing the next move. The decision is yours. She is betrothed to John and has received your blessing. If she doesn't go to John, the sheriff will try again to see her. Taylor is no fool. He is a good man, but even good men can have bad ways and find for themselves wrong direction."

The two men walked a short distance as the pastor prepared to leave. He added, "Those of us who still desire religious freedom are outlaws. It is our prayer that God will open the door for us to have the spiritual freedom we desire. Till that day comes, we have few choices. Many have escaped to America for such freedom, while the rest of us meet secretly. We must remember the law is on the side of Taylor. If he should find us out, we can be arrested, and the earl would be placed in a questionable position. Taylor might even pursue Chastity, forcing her to marry him by threatening to turn us all in."

Thomas remained in deep thought. His question to Elijah revealed it. "How could this be? Isn't God for us?"

Elijah felt led by the Spirit in his answer. "The Bible is filled with examples of those who struggled for the right to worship God freely. Elijah, Esther, Hezekiah, Daniel, and others stood up and lived their faith. God saw fit to deliver and even prosper them, but the struggle to gain that freedom was costly. We are presently in that struggle. I believe in time, if we remain faithful and trust in the Almighty, we shall have that freedom."

Elijah extended his hand to Thomas. "Come, Brother, there is much to do. I urge you to prepare your daughter and family for the journey ahead."

The two men stood for a moment and embraced each other. Elijah mounted his horse and rode away. Thomas slowly began the heart-wrenching walk to his house. He now faced the most difficult decision of his life.

The ship continued to lumber across the Atlantic. The crew was exhausted from the constant commands and the care of the ship. Timothy and John were caring for the ship at all hours, doing all they could to keep the ship afloat.

Timothy mused to John, "The ship, she be in need of dry dock. The captain has pushed this old vessel way too far. We may have to divide our time so that at least one of us can get our rest. We will have to stay up through the night to tend to all the ship needs."

John understood and willingly volunteered to stay up through the night. The success of this voyage was dependent upon Timothy and John keeping the ship afloat.

Then came the unexpected. During the crossing, they encountered three days of a violent storm. Henry's skills as first mate, as well as the captain's experience, were put to the test. Timothy and John were kept busy making repairs to the *Elizabeth Marie*. At least two of the crew were constantly at the pump to rid the ship of water. Some of the crew wanted to lighten the ship, but the captain refused. When the storm finally passed, Timothy and John continued to patch holes and cracks. The two men hadn't slept through the entire storm.

When the final patch was made, Timothy proclaimed to John, "Come, lad. We are going to our hammocks. If the ship sinks, I very much doubt it would be worse than I feel right now."

Forty-five days into the journey land was sighted. The men were surprised that land was spotted so soon. It usually took eight to twelve weeks to cross the Atlantic. Some thought the storm pushed them faster.

Little did they know that they had been pushed into currents that would not be discovered for another two hundred years.

The sailors wanted to make land in order to recover and make repairs, but the captain remained insistent that they press on to their destination. The men were weary and exhausted, and they wanted this journey done with. The land sighting did not cheer them. The sighting of dolphins and the circling of seagulls did little to lift their spirits. They were troubled, because they knew the dangers of the waters they now sailed.

The seas all around them were full of pirates and on the verge of war. Tensions continued to mount between the sea powers. The Dutch would fire on any ship that threatened their newly acquired trade and settlements. The English were pressing their interests in the Americas. Pirates attacked whatever ship they wanted to plunder. Lastly, there were the Spaniards who had established themselves since the days of Columbus. They were not about to give up what was theirs.

The sailors on board the *Elizabeth Marie* knew they could not outrun or outmaneuver anyone. They were too heavy, and there weren't enough guns to fend off a skiff. If anyone wanted to attack them, the attacker could easily defeat them. The knowledge of their situation gripped the men with fear—even more than the sea and the difficulty of the final leg of the journey they still had to endure. They were not fighting men, and they wanted no part of a battle.

It took another five days of sailing before the men finally spotted Port Royal. The island port was still in Spanish control but suffered greatly since the defeat of the Spanish Armada. The officials of Port Royal needed goods from other nations and pirates—goods that were necessary for living. In exchange, handsome prices were paid out in gold and jewels. Such payment was never kept secret.

When the ship finally docked, the order was given to secure it. As soon as he could, the captain left the ship to make arrangements with the authorities. Nearly half the day was spent in negotiations before his return. He ordered the men to off-load the cargo. With every little bit that was off-loaded, the men could actually feel the ship rise in relief. It took nearly three days for the cargo to be completely removed. When the task was complete, the captain paid the men and offered them shore leave. Every man saw what he was paid and felt it wasn't enough for the danger they'd just come through. Several sailors stated that they would not be joining the ship when it departed but would offer their services to a worthier captain.

Captain Wise called for Henry to bring John before him. Together, they entered and stood before him.

A fiendish smile crept over the captain's face. He looked at John. Addressing him, the captain said, "Mr. Devine, thank you for joining me. As you can see, we have made the journey and have safely arrived at Port Royal. Your fears were unwarranted, but I chose to reward you for your remarkable service. I know that it has been a long time since you have been ashore. How would you like that opportunity?"

John just looked at the captain with disdain in his heart. "Aren't you afraid that I would escape?"

The captain reared back and laughed heartily. "Escape? Did you say *escape*? You're on an island, man. How far can you go? And with what? You have no money, and all your positions are aboard this ship. No, you won't escape. Besides, I own the bill of your indentured service to me."

John cast his eyes to the ground. He was not a servant, but every bit a slave. He took a shallow breath. When he exhaled, he said to the captain, "I would enjoy a bit of shore leave."

The captain smiled and then looked at Henry, "Release him from his irons."

Henry took the key ring from his side and removed the iron shackles. John rubbed his wrists, thankful that the cuffs were removed. The captain then gave order to John while tossing him a Spanish doubloon. "Enjoy yourself, Mr. Devine. Make sure you are back on ship by the end of the day, or you will be offered no other freedom."

Looking to the captain, he replied, "Thank you, sir." He then turned and walked from the cabin without saying another word.

Captain Wise turned his attention to Henry. "You served me well. The way you handled the ship and the men was outstanding. Here is your pay. The captain laid out five gold Spanish coins. The value was little more than what he would have been paid in silver. Henry lifted his eyes to see the greedy smile cross the captain's face. "As promised, I have paid you in gold."

Henry looked back. "And I was a fool to think you would reward me handsomely."

Captain Wise laughed again. "Mate, I have done you no wrong. Now enjoy your stay in Port Royal."

Henry leered at the captain. "I am no mate of yours, and I shall never be tricked again by you." Henry stormed from the cabin as the captain laughed greedily.

John took the final step from the plank to shore. How strange solid ground felt beneath his feet. He looked at his rags. When he had boarded the ship nearly two years ago, he did so in fine clothes. Now he departed in dirty, worn rags. John did not know what the coin would buy, but he knew he wanted a good meal, a hot bath, and new clothes. He stood on the dock a long while. From behind, he heard the familiar rattle of the plank. Henry was leaving the ship.

Henry reached the dock and stood beside John before expressing his apologizes. "I'm sorry, Mr. Devine, for all the hardship. I hope you will forgive me."

John looked at Henry. "How many times must I ask you to call me John? You have nothing to apologize for. We are trapped in the captain's game. He has calculated his moves very carefully."

Henry looked puzzled. "How so?"

John continued. "We are at an island port exchanging goods. The captain has the pay he wanted for this treacherous journey. The crew shall soon be in need of his service. Even though they vowed not to return, most will, because they have no choice. The captain said it well when he said we have no escape. So we best make the best of it." Then, flipping the gold coin in the air, John added, "I plan to spend what the captain gave me without regret. Care to join me?"

Henry smiled and said, "Aren't we a pair?"

The two men looked at each other up and down. They looked every bit seamen. The two warn and ragged men walked about the town to find a place where they could buy much-needed clothing. John found a cobbler and left his boots to be repaired. In this tropical port, it wasn't unusual to see a man walking barefoot, but John preferred boots. The cobbler told them of a local bathhouse and promised to deliver the boots to John there.

The two men went directly to the bathhouse and were soon neck deep in steamy hot water. How soothing it felt to have the hot water wash away the salt and grime. The oils used in the bath relieved the aches and pains of worn muscles and soothed cuts on the hands. John decided not to shave his beard. He left it as a reminder of the days in the service of Captain Richard Wise.

The men were still enjoying their baths when the cobber brought the boots. John exited the tub and dried himself before putting on his new clothes. He then pulled on his boots. He stood and peered into a looking glass. He had aged considerably, and marks on his face showed the strain. His youthfulness was disappearing. John pulled his hair straight back and tied it. He combed his beard. Looking again in the glass, he realized that John Dairyman was truly gone. He had become a new and different man.

John and Henry emerged at about the same time. Henry couldn't help but admire the change in John. Smiling, he said, "John, you look rather distinguished. Save that beard, and you could pass for a British officer."

John laughed. "I thought I looked more like a vagabond."

Hunger gripped them. They left the bathhouse to walk the street, hoping to find a place worthy of their appetite and budget. Together, they took a table outside a tavern and were quickly greeted by the owner. He only spoke Spanish but understood the men wanted to eat. Henry slapped a silver coin on the table. The owner snatched it up, and soon, bowls of soup were served followed by plates of seafood and local vegetables. Mugs of beer washed it all down. When the meal was done, the men paid the remainder of what they owed. John was broke but enjoyed the feeling of being full and relaxed.

John sat back in his chair. He looked over at Henry. "I have enjoyed this lone day of freedom. It has been so good to be released from my restraints even if it has only been for one day."

Henry looked keenly at his young friend. "John, I am surprised to hear you say this. Why would you refer to today as a day of freedom?"

John quickly answered, "Am I not a slave? Am I not here because the captain gave me a momentary reprieve?"

Henry thoughtfully responded, "My friend, you are only a slave if you allow yourself to be. Have you noticed that I never treated you any different from the moment I was told you were an indentured?"

John nodded his head in the affirmative.

Henry continued. "You were indentured in the employment of Mr. Howell. Now you are indentured to Captain Wise. You are an indentured servant, not a slave. This time will pass. Even maritime law will support you."

John thought carefully about what Henry had to say and then asked, "What's the difference? I can only move so as long as the captain permits."

Henry leaned forward and sipped his beer. "John, how did you become a smith?"

John stated, "My father made an agreement for me to learn the trade with the local blacksmith. I served him, and he trained me."

Henry replied, "So I take it that you lost your freedom when you became an apprentice."

John shot back. "No. How could you think such a thing?"

Henry remarked, "I don't. You do." There was an awkward pause before Henry continued, "John, don't you see that you gave of yourself to be a student? The blacksmith did not own you, and neither does the captain."

John stated, "But my shackles—

Henry cut him off. "Were put on you by the captain to make you feel like a slave."

Henry was making sense. John had never thought of it in these ways. Henry took another sip. "Do you know how I became a sailor?"

John shook his head. "No. You never told me."

Henry continued. "I was a foolish lad and left my home to get away and find adventure. I found it all right. I visited a pub and was served a Mickey Finn by some press-gangs. Next morning, I had a terrible headache and found myself aboard a ship of one of His Majesty's Royal Navy. At first, I was angry and bitter. I thought someone stole my freedom."

John replied, "That is how I feel now."

Henry replied, "It wasn't till I realized that my dreams were just being detained that I looked at things differently. I soon realized that no man can steal your freedom. You can only give it up."

The thought made John realize that's what was happening to him. After a moment of thought, he looked to Henry and studied the face of his friend.

John asked, "You mean, that is what I am allowing of myself?"

Henry gave a familiar half-cocked smile. "That's exactly what I mean. You know what I did?"

John replied, "No. What?"

"I accepted my position and began learning how to be good seaman. Eventually, I became an officer on the ship, learned navigation, and even commanded a few vessels. When my seven years of service were up, I stayed on for another fifteen years. I now choose to serve aboard Captain Wise's ship because I want to—no more and no less. You have a little less than three years left in service. How will you spend it?"

John stated, "Not as a slave."

Henry posed another question. "Before you have to return to the ship, let me ask you one more thing. Would you fight for the woman you love?"

John was surprised. "What do you mean?"

Henry continued. "It's quite simple really. If someone were to attack the woman you love, would you fight to protect her?"

John didn't hesitate. "Of course I would. I would protect her and our children the best I could."

Henry made his point. "My friend, you would fight for them because of the love you have for them and the principle of the matter. What about freedom? Don't you know that we have the freedom we have because someone fought for it? If you believe strongly enough about something, you will fight for it as well. Be willing to stand up and fight for what you believe in."

John thoughtfully added, "I think you will have to teach me how."

As promised, the two men returned to the ship and walked up the plank together. John approached the captain.

John looked the captain square in the eyes. "Mr. Jonathan Devine reporting as commanded."

Captain Wise looked him over. "I see you bought some sensible clothes." Turning to Henry, the captain ordered, "Put Mr. Devine back in irons."

John just looked at the captain. "There will be no need, Captain, but if you feel it necessary …" With that, John extended his arms and waited for Henry to clamp the irons shut.

Pastor came to the Shepherd home with news for Chastity about the position available for her in the New World. The talk was sensible and very much to the point. Pastor Elijah had arranged for Chastity to join the group of believers leaving the following week from London.

Sorrowfully, Ruth spoke up first. "I knew this day would come, but I thought it might be another year or so. Now that it is upon us, I don't know if I can do this."

Thomas sat close to her and placed his arm lovingly about her. "Sweet Ruth, it is no easier for me. Our daughter is not in danger just yet, but the sheriff could make things hard for her. He might do the same against us. We have raised Chastity to the best of our ability. I think it's time."

Ruth looked up at her husband with tear-filled eyes. Her voice quivered as she stated, "But she's our daughter."

Pastor Elijah told them of the arrangements. In America, a Mr. George Abernathy and his wife, Susan, needed a governess. They would benefit a woman coming to America if she had the education and ability to serve in this capacity. They were asking for five years' service with opportunity to stay longer if the lady so chooses.

Pastor explained what he had learned of the situation. "George Abernathy is well established outside Plymouth in the new town of Boston. He works there for the Massachusetts Bay Colony's investors. Shipping is being established in the port area. George builds some of the finest houses in the growing town. With each new arrival comes the need for housing. His houses are built to suit the new arrival's need. With more and more people arriving on a regular basis, the need for houses has boomed. George is a very busy man and works long hours. His wife is left alone. So, Chastity, in added ways, you will also be company for Susan."

Pastor strolled about the room. "I don't know how many children they have, but they want them to be educated." Turning to Chastity, Pastor stated, "I have arranged for you to travel with Paul and Leah Stitch."

Chastity sat up excitedly. "I know them. They are part of our congregation."

Pastor smiled. "Yes, they are. They were married last fall and are expecting their first child. It will be good for the three of you to travel together. I also believe you will be a big help to Leah and she to you."

Thomas rose up and walked over to his daughter. He lifted her to her feet. He stood with her and admired his beautiful, young daughter. His mind was filled with thoughts of the past. He remembered the little toddler who made her first steps calling out "Dada" as she walked to him. He thought of how pretty she was as a little girl sitting on a rock in the field as she basked in the sun. Memory upon memory flooded his thoughts. Now he beheld the woman she had become. She was pious and pure. She was mature beyond a woman of her age. Thomas knew she had a deep, devoted love for John and that she would be a loving wife and mother.

Thomas finally spoke. "My precious daughter, I, like your mother, dread the thought of this coming day. Now it is upon us. We taught you, but you had the heart to learn. We challenged you, and you found the courage to accept each challenge. We did our best to prepare you for your life. You have all the abilities, but the decision is yours to accept or reject this offer. I tell you now that you may face great hardship and sickness. You may have to face this alone. You do realize that we don't know John's whereabouts." Thomas then pulled her into his arms. "My girl, do you truly love John?"

She looked up to her father. "With all my heart."

Thomas smiled. "Then remain true to him always. I am sure he will find you."

Thomas called for all the family to come together, and while they embraced each other, Pastor led them in prayer.

Chastity realized life was an adventure. She didn't know where it would lead her or how things would turn out. The prospect of leaving family for a distant place was beyond her comprehension, especially given the fact that the ocean travel would be treacherous and the destination was still a wilderness. But this was Chastity's new beginning. She busied herself preparing her clothes and belonging for her departure. She had a small wooden box in which she put what clothes and few belongings she had.

This wasn't a pleasure cruise. There would be little privacy, and few could afford a change of clothes. When clothes had to be washed, a modesty curtain would be hung. Women removed their garments to wash them. Then waited for them to dry before dressing again. Children didn't seem to mind, but most found it quite embarrassing.

While Chastity was packing, her mother came to her with a sampler. The sampler was hand stitched and bore the names of grandparents, parents, and family members. There were other details of her life sewn in beautiful colors.

Ruth handed the sampler to her daughter. "I thought long and hard as to what I could give you to remind you of our love for you. Many years ago I began working on this to keep a record of our family. I started it when your father and I married. I want you to take it with you to remember us by."

Chastity replied, "Mother, I cannot take something that means so much to you."

Ruth smiled. "You are embarking on a new life. Someday your children will want to know about us. I want my grandchildren to know me. With this, you can tell them the story of us."

Later that afternoon, James and Martha came to the Shepherd home. From the time John had departed, Chastity made regular visits with the Dairyman family. James and his family loved Chastity like one of their own.

After a good visit, James handed her a letter. "I want you to give this to John when you see him. I wrote it with my own hands. Truth be told, Adam had to help me a little, but it's my letter. Thanks to you, I can write him now."

Martha then gave her two pewter plates and cups. "We haven't much, but you will be needing something to eat on. These are from our table to yours."

Chastity knew how valuable these gifts were. From their meager belongings, they were giving the best they had. She took the items and laid them down. She addressed James and Martha. "Mum and Dad, I love you so. I promise to make you proud."

By morning, Pastor drove his carriage to pick up Chastity. Paul and Leah were with him. Paul quickly exited and helped Leah down. Pastor loaded Chastity's lone box onto the carriage. The family came out to say their final goodbyes.

Pastor spoke words of comfort and purpose. "Once again, we see our loved ones parting from us to go the New World. When the first ones left here, they thought they would land at Jamestown. God, however, saw fit to push them much farther north to the place we now call Plymouth. Those early believers endured hardship, but by the Almighty's grace persevered, and the new colony survived. Even now, the people grow in number. You three will be added to that number, and it is our prayer that the Lord will bless you."

Then Elijah gave a charge to them. "Paul and Leah, may the Lord bless the child you now carry. Raise the child in God's own way. May the Lord prosper you and give you increase. Chastity, I pray that you will find John soon. Till that day, show the family you will be with the Spirit of God in all you do. When the time comes for your marriage, remember all that you have been taught and teach your children in the nurture and admonition of the Lord."

One by one, they all embraced before loading into the carriage. It was Thomas who whispered into Chastity's ear. "I want to be the one to give you away when you are married. That seems impossible. There is one thing I can give you. I give you my blessings. Remember our love for you, forever and always."

It was time to depart. The four climbed into the carriage, and Pastor urged the horses on. The New World awaited their arrival.

Two days later, the ship set sail. Their destination was Boston. Chastity, as with John, loved all she saw. There were a few women on board the ship, and they were quickly shown to the lower deck. There were no private rooms, just an open deck. Women were generally a distraction to the crew. For that reason, they were not permitted to walk about on the main deck. The entire journey across the Atlantic, for the most part, would be spent out of sight and out of mind. This was necessary for their protection against the elements and sailors who might be less scrupulous.

The *Elizabeth Marie* remained at Port Royal longer than expected. Sure enough, many of the crew refused to set sail with Captain Wise. New crewmen were recruited to join those who chose to return. Immediately, the balance between crewman was lost. The captain pushed the men to get the ship loaded. The newer crewmen were reluctant to help. To John's surprise, a horse was also loaded aboard.

Captain Wise took great pleasure in the horse and commented to Henry, "Isn't he beautiful?"

Captain Wise wanted to leave Port Royal as soon as he could, as he too was feeling suspicious. Many along the waterfront were taking notice of the cargo being loaded. The captain displayed an edginess, and the crew who knew him could see it. He wanted out of Port Royal. Still, only he knew the destination and the route he intended to take. The cargo was gold and jewels. He had been able to trade for more than he planned and congratulated himself on his success. He trusted that John's work would present him a greater fortune. He would be wealthier than even he could ever image.

John was glad that some of the regulars returned. He watched as Henry, Timothy, and Samuel boarded with a few others. Samuel and Timothy spent all they had on women and drink. Henry returned out of loyalty and love of the sea. As soon as the rest of the men boarded, the captain began giving orders. The old crew prepared for the departure, but the new crew seemed less inclined to do so. Many of the new men did not understand the commands. Henry called them landlubbers. Fact was, some of the men did not speak English, making it more difficult to communicate. The *Elizabeth Marie* was in chaos, to say the least.

Captain Wise paced the deck anxiously. He could see the lack of organization. Before, his crew had worked as one. They had been together a long time and only added new members from time to time. Now, the men did only what they were told to do. To make matters worse, none of the new men knew the cannons. On the crossing over, Henry had taught most how to use them. Those who did not return had been instrumental in Henry's organization. Now only four returned—barely enough for one cannon. Henry very much doubted the newcomers and their willingness to fight if necessary.

After being clamped in irons from his shore leave, John returned to his work on board ship. Long before the ship sailed, John went about making the much-needed repairs to the *Elizabeth Marie*. The old ship had taken a beating on the crossing. While at port, no major repairs were made. Even Timothy shook his head at the poor condition of the ship. "I fear a strong wind will shake her apart," he noted.

John's time alone on ship offered him one opportunity to escape. Much of the time while in port, John had been left alone. When no one was around, John made a key—a key that would unlock his restraints.

John knew that as long as he stayed busy, the captain would have little reason to suspect him. Whenever the captain looked for John, he would find him repairing the ship. When the captain left the ship or went back to his cabin, John would go to the bench and begin working on the key. Henry had allowed John to see the key, and John traced it quickly on a piece of wood. From that image, John created a replica. It took days to complete. Many first attempts failed. Those that failed he hid in the waste bucket, which he conveniently dumped over the side of the ship. Finally, he made a key that began moving the lock. He made small corrections until the lock opened. He tried it several times. More than ever, John felt like a free man. When the opportunity came, John would escape.

Captain Wise considered his course carefully. It was common knowledge that the Dutch would pester any ship that sailed too far south. Pirates watched ships leaving Port Royal. Wise hoped to fool the pirates by sailing west and then north around the island before heading east. The captain shared his plans with Henry and gave orders for him to carry them out.

At first, the plan looked flawless. The ship passed almost unnoticed as it sailed west and then north. The newly acquired map listed the names of the islands by their original names. They sailed east, passing north of Xaymaca. The waters were quiet. At night, the captain ordered the men to silence. In the morning, they resumed their journey, passing between the islands of Juana and Hispaniola.

John was restless and had a difficult time falling asleep. The breeze made the deck bearable, but below deck, the air was hot and stuffy. He was awakened by the sound of someone near. A soft feminine voice called out to him, "John, John darling." Chastity came to his side. She touched his shoulder. "I am on my way to you. I am making my way to America. I love you, my beloved, but I have come to warn you. Danger is near. You must be careful." She leaned over to kiss him. She was about to press her lips to his when he was shaken awake by Timothy.

"We must be vigilant, John. Hurry. Come with me."

John had been awakened from a beautiful dream.

Come dawn, the waters were still and the breeze gentle. John and Timothy busied themselves. The things spoken to John in the dream stayed with him. He thought to himself, *It was so real. Was the dream from God?* John did not take the dream lightly. He had learned to trust his instincts and any warning he got from God.

The ship sailed along on smooth waters, taking advantage of the gentle tropic breezes. By midmorning the ship approached the straight between the two Islands. A short time later, the captain commanded a more northeasterly direction. Richard Wise was congratulating himself on a well-laid course. The captain was heading for open seas. Then, as they were about to pass the last of the Caribbean Islands, a shout from above stirred fear within him.

A sailor perched high above shouted, "Ship on the starboard side!"

The captain rushed to that side of the ship. He could see nothing. The far-off ship was below the horizon and only visible from high above.

The captain ordered the sailor to keep watch on the ship and report its whereabouts. At first, he decided to make a run for it, but from the reports shouted from above, it was obvious that the distant ship was on a collision course to intercept them.

The captain ordered Henry to keep course, while he returned to the cabin to look over his maps. He carefully studied them. He determined that he could race up the coast for Virginia much quicker than trying to outrun the ship to England. It would be risky, as the course would take them through Spanish-controlled waters, but it was a risk he had to take. The captain left his cabin and called for Henry to take a reading. Henry plotted the ship's position and made his report. The captain was shocked that the winds did not favor their situation for a run to England.

The captain commanded, "Then take us north, Mr. Finch. We sail for Elizabeth City."

Though the cargo on board ship was lighter, which made the *Elizabeth Marie* faster than when heavily loaded, she was no match for her pursuer. The captain and Henry determined that it was much too fast for a Dutch ship. That could only mean one thing. It had to be pirates. Captain Wise realized that someone had tipped them off about Wise's cargo. Now it was a matter of experience. Captain Wise's abilities as a seaman and Henry's knowledge as a navy man was all that stood between disaster and success.

Throughout the day and into the night, they sailed. Constant course corrections and sail changes were being issued. The waters in these parts were treacherous, but they had no choice but to sail as far and as fast as they could. By dusk, the enemy was now in clear view. Henry guessed they were about seven miles away. Whoever the captain was, he knew these waters and how to make speed. The men were exhausted, and they needed rest. Henry ordered half the crew below to rest a while. He would schedule the relief of others in a few hours. Those who went to their hammocks found it hard to sleep. They only had a few hours of rest before relieving others. Many never slept, but a little rest was better than none.

Morning came, and a haze prevented anyone from being able to look too far behind the ship. Men took their positions. One man was ordered to climb the mast for a better view. Men were at the rail, gazing into the fog for any sign of their pursuer. All eyes were scanning the ocean. Men listened keenly for any sound that might prove to be a ship, but all they could hear was the waters being broken by the hull of the *Elizabeth Marie*. Any unusual noise made the men look, whether it was the buffing of the sails or the familiar groans of the ship.

Suddenly, someone sounded an alarm high above the ship. "Ship to starboard! Ship to starboard!"

The enemy had not only overcome the *Elizabeth Marie*, but its captain had managed to intercept them. He positioned himself as though he knew exactly what side to make his attack on. Captain Wise was in complete shock. He stood transfixed, looking into the haze. He could see nothing. Fear took his voice and reason.

Henry yelled at him. "Captain, your orders? Captain!"

There was no answer. Henry recognized this condition, having served with men newly acquainted to combat. He saw it firsthand years before when a young officer froze in battle and could not usher a word. In that moment, Henry had to take command. It was necessary to do it again.

Henry began ordering men to station. He needed time, because the cannons were on the port side, per Captain's orders. Quickly, he ordered two groups of men whom he had trained on the cannon below to move their stations to the starboard side. The men immediately rushed below and began the arduous task. On deck, Henry ordered others to prepare the ship for battle. Cutlass and pistol were given to every man. Henry knew that they were not trained in combat, and he had but one chance— one chance to attack and run away.

John was forgotten. Hearing the sounds around him, he knew he had to be free of his shackles if he was to be any help to Henry. John went to the place where he'd hidden the key. Within seconds, he released the lock of his shackles. He raced to the deck to see what help he might be. The haze was clearing, and the enemy could be seen a short distance from them. The captain was regaining his composure. He was surprised to see John free and upon the deck.

John called to Henry, "What do you need me to do?"

Henry replied quickly, "Grab a cutlass and pistol. You may have to defend yourself. Then check the charts. Make yourself aware of our position."

The captain called to John and Henry. "Delay that order."

Henry stood up to the captain with determination in his eyes. "There is no time to argue." Henry pointed to the enemy ship. "He will not wait, and you, Captain, are not fit for command, so stand aside. We have one chance of escape, and I haven't the time to argue with you."

The captain called back, "Escape?"

Henry replied, "That's right. Your opponent is a man of war. You are a merchant. Those men are used to attacking and plundering. Your men know how to sail. We need to strike fast and run. The longer the battle, the more likely we will lose everything."

The captain did not like what was being said, but he understood.

The enemy began to slowly close the distance. He tried to lure the *Elizabeth Marie* into firing her guns. Like a cat playing with a mouse, the enemy moved in and out of range. The pirate captain tried to get Henry to show his hand, but Henry would have nothing of it.

"Why haven't you fired at them?" Captain Wise inquired.

"That is exactly what he wants me to do," came Henry's reply.

"That man knows too much about us."

Captain Wise was stunned. "What do you mean?"

Henry responded, "For one, he knows that our vessel is not heavily armed. He knew which side the cannons were on. How did he know to approach us starboard side? I'll tell you why. Some of his crew are on board with us right now. Either that, or some of the men you disrespected turned informant. He knows what you are carrying on this ship, and he will have it."

Captain Wise turned pale at the news.

Henry assessed the situation. The enemy had their cannon ports open. The boarding party was armed and ready for the signal to attack. Henry also knew that he could not outmaneuver the enemy with so many sails deployed. He ordered sails in until only the main sail was pushing the ship. He ordered those that were taking in the sails to remain in the rigging.

John ran to his friend. There was a panic in his voice. "What are you doing?"

Henry remained focused, "Luring him in, Mr. Devine. He thinks we are about to surrender. Just watch and learn, my young friend."

Onward came the enemy. They were nearly in range. Without warning, two cannon shots were fired but fell short of their target.

Captain Wise screamed, "Fire back! Fire back!"

Henry shot an angry glance back at him. "Quiet, man!" Henry knew that the enemy wanted the *Elizabeth Marie*'s cannons empty. Henry would not bite or be baited. His experience at sea was the only hope the *Elizabeth Marie* had.

The enemy was in firing range. Henry heard the enemy's captain issue a command to aim, and with that, the cannons were immediately rolled back into position. While the enemy cannons were being rolled forward, Henry ordered a countercommand. "Open the gun ports. Ready the cannon."

The enemy captain was taken by surprise. His shouts of urgency were heard loud and clear.

Henry looked at Captain Wise and ordered, "Keep this course." Then, calling to John, he commanded, "If the captain or I fall, take over. I know you can do this." Henry raced below to command the cannons.

Suddenly, three of the crewmen on board the *Elizabeth Marie* pulled their swords and were about to attack some of others. John shouted the alert in time for the crewmen to avoid the attack. A short skirmish followed before the three assailants were forced overboard. The pirate captain had hoped his crewmen aboard the *Elizabeth Marie* might take out a few of the men aboard, thus disheartening the rest. Then the cannons from the enemy ship began to roar. The shots were true. The first shot hit the railing around the helmsmen, killing him instantly. Shards of wood shot through the air, seriously wounding the captain. Seeing the abandoned whipstaff, John rushed to the helm, grabbed it, and took over the duties of his fallen mate.

John saw the enemy pull back the cannons for reloading. Now it was Henry's turn. John heard the two guns of the *Elizabeth Marie* being fired. Both cannons were aimed at the main mast of the ship. One hit it, and the sturdy timber cracked. As quick as the guns were fired, Henry ordered them reloaded. The cannons were being rolled back at the same instant the cannons of the enemy ship were being rolled back in place. Once again, they roared. One shot hit the deck, killing two crewmen. John held the course as ordered by Henry.

Captain Wise uttered, "Take evasive action."

John ignored him.

The *Elizabeth Marie's* cannons, now reloaded, were rolled back to place. Quickly, they were aimed and fired. Both shots hit the enemy ship at the waterline. Henry rushed back on deck and shouted to the men at the sails. "Deploy full sails!" He knew his shots into the enemy ship had reached their mark.

However, the enemy was not done. The pirate captain ordered the cannon reloaded, aimed, and fired. The angry roar echoed all around the *Elizabeth Marie*. One shot hit the deck, and Henry fell. John was shocked to see his friend lying on the ground.

John called to the crew, "See to Mr. Finch and take him below deck. Then come back and take the captain down. Ask Timothy to take care of them."

Henry's skills as a sailor had given them time to escape. The enemy ship was damaged and taking on water. The strategic shots would soon reveal Henry's plan. The enemy's captain was in a rage. He watched his prize pull away and ordered sails dropped. A heavy gust of wind hit the main sail, and the mast snapped, causing the great timber to fall across the deck. Pirates rushed away from the timber. One man who was in the rigging was catapulted into the sea. The pirates recovered quickly from the sudden shock of the falling mast and returned their attention to the escaping *Elizabeth Marie*. The captain was angry and demanded satisfaction.

The *Elizabeth Marie* was gaining speed and pulling away. The pirate captain ordered one more round of cannon fire. John thought the ship was free and clear when a sudden broadside hit on the aft part of the ship. The shot left a gaping hole, and water was rushing into the *Elizabeth Marie*.

With the captain and Henry down, it was up to John to get them out of danger. He was now in charge and alone at the helm. The deck was full of debris. John could not take his eyes off the place where Henry fell. A lump was in his throat, but there wasn't time to think about it. He fought the whipstaff. Adrenaline and fear gave him stamina that he had not known before. John gave orders to organize the ship and clear the debris. He called for full sail in hopes of putting distance between them and the enemy. As each sail dropped and filled with air, the ship seemed harder to handle. Still, he had to escape, and distance was the only hope. He was afraid to even look aft. It wasn't till much later that one of the crew informed him that the attackers were nowhere in sight.

From the helm, he ordered men to begin inspecting the ship. Below deck, Henry and the captain were fighting for their lives from the wounds they'd received. Four crewmen lost their lives in the battle, and five more were wounded, but they would mend. Then came the shocking news. Timothy sent word that the ship was taking on water from a large hole made by the last cannon shot.

Things looked dire, but John remembered the last command made to him. "If I or the captain fall, you are to take over the ship."

Crewmen were looking for leadership. John realized he had to be that leader. There was no time to think about Henry or the captain. John had to consider the safety of the men, and they were looking to him to lead.

John cleared his mind. He could ill afford any form of distraction. Right now, the men needed leadership, and he was the one called upon to give it. John started issuing commands. Where he found the clarity to take command no one knows, but none of the crew questioned his authority. That was good. The last thing anyone needed was a struggle for command during times of crisis. John took count in his mind the remaining crew and who was doing what. Eight capable men were all that remained. If Timothy was making repairs, another crewman had to be tending to the wounded. John surmised he could handle the ship with three men on deck. One of the orders issued was to check on Timothy. John knew Henry and the captain needed care, but there was one other patient who needed attention. Her name was *Elizabeth Marie.*

The report was clear. Water was coming in aft and to the starboard side. John knew what had to be done. He called for Samuel to come up. When Samuel arrived, John ordered him to take two men below to move the load to the port. He ordered the cannon to be moved first and then the rest of the cargo. He hoped that by shifting the load, it would force the ship to port, thus lifting the hole above the waterline. It took several hours, but to everyone's surprise, it worked.

John order another crew member named Philip Martin to the helm. Philip was strong and possessed some knowledge of the sea. John knew he had to make a full assessment of the ship, and he couldn't do it as long as he was at the helm. Looking to Philip, he commanded, "Take the whipstaff, Mr. Martin."

Philip was hesitant. "I don't know how to handle the ship."

John looked sternly back at the crewman. "Philip, I need you to do as I say. I have every confidence you can do this, and there is no time like the present to learn."

In short order, John showed Philip how to firmly handle the whipstaff and keep course. John gave one final order. "You have open sea ahead of you. Don't hit anything."

Philip became wide-eyed.

Feeling confident that above deck was secure, John raced below to see what needed done. He found Timothy making repairs to the ship's hull. Timothy's complaint was there weren't enough materials to fix it properly. John understood and told Timothy to do the best he could. He then went below to see how Samuel progressed with the shifting of the load. He and the crew were nearly done. As John headed back topside, he took count in his head. One man was unaccounted for. He searched the ship and found the lone crewman cowering among the cargo.

John approached him. "What are you doing here?" he asked. John knew this man was one of the replacements and sensed something was wrong. Without warning, the man lunged at John with a knife in his hand. The man yelled something in Spanish. There was no doubt in John's mind that this was another assailant who escaped the attention of the crew earlier.

The Spaniard slashed at John with the knife. John managed to step aside but not before receiving a cut across the side of his left arm. The cut hurt, and John quickly covered it with his right hand. There wasn't any time to consider the wound. The Spaniard came charging again, thrusting the knife in the direction of John's stomach. John managed to avoid each thrust, but all of a sudden, the attacker slashed back at his stomach, inflicting another cut.

John felt anger like he'd never known before. In his mind, he began seeing the bodies of the dead sailors killed in the attack. From John's lips, escaped the words, "You brought all this on us. You would steal from us what we risked our lives to gain. If that wasn't enough, you would kill me for no reason."

The Spaniard looked confused by what John was saying. John showed no fear and kept his composure. John found a piece of wood that was once part of the ship's hull and picked it up. He approached the assailant slowly and deliberately. It was the attacker's turn to deal with fear. He looked into John's eyes and saw John meant business. Then, seeing the crimson stain on John's shirt, he attacked wildly once more. The Spaniard wildly slash at John with the knife. This time, John swung back, striking the assailant's side. Then, swinging back, he caught the man beside the head. The Spaniard fell to the deck. The man began to lift himself up when John hit him once more, knocking him out cold.

John reached down and took the knife from the Spaniard's hand. A leather sheath for the knife hung to his side. John took them both and proclaimed, "You won't be needing this anymore."

John approached two crewmen. He told them of the Spaniard and where to find him. Then he ordered, "Tie him to the mask so everyone can see the enemy up close." John returned to see how Timothy was doing. To John's relief, his friend had managed to slow the water flowing in. Everyone's efforts were paying off. John inspected the work. Additional patching might help, but with everything else that needed attention, there just wasn't time.

John quickly made his way to the captain's cabin. Maps lay strewn across the floor. He quickly gathered them. There were marks made by the captain that showed his position, but from the moment of the chase, no additional marks had been made. Navigation was dependent on time and distance. Without this information, it was a guessing game. John went on deck, took measurements, and returned to the cabin. As best as he could determine, the ship was somewhere off the coast of Florida. His calculation put them about thirty miles east of the Spanish Fort called Augustine.

John wanted nothing to do with the Spanish-held fort. He went to Philip to show him how to make a course correction. John was glad the ship responded to the whipstaff. Slowly, the crippled vessel changed course. The new course was northeast. As soon as it was obtained, John ordered Philip, "Keep her steady, Mr. Martin. I shall return shortly."

Philip wrinkled his brow. "Might you find someone to spare me, Mr. Devine—er, I mean, Captain?"

John answered, "I will do my best. This I promise."

John surveyed the ship. The remaining crew were working well together. Many were men who served the ship for years. They were fewer in number, but they knew their duty. John was grateful for all for their efforts. He wanted to thank them, but time didn't permit it. He sought out Samuel and asked him to prepare food. John then went to Henry and Captain Wise. Henry was still unconscious. The captain was awake and pale.

The captain nonetheless remained defiant. "What think ye be doing? This is still my ship."

John looked at him and firmly replied, "Which I am doing my best to save." John leaned over the man to make sure their eyes were fixed. "A lot of good men died today thanks to you. Your precious cargo is safe. That is, for now. Know this: I am fighting a new enemy. An enemy called time. I don't know how much time we have before we lose everything." John turned to walk away but called back, "I will not lose another man."

The captain did not hear, because he'd fallen back unconscious, overcome by the pain.

John found Timothy making final repairs to the hole in the hull. Approaching the carpenter, he said, "Thanks for all you've done.

Unfortunately, there is much more to do. I know you are exhausted. Will the repair hold?"

Timothy answered candidly. "The captain did not replenish the necessary supplies to make repairs. I took from other parts of the ship to do what I could. We need to make landfall in order for me to gather the materials."

John looked at the old carpenter. "I'm afraid that will be impossible. We are still in enemy waters. More importantly, I don't know which enemy we might face next."

All through the day, the *Elizabeth Marie* struggled to stay afloat. John divided the crew into shifts so they could rest. John took advantage of the moonless night and ordered a northwesterly course. Order seemed to finally come to the crew. There was still a lot of anger, and some of the men wanted to throw the Spaniard overboard. John did not trust the man, but he could not bring himself to do that. He talked the men down. He would not be guilty of murder.

John went on deck to take over for Philip. "Take your rest, Mr. Martin. I shall send for you later."

Philip relinquished the ship to John. He immediately grabbed his arms. The ache from the exertion seemed to cramp his suddenly relaxed muscles.

John laughed. "My friend, I very much doubt you'll ever forget this experience."

"Friend." Philip felt honored to be entrusted with such great responsibility and to be called John's friend.

Some six hours later, Philip returned to take over for John. Weary men rose from their hammocks to give relief to others. Those who slept relived the events of the day in their minds, causing them to jerk awake.

John's sleep was anything but restful. He wanted Chastity to come to him again. She did not come. He whispered to her, "Your warning saved us. Pray, my love, that we might be delivered."

John was shaken awake. Timothy looked down on the new captain and said, "Land has been sighted. We are getting close to the coastline."

John hurried on deck. From this distance, the land looked green and lush. There were no ships in sight. A heavy wind was blowing up from the south, and John feared that a new menace was approaching. This time, nature was about to usher in her own challenge.

John noted that the ship was riding lower. He went below and discovered the water was more than waist deep. Virginia seemed less likely. Returning to the deck, he found Philip exhausted. John took over for him and ordered, "Hurry down and bring the carpenter here."

Philip did as ordered.

John fought the sinking ship with all of his strength. As soon as John saw Timothy, he ordered him to come up. "Mr. Bowman, we are sinking, and there is a storm approaching. How are the longboats? We may have no choice but to abandon ship. Prepare the longboats in case we have to do just that. Load Henry and the captain into one. Hurry, for I do not know how much time we have."

Timothy hung his head. John asked what was wrong, to which Timothy replied, "I made repairs to the ship from one of the longboats. It will not hold in a storm."

John understood. He tied the whipstaff such that the rudder was straight. He hurried down and brought individual bags of gold for each man. Racing back on deck, he handed each man one of the bags.

John stated, "I wish I could give you more. You deserve it. I hope we all make it. John watched as the unconscious Henry was loaded into the boat. When the other men were loaded, it was obvious that there wasn't room for another lifeless body. John ordered Samuel to bring the Spaniard. As soon as he was released, the Spaniard pushed Samuel aside, rushed to the deck, and threw himself into the ocean. Samuel ran after him. He leaned over the rail, but there was no sign of the man.

John saw how full the craft was. It wouldn't be safe to add another soul. Addressing Timothy, he commanded, "Join the men, my dear friend. Get them to safety."

Timothy looked with admiration at young man he once thought so little of. Now he asked, "What about you?"

John pointed. "See for yourself that there is no room. I will stay with the captain. After all, he is my master." Timothy started to argue, but John cut him off. "There is no time to discuss this more." Then, pointing to the approaching storm, he added, "That will be upon us before long. Go, Timothy. May God be with you."

Reluctantly, the old man boarded the longboat and shoved off. It was now just the captain and John left aboard a sinking ship.

John watched the vessel pull away. He remained concerned for their safety and wondered if Henry would make it. The longboat was safely away. There was no time to waste; he set his attention to the task of making for the shore. He estimated the distance to be about twelve miles. From the south, the dark clouds rolled in. The jagged slashes of lightning stabbed at the ocean. John struggled to turn the ship. Slowly, it responded to rudder. John did not have time to check the depth of the water in the hull. How low the ship rode let him know the ship was being pulled downward. Once more, he secured the whipstaff. The wind increased, and the waves grew more intense, but the weight of the boat made it plow through the water instead of rising over each one.

The skies grew darker and darker. Lightning flashes illuminated the shoreline. John could not see waves crashing upon it, though the smooth surface assured him it was sandy. The last thing he needed was a rocky shore. John estimated the distance to be about five miles.

John rushed back to check the captain. He was still out cold. John secured him to the deck as best he could with ropes. He didn't have time to take the man to his cabin. Then he rushed forward to measure the depth of the water. He dropped the lead line. He counted the marks. *One, two, three ... only three marks. How can this be?* He was still a mile or so from shore. The fierceness of the storm was driving the *Elizabeth Marie* toward land. John kept checking the depth, *Two marks*. He thought, *The ship will run aground very—* He didn't even have time to finish the thought. John was thrown forward and landed hard on his back and head as the ship ran aground.

John lay upon the deck for a long time. The rain on his face brought him to his senses. The wind was blowing harder, and he felt cold. A heavy downpour of rain nearly choked him. Rolling over, he got to his knees. His forehead received a cut when he was knocked to the ground, and from it, a small trickle rolled down his face.

He crawled over to the captain. The impact also threw the captain forward. Captain Wise was still covered, but his clothes were soaked. John stood and staggered to the captain's cabin to retrieve blankets. Returning, John covered the captain to shield him from the pouring rain. The storm was becoming more intense. As long as the sails remained deployed, they would drive the ship inland. The waves lifted the ship, and the filled sails drove it toward shore. It seemed like Mother Nature was punishing the ship for daring to cross her ocean.

John got to his feet and pulled the Spaniard's knife from its sheaf. He began cutting the tether lines to the main sail. As soon as the lines were cut, the sail began whipping freely in the wind. Without the largest sail, the ship seemed to settle down into the sandy bottom. John staggered forward to cut the lines on another sail, but a boom still attached to it broke free, striking John in the back of the head. John hit the deck with a great force. All was black.

The morning sun shone heavy on John, and he felt the warmth of its radiant heat. He came to slowly. He wiped his face and felt the dry salt and sand left on him by the ocean. The waves receded from the shore, and the ship was steadfast. The hull was still in the water. John rolled over and slowly stood to his feet. He staggered and fell. He shook his head and stood once more. His attention was directed skyward from the sound of the torn sail flapping in the morning breeze.

John made his way to the captain. He was very pale but still clinging to life. John uncovered the captain and looked over his wounds. The bleeding had stopped. His body was dry and cool. John knew they needed nourishment and dry clothes. There would be time enough later to inspect the ship.

John released the captain from the ropes and carried him to his cabin. He carefully lifted him into his bunk and then he removed his boots and wet clothing. The captain's skin was wrinkled from being wet too long. John fetched water to wash the salt and sand from the man. By the time John finished, the bucket of water was milky. When he was all done, John covered Richard. It was now time for some food.

John went below deck and looked over the galley. He found enough dry wood to start a fire. He boiled water and put some salted pork in it, and the water slowly became a thick broth. He brought the soup to the captain. Looking around the cabin, he found a bottle of wine. He sat next to the captain and spoon-fed him small amounts of broth and wine. The captain naturally supped each spoonful. It took a long time, but the captain drank it all. John made a little more, and the captain took that nourishment as well. For now, that was all John could do. When the captain finished eating, he drifted off into a deep sleep.

Once the captain was stable, John began the arduous task of inspecting the ship. John went below to the hull to check the condition. Much of the water had escaped, but it was still knee-deep. The opening made by the cannon shot was too much for the ship. The repair made by Timothy kept the water from rushing in and gave sufficient time for their escape. John walked forward in the hull. He heard a stirring. John feared that there was another stowaway on board.

He called out, "I don't know who you are. Come on out, and no harm will come to you."

No one came out or made a sound. Then he heard a stomping sound. John moved forward and was startled by the whinny of the young horse. The young Appaloosa was calling for attention. The sight of the horse made John smile for the first time in a long time.

He walked over to the horse to inspect his condition. It was obvious that the horse had been in water up to his chest. How the animal remained calm during the day's ordeal he did not know. John pondered who was in charge of caring for the animal. Then it occurred to him that the Spaniard he found below deck might have been brought on for just that purpose. John now questioned if the man really had been an enemy. John realized that he had another to care for. The horse was hungry and needed water. All the hay below was wet, and the only water he could find was salt water. The horse needed care, and he had to get it off the ship soon.

John was thankful that he had watched the crew load the horse. It took several men to do the job. John didn't have that luxury. He would have to find a way to do it all himself. There was no way for John to walk the animal to the deck. He would have to find a way to lift it from the hull. Right now, the issue was much-needed food for the animal. John climbed back up to the deck and made his way to the ground. He walked over to some grass and sea oats. He gathered as much as he could carry and took it back to the horse. As soon as it was laid before him, the horse began chomping away at the special treat.

While the horse ate, John set about surveying the damage. The four cannons had been thrown forward by the impact, but the rest of the cargo was still secure. Then John came upon the gruesome sight of those who died in the fight. The bodies of the dead men were still lying side by side just as they had been laid. John was unprepared for such a sight. It made him sick. He rushed from the men to another location. His stomach lurched, and he gasped for air to settle his stomach. Tears filled his eyes.

John regained his composure. He left the ship with a shovel and walked inland. Finding a place where he was confident flood waters would not reach, he dug a common grave big enough for the four men to be laid. Once the task was done, he returned to the ship and set up a boom to lower the bodies to the ground. He laid each man down to his final resting place. He made four separate trips, interrupted each time with a visit to the captain to check on him.

When the task was done, John stood overlooking the grave. He felt very much alone. He was tired and exhausted, but he knew there was so much more to do. He had to decide what to do with the ship, the captain, and the cargo. Looking at the grave, he struck upon the solution. He must bury the wealth and other precious items. He would draw a map and retrieve things as he needed them. He would also dig a dugout and make it livable so that the captain could recover. Once everything was removed, he would find a way to destroy the ship.

John took time to survey the land. He walked east from the ship and traveled a little more than a mile. On top of a sandy dune, he learned that he was on an island. Before him was more water. He began to question his navigation. Had he miscalculated? He saw the charts and took measurements. He second-guessed himself. Surely, he was farther north than Florida. He had little time to think about it and hurried back to the ship. There was enough space on the island to do what he wanted. His fear was that pirates or Spaniards might pass this way. If he were discovered, he was a dead man.

John was careful not to stay away for very long. With each and every trip away from the ship, John returned to first checked on the captain. The captain was still very pale. After returning from his island exploration, John went to him and offered him fresh water. This time the captain refused. Thinking the captain did not like water, he tried wine, but once again, the man was aware enough to not want any of that either.

John called to Richard, "Captain, can you hear me?"

Richard Wise only mumbled. John took hope. This was the first sign he'd had that the man just might recover. John let his captain rest.

He stood and walked over to look at the maps. Selecting the right one, he tore a large enough piece from it. He drew upon it a five-pointed star. He would add the details to it as he went along. His first mark would be the grave he dug for the four crewmen. From that point, he would coordinate the remaining points on the star. His idea was to bury the items and build a dugout within the pentagon of the star. He would then establish points on the star to remind him of the location of all that which he buried. Hopefully, he was being cunning enough to ward off strangers and treasure seekers. If they happened on one part, they might not find the rest.

John turned his attention to getting the horse off the ship. The *Elizabeth Marie* was no ark. There was no side door for animals to exit. John recalled that when the horse was loaded, a harness was used. He tried to remember how the sailors were able to get the horse loaded to begin with. He recalled that a boom was attached to the main mast, and block and tackles were used to lift the cargo from the hold. Once clear of the deck, the cargo would be swung clear of the ship and lowered to another ship or dock. He thought, *I don't think the horse will like it.*

Scouring the cargo holds and hull, John found what he was looking for. A large piece of leather that would fit the animal's girth was hanging near where the horse was tied. Metal rings were attached to each corner. John understood how the horse could be safely lifted. The difficulty was that no one would be able to assist in keeping the horse calm. Being lifted in the air would spook the animal for sure. If the horse fought, it could work itself free and fall, thus breaking the horse's leg.

As soon as the rigging was ready, John walked the horse to the hold. The horse reacted just as he suspected. When lifted the least little distance, the horse pawed the air, turning this way and that. John realized he had to calm the horse first and find a way to keep it that way.

John lowered the animal but kept the large leather harness in place. He found a cloth bag and cut the bottom out of it. Returning to the horse, John slid the bag over its nose and up his head, covering his eyes. At first, the horse tried to resist but soon settled down. John tied the bag above the head. A few minutes later, the horse was quiet. Once more, John began lifting the horse from the lower deck. John breathed a sigh of relief because the horse remained calm.

Slowly, carefully, and ever so gently is the only way to describe the way John lifted the horse. John realized that as long as the horse remained in the harness, it would be difficult for it to breath. He knew if he raised the horse too fast, the movement might startle it, causing it to fight for its freedom. To calm the horse, John kept talking to it and patting it from time to time for reassurance.

After several minutes, the horse was lifted above the deck. Painstakingly, John moved the boom over the side. Then he began reversing the order, lowering the horse toward the beach. Finally, the horse touched down on land. The sensation caused the horse to move in circles. John hurried over the side of the ship to the horse and removed the large leather harness before removing the bag. As soon as the bag was removed, the horse began surveying its surroundings. John led the horse over to where some fresh sea grass was growing. Immediately, the horse sniffed at it and began to pick and pull grass to curb his appetite. John took a deep breath. *So far, so good.* John tied the horse to a nearby tree and let him graze.

That evening, John went again to the central part of the island. He went north from the grave he had dug for the sailors. The location he fixed upon was covered with tropical grasses and trees. He felt he could accomplish his plan there and leave the earth relatively unscarred, thus concealing all that he planned to do. He determined where the dugout would be and immediately began digging an eight-by-eight pit. The pit would only be a little more than five feet deep. The sand moved easily, and by late evening, he had finished what he started. He stopped, knowing that he had to get back to the ship and care for the captain and himself. For the first time in days, he was hungry.

John made more broth for the captain and prepared for himself some vegetables to go along with the salt pork. John ate heartily. It felt good to have a full belly. Returning to the captain, he tried to feed him broth. The captain refused any nourishment. John drank a little wine and offered some to the captain. Again, the captain refused.

John went below and gathered his Bible. It had been days since he'd last read from it. He opened the book and read from the Psalms. "The

Lord is my Shepherd, I shall not want." The old psalm spoke to him. He was cared for and protected by the Almighty. He then recalled that he prayed to be delivered to America. He prayed for deliverance. Both had been accomplished. Not in the way he suspected, but indeed, his prayers had been answered.

John realized that he felt no malice toward the captain. He knew the man was growing weaker. Even now the captain struggled for each breath. John knew he had to convince the captain to take nourishment, or surely, he would die. John wanted the captain to recover.

John lit a single candle. In the darkness, the captain stirred. He called out, "Elizabeth! Elizabeth!"

John went to him. "Captain, I am here."

Richard Wise was crying. He looked at John, and just above a whisper, he asked, "What has happened?"

John replied, "We were attacked and nearly taken. Henry managed to secure our escape. In so doing, several have died. Henry was also severely wounded. The ship was nearly sunk, and we had to abandon ship. Only you and I could not fit in the longboat. I stayed with the ship and managed to run her aground. You and I are alone on an island. Alone, that is, unless you count the horse."

Richard looked at his caregiver. "John, I know I am dying. Why didn't you leave me to die?"

John replied, "I could never do that. You are my captain, and I serve the living God. He was ever with us, and it is by His grace that we have made it to shore. As my Father in heaven has never left me, I would never leave you."

Richard cried, "Even after all I did to you?"

John smiled. "Even after all that."

Richard struggled with each word he spoke. "Would you do something for me?"

John answered, "Of course."

Richard pointed to a box and asked him to retrieve it. John brought it over, and Richard directed him to open it. He explained, "I free you of all debt on one condition. That you see to the care of my wife and daughter." Tears began to fill Richard's eyes as he told his story. "I left years ago to be a sailor. I know Elizabeth never divorced or remarried. From time to time when I returned to England, I would check on her and always leave her with enough money to live on. I managed through a broker to see to her finances and care. We have one child."

John interrupted. "You named her Marie."

Richard smiled. "Yes. I ask that you continue to see to their care. I know I cannot." Richard struggled to get the next words out. "I still love her, you know. She came from a family of stature and means. Her father never approved of our marriage. I was a failure in business, and that drove me to become a sailor. I wanted to make her proud, have her family's approval, and provide for her as she deserved."

Richard choked and struggled for a breath of air. "Please do this for me. This was to be my last voyage. I hoped with the wealth I had gained to return to England and live the rest of my life with Elizabeth and Marie. I even bought the horse for my daughter."

John smiled. "Well, that explains the horse."

Richard's eyes began to fade. "See to my loved ones' care. Tell my wife that I am dead and encourage her to remarry. Tell her I ... I still ..." Richard fell into unconsciousness.

John took Richard's hand. "All right. This I promise. I will find a way."

John held Richard's hand as he prayed silently. When he finished, he looked over at the captain. Richard Wise's journey on this earth had ended. The death of Richard Wise was another blow John was not prepared for. John had never experience death so closely as he had the past few days. There was no joy in seeing the lifeless body of his captain. John had come to realize in the last few moments of the captain's life that he was a broken man—that he wanted to prove his worthiness. John could only imagine the pain Richard had gone through—pain that manifested itself in anger and greed.

John began looking at the contents of the box. For a long while, John read over the records of the ship's logs. Then he chanced upon a letter written by Elizabeth several years before.

Richard,

I woke this morning touching your side of the bed. It was so cold and lonely. My love, what did I do that made you want to leave me? Am I not a good wife? I learned you became a sailor. When you come to port, please come to me. Little Marie wants to see her papa. She cries all the time for you. I want to be held by the man I love. I don't care want my family thinks. I love you, and I will have no other. Please come home. Come home, my darling. Come home.

Elizabeth

John looked at the lifeless body of Captain Richard Wise. "It will be my pleasure to do all I can, Captain."

The next day John buried the captain near the others. He made up his mind that before he left the island, he would make markers for the graves. He took out the paper he was making into a map and marked the exact locations of the graves. John was feeling the despair of his situation. He knew he had to stay busy or be overcome by reality. He hurried back to the ship. On board, he made his way down to Timothy's tools and gathered saws and hammers. He climbed back on deck and began marking sections to cut out. He would use each piece to line his dugout. The captain's cabin was the logical choice for what he needed. John began cutting out panels of the wall that he could handle. It took a lot of time just to free up one section. Once finished, he lowered each section to the ground and then went down and dragged each to the dugout. It took the greater part of the day, but by evening, the flooring and four walls were in place. Tomorrow, he would see to the roof and trapdoor.

The morning light revealed John making the first cuts of the day. His arms ached, and his back was sore from the previous day's labors. A sense of fear drove him. He sawed away at what would become the roof. He tied ropes to the section and secured it to the rigging before making the final cuts. The first roof piece now dangled freely in the air. Over the side, he swung the panel and lowered it to the ground. Climbing down, he just stared and knew it would take a lot of work to move the heavy roof. He spoke out loud to himself, "Well, it isn't going to get there on its own."

He began pulling and dragging the roof to its location. It took two hours, but he finally got it to the sandy pit. He was exhausted. Throughout the day, he repeated the process. He was ever so thankful when the last cut was made, and all parts were finally delivered to the dugout.

It was late in the day before John was ready to place the roof on the concealed hideaway. He removed the boom and tackle from the ship and took it to the location. John climbed one of the trees overlooking the walls with a block and tackle in tow. The tree was large enough to hang a boom to it. Once the boom was secured, he attached the block and tackle to the end of it. Now he could swing each panel over to the dugout. He climbed down and secured the line to the first piece. He pulled on the rope, lifting the first about waist high. Then he swung the panel over the pit. He lowered it in place and then climbed into the dugout to secure it to the walls. He repeated the process for the second and third sections as well. When night came, John saw that everything was where it was supposed to be.

Still, he pushed himself. He made an opening in the roof for an access door. When this was done, he surveyed it all, satisfied with his underground hideout. It was a place for rest, storage, and safety. John was worn and weary. Now was the time to rest. Tomorrow he would conceal his hideaway.

# Peril

Danger can come in many forms. It can come in nature or manmade disasters. It can also come in beastly form or as a person. People can find themselves in peril without any doing of their own. Chastity was about to experience such an event.

Paul and Leah Stitch were wonderful traveling companions. While the women were for the most part separated from the men, Paul and Leah found time every day to be together. Chastity admired the way Paul doted over his wife. It was obvious that he loved Leah. From time to time, Chastity would catch them in a loving embrace or find Paul rubbing Leah's shoulders or tummy. Chastity thought about how much she wished it was John and her taking this trip. She imagined John would be just as loving to her as Paul was to Leah.

Their trip to America was now in its fifth week. The passengers spent nearly all the trip below deck. On this day, the passengers were invited to come on board for fresh air and sunshine. As the passengers came on deck, they shielded their eyes from the bright sunlight. The warmth of the sun, the freshness of the wind, and the taste of salt in the air made everyone appreciate the opportunity. When the women came on deck, some of the less disciplined sailors made inappropriate jesters and comments. Such things angered the men and made the women uncomfortable. To everyone's surprise, the captain said nothing.

Captain Noah Barkley informed the passengers that if the prevailing winds remained favorable, he hoped to reach their destination in two weeks. The news brought a sense of joy to all those aboard. They could not wait to be back on dry land. They hated being kept below deck. The huddling of people, the smell of human waste, the limited ventilation, and the lack of hygiene added to the discomfort. While on deck, the sailors made the women feel uneasy by their lewd comments.

One of the sailors approached Chastity. The way he looked at her caused her to hide behind Paul.

The sailor uttered, "Eh, Lassie, how about a bit of slap and tickle?"

Other sailors had a hardy laugh at Chastity's expense. As soon as the words were said, the sailor was spun around and received a serious backhanded slap across the face from one of the male passengers. The sailor fell to the deck.

Nathan Porter loomed over him. "How dare you talk to a lady like that." The sailor started to rise, but Nathan placed his foot on his neck. "Apologize to the lady."

The sailor tried to move Nathan's foot.

Nathan stepped harder. "I said, apologize!"

Chastity came forward. "Please don't hurt him."

Nathan smiled and responded, "I shall do more than that if this rogue refuses." Then, turning his attention to the filthy little man, he demanded, "Out with it."

Reluctantly, the sailor responded, "Sorry, miss."

Nathan raked his boot down the man's throat. "I best never hear of you disrespecting this lady here or any other place."

The sailor grabbed his throat, rose to his feet, and went back to his duties.

Nathan turned to Chastity and tipped his hat. He introduced himself. "I am sorry that you had to experience such rude behavior. My name is Nathan Porter, and may I have the pleasure of knowing whom I am addressing?"

Chastity was very much taken by Nathan's gentlemanly ways. Dipping her chin, she answered, "My name is Chastity Shepherd. Pleased to make you acquaintance."

Nathan assured, "The pleasure is all mine."

Taking her right hand, he kissed her fingers. Chastity held her left hand across her stomach. Nathan took notice of the beautiful ring but said nothing more. Nathan stood tall and looked about for the captain. When he found him, he called with authority, "Captain, a word, if you please."

Nathan once more tilted his hat to excuse himself and then walked over to Captain Barkley.

Nathan made his way to the captain, but all the while kept glancing back at Chastity. He was taken in by her beauty and innocence. Chastity had never experienced such gallantry. She was thankful to Nathan for his intervention but had no other interest. Chastity was raised believing women were to be respected. She did not know that some women in London society would seek a man's attention, oftentimes by provoking a situation. Chivalry was always appreciated. Nathan's dress and manner suggested that he was a man of culture. If she had known Nathan's thoughts, she might have been more alarmed.

The passengers remained below deck for the remainder of the trip. Just as the captain predicted, the ship made sight of Cape Cod within two weeks. The Dutch settlement of New Amsterdam was his present concern. English shipping kept clear of the Dutch if at all possible. They passed the Cape and were relieved to be in safer waters. The captain headed the ship east, around the horn of the cape. Once beyond that point, he headed for the new settlement of Boston. By evening, the tiny lights of the town were visible. The news made the passengers extremely excited. Chastity's emotions ranged from excitement to loneliness and fear.

The shores of Boston represented a new world—a new beginning. Far behind her lay the green shores of England. The land before them was that of vast forest and wilderness. Chastity thought, *Who would have ever imagined a poor country girl moving to a faraway land?* Her heart ached for her family more than she could have ever imagined. She missed the morning chill, the smells of fresh bread baking, and her father pulling on his boots. Tears welled up in her eyes as she thought of her family, while at the same time, her thoughts were filled with joy because of John.

Where was he? She thought how great it would be if he was there to greet her on the shore. She could imagine the wonderful surprise of him standing waiting for her, but she had no idea where he was or even if he was alive. The thought that he might not be alive scared her. She pushed the thought from her mind and proclaimed to herself, *No, I can't think like this. He is alive. I know it.*

The ship was still a good distance from the shore when the captain gave the order to drop anchor. The ship dropped anchor at Mill Cove.

Sailors hurried to take in sail and prepared longboats to be lowered. Passengers could hardly wait to begin their decent to the longboats that would take them to shore. The captain invited the passengers up on deck as soon as it was safe to do so. On top deck the passengers squinted their eyes against the afternoon sun. In the distance they could see boats and barges leaving the dock to meet the ship and to help with the off-loading of cargo and goods.

In town, word spread of the ship's arrival. Settlers knew that arriving ships would bring precious cargo and loved ones. Items from England were highly desired. There was also a sense of excitement to see newcomers who came to join the ever-growing population. Bostonians knew passengers brought news from home. It did not matter if it the new folks were family or not. All that mattered was word from England.

For nearly four months, one of the residents of Boston, a Mr. George Abernathy, expected a governess's arrival. George and Susan Abernathy were very excited to have a governess to help with the care of their children. George's request was that the woman who came was of the greatest moral character and intelligence. So news of the ship meant the governess might have arrived. Mind you, they had been disappointed before when no governess came. They were nonetheless hopeful as they made their way to the dock that today would be different.

On board the ship, Nathan approached Chastity and offered to escort her to shore. Chastity politely refused. "Thank you, Mr. Porter, but I am here with Paul and Leah Stitch and will be accompanying them."

Nathan smiled. "There will be plenty enough room for all of us. It's just that I would like the privilege to get to know you more."

Chastity politely refused. "That will hardly be necessary. You see, Mr. Porter, I am betrothed to Mr. Jonathan Devine, and we hope to be married soon."

Nathan, in coy fashion, replied, "I find it hard to believe that the man you are betrothed to would send you on a dangerous voyage unaccompanied."

Chastity did not like the insinuation or the way the conversation progressed. Looking sternly at Nathan, Chastity rebuked him. "Mr. Porter, you know nothing of our situation, the ordeal that we have endured, or the strength of the character I possess. I shan't need your help. I am not a delicate, helpless woman as you would like to believe. If I were, I would not have taken this journey alone. I bid you a good day." With that, Chastity sharply turned away and joined Paul and Leah.

Nathan remained resolute. He thought, *A spirited girl indeed. I shall have to find a way to endear her to me.*

Once on shore, Chastity looked about to see if anyone was there for her. Boston was still a small settlement, but the shore was a buzz of activity. People were moving here and there, some looking for friends and relatives and some escaping from the crowd. Others were hauling in cargo from the newly arrived ship. Navigating the crowed dock was a challenge; however, Paul, Leah, and Chastity managed and were soon standing on the shore.

The Abernathys were of strong moral character, and George was ensconced as a town leader. George and Susan wanted a woman of education and moral character in their home. When they arrived at the dock, George left the family behind to look over the crowd for a woman whom he expected to be in her forties.

A young dockhand approached him. Behind him, Chastity followed, "Mr. Abernathy, this young lady is looking for you. She says that she is your new governess."

George was completely surprised. He tipped his hat and stated, "'Tis a pleasure to make your acquaintance. I am George Abernathy."

Chastity politely bowed. "The pleasure is all mine. My name is Chastity Shepherd."

About that time, Nathan Porter came from behind and, with a tone of arrogance, stated, "Ah, Miss Shepherd, I see you have someone to welcome you. Very good. Should you need me, I will be staying at the local inn."

George did not like the way Nathan spoke so presumptuously. Before George could say anything, the young libertine turned and walked away. Looking after Chastity, George stated, "Young lady, I hope this kind of character is not approved by you."

Chastity replied with a tone of anger. "Not in the least, sir. In fact, I know nothing of the man."

George escorted Chastity to the family carriage. Susan climbed down to meet her. After introductions, George returned to speak with the dock master about Chastity's belongings and a shipment he was expecting. In his absence, Susan gleefully took Chastity's hands. "Pay no mind to George. He is gruff on the outside, but I assure you he is quite the gentle soul on the inside. I am so glad that one so young would come to us. I know we shall have a wonderful time together. Come, let me introduce our children." She called back to the carriage. "Children, come meet your new governess, Miss Chastity Shepherd."

From the carriage, came five young children ranging from seven to two years of age. Isaac was the oldest and tried his best to imitate his father. Next to him was Sarah, followed by Enoch, Esther, and two-year-old Faith. It took just a few minutes, and all the children began asking all kinds of questions, doing their best to capture their governess's undivided attention.

When he returned, George was surprised to see all the children, including Isaac, playfully attending to Chastity. It brought a smile to his mostly stern expression. He quickly wiped it away before anyone noticed. George commanded, "Everyone into the carriage. We must return home, for there are still chores to do."

Little Faith came up to her father. "Papa, we keep Miss Tasty?"

George could not contain his amusement. "Miss Tasty, is it?" With a humorous response, he looked at Chastity. "Seems you have a new name now. Welcome to my home, Miss Tasty."

The trip to the Abernathy home was most enjoyable. Chastity was surprised to find that George and Susan were loving and playful with the children. They all laughed every time Faith tried to say Chastity's name. Pretty soon, all the children were calling her Miss Tasty. Susan apologized, but Chastity took it in good humor. "I always admired people who had pet names. I never knew mine would be so delicious." Her response brought laughter to everyone.

Chastity noticed many small dwellings along the road to the house. She wondered if large families were crowded in such small houses. Along the street were small, two-story houses built side by side to each other. Then, farther along, the houses were larger, though still small for large families, and many Bostonians had large families. The structures looked very English with thatch roofs and mud walls. Others resembled Tudor homes with a definite American twist.

In just a few short years, Boston had become larger than Plymouth and showed more promise. Boston, like Plymouth, was a very religious community. Folks shared in the common good of the town. At the center of the town was the Commons. It was a fine pasture for livestock of the townsfolk. Another important desire of the people was to keep the town clean. Chastity soon realized that the religious nature of the settlers dictated the care for all who would live there.

The carriage ride went out into the country. On and on they traveled until they reached the very edge of town. The coachman turned the carriage up a road marked by twin pillars. At the end of the road was the house that George had built for his growing family.

Chastity was pleasantly surprised. The house was large and very different from those she saw in town. It was a two-story wooden structure with clapboard siding. On the side of the house was a smaller structure that served as the kitchen. Chastity could hardly contain her excitement. She wanted to see the inside of the home and explore the surrounding grounds. Then she noticed a small cottage at the rear of the house. It was quaint and charming.

Susan watched Chastity's expressions and was very aware of Chastity's interest. "Welcome home, Miss Tasty."

When the carriage arrived, the children rushed from the carriage with George's charge to begin their chores. The ladies exited the carriage, and Susan immediately began showing Chastity around the gardens and finally into the house. The house was warm and inviting. A small fireplace was set in the center of the main room. The hearth extended a short distance from the fireplace. A table with benches and chairs was placed just right. Here the family would take their meals and the children their lessons. There was a door to the left of the room that led to the family room. George had built a modest library of books. A rocking chair was nearby. Chastity imagined the family spending time reading to each other. She was surprised to see a virginal harpsichord along the wall, as well as a violin.

Susan asked, "Do you play, my dear?"

Chastity gently shook her head no before answering. "I could never imagine someone having an instrument in their home."

Then Susan inquired, "Would you like me to teach you?"

Chastity turned to Susan and excitedly replied, "Would you?"

She reached to give Susan a hung when she saw something that brought immediate tears to her eyes. She gasped as she stated, "Oh my."

Susan stepped back and said, "What is it?"

Chastity slowly walked over and touched the spinning wheel.

Susan commented, "That was my mother's. I have never used it. Frankly, I don't know how."

Chastity responded, "Then I shall teach you. Have you any sheep?"

Susan replied, "We have a modest flock of about ten."

Chastity smiled. "Then what fun we shall have learning from each other."

The ladies continued the tour of the house. Chastity was amazed at everything. She loved the kitchen and the bedrooms. She imagined that someday she and John would have a house like this for their own. Chastity was completely lost in her imagination when there came a knock at the door.

A dockhand stood with hat in hand. "I have Miss Shepherd's belongings. Where shall I put them?"

Susan smiled. "Your timing is perfect. Please follow me." Susan led the way to the little cottage in back of the house. She opened the door and invited the man to bring in the box. After thanking the delivery boy, she kindly dismissed him. Chastity slowly entered the quaint little cottage. The room was cozy with a small fireplace at one end of the cabin. A bed sat opposite it. There was a little table next to the window. It was all Chastity would need, and more than she could have imagined.

Susan told the story of the little cottage. "When George and I left for America, we had only the clothes on our backs and his carpenter tools. As soon as we arrived, he secured this piece of land with a promise to build houses for those willing to pay. First, he built this cabin. Shortly after that, I found out that we were going to have a child. Isaac was born eight months later. George's skills were in high demand, and he built several houses for people in town. When word spread of the quality of George's work, he had more than enough to do. We saved until we had enough money to build our home." Looking back at Chastity, she stated, "I do hope you will like it here."

Chastity smiled and hugged Susan. "I already do."

In town, Mr. Nathan Porter checked himself in at the local tavern. He was glad to be off the ship, but as he looked about, he felt a great deal of disgust. He'd secured a room where he would stay several days before seeking out his opportunities in Boston. Nathan came from a family with means, but he had managed to lose most of his inheritance through loose living. He fancied himself a lady's man and enjoyed gambling, both of which nearly ruined him. It had been his father's idea to send his son to America. He realized that his son needed to be separated from the temptations of London. His father's hopes were that Nathan would be free of such temptations, especially around the religious order of Boston.

Boston was being built on hard work, faith in God, and righteous living. Those who established Boston saw the opportunity in the great hardwood forests. Those who knew how to work timber were in high demand. Apart from that, education and skill were also favored. A man skilled in building houses, boats, or any wooden structure was desired and found employment almost at will. Hunters, farmers, tanners, fishermen, and other trades were nearly everywhere. Nathan was ill-equipped for any of these opportunities. There was nothing here for a dandy.

The entire setting just made Nathan loath Boston. The more he saw, the angrier he became. Under his breath he cursed his father for making him come here. Nathan could not escape the moral character of the citizens. In his heart, he mocked them. He surmised, *A clever man might exploit these people. All I need is the right opportunity.*

After a few days, Nathan saw some very rough-looking sailors buying goods around town with Spanish pieces of eight. He took immediate interest and followed them much of the day. By late evening, the sailors were keeping to themselves at a table in the same tavern where Nathan was staying. He approached the table and offered to buy them drinks. That's all it took before the men invited him to join them. One of the men would only introduce himself as Jonas. Jonas was the most cautious of them all. He was leery of Nathan, especially when he began asking questions about the Spanish gold.

Jonas could stand no more. He was agitated by the questions Nathan asked. Wiping his mouth on his sleeve, Jonas inquired, "What's all this about, Mr. Porter?"

Nathan sensed the Jonas's caution. "It is just that I would like to acquire some for myself. I prefer Spanish gold and silver over wampum. Can you blame me?"

Jonas leaned back in his chair before answering. "It's that I know when men begin making such inquiry, they be after something. So what are you after?"

Giving thought to the matter, Nathan beckoned the men to lean in closer and quietly spoke. "I see occasion here among the citizens of Boston. There is no bank that the people trust. I wager they would prefer Spanish gold as well. I watched today as many of the merchants offered you much more in hopes of being paid in doubloon."

The men nodded in agreement.

Nathan continued. "It is obvious by your clothing that you are pirates."

This statement made the crewmen laugh heartily.

The corners of Nathan's mouth rose as he added, "I could convince the people that you should be employed to protect them."

Jonas sneered, "And why would they need protection?"

Once more, Nathan felt the wiser. He explained, "The Dutch will soon be at war with England. Your trade and protection might ease the fear of the people. They will want protection and currency, especially if it's English or Spanish. In turn, I could make sure your money buys more of what you want at favorable prices."

Jonas asked, "How do you plan to manage that?"

Nathan folded his arms before answering, "Just leave that to me."

Jonas stared at Nathan, doubtful of his intentions. Jonas asked, "So let's say that after I speak with the captain, he refuses?"

Nathan replied, "That will be simple enough. I shall report back to the king that the pirates in this region have sided with the Dutch."

Jonas jumped to his feet and put his hand to his knife. With anger in his voice, Jonas snarled, "I'll slit your—"

Nathan shot back. "You'll do nothing of the sort. Sit down. I am not afraid of you in the least." Nathan lifted his arms from beneath the table to reveal a cocked pistol.

Jonas removed his hand and returned to his seat.

Nathan continued. "I need you alive, Captain Jonas. Oh, don't be surprised. I have known all along. As I said, I can make this agreement very profitable for the both of us."

Nathan revealed his plan. "It's quite elementary. When the war begins, the English can ill afford to have a Dutch settlement here in America so close to Plymouth and Boston. A settlement, I might add, that separates these two towns from Virginia. What I propose is that you block off any Dutch ships from coming to New Amsterdam. Raid the Dutch ships, sink them, or chase them off; I do not care. Soon the people of New Amsterdam will depend on us for items that you plundered from them in the first place. Funny thing is they will be paying twice for these things—once to have them shipped, only to be taken by pirates, and then again when they're resold to them from my stores. I will sell them back to the people, and we will double our profits. I shall report to the king that you are loyal sailors. Who knows, the king might even secure a commission for you."

Jonas thought for a moment. "What about the Dutch ships in the Caribbean?"

Nathan laughed. "The Dutch? Bah. Already they are disposed due to their loyalties with Spain. The Spaniards need protection from pirates out of Tortuga. No, the Dutch fleet will not bother us so much. So are you in?"

Jonas gave thought. He looked at his men and then back at Nathan. "Aye, we be in."

Chastity busied herself as soon as Susan left the cabin. She began unpacking the box and hung out her clothes to air. She put the pewter plates and cups given to her by Martha on the table. *Soon, she thought, John will come. I want everything prepared for him.* Chastity went to the main house and asked for some hot coals to begin a fire. Before long, a fire burned in the small fireplace. A metal pot hung on the swing arm. She filled the pot with water from the well and swung it over the flames. A washtub leaned in back of the cabin. She brought it into the cabin. As soon as the water was hot, she poured it into the tub. She repeated the process until the tub was filled. When the final pot was poured into the tub, she undressed and stepped into the bath. How good it felt to be out of the same clothes she'd been wearing for so long. How soothing the water felt on her weary body.

Chastity woke when she realized the water had become cool. She washed quickly, dried herself, and put on the only other dress she had. It felt good to be clean and to get into fresh clothes. She dumped the water and set another pot of water to heat. Her next job was washing her clothes.

When night came, Chastity climbed onto the straw tick mattress. It felt both comfortable and strange. Comfortable because it had been a while since she last slept on a bed. Strange, because she had gotten used to sleeping on the floor. Sleep did not come quickly, perhaps because of the nap she'd taken in the tub. For the longest time, she tossed and turned. John was on her mind. Then, from out of nowhere, Nathan came into her mind. She took in the things he said and the way he defended her. She could not make up her mind if he was a good man or bad man. The thought of him made her afraid. She wasn't sure why.

Morning came with the sound of someone knocking on her door. "Miss Tasty, Miss Tasty, bake-fust is ready."

Chastity knew immediately that it was little Faith. Chastity had not intended to sleep as long as she did and called to Faith, "I'll be right there!" She jumped from her bed and quickly readied herself. She opened the door to the golden-haired little girl with sparkling blue eyes. Chastity invited her in. "Come in, Faith. I shall be ready post haste." Chastity brushed her long dark hair and washed her face. She took Faith by the hand, and together, they rushed to the house.

When the two entered, George looked stern. "Are you accustomed to rising so late, girl?"

Susan quickly interrupted. "Hush, George. She had a busy day yesterday, and you know it. Give her time to adjust." Then, with a wink toward Chastity, she added, "Besides, I told her that she could start the children's education on Monday." Afterward, Susan invited her to the table.

As soon as they were beckoned, all the children came rushing in laughing.

George gave a hearty command. "Sit down, children."

They all took their seats at the table. Faith took her seat on her father's lap.

George lifted up a prayer of thanks. "Father, we thank thee for the food before us, for life, health, and the safe arrival of our governess, Miss Tasty." The children chuckled. George continued. "Bless this food for our bodies, and bless the endeavors of the day. Amen."

On the table a pot of hot pottage was placed, which had cooked overnight. There was also corn mush sweetened with molasses. Chastity watched the good humor of the family. The children waited for Mother to dish out each portion, except for Faith who picked out what she wanted from her father's bowl. There was a loving playfulness between father and daughter. It was obvious that George took special delight in his little girl. The food was washed down with apple cider. George had a cup of sassafras. Chastity sat in silence watching all. She was amazed to see such happiness and togetherness, all of which made her long for home.

There wasn't a lot of conversation, but from time to time, something was said about work to be done or something that struck someone funny. The children were encouraged to speak and share as well. The children displayed a maturity not normally seen in others their age. From time to time, they would ask Chastity about England, the ocean crossing, and John. When she showed them the ring he made for her, they all marveled at the craftsmanship. Susan could not take her eyes off the beautiful ring.

George commented, "Someday, I may have this man make a ring for you, my dear. Would you like that?"

When breakfast was finished, George lifted Faith from his lap and sat her on his stool. He walked over and gathered the family Bible. He returned to the table and sat Faith back on his lap. "Today, children, I want to tell you of Ruth." He opened the Bible and read from the book of the same name and told how she had left her country to be with her mother-in-law who had lost everything, including her husband and sons. After reading the first chapter, George commented, "Ruth saw that she was needed and had fallen in love with the God of Israel, the same God who is our God. Ruth left the land of Moab to go back to Judah. She was willing to give up the life she knew to help the woman she loved like her own mother. I tell you now that Miss Tasty left the home and family she loves very dearly to come and help us by teaching you." He closed the

Bible and looked straight at Chastity. "We are honored to have you as part of our family. We hope you will always find a home with us, even when your John comes for you."

Tears filled her eyes. Chastity had come to a family who would love her and care for her.

George closed the Bible, and the family joined hands. Without a word, every head bowed, and George offered a pray of thanksgiving to God for His blessings and the safe arrival of Chastity.

# Survival

For days on end, John worked to off-load things from the ship. His idea to bury the treasure was good but required a lot of labor. It proved to be hard, backbreaking work. Accomplishing the arduous task of unloading the ship, dragging the items to the selected location, and burying them. At strategic points, he buried all that was valuable and important. His map of the five-pointed star was all that indicated where items were located. He used encrypted marks that only he understood. Then he carefully stowed the map in the dugout. Each night he retreated to his earthen shelter. Here he found rest for his weary soul.

John enjoyed caring for the horse. He built a corral from existing fallen trees and branches. Each day he took the horse for grazing and began training it to pull and carry loads. After a while, John let the animal run around freely. John laughed as he watched the youngster run, stomp, twist, and turn over the lush grassland. From time to time, John joined his friend by running alongside. When exhausted, John would lie on the ground. The horse would come to him and just to be touched.

John named the horse Spirit.

John was surprised how strong the storms could be. Once a storm was so great that it even pulled the ship back from the shore. With the load removed from the ship, it actually rose and settled a bit with the rising tide. This made John think about how to dispose of the ship. At first, he feared he would have to take it apart piece by piece. Now that it was more buoyant, he thought he could somehow move the ship back out to sea. If so, he would sink it rather than dismantle and burn it.

He was afraid to burn the ship. He knew that if he burned the ship, the flames and smoke would be seen for miles. He also thought that if the ship was burned, the sand would be blackened, and anything made of metal would remain. If the ship was sunk, all evidence would be gone.

There was one remaining longboat, but it was not in very good shape. Some parts of it were cut away by Timothy to make the repair to the hole in the ship. John decided to make repairs as best he could. How long it would last afterward, he did not know, but he needed it if his plan was to succeed.

The ship had two anchors. John planned to use the anchors to help pull the *Elizabeth Marie* away from shore. Once it was afloat, he could take it out to open water and sink it. It would be a difficult task, but with patience and perseverance, he was sure he could get the ship away from shore and out to sea. Then he would use the remaining gunpowder to blow a hole in the hull, sending the *Elizabeth Marie* to the bottom of the ocean.

John knew even this was a risky plan. If pirates or Spaniards were nearby, they could hear the explosion. Should the ship catch fire, they might see the flames. He had to risk it. He was losing too much sleep thinking about possible attacks. It was now or never. He had to take the chance.

Early next morning John set his plan into motion. He made final repairs to the hole in the ship. When finished, he rowed the longboat to the back of the ship, tying it as close as possible to where the anchor would drop. He swam over to the rope ladder of the ship and climbed aboard. Carefully, he lowered the anchor into the longboat. Then He returned to the longboat and rowed as far out as the tether line on the anchor would allow. Next, he threw the anchor overboard. Afterward, he returned to the ship and repeated the process with the other anchor. Only after this was done did he return to shore. It had been exhausting work, but he was prepared for when the next storm came. Then he would attempt to pull the ship from the shore.

Just two nights later the opportunity came. A severe storm rose up, and the surf rose high. Spirit did not like the heavy tempest and cried his displeasure. Heavy waves pounded the old ship, and it began to lift. John fought his way on board. He raced to begin the difficult task of weighing in the anchors. Grabbing the anchor bar, he placed it into the eye of the chain. He watched a great wave approach the ship. John timed it so that when the wave was beneath the ship, he pulled with all his strength. He managed to budge the ship just a little. Throughout the night, he repeated the process. He strained his muscles to gain inches, but his plan was working. By working both anchors, John managed to free the ship and get it away from the shore. By dawn, the ship was afloat in about ten feet of water. John collapsed on the deck from sheer exhaustion.

He did not rest long. John lifted himself and looked at the mast. There was one good sail left. He climbed the rigging and lowered it. He raised one anchor, allowing the other to keep the ship from heading back to shore. He pushed the whipstaff to turn the ship. Once the ship was headed in the right direction, he lifted the other anchor. The ship protested with creaks and groans, but it gradually made its way toward deeper water.

The sun was high in the sky when John dropped the ship's anchors for the final time. The ship was in much deeper water now, and it could be sunk out of sight. One small keg of black powder was placed in the lowest part of the ship. He laid a trace of powder to it. Once the trace was lit, he would have just enough time to get to the longboat and make his escape. If his plan worked, the powder would blow a big enough hole in the hull, and the ship would sink. John lit the trace with the flint he carried. The powder trace ignited quickly. John hurried to the deck and dove overboard near the longboat and climbed aboard. John lifted the small sail on the longboat and headed back to shore. John had no idea how long it would take for the powder to explode, if it exploded at all.

John was about a hundred yards from the ship when a deep rumble and muffled boom was heard. The ship rocked in place, and then a fire flash shot into the air. The main mast dropped across the deck. Water shot up into the air as the volume of air decreased. The powder had done its job. In less than two minutes, the ship was claimed by the sea. The *Elizabeth Marie* was gone.

John had never seen a ship go down before. He felt a pang of sadness. This ship had been his jail and his means of escape. The ship lasted long enough to save the crew. The ship was his school. From its deck, he had learned to sail and navigate. On this ship, he learned how to command. He even learned the value of forgiveness. He forged lasting friendships on her deck. He stepped aboard a boy. He had grown on the ship into manhood. Now the ship was gone. For his protection, he knew it had to be sunk, but he would never forget the name *Elizabeth Marie.*

John turned his attention to the task of sailing back to shore. The longboat was anything but watertight. He bailed bucket after bucket of water. He was already exhausted from the long night. He just wanted to get back and rest. It seemed to take forever to return to shore. John was thankful that there weren't any threatening storm clouds. He doubted the longboat could take it. He looked back and saw nothing but calm waters.

It took almost three hours to return to the beach. John lowered the sail, and the boat stopped on the sandy shore. He took the small anchor and buried it in the sand. He went to the corral to check on Spirit. The horse was fine and welcomed John by running to the removable opening. John walked Spirit to a grassy area and tethered him to the ground near fresh green grass. John lay down nearby and quickly fell asleep.

It was dusk when John woke to Spirit's neigh. John sat up and looked about for danger. Thankfully, all was quiet. Spirit welcomed John with a nuzzle and then returned to pick some more at the fresh green grass. John got to his feet and began rubbing Spirit's neck. A smile crossed his face as he said, "Tomorrow we shall begin our journey off the island. Think you're up to it?"

When morning came, John inspected the longboat. It was in no condition to get him off the island but would suffice for a little exploration—that is, *if* he stayed close to shore. He could sail north to possibility find a way to Virginia. He would travel as far as he could, spend the night, and return the next day. He sat to work making repairs to the longboat and then loaded it with supplies. Afterward, he went to Spirit to make sure he had plenty to eat and water to drink while he was away. Before leaving, he petted his young partner and said, "I will be gone a day or so. Don't make a pig of yourself. I will be back as soon as I can."

As he was about to shove off, Spirit whinnied his disapproval. John hated to leave him, but he had no choice. John turned. "Sorry, big fellow, but I have to go alone."

John pushed the longboat out and rowed into deep enough water before raising the sail. He felt he had risked his life in sinking the ship. He wasn't about to risk it again by going out to water that was too challenging.

John sat in silence. The longboat sailed along uninhibited on the unusually calm surf. This left John with his thoughts. The last few months had been a struggle for survival. Each day was a fight within to push himself. There had been no time to grieve or to even think about his loneliness. Even though this trip was to secure his escape, the inactivity offered his mind the realization of his circumstances. For the first time, John felt despair. He knew he was alone and wondered within himself if anyone cared.

John took account of all that led to his being here. He thought of the ill treatment of the blacksmith and Captain Richard Wise. He reflected on the pirate attack that eventually led to his exile on the island. He recalled the aftermath—the death of fellow sailors and the captain and the unknown condition of Henry Finch. It all depressed him. His mind flashed back as he thought of the men who escaped the ship and the lifeless body of his friend. He wondered if they survived the escape and made it to Virginia or if they'd died in the vain attempt to escape.

John's mind took him to a place of darkness and despair. A raging storm of the mind brewed, causing him to fear the unknown. Depression overtook him. He thought of his mother, father, and Chastity.

The deceiver whispered, "What would your parents think of you now? They have moved on without you and are living their lives without a single thought of you. And Chastity ... Do you think she is really waiting on you?"

He thought of Chastity and the dream telling him she was on her way. Had she really departed for America? Was her plight as difficult as his? Or was it just wishful thinking on his part that she might truly be taking the journey? He bowed his head and prayed to God for her care. Years of heaviness within came pouring out of his soul. John felt cheated that he had been taken advantage of. He felt that in the past two years he had been deprived of Chastity's love. He yelled into the sky, "Haven't I done all you wanted of me?"

There was no answer. John began to think that his worth to others was nothing. He even wondered if Chastity would want him now. He hung his head and wept.

The loneliness heightened his desperation as he cried, "Father, you know I love her, and I want to marry her. If I should die, then give her a man who will care for her. Let her find a man who will love her as much as I do."

John remained with his head down. A solitary sound was heard from above. John looked up, and there, circling the mast, was a lone white seagull. John recalled Henry's words to him when they left England's shores: "It's a good omen."

In response, John called out, "All right, Father. I get it."

He looked to the port side and saw the beach. To his amazement, the shoreline did not end. He took his measurements and plotted his course. He determined he was traveling close to ten knots an hour. He left midmorning, and now with the sun high in the sky, he figured he had traveled more than fifty miles up the coast. He had not run out of shoreline. The continual shore turned despair to hope.

*Maybe*, he thought, *the journey may not be that impossible.*

By midafternoon, he discovered the island ended and another island began. He headed inland to investigate. The water was shallow, and the distance between the two islands was about a hundred feet. John anchored the boat and got out. The water came up to his knees. He wasn't sure if the tide was in or out. The separation between islands seemed to him his greatest challenge. He questioned whether Spirit would go into water. Would the young horse trust him enough to make this crossing?

After a while, John returned to the boat and continued north. Beyond the separation, the shoreline continued. He sailed on for about an hour until he was satisfied that he could make the trip by land. He reversed directions and began the return trip back. By nightfall he had passed the watery divide. He headed for shore at the same place he had stopped earlier. He anchored a short distance from land. John did not know what dangers might be on the shore, so he decided to stay on the boat for the night. Providence had smiled on him to this point, and he wasn't about to challenge it now.

A hint of sunlight was all that was needed to stir John to his senses. John did not sleep well. He woke because his clothes were wet, soaked from the leak in the boat. He was chilled and shivering. The longboat held about six inches of water. The repairs he'd made were not holding. The boat was still floating but in desperate need of bailing out.

John spoke to the old boat as if it could hear him. "Just get me home, okay?"

The sun was coming up on the horizon by the time John had finished bailing out the water and patching the hole. John raised the sail. The morning breeze quickly filled the canvas, and the boat accelerated toward the south. The return was much slower. It was late afternoon when he finally arrived back at the camp. As he pulled the boat ashore, a high-pitched whinny greeted him. John smiled and called back, "Yes, Spirit. I'm back." He let the horse out of his corral, and Spirit ran up and down the shoreline while John stowed the boat and his belongings. Spirit enjoyed the reprieve from his pen. John thought only of the trip to Virginia.

The next morning John exited the dugout with map in hand. He wanted to chart out his planned trip. He walked over to the corral and was shocked to find that Spirit was gone. Looking on the ground, he discovered a set of footprints much smaller than his own.

John thought, *Why didn't Spirit warn me that someone was approaching?* He followed the tracks. The horse was being led by whoever had taken him. John followed the footprints to the grassy area where he often let Spirit graze. He approached and found a man of darker complexion just sitting nearby watching over the horse. His clothes were badly worn. John walked toward the man. When he saw John, he stood to his feet. It was the Spaniard!

John sized up the situation. The Spaniard raised his hands, showing he meant no harm. Approaching, John asked, "Do you speak English?"

The Spaniard replied, "Si, senor. I speak a little."

John questioned, "What is your name?"

The Spaniard replied, "Enrique Gomez. Most people call me Rica."

John was not wearing a weapon. He felt no danger. He pointed to the ground to suggest that they sit together. As soon as they sat down, Spirit came over to greet John. He rubbed his nose, and the horse, sensing everything was all right, went back to grazing. John turned his attention back to the Spaniard. He asked, "How long have you been watching me?"

Rica replied, "Oh, maybe a week or two. I see you work around, burying this and that. I saw you sink the ship. I wonder what you were doing."

John replied, "I have my reasons. Why didn't you make yourself known to me before now?"

Rica responded, "The last we saw each other we fought, no?"

John smiled. "Yes, we did." Then, looking at the man, John suggested, "I haven't had anything to eat. Care to join me? Don't worry, the horse will be fine."

John made some food from what was left of the dry goods. Rica ate heartily.

John said, "I didn't think my cooking was that good."

Rica replied, "You're right. It's not, but I have eaten little the last few days."

Rica's answer made John laugh. "Fine, next time you cook." While they ate, John asked Rica why he had attacked him and fled the ship when they were trying to escape.

Rica answered, "When you came below, I thought that you were one of the pirates who came on board at Port Royal."

John wrinkled his brow. "But I'm not Spanish."

Rica replied, "Pirates come from all places, senor."

Thoughtfully, John agreed.

Rica continued. "When I saw the men leaving the ship in the boat, I was sure I was right."

John then asked, "How did you manage to survive the storm?"

Rica stood and demonstrated. "When I jumped, I clung to a rope dragging in the water. I held the rope until I saw a piece break from the ship. I swam with the board and the wind. It blew me away from the ship. A day later, I landed on a little island that way." Rica pointed to the south.

John poured Rica some wine. He handed the cup to him and asked, "What changed your mind about me?"

Rica responded, "When I came here, I see you are all alone. I also saw how you treated Estrella."

John had the same questioning glare. "Who is Estrella?"

Rica answered, "Why, the horse."

John questioned, "What does it mean?"

Rica answered, "The little lights in the sky."

John's eyes grew wide. "Ah, Stars. Why such a name?"

Rica smiled and pointed to his eyes. Then, leaning forwarded, he remarked, "Have you not looked into his eyes? What do you call horse?"

John replied, "I call him, Spirit."

"Ah." Rica seemed to approve. "Espiritu. That is a good name. Maybe we combine the two, eh?"

John nodded. "Sure, why not."

After a while, John told Rica his plan for leaving the island. He also told him what he discovered when he sailed north. When Rica asked him why he sunk the ship, John told him it was because he feared the pirates. Rica considered what John said and agreed that it was a good decision. On and on, through much of the day and into the evening, the two men spoke. John was glad to have Rica's company. He showed Rica the dugout, but being careful, he chose not to show him the whereabouts of things buried. He told of his plans to go to Virginia.

Rica took it all in. When night came, John invited Rica to stay in the dugout with him. Rica was grateful for the invitation. It did not take long for the both of them to fall fast asleep. That night, they felt safer than they had in long time.

John woke to the smell of freshly fried fish. Rica was cooking, and the aroma was wonderful. Rica had gotten up early and made a ring of sand and wood close to the increasing swell of the tide. When the tide came in, it filled the makeshift pool with water and a few fish. Rica quickly closed the pool from the retreating water, thus preventing the fish from swimming back out to sea. He had managed to catch five beautiful fish.

John enjoyed every bite. With gratitude, he stated, "You are right, my friend. You are a much better cook than me." After breakfast, John took Rica to where the captain and the four sailors who died in the battle were buried. John spoke. "Before we leave, I have something I need to do. I will make markers for the graves. Care to help me?"

Throughout the day, the two men prepared for the trip off the island. John made a travois for Spirit. He knew that there were things he would be needing for this trip, but he had to be careful not to overburden the young horse. John decided to take the money he was given by Mr. Howell plus a little more from the rest of the treasure. If he was careful, he would be able to set up at shop with this money in Virginia. He decided he would leave his tools behind. He did not want to overburden Spirit.

One thing weighed heavily on John's mind. There was still something that had to be done. Call it respect. Call it dedication. Whatever you might call it, it was something he felt he had to do.

John called for Rica. With tools in hand, they went to the longboat. John stated, "The old boat won't last much longer. I can put it to one final use. After I take from it what I want, I would like for you to continue cutting it up in pieces so that we can burn and dispose of it.

Rica looked puzzled. "Why we do this to the boat?"

John explained, "I thought about the pirates who attacked us. They may still come looking for us. I don't want them to find any evidence of our being here. If they should stumble on this shore, the only thing they will find are two graves."

John touched the boat and looked at the water in it. He thought of the longboat in which others escaped. He continued to explain. "I want to honor those who have died, and I need the boat for that reason. Those who died deserve to be respected."

Rica asked, "Even the captain?"

John nodded. "Even him."

Rica seemed to understand. "Then I will do as you ask."

From the flattest part of the boat, John cut out two square sections. He carried these pieces to a place he could work. He returned for the four oars, walked back to the camp, and continued. John cleaned up the edges of the cuts to the wood. Next, he took chisel and hammer and began carving words on each board. A short distance away, Rica was burning small pieces of the boat. Back and forth, Rica traveled to cut small pieces of the boat and then burn them on a low fire.

When John was finished with the carvings, he took a set of oars and attached them to the boards. The paddle part of the oar stood straight up with the writings beneath it. John took the first one and stood it erect at the mass grave of the four sailors who died during the battle with the pirates. The second one was placed at the head of the captain's grave. The captain's marker bore the image of an anchor. Below the anchor John wrote: "Richard Wise, husband, father, and captain of the *Elizabeth Marie*, who gave his life in battle when pirates tried to take his ship. May he rest in peace."

John called Rica. Rica could not read English, so John read for him what was written. Rica replied, "This is a good thing that you do."

John replied, "I promised to do more for the captain, and by God's grace, I shall do it." With that, the two men bowed their heads as John prayed.

Virginia. Where was Virginia? This was the question that ran through John's mind. The maps he had were not detailed. From his measurements, he was certain that he was south of Jamestown and Elizabeth City. The map bore a, *X* representing Jamestown. The *X* was made by the captain when he planned his escape from the pirates. The map was old and detailed Spanish territories. Therefore, the captain's mark was really his best guess. John decided that he might be on a chain of islands or on one long, narrow strip of land not yet known. John decided that he would detail the map as he went. He would need it later upon his return, and others would benefit from what he discovered.

By day's end, all the preparations were made for the journey ahead. If the weather was fair, they would leave the next day.

Morning came, and the two men walked Spirit close to the water. It was low tide. John knew that the hoof prints and the travois drag marks would be washed away when the tide rose. John made sure they had good enough clothes for the journey, but nothing too posh, as that would only draw unwanted attention. He secured the items he planned to take onto the travois, including food and a few cooking items.

Rica argued, "I catch fish and make better food."

John laughed, "Maybe, but we will take his just in case."

When all was loaded, the two men tore down the corral and used the debris to sweep away their tracks. Mother Nature would do the rest. They made sure the fire pit was buried. As best they could, they removed all evidence that anyone had ever been there. The only indication was the grave markers. John felt both sadness and excitement. He had come to love this location and thought to himself that this would be a good place to build a home. On the other hand, he was excited to be traveling to Virginia and on his way to find Chastity.

It was time for the three companions to begin their journey. At first,

Spirit resisted the travois. Rica and John managed to encourage him. With gentle guidance and care, Spirit soon accepted his burden. Along the way, John and Rica talked and commented on things they saw—the barren shores, the beautiful ocean, and the large body of water west of the island, which seemed completely untouched by human hand.

At one point, Rica asked John, "Senor John, what will you tell the people about how we came to be here?"

John answered, "I have given much thought to that. I will tell them the truth. I will tell them that we were part of the crew of the *Elizabeth Marie*. The ship was run aground, and we managed to survive the ordeal. I will tell them that some of the men escaped by longboat, but the other boat was not seaworthy, and we took our chances along with the captain of the ship."

Rica thought for a moment. "But I am Spaniard."

John replied, "And the best horse trainer to ever be brought to America. The captain personally hired you to care for horse."

Rica smiled, "Si, senor. I am a good horse trainer, no?"

John laughed. "Yes, you are. If I am asked about the captain and crew, I will tell them that we narrowly escaped an attack by a pirate ship. During the battle, the captain was mortally wounded and later died of his wounds where we landed."

Rica looked at John with admiration. "I have seen your skill with wood. You are a carpenter, eh?"

John answered, "I am a smith and work with precious metals." With that, John took the knife from his side. He paused and handed it to Rica. "This belongs to you. I took it from you when we had our first meeting."

Rica looked at the knife. It was shaped like his, but the handle and blade had been changed to bear special markings. Rica commented, "It looks like mine, but it is different."

John thoughtfully commented, "How does it feel in your hand?"

Rica smiled. "Very good."

John pointed out, "I balanced it and made a few changes. Then I added the engravings. It's your knife, and I want you to have it back." With that, John untied the sheath and handed that to Rica.

Rica was sad. He hung his head before saying, "But I attacked you with it."

John understood. "It's all right. You did not know my own intensions and fought to defend yourself. My friend, this knife is yours. Please wear it and accept it back."

With true gratitude, Rica strapped on the knife. Smiling, he asked, "It looks good, no?"

Their first day's journey ended on the shore where they would have to cross the narrow waterway. They'd covered about fifty miles of coastline. Before retiring for the night, John decided to walk across the watery divide. He stripped himself of his clothing and began walking over the watery divide to the other side. It was low tide. The water was warm, and the sandy bottom felt good beneath his feet. He was tempted to start swimming and had to remind himself why he was making the crossing. The deepest waters came to his chest. This lasted for only a short distance before the waters became shallower. When he made it to the other side, he waved back at Rica. It took nearly an hour to make the crossing and, naturally, an hour to return. His only concern was the horse. Spirit had never been in water before, and John did not know how the horse would react. The depth could spook him.

When John got back to camp, he dried himself and put on his clothes. Rica was putting final touches to their supper. John sat down and ate heartily. It had been a long day.

John shared his concern. "The way across can be done easily by you and me. I think we can carry the items from the travois across. Once across, I would have you watch over the goods, while I will return for Spirit."

Rica replied, "We could bring him together."

John replied, "True, but I am still cautious. Though we have not seen Indians, this is their land. I want to make sure we protect what little we have."

John looked over to the horse. "I am not sure how Spirit will respond to being in water for the first time."

Rica smiled. "Senor John, we should take him to the water tonight. If he sees we have fun in the water, he will be less afraid. Come, let us show him together."

John rose to his feet and walked to Spirit. He led him to the water's edge. When he tried to walk him into the water, the horse resisted. Each time, he would rear up and pull back to the camp.

Finally, Rica came to him. "We take him together. I cover this eye, and you cover that one."

Spirit calmed down immediately. The three walked into the water. When it was about chest deep on him, Rica said, "Uncover his eyes."

Spirit looked about but did not panic. The two men began taking handfuls of the warm water and pouring it on him. Spirit did not shy away. Before long, the two men began splashing water at each other and then onto Spirit. To John's total surprise, the horse joined in the fun.

The morning sun beat down upon the three companions. It was late in the day before the tide receded. John left Spirit tied to some high brush, while he and Rica moved everything across. The water came up to Rica's shoulders.

He explained, "The horse will not like this. So take a rope and walk far ahead of him. He will swim. Pull the rope so that he will not turn back but come to you."

It was good advice. Once everything was on the opposite shore, John returned for Spirit. Just as Rica suspected, Spirit began swimming as soon as he became buoyant. John held the rope farther ahead of him and kept it taunt. Spirit had no choice but to go toward John. It was only a short swim before the water became shallower. At that time, Spirit began to quicken his pace to reach the other side. John and Rica hurried to congratulate Spirit and rubbed the water off him. They loaded Spirit with the travois and continued on their way.

John took mental notes that some parts of the shore were so narrow they could see water on both their left and right. He was sure the island would end soon, but to his amazement, the land became wider and wider. Off in the distance he could see the waters to the west were part of a bay. They would soon be on the main body of land. There was no bay charted on the maps they had. *Where are we?* he wondered.

When they stopped for camp, John removed the map and made notes and changes to it. John took time to explain to Rica what he was doing and what it meant. That night, around a small fire, John shared his thoughts. "I think we are getting close to our destination. The land is wider." Pointing to the map, he stated, "There is a wide inlet that leads inland and is called the James River. This river leads to the first English settlement known as Jamestown."

Rica asked, "How far away is this river?"

In response, John answered, "I don't know. I just know we have to be getting close."

The next day they were glad to have found some fresh water. Their supply was nearly out, and besides that, it was tasting stale. They drank their fill of the sweet, fresh stream. They dumped what remaining water they had and filled up with fresh water from the stream. Rica was able to spear several nice fish. They could have gone farther but decided this was a good place to stop and rest. Spirit was glad to have his burden removed and the opportunity to feast on green grass. It was a rewarding day. They hoped the next day would be much of the same.

The coastal land was becoming denser with trees and shrubs. There was no doubt about it; they were on the mainland. The only thing west of them was land. John continued to follow the shoreline. He was growing a bit impatient. He figured they should be seeing the James River by now. If Rica sensed any change in John, he did not say. John was becoming hopelessly restless.

Suddenly, Spirit stopped and whinnied. Someone or something was nearby. John's heart began to race. He peered ahead and saw four men with spears entering the water. It was obvious by their dress that they were natives. There was no way of knowing if they were friendly. John quietly directed Rica away from their line of visibility by moving inland to hide. He wanted to avoid the Indians if at all possible. John knew they would be forced to journey west into unknown territory.

Moving west, they soon found the land became marshland. The pungent smell of the salty brine reminded John of the day he first came to London. They were able to move out of sight by hiding in the marsh grass. The air was filled with insects, especially annoying horseflies. In some places, the horse sunk up to his hock. This condition startled Spirit, but Rica and John stayed with him to keep him calm. They traveled a little over a mile before the ground beneath their feet was dry. John was convinced that they were in Virginia. When he felt it was time, he redirected their course due north.

It was beautiful land. He now knew why this place was chosen for the first settlement. John filled his lungs with the fresh, clean air. How different it was from the coastline. He was mesmerized by all he saw—so much so that he forgot about the Indians. The men remained cautious. They relied on Spirit to warn them of any danger.

The air was becoming saltier. They had gone about two miles north when they heard gulls making their familiar call. Suddenly, Rica stopped and pointed. "John, look!"

There, above the treetops, was the top of the mast of a sailing ship. The two men looked at each other and embraced. They hurried their pace, stopping when they reached the south shore of the river. The ship was newly arrived and was moving slowly up the wide waterway. John figured the ship must be heading for Jamestown.

John could not contain his excitement. He turned to Rica, and the two men hugged each other. They hopped up and down in a makeshift dance. They included Spirit in the celebration by patting him and rubbing his mane.

Rica whispered, "Espíritu de la estrella que lo hizo."

Then, realizing the ship was still moving, they gathered themselves and walked the riverbank toward it. Men on board the ship spotted them. Those who could, pointed at them. Together, they shared in a greeting by waving. John would call to the men on deck, but they were much too busy to respond. They followed the slow-moving ship on its upstream course. The river was much too wide to cross. They figured that there would be a place to cross closer to the settlement. John and Rica saw a few Indians, but neither took notice of the other. The natives were accustomed to the strange sight of the white settlers.

From time to time, they had to walk around small inlets. These diversions allowed the ship to move farther ahead of them. They did not know how far upstream the town was, but they knew they were on the right course. Sooner or later, they would find Jamestown.

When evening came, they were still a good distance from the settlement. The riverbank was rockier now, and the trees were denser. The endless inland walking to find a place to cross made the journey seem much longer. It was nearly dusk when they decided to camp for at least one more night. They felt comfortable enough to build a small fire and make a meal of dried fish and meat. They kept Spirit close to them. John and Rica trusted Spirit to warn them if anyone tried to approach. The horse was their best security. They welcomed sleep. The trip had been a rush of emotions and challenges. They hoped they would reach their destination the following day.

John woke early. Spirit was looking inland as though something or someone was approaching. The land was teaming with game. This made John think that there might be bear or wildcats nearby, so he got to his feet and carefully looked in the same direction as Spirit. He could not see anything. The morning mist and the stillness of the dense woods made it hard to detect any movement.

John called to his friend. "Rica, get up. I think we are being watched."

Rica moved quickly. The two men hurriedly worked to clean up the camp. No sooner had Spirit been loaded when they heard, "What do you know about that? It is a horse."

John quickly turned to face a rugged-looking man. John questioned, "You're English?"

The man was Benjamin Baker. He responded, "From the time I was born. And who might you be?"

The answer brought welcome relief to the travelers. John made introductions. "I am Jonathan Devine, and this is my friend Enrique Gomez."

Benjamin looked at the men questionably. "How did you all get here?"

John answered, "We were shipmates on the *Elizabeth Marie*. We were attacked by pirates. Several of the crew escaped by longboat, but we were not so fortunate. We ended up shipwrecked on a distant shore. Rica and I, along with our horse, survived the wreck."

Benjamin then asked, "Then where ya be heading?"

John replied, "Jamestown for a start and eventually Elizabeth City."

Benjamin laughed. "I can help ya then. I have a homemade flatboat that I used to cross over to here. I can getcha across the river if you like. The flatboat will handle us and the horse. We heard tell by the captain of the ship that came in yesterday that they saw two men and a horse walking along the shore. When I heard the news, I had to come see for me-self. Besides, I am the only one who could help you cross. You'd have to go way upstream into Indian land to find a place shallow enough to cross the river. And I hear tell that the river is tricky. Full of rocks and drop-offs. Nah, you're better off with me."

Benjamin showed them the way to his flatboat, which was just a bunch of logs tied together. The men climbed aboard. When they did, they felt the boat dip and twist in the water. Spirit was led onto the boat and did not like the instability of the contraption. The crossing to the other side was at least a mile wide. John and Rica kept looking at the dark water they crossed to see if they were sinking. Even Spirit looked at them, wondering if they'd lost their minds.

The homemade contraption finally made it to the north side of the river. When they reached the other side, John and Rica breathed a sigh of relief. They were ever so thankful that they had safely made it to the other side. They offered to pay Benjamin, but he refused. He grinned at the men and said, "Just glad to be of service."

Benjamin led them to the fort. When they entered, the men and women were surprised to see the newcomers and especially the horse. They took little notice of Rica. A horse, however, was of great value to those doing farming, transportation, and other types of work.

Benjamin took John and Rica to meet Sir William Berkeley. His residence was on the northwest side of the settlement. William's house was larger than the others, but John thought it lacked in style and elegance, which ought to be for a man of his importance. Since becoming governor, William had built his plantation and established farming among the settlers as a way of life in Jamestown.

Sir William welcomed the newcomers to his home. John and Rica were ill prepared for this meeting, as they were wearing the same clothes they had been wearing since leaving the camp. William offered them seats and ordered cups of beer from his servant. William was quite interested in their story. He wanted to know all about the shipwreck and details of their coming to Jamestown.

When asked about the location where the ship settled, John explained, "The ship no longer exists. You see, sir, I was afraid the Spanish or pirates would come looking for us. We were able to move the ship out to sea far enough to sink it. Only Rica and I know the true location of its whereabouts and the island we were stranded upon. In time, I will return there, because there is something I must do."

Sir William narrowed his eyes before inquiring, "What might that be?"

John thoughtfully replied, "Sir William, I plan to make two stone grave markers for the men buried on the island. I plan to replace the wooden ones I made with stone. I never want these men to be forgotten."

Sir William was taken back. "Amazing. Truly amazing." Then, in greater respect, he added, "You said you would make these stones?"

John nodded his head. "If I cannot find someone to do it. You see, sir, I am a smith. I was trained as a blacksmith and honed my skills as a silversmith. I know carpentry too, thanks to the ship's carpenter. That is how I learned to make the present grave markers."

Rica interrupted. "Si, Senor Jonathan is a great smith." Rica pulled his knife with such quickness that the governor was startled. Rica flipped the knife before handing it to the governor. "Look here. This knife is what John did for me. Is it not good?"

The governor took the knife and handled it with care. He was very impressed. The things he said next shocked John. "I heard tell of a man who was kept as a slave aboard a ship making wares for his master. Do you know anything about this man?"

John was thoughtful before replying. "I was that man. I will never be that man again."

Sir William responded, "So what are your plans here in Virginia?"

John answered, "My original destination was Elizabeth City, and I intend to go there tomorrow. There is a man I must see. I have been kept from my destination for so very long. I think he may have letters from my family. They were told he would be my contact in America. I also have to get letters to my love ones and my betrothed. Furthermore, I want to set up shop in Elizabeth City and procure land on which to build a house."

Sir William asked, "Why not stay here? There is plenty of opportunity and work to be done in Jamestown."

John answered, "That is a most admirable offer, but I feel my destiny lies closer to the coast. My betrothed may also be in Elizabeth City, Boston, or Plymouth."

William was surprised by the answer and asked, "You don't know? Then how can you be sure? How might she have arrived there?"

John replied, "She would have come as an indentured servant under the authority of the Earl of Sussex. We both grew up in the farming community of Haywards Heath. I left as an indentured, and she was supposed to follow me when I sent for her. I don't know why, but I feel she has already come to these shores. One way or another, I will find her. When I do, I hope to purchase her debt so that we can be married."

Sir Berkeley sat back in his chair and supped the warm beer. He stated, "Ah, many are coming here by that means. So you were an indentured?"

John was thoughtful. He crossed his arms and looked intently at Sir Berkeley. "I was endured to a Mr. Robert Howell. Two years ago I was supposed to arrive here to begin serving my time. The captain of the *Elizabeth Marie* bought my services, and I served him. Before he died, he forgave my debt if I would honor him in one thing."

William was surprised at John's honesty. He asked, "What might that be?"

John answered, "That I provide for his wife and daughter in England. It is my intention to keep my promise to him."

William thoughtfully replied, "I believe you will keep your commitment. Most men would have left that part of the agreement out of their conversation. I agree with your captain. You are a free man. I have no doubt in you. Furthermore, I will aid you in your journey to Elizabeth City." William then leaned forward as he cautioned, "I urge you to say no more of this agreement between you and your captain, or you having been an indentured. Some may try to circumvent your work and claim you are indentured to them. Without documentation, it would be their word against yours. May you truly prosper in your endeavors."

John agreed. "I thank you. As soon as I can, I will secure the documentation with Mr. Howell."

Sir William turned and asked Rica, "And what of you, my fine fellow?"

Before Rica could speak, John replied, "Rica is the greatest horse trainer in the Americas."

William's eyes widened. "Really now. Then come with me, gentlemen, for I have a modest selection of horses."

As the three men left the plantation house, William stepped from the porch and fixed his gaze on Spirit. Spirit was picking at the grass near the house. Immediately, the governor gasped in amazement before uttering, "Oh my."

John could see the look in the governor's eyes and called Spirit to him. Spirit raised his head and walked over. The horse was still dragging the travois. The horse stopped in front of John and accepted his gentle patting. He shied just a little when the governor tried to do the same.

Sir William was impressed. "Beautiful. Simply beautiful, and his markings are like none I have ever seen." Turning to Rica, the governor asked, "You trained him?"

Rica smiled. "Si, is he not magnifico?"

Sir William slapped Rica on the back and asked, "How would you like to be my personal horse trainer?"

A broad smile crossed Rica's face. "Indeed I would, but I owe Senor John so much."

John took Rica by the shoulders and looked into his friend's eyes. "You owe me nothing. We are friends, and that will always be. This is a wonderful opportunity, and serving the governor would be a great honor."

Rica smiled back at John with gratitude. He then turned to the governor and said, "Then I will accept."

Sir William was pleased. He asked the two men about their plans for the night. John said they would camp nearby, to which the governor protested. "Nonsense. You shall stay here with me tonight in my home. Tomorrow, I shall send you with an escort to Elizabeth City with a letter to the governor there."

John thanked Sir William and asked his reason for the escort. Sir William informed him that there had been some attacks by the Indians recently upon some of the villagers. William stated that the escort was for John's protection and added, "The Indians would prize a horse like yours."

The distance between the two settlements was only about twenty miles, but once again, the dense forest marked only by deer trails made the trip slow and difficult. John loved everything he saw about the undeveloped country. Great hardwoods were everywhere. The land was dark and so was the soil. It would be good farmland. Truly, this was a land to be prized.

The sun was high in the sky when John and his escort arrived in Elizabeth City. The new settlement had blossomed into a real town. A beehive of activity was the best way to describe the movement. There was a different feeling among the coastal folks. John could see more than one ship anchored in the bay. Men were loading and off-loading goods, and John could hear carpenters busy at work as they built a new structure for business.

No one seemed to take notice of John or the escort. Unlike Jamestown, the people here seemed more dedicated to making this land their own. In less than thirty years Elizabeth City was establishing trade through farming, fishing, and other ventures. The town welcomed skilled tradesman. John had no doubt that this town needed his talents, and he knew he would soon establish himself.

It was late in the day before John met with Captain Raleigh Croshaw. The captain welcomed John into his chambers. Captain Raleigh sat behind his desk reading the letter from Sir William. The captain engaged John in conversation. He took great interest in John's story.

He commented, "I'm afraid your tale is a common one for these waters. In fact, one of the ships in our harbor is being tended to after she was attacked much like you were. Have you heard that England is now at war with the Dutch? Dreadful business, war. It has made us all a bit concerned." Captain Raleigh poured a glass of wine for each of them. Then he picked up a long white stick with a small pot on the end. He stuffed the pot with ground, dry leaves before lighting it with the flame of a candle. The captain took a puff of the smoke, which he sucked through the stick. The air in the room was then filled with the aroma of the pungent smoke.

John gave a subdued cough. The captain replied, "Oh, so sorry. Would you care for some?"

John looked inquisitive. "No thank you. May I ask what it is?"

The captain chuckled. "The leaf is called tobacco. The natives taught us how to grow it. We drink in the smoke, so to speak. It has become quite the rage, and many are making handsome profits with its sale in England."

Surprised, John stated, "Amazing."

Captain Raleigh continued. "Let's address your circumstances, shall we? What makes your story so interesting to me is that it matches one told to me by a dozen or so sailors who managed to escape such an attack. They told of their escape and of a shipmate who saw to their safety. These men were picked up a few days later by another ship. The reason for my interest is they had Spanish coin in their possession. They told me that they were paid by the same shipmate who took command when the captain and first mate were badly injured. They stated there was no room on the boat for everyone, so their new commander chose to stay with the sinking ship." Then, looking more intently at John, the Captain Raleigh stated, "I presume that you are that man."

John's widened his eyes. This was remarkable news. With a low voice, he inquired, "Are the men ... all right? And what of my friend, Henry Finch?"

The captain sat back in his chair. "Ah, Mr. Finch. Did you know that he served in the King's Navy?"

John replied, "Aye, he told me of his service, and he was the one who instructed me in sailing and navigation."

Raleigh continued. "Good man, this Mr. Finch." With that, the captain called out, "Orderly, come here at once."

In short order, a side door opened, and in walked Henry Finch. When the two friends laid eyes on each other, they rushed together, hugging and patting each other on the back like two lost brothers.

Henry pushed back John and stared at him. "John, you made it!"

John replied, "As have you, my dear friend."

Henry became aware of his bearing and snapped to attention. "Sorry, sir. You called?"

Raleigh laughed. "Relax, man. I called you in because of Jonathan here. Is this the man you claim to have saved your life?"

Henry had a fiendish grin come over his face. "Can't be sure, sir. I was unconscious, you know."

John just shook his head. The three men laughed heartily at the pun.

After a brief visit, Raleigh asked Henry, "John here tells me that he is a smith. Is he any good?"

Henry replied, "Captain, John is the finest silversmith I have ever known. He is a craftsman for sure. It is in his heart to do his best at all he does. Even when in the restraints of Captain Wise, John gave his best. Our town needs a man like this."

Raleigh responded, "Excellent! Jonathan Devine, welcome to

Elizabeth City." Turning once more to Henry, he charged, "I shall put him in your care. Take the day and see to his needs."

John protested. "Oh, no, sir. I could not be a bother even to my dearest friend."

To which Henry replied, "John, you have cared for me and offered your life for mine. Please allow me the honor to care for you."

Humbly, John accepted.

Captain Raleigh dismissed the two by saying, "I want to hear more of your story, Mr. Devine. I will call for you after you get settled. Is there anything you need?"

John replied, "Just one thing. Where can I find Mr. Charles Briargate? I have some business I need to discuss with him."

The next morning, John found himself standing in front of the door of the office of Charles Briargate. The sun rose high in the sky, and still Charles had not arrived. It was the early afternoon before the man finally came in. It was obvious Mr. Briargate had spent the night in a tavern somewhere. He looked bedraggled. The smell of strong drink was upon him.

John stood when Charles approached. "Mr. Briargate, I presume?"

Charles was less than accommodating. "Maybe, and who might you be?"

John was leery. "Let's just say I am here on behalf of Captain Croshaw. Have you a moment?"

Charles opened his office door and led the way into a disheveled room. Charles took a seat behind a dusty old desk. He looked back and asked, "What can I do for you? May I ask who you might be?" Charles waited for John to provide a name.

John continued. "Who I am is of little consequence to you. Have you any letters of correspondence for a man named Jonathan Devine?"

The question troubled Charles. He had heard the name before, but he could not recall from whence. After all, a man of his position dealt with a lot of newcomers, but this name unnerved him. Charles thought that there might be an opportunity of sorts. He had benefited from others he knew nothing about.

He inquired, "What is your interest in this man?"

John remained stoic and aloof. "Mr. Robert Howell has a keen interest in Mr. Devine's whereabouts. Mr. Howell has been awaiting correspondences from him and has received nothing. I am here on his behalf. Likewise, Mr. Devine's family has been inquiring also. His family has not heard from him. I have learned that letters were sent to this office. I am to report to Mr. Howell on my findings." John looked at the deplorable condition of the office and added, "From what I see here, Mr. Howell would be most interested in my report."

Charles's heart raced, and sweat began to bead on his forehead. He removed a soiled handkerchief from his sleeve and wiped away the watery drops. He wanted to ask John about himself but was afraid to ask. John was bluffing, but Charles did not know that. Charles moved some things about on the desk. John stood erect and unmovable.

Charles responded, "I will have to find the letters. If they are still here."

John then replied, "Jonathan Devine was indentured to Mr. Howell, and he is concerned that he has never heard from him. Mr. Howell is also concerned because you haven't sent money to him from what Mr. Devine has produced."

Charles's head was whirling. He tried to make an excuse but couldn't think of one.

John continued his barrage. "It was suggested by Mr. Howell that you might be stealing from him, and if that is the case, you should be reported to the magistrate."

Charles continued to fumble around the office. "Can you give me a little time? I can have everything ready by tomorrow."

John looked steely eyed at the man. "I will be back first thing in the morning. See that you have everything ready." With that, John stormed out the door, slamming it behind him.

John's heart pounded severely in his chest. He felt so close to finding answers and yet no closer to the truth. He fought for composure. John took a stroll about the town. Shops were established on the waterfront. Men were moving goods from the dock. Carpenters were busy everywhere, completing buildings or starting new ones. It seemed to John that everyone was dedicated to the success of this new community—well, almost everyone.

John joined Henry, and together, they made their way to the local tavern for some lunch. John asked him about his recovery, to which Henry offered, "We were just a day out from casting off when I came to. I was still woozy from my condition. The men told me of your sacrifice. They said that they owed their lives to you."

John proclaimed, "Nonsense! The hand of the Almighty was upon us all."

Henry continued. "Be it as it may, they knew it was your skills that helped them escape."

John stopped a moment before speaking. "Henry, I did what I could, but every man pulled together. You have to know that. Had we not, we all would have perished."

John feared the fate of the others and asked, "Where are the other men now?"

Henry laughed. "Where do you think? They are sailors. They all have joined other ships. Sooner or later, they are bound to return. That is the nature of the trade. When they do, I am sure they will come to see me. I can hardly wait to see their faces when they find you here."

John was surprised at the thought of them returning to the sea. He asked, "Were they not afraid to board another ship?"

Henry shook his head. "The ocean and sailing are their lives. A true sailor loves the freedom and adventure the ocean offers. I fortune that deep down you already long to be back on board ship."

John hadn't given it much thought, but he knew Henry was right.

Throughout the night, the men exchanged stories. John told Henry all about his ordeal on the island, the captain's death, and of Rica and Spirit. John also told him of the captain's last words and his charge to John to see to the care of his wife and daughter.

Henry told of his recovery and what he knew of some of the men of the *Elizabeth Marie*. Then when the moment was right, Henry sat back in his chair before announcing, "John, I have met someone. Her name is Abigail."

John smiled. "You? You have met a lady?"

Henry was surprised at John's question. "Why does that seem so hard to grasp?"

John could not help himself. "Me thinks the blow to your head has done you good. It got you off the ship, placed you in a new position, and provided you a wife."

Henry retorted, "Now wait a minute, John. I'm not married."

John cut him off. "Yet."

Henry tried to look stern. It was no use. Together, they busted out laughing.

John arrived at Charles's office early the next morning. To his surprise, Charles arrived at the appointed time. He looked more presentable than before. Charles rushed up to John.

"Good morning, sir. I hope you slept well. Please come in. I have found what you have been waiting for."

They went into the office, which had been tidied up a bit. On the desk was a small pile of mail tied together with a string. John nearly lost his composure. He so wanted to grab up the letters and read them, for they contained news from home. Most of all, he hoped to have a letter from the woman he loved.

Charles went behind his desk. He lifted the bundle and handed it to John. "All of them are for Jonathan Devine."

Some had been opened. John's countenance fell. He fixed his stare at Charles. "Who opened these?"

Charles hung his head. "I did. I thought—"

John shouted back. "You thought nothing! Those letters belong to Jonathan Devine, and you, sir, dishonored him by reading what was intended for him in private. I ought to have you whipped."

Charles retorted, "But I didn't know how to get them to Mr. Devine."

John asked, "What did you do with the man?"

Charles felt trapped. His stomach was in knots. His greed had caught up with him. He never expected his actions would be called into question. Charles wanted a drink. His mouth was dry, and his nerve was gone. He began to shake. He moved his hand to a book and turned the page to a single entry. He pointed his finger to what was written. "I sold his services to a Captain Richard Wise. The captain promised he would fulfill the agreement made between Mr. Devine and Mr. Howell."

John did not flinch. "And how well do you know Captain Wise?"

Charles answered, "I had never met him before. He offered a handsome sum, which I was able to send to Mr. Howell."

John walked up to within inches of Charles. John's cold glare made Charles quake in his boots. John gritted his teeth and asked, "What did you tell Mr. Howell when the money promised him stopped coming in?"

Charles turned his head away, "I said—"

John stopped him. "You told him I was dead."

Charles staggered back. He looked into the eyes of the man he had unknowingly betrayed. "You?"

John stood like granite. "I am Jonathan Devine. You sold me, stole my life, and reported falsely against me. My family and betrothed may even now think me dead."

Charles was shocked, and his mind was in a whorl. "What do you—"

John cut him off. "Plan to do with you? First, you will write a letter to Mr. Howell telling him that you were misinformed. You will tell him that Mr. Devine is very much alive. There is a ship leaving for England soon. I expect that letter to be on that ship before it departs. Next, according to my service agreement, I am to be given a plot of land. You will buy that land for me. We will select it together. Your days of stealing are over. Consider yourself indebted to Mr. Jonathan Devine."

# A Time to Prepare

John sat alone at a small table. Henry's home was small in comparison to many new homes being built. He was pouring over the letters he'd gotten from Charles Briargate. All the letters were open and spread across the table. John sat with his elbows posed so that his head rested in the palms of his hands. The letters were all marred by his tears. Each teardrop caused the dried ink to explode on the page. The most touching letter was one from his father.

> Hello, Son. Yes, I am writing a letter to you. Chastity has taught me to write and read a little. I love you and pray you are well.

John could hardly imagine that he was reading something from his father's hand. There were letters from Pastor Elijah, Adam, Thomas Shepherd, and even from Emit Browning, but the one he read over and over again was from Chastity.

> My beloved John,

> How much I miss you. Every day my thoughts are filled with you. I have not heard from you but once, and it is hard. It has been six months since you departed for Massachusetts. Have you begun your work as a smith? I can't wait to see you. I hope to be making the trip soon. Oh, how I hope you are there waiting for me when I come off the ship. I know it isn't proper, but I want you

to take me into your arms and welcome me. I am praying
for us, and I cannot wait to be your wife.

John read the letter over and over. Each time, new tears filled his
eyes from a heart that felt very much alone. Could his sweet Chastity
even now be in America? John fought the anger that welled up inside of
him, because this was one of the letters that Charles had opened. Charles
opened one other letter—one from Emit. In that letter, Emit spoke of
their budding friendship and even wanted to commission some of his
work for sale in England. John thought, *Does Emit think I am dead?*

After regaining his composure, John hurried to write letters. He
knew that the ship leaving for England would leave with the tide. He
wanted these letters, no matter how brief, to be on the ship when it
departed. He took out paper and pen from Henry's table and quickly
wrote letters to Emit, his family, Chastity, and Thomas Shepherd. Each
letter had to be to the point. He would send them to the attention of Emit
Browning, knowing full well that he would get the letters to the others.

John wrote as fast as he could. It was hard for him to contain his
energy. So quickly did he write that he took little notice of grammar.
He had little time to make sure everything was correct. He would make
sure future letters were carefully scripted. Finally, after he had penned
what he could to all intended, he wrote to Chastity. He closed the letter
by writing, "I'm ready for you to come to me or me to you."

John hurried with the letters to the dock. The shipmaster was about
to board the boat that would take him to the ship when John approached
him. "I am glad I caught you. I need these letters delivered to Mr. Emit
Browning in care of Mr. Robert Howell. The address and location are
both there. I need these letters delivered to him as soon as you arrive.
This is for your efforts." John handed the shipmaster a Spanish gold coin.

The shipmaster's eyes widened and assured John by saying, "Yes, sir.
I shall see to it."

John continued. "Bring me word from him on your return, and I shall
reward you equally."

With a tip of his hat, the shipmaster responded, "It shall be done."

Susan and Chastity sat at the table in the early afternoon. The sun beamed through the window, while Susan made a hot drink called sassafras. Chastity had never tasted a drink like this before. Susan sweetened it with a little honey. As the two women supped on the drink, Susan explained, "The Indians introduced this drink to some of the early settlers. It takes some getting used to, but I have come to enjoy it."

Chastity tasted it and then proclaimed, "Very interesting. I agree that I will have to get used to it."

The girls giggled at the statement.

In no time at all, Chastity and Susan's relationship blossomed into a great friendship. Susan shared how they had come to America.

"You know of our faith in God and our desire to worship freely, but I have not told you how we came to be here."

Chastity was truly interested in what Susan was about to say. She sipped on her drink as Susan continued.

"George was a carpenter's apprentice near Smithfield. He showed great promise and had introduced some new designs in his buildings. The pay he received was very little. We knew we could not afford to live on what he earned but did not want to be a burden to either of our families. My family is somewhat prominent in London. My father owns a money-lending business and has profited by it, but even so, he could not afford to give continuous aid to us. We wanted to get married. Father could not discourage us, though he tried. He wanted us to wait. Eventually, it was his idea that we come to America and offered to pay for our passage."

Susan drank from her cup and then let out a sigh. "That was nearly ten years ago. It was common knowledge that the new town of Boston was in need of carpenters. Once we left, a new hardship presented itself." With a deep sigh she added, "I haven't seen my family since."

Chastity took Susan's hand. "How have you managed? Not seeing your family, I mean."

Susan tried to hide the pain. "I try not to say anything to anyone. I would never let on to George. He is very loving, but he would not understand. In fact, I think he sent for a governess more to be a companion to me than for the children. Even he is surprised how quickly we became fast friends."

Chastity squeezed Susan's hand in agreement. She thought for a moment before commenting. "I am surprised that George didn't ask a family member to come. Have you any sisters?"

Susan turned her face a little to the left. Her answer was chilling. "There is more to the story. Our desire to worship was not met with approval by certain members of the family. Some are staunch Anglicans. I have one sister, and she has married. She and her husband live near Dad and Mum. He is a magistrate in London." Wrinkling her nose, she stated, "Her husband isn't a very handsome bloke."

Chastity had just taken a sip of her drink and nearly choked on the unexpected comment. Suddenly, the solemn mood turned to laughter.

Chastity looked about the room. "You have been blessed. I truly hope John is as successful in his endeavors."

Susan remarked, "From what you have told me of your young man, I am sure of it. Seems that in this land, if you have a mind to work, you can prosper." Then Susan reached for Chastity's left hand. "Men with the skills of your John ought to do well like my George." Susan stood with an air of excitement. "Now it is my turn to give you something."

Chastity looked at her with surprise. "What?"

Susan hurried to the next room and reappeared with some papers that she laid upon the table. Upon the papers were lines filled with dots and marks. Susan explained, "Do you know what this is?"

Chastity replied, "No, I don't. What kind of writing is this?"

Susan chuckled. "It is called music, and it is time for your first lesson." Then she took Chastity by the hand and rushed to the harpsichord.

Many missteps and misgivings have been made for being too rash. Oftentimes, things said and done too hastily result in unintentional trouble. John had time to calm down and think about things he had said to Charles Briargate. John and Henry were making their way to Charles's office. John told all that had transpired and some of the things said in haste. He then remarked, "I have thought it over, and I believe I should apologize to Mr. Briargate. If he is so inclined, he can continue to work with me under my personal direction. I will need your assistance in helping me make my point."

Henry was stunned. "Me? How so?"

John continued. "Your presence will supply added proof that I am no longer obligated to Richard Wise. Charles will soon learn that I have the knowledge and talent to accomplish what I want."

Henry looked puzzled. "I don't understand."

John replied, "You will, my dear friend. You will."

The three men sat in front of Charles Briargate. Charles positioned himself behind his desk, appearing less shaken than before.

When everyone was seated, John introduced Henry. "Charles Briargate, this is Henry Finch, an officer in the service of our governor Captain Raleigh Croshaw. Henry is also my trusted counselor and advisor in my business affairs."

Henry was surprised and felt a great deal of honor at the proclamation.

John continued. "Should you have any doubt that my debt has been paid in full, I present Mr. Finch as proof to the matter."

With that, Henry nodded in agreement. This announcement caused Charles to sink lower in his chair. It was as if he planned to challenge John when next they met concerning his indentured service being ended. Now that opportunity was gone.

John stood up from his chair and began walking around the room. He stopped at a bookshelf and wiped the dust from it with his fingers. He turned to look at Charles. "I have had time to think about what I said to you. I was a bit hasty and full of ire. Some of my anger has subsided. However, you invaded my privacy by opening and reading my letters, and I cannot excuse such behavior."

When Henry heard that Charles had opened John's letters, he looked at the man and scowled.

John turned to face the desk and continued. "I am willing to secure your employment. I offer you to partner with me after a different fashion."

Charles was unsure of what John was saying and asked, "What do you mean, employ?"

John replied, "It is quite simple really. I have dispatched a letter to Mr. Howell stating that you are now in the employment of Mr. Jonathan Devine. From this time on, I will be the liaison and representative of all newly arrived indentures. I now manage this business. If you want to continue in your situation, you will work for me."

Charles was stunned. "I now work for you?"

John answered, "Yes, dear fellow, and with that, I have certain requirements."

Charles did not know if this turn of events was good fortune or not. He was suddenly aware that Jonathan Devine was not a man to trifle with. He never imagined that he would be held accountable for his actions, especially so far away from England. He knew that if he rejected the forthcoming proposal, he wouldn't have the means to live. A much humbler man looked to John and asked, "What do I have to do?"

John replied, "First, I want this office cleaned. Then I want to look at the books and receipts. I trust they are in order. Mr. Finch and I will oversee the operations until I am sure of your work. You might say that I am placing you on warning. Finally, Captain Richard Wise charged me in the care of his wife and daughter in England. We will see to their financial security and well-being."

Charles questioned, "How?"

John replied, "That will be my problem. Now, as for my property ..."

Susan showed Chastity how to read the music and how the notes correlated with the keys on the keyboard. Soon, the sounds of plucked notes could be heard from the harpsichord. Chastity's mistakes and amateur playing caused the children to come running into the house to see for themselves what was going on. They could not imagine their mother playing so poorly. They were all surprised to see Chastity sitting and struggling to play the beloved instrument. The older children began to chuckle at the many mistakes.

Faith climbed into her mother's arms. "Is Miss Tasty all-white? Did she break the hop-si-cord?"

Susan laughed. "No, Faith. She is just learning."

Faith whispered in her mother's ear. "I hope she werns fast."

In spite of their friendship, the new governess took her responsibility with the children seriously. It wasn't long before the children settled into their new routine. The family was already used to getting up at dawn. After a hearty breakfast, George would leave to go work on whatever building he was hired to build, and the rest of the family worked on chores. When everything was cleaned up and chores were completed,

Chastity would begin teaching the children. She emphasized reading and utilized the Bible for most of the assignments. She also taught the children mathematics. All the while, she thought of the lessons she'd given John.

Isaac consumed all things dealing with numbers, and Sarah loved reading. Chastity also made the children practice their penmanship, stressing the importance of proper handwriting. She always made sure that there was room for fun. At least twice a week she taught children songs from the Bible. From time to time, she would take the children outdoors to look for rocks and leaves, to watch animals, and even to look for fossils.

One day Isaac surprised the others by saying, "I would like to play the violin like Papaw."

Chastity replied, "Then I shall approach him for you. If you would like, Master Isaac."

Isaac like the sound of being called Master Isaac.

Chastity was also learning. She practiced the harpsichord constantly, even though the children poked fun at her. More importantly, she was learning how to raise and teach a family.

Susan and Chastity became inseparable. Whether it was to church or into town, they were always together. George was glad for their friendship. It had been difficult for Susan to be so far away from her family. Now that Chastity was there, he could see the sisterly relationship they built together. In fact, George felt more comfortable leaving for work knowing that Susan would not be alone.

Sunday was a day of worship. In seventeenth-century Boston, there was little fear of persecution. Believers could openly worship and praise the Lord. Chastity was surprised that this freedom offered something more. One way in which she saw this freedom was in the music. People sang from the heart. The church did not use instruments, because the church could not afford them. The pastor led by singing a verse. Afterward, the congregation would repeat it just as they heard it sung. The congregation lifted their voices in vibrant praise. How unlike her home in England where praise would lead to persecution. Chastity had never heard anything so beautiful. It was her delight to add her melodic voice to the number.

The church members were pleased to have a young and energetic woman in their congregation. Many of the young men were heartbroken to find out that she was already betrothed to another. While envy is a sin, some of the women were jealous of her when they saw for themselves the beautiful ring John had made.

But rainbows do not appear without a storm. Little did Chastity know that there was one who would gladly cause such a storm in order to capture her attention. One Saturday George brought the family into town for shopping and a time of relaxation. The outing was just what the family needed. It was a rare occasion when Chastity was separated from the family. However, on that day, she roamed the town alone, while George and Susan visited shops with the children in tow. It was all the opportunity that Nathan needed. He followed her into one of the shops before snaking his way toward her.

When he was close enough, he announced, "Miss Shepherd, so good to see you again. Now where have you been keeping yourself?"

Chastity was alarmed to see Nathan Porter and responded, "Mr. Porter, I-I am surprised to see you."

Nathan replied, "But good surprised, I hope."

Chastity wasn't sure what to say or how to react. Stepping back, she added, "It's just that I wasn't expecting anyone. I am here on an outing with the family I care for."

Nathan retorted, "Do they own you? Haven't you any time for yourself?"

The remark angered her. "Mr. Porter, do not assume you know anything about my life. I am here on their behalf, and I am more than grateful to be with them. I love the family as my own and enjoy being with them, not out of obligation, for I have all the time I desire. I would thank you not to refer to Mr. and Mrs. Abernathy with disrespect, which I very much doubt you are capable of."

The people nearby took notice of what Chastity said, and displeased looks were directed at Nathan.

Nathan sheepishly retreated. He raised his hands. "I meant no disrespect. I just thought a girl like you would enjoy some time away with someone else."

Chastity replied, "Like me? I suppose you think I would be entertained by you? You said a girl like me as though you know me. Well, sir, you don't know me, and I will see to it that you never will. No thank you. I much prefer my family's company and that of the church to which we belong."

Nathan smiled. "A church girl, eh?"

Chastity replied in offense, "Yes, a church girl, and one who loves God. The way you just said it proves all the more your disdain for believers in the Almighty."

Nathan stopped her. "Once again, I have unintentionally offended. I too go to church from time to time. Perhaps I shall see you there."

Chastity replied, "We shall see, shan't we?"

That evening the family loaded into the carriage. In the shadows, Nathan remained hidden. When the carriage pulled away, he followed at a distance. He wanted to know where Chastity lived. He watched as the carriage turned up the way toward the Abernathys' home. He rode his horse near the hedge of the road to conceal his whereabouts. He was careful to keep his distance and watched as the family climbed from the carriage and entered into their home. He was about to leave when he saw Chastity exit the house and enter the cabin.

An evil grin crossed his face. "So this is where you live, eh, Miss Shepherd? Prefect."

John returned the next day and found Charles with the legers at the ready. Charles had spent time cleaning the office. He had to if he were to find all the necessary items that John sought. John looked over the ledger and from time to time inquired about certain persons who were sponsored by Mr. Powell only to have their service sold.

Charles answered, "It is a common practice. As goods are traded, so are contracts."

John was puzzled. "The sponsors in England are not bothered by this?"

Charles replied, "Some are, but usually, once they receive their money, they accept the transaction."

John slid his finger down the page. John stopped when he came to his name. Unlike the others, a line was marked across it. There was no transaction as to what became of him. John looked at Charles. "What does this mean?"

Charles stated, "You did not arrive. If anyone inquired about you, I would say that you never made it."

John looked at him. "Therefore, I am presumed dead?"

Charles began to wring his hands and pace the room, "Your captain offered me a good sum of money for your services. Men die at sea, you know, and—"

John shot back. "And you wanted anyone who inquired to assume I was dead? How dare you!" John clenched his fist. His face reddened with the anger he felt. He walked over and laid his hands on the back of a chair to regain his composure.

John breathed slowly in and out. He gripped the chair so tight that his fingers and knuckles turned white. His grip caused the wood to crack. He announced, "Sit down, Mr. Briargate."

Charles responded, "Sir?"

John repeated himself slowly and directly. "I said, sit down."

Charles took his seat.

"I want you to write a letter to Mr. Howell letting him know that I am not dead. Tell him that my services were purchased by Mr. Henry Finch."

Charles gave him a questioning look, but without uttering a word, he did as he was told.

Silence filled the room except for the scratching of the pen tip to paper. When Charles had completed the letter, John asked, "How much did the captain pay you?"

Charles answered, "I ... I ... don't recall."

John placed his hand on the desk. "How much did he pay you?"

Charles hung his head and then replied, "He gave me five hundred pounds with a promise to deliver me another one hundred pounds each year for the next five years."

John found it hard to contain his anger. He asked, "Was the soul of another worth the price of enslavement? You, dear fellow, allowed your lust for money to—" John stopped himself. His chest heaved from the deep breaths he took. John wanted to be rational but found it hard. Finally, he asked, "How much did you send to Mr. Howell?"

Charles was afraid to answer but finally said, "Nothing."

John smiled. "Well, my dear fellow, that is about to change. You will send Mr. Howell the five hundred pounds you received from the captain."

Charles stammered, "I … I … I don't have it."

John gritted his teeth and slammed his fist on the desk. He shouted, "Then you better find it!" Then sternly he added, "In the letter, I want you to promise that Mr. Finch will pay one hundred pounds a year till the debt has been fulfilled. Did you get that, Mr. Briargate?"

Charles stated, "I don't know what he will say."

John said, "I don't care. You took my life from me. I want my life back."

When all was done, John took the letter and sealed it. He told Charles to have the money ready before the next ship to England sailed. Afterward, John paced the room till he was calm enough to continue.

John explained, "Before the captain died, he made me promise to see to the care of his wife and daughter. I intend to keep that promise. I have prepared letters to Emit Browning in London to serve as my broker. You will keep ledgers of all transactions. I expect reforms in this office, Mr. Briargate. Men will not be lost to unscrupulous dealings. Do you understand?"

Charles considered all that John was purposing. He wanted to ask questions but didn't know where to start. He simply nodded his head.

John returned to his seat. He leaned back in it before continuing. "Our office will offer financial services for qualified individuals. If all goes well and you prove yourself, from time to time, I will be sending you back to England to report to Mr. Howell about our service. My intention is to make our office profitable and worthy of people's trust. This place has been a bleak and dire place. Never again will I let this happen. I will see to it that people are made aware of the new service."

Charles asked, "Where shall I find the money to begin such an operation?"

John stood, preparing to leave. He walked over to collect his hat and then made his way toward the door. Turning back toward Charles, he stated, "That will be my responsibility." He then placed his hand on the door latch. "Most men in my position would have you publicly flogged. I am willing to give you a chance. Make the most of it, Mr. Briargate. I am a patient man, but I will not tolerate laziness or incompetence." With that, he opened the door and announced, "Tomorrow I wish to see the land I was promised by Mr. Howell."

Late one night there was a knock at the door. Chastity wondered why Susan needed her attention after everyone was in bed. Maybe one of the children was sick. Call it a woman's intuition, but Chastity went to the door and immediately felt guarded. She knew that it wasn't Susan. Susan had become accustomed to knocking and announcing herself. If it was one of the children, they would keep knocking and calling, "Miss Tasty!" George would never come to the door, as it would be most inappropriate. She hadn't a clue who it might be.

Cautiously, Chastity called out, "Who is it?"

There was no answer. Whoever the visitor was, he or she was not about to give themselves away. Again, there was a knock at the door.

Chastity called back, "It is much too late to be receiving visitors. Please come again when the hour is more acceptable."

The stranger knocked again. Now Chastity feared that someone in the house must be hurt, but she knew better than to open the door. No, whoever it was must speak first.

Chastity called out again. "Seeing that you refuse to answer, I shall refuse to open my door. Good night."

The next day Chastity told Susan of her ordeal. Susan commented, "Oh, I bet it was a limb from the tree tapping the door. There was a gentle wind last night, and I suspect that was the knocking. Either that or a bear." Chastity tried to mask her concern with laughter but remained unsure and afraid.

When the day was done and night chased away the light, Chastity once again made her way to her cabin. She was about to open the door when she heard from behind, "Good evening, Miss Shepherd."

Chastity turned to face the masculine voice. There, standing in the fading light, stood Nathan Porter. She felt like screaming, but Nathan sought to silence her. "Please do not be alarmed. I only wanted to make a social visit."

Chastity shot back. "As you did last night?"

Nathan smiled. "So you knew it was me?"

Chastity angrily proclaimed, "Do not flatter yourself, Mr. Porter. I was not sure who it was, but you had no business coming to my cabin. Even now, this is most inappropriate, and I bid you good night."

Chastity turned to leave. Nathan did not like her tone. He was not accustomed to women halting his advances. His countenance changed, and he more directly stated, "Do not be so hasty, Miss Shepherd. I can cause a great deal of trouble for you in town and even among the church members you put so much stock in."

Chastity turned quickly. "What do you mean?"

Nathan stood smugly. "Now what would a single woman be doing here in Boston? A woman who is of marrying age. I am sure that some of the women are already suspicious. If a rumor was to be started that you are entertaining men late at night …"

Chastity shot back. "That is a bold-faced lie."

Nathan looked evil in the pale light. "Am I not here?"

Chastity ran to her cabin as fast as she could. Nathan did not chase her. To do so might cause her to scream. He would be patient and allow his words to take their course. She would either begin seeing him, or he would mar her name throughout the town of Boston. He congratulated himself on his craftiness. He had no doubt that she would see him, or he would destroy her in the process.

Chastity paced the floor. No matter how tired she was, she could not sleep. She went to bed and prayed for sleep to come, but over and over, she thought of what Nathan said. It was nearly morning when she finally fell to sleep, but any noise would quickly shake her awake.

At breakfast, Susan could tell something was wrong. Chastity was not her usually buoyant self. Susan invited her to sit and talk, but Chastity declined politely. "I have so much to do," she said. Even the children could not make her smile.

When the day was nearly done, Susan seized upon an opportunity to speak to Chastity. Faith was taking her nap, and the other children were busy with chores. Susan came to Chastity with a cup of sassafras. "I have a friend who loves talking with me. Do you know where I can find her?"

Chastity had tears streaming from her eyes. Susan put down the cups and took Chastity in her arms. "What's wrong?" she questioned.

Chastity sobbed. Susan held Chastity till the crying subsided. She led her to a chair, and they sat down together. Through sobs, Chastity told Susan about who it was who knocked at the door and his return visit last night. Chastity cried, "I don't know what to do."

Susan calmed her. "One thing is for certain. We must tell George."

That night, after the children were in bed, Chastity recounted the story for George. In anger, he marched about the room and proclaimed, "Who does this libertine think he is? I knew the moment I laid eyes on him I did not like him."

Chastity cried, "I fear I have no choice but to flee."

George quickly turned to face her. "Nonsense, girl. You will stay in our house from now on."

Chastity explained, "I thought of that, but that is exactly what he wants me to do. If I do, he will say that I have become your mistress. If I go to my cabin, then he shall try and approach me again. I just know it."

George paced the floor, mumbling to himself. Then he turned and explained, "Then we shall give the man what he wants."

Evening gave way to night, and a lone figure wearing a cloak rushed to the cabin. The light remained low. Hiding within the garment, the body moved about, adding dry wood to the hot coals. Soon, a soft glow filled the room. Shadows revealed gentle hands touching a dry, thin stick to the flames. Once lit, the tiny fire was carried to the table and touched to the wick of a candle, bringing its flame to life.

A man peered through the window from outside. The outside menace could see no one, but he knew the girl was in the cabin. Nathan walked to the door and tapped lightly. Without warning, the door flung open, and two great hands grabbed Nathan and flung him into the room.

George threw off his wrap and head covering. "So you are the worm who dares to challenge the honor of an innocent woman."

Instantly, Nathan felt the pain applied by George's backhand. Nathan was stunned. "Who do you think you are?"

George gritted his teeth. "I am George Abernathy, and Chastity Shepherd is in my governess. You are not welcome here, and I demand you leave her be."

Nathan glared at George. "And how do you know I was not invited here by her?"

George gripped Nathan's lapel tighter. "It is enough that I know the testimony of her father and pastor. What they have to say is honorable. I trust their word over a loathsome creature like you."

Nathan was not done accusing. "Perhaps you just want her for yourself."

George reared his hand back to apply another strike. This time, Nathan stopped his hand short. "I would not do that again. My father has influence with the king."

George snarled, "A king who sent you here to get rid of you like vermin from England's shores."

The moment was tense, and the men stood toe to toe, glaring at each other. George calmed himself long enough to issue his warning. "Never show your face around my house or my family again. That includes Miss Chastity Shepherd. If I find you anywhere near here, I swear that I shall beat you like the rodent you are."

Nathan straightened his clothes. He gave a huff before exiting the cabin.

John and Henry met for dinner at the tavern. Soon, John spoke to him about returning to the location of the shipwreck. "I need a boat big enough for us to make the trip back to the location where I buried the captain."

Henry asked, "Are you sure you can find it?"

"I'm sure," John replied. "With favorable winds, we could be there in two, three days tops. It will take me a day to gather what I am after. Then another two or three days back."

Henry thought, *I could ask Captain Raleigh for the time. I'm sure he would aid us in our journey.* Then Henry sat back with his mug of beer. He looked over at his dear friend. "You know, the longboat from which we escaped is still here."

Surprised by the information, John asked, "Is it seaworthy?"

Henry laughed. "Well, it got me here, didn't it? You can check it out in the morning. If all goes well, we could leave less than a week. What do you say?"

John thought it over. "Yes, that will do. I have more work to do here.

Secure your time, my friend, for we shall soon travel south." Then John smiled. "Now when do I get to meet this Abigail?"

Just then, a woman spoke up from behind him. "Right here and now."

John turned to see a very pretty woman who appeared to be about thirty-five years old. John rose to his feet, removed his hat, and extended his hand. "Miss Abigail?"

She fixed her eyes on the young man. "So you be John? Henry hasn't hushed about you since your arrival. He tells me you are quite the craftsman, but he never mentioned how handsome you are."

John blushed. "Thank you, madam. I think."

Abigail Landry had come to America ten years prior. After they arrived, she and her late husband built the tavern. Her husband knew how to make beer. He even found a good source of wild muscadine grapes and made wine. They had hoped in a few years to begin a family, but five winters later, her husband caught pneumonia and died. She had managed to run the tavern by herself, even continuing to make the beer and wine. When Henry first darkened her doors, he was still recovering from the wounds he received during the battle. Abigail took compassion on him and nursed him back to health. She even introduced Henry to Captain Croshaw and got Henry's appointment. In due time, Abigail and Henry had fallen in love.

Henry sat back. "Jonathan here wants me to join him in a little trip, love. Would you mind?"

Abigail smarted back, "Why should I care? You're a man and apt to do what you want anyway. Am I right?"

Henry laughed. "Reckon so. We will be gone about a week."

She leaned forward on the table to him. "Just be sure you make it back to me."

John couldn't help but smile.

Before leaving for the night, Henry asked John about the meeting with Charles. "I don't think I fully understand what's going on with him or your intentions. Tell me, John, what are you planning?"

John sat forward in his chair. His face revealed deep thought on the matter. He chose his words carefully. "Charles was employed by several clients to oversee those who came here as indentured servants. While there is no law protecting those who have indentured themselves, they came with a sealed agreement. Charles profited by selling their services to others. I discovered that he pocketed large sums of money by selling their services to those willing to pay handsomely. In the ledgers he keeps, he would mark through their names, indicating that something happened to them."

Henry asked, "So is that what Charles did to you?"

John nodded.

Henry's anger grew, knowing what John went through with Captain Wise. He was also confused as to why John would consider continuing Charles's service. Henry expressed his concern. "How then can you trust a man like that and continue to allow him to be involved?"

John answered, "It's simple, really. Charles is the one man the sponsors know as their contact. If I was to interrupt this contact, those in England might become suspicious. Besides, it would take months to make the change. I will use him because he understands the system, has the contacts, and knows how it should be done. You, my friend, will play an important role, because of your contact with the governor of our settlement and his law enforcement. Charles wouldn't dare go against Captain Croshaw, and he wouldn't want the captain investigating his activities. By your involvement, you will receive a bit of financial reward for your assistance. You wouldn't mind that, would you?"

Henry just smiled. "You have a very intriguing mind, John. I must make sure I am careful should I ever sport a game with you."

John smiled. "This is more than a game. This is life."

The departure day would come soon enough. John had much to do before they could make the trip back to the camp. For one thing, there was the land that he wanted to procure for himself. John met with Charles, and together they looked at several properties. About midafternoon, they went to a fifty-acre plot belonging to Mr. Howell for those who completed their service.

Charles commented, "This is one of the parcels of land available to you. I looked at all the different plots, and this seemed to me to be the best."

John left Charles to survey the property. It was plush with hardwoods and grasslands. John imagined the kind of house the oak would make. From a rising knoll, John could see the ocean. He imagined his own sturdy house for him and Chastity. The grasslands would support livestock. He thought of Spirit enjoying the green grass while being annoyed by sheep grazing nearby. He took a deep breath and smelled the amazing mixture of grass and salt water. He walked back to where he had left Charles. John stopped to look back at the land and then turned to face Charles before stating, "Secure it for me, Mr. Briargate."

John found the only stonecutter in town. He inquired as to his abilities to make headstones for two graves. The man agreed that he could make the headstones but bulked at the idea of having them ready within a week. John explained that this was a matter of great importance. The stonecutter continued his protest until John laid before him a gold Spanish coin. The yellow hue quickly caught the man's attention. If John's persuasion had not convinced the man, the gold did.

John explained, "I will pay you this gold coin if you have the work done by the desired time."

The stonecutter responded, "It shall be done."

Another time John met with Captain Croshaw. John needed a good place to build his shops. He inquired as to the best possible location. The captain rose from his chair and walked over to gather his coat from the wall peg. Putting on his coat, he invited, "Let's go look for ourselves, shall we?"

The two men left together to see the hustle and bustle of the little town. John enjoyed the company of Captain Raleigh. The captain was proud of the town's development. As they walked together, many tipped their hats in greeting. People took notice of the man who accompanied the captain. They thought to themselves that this man must be of real importance to be associated with the governor. People could see a confidence in John. He also felt more alive than he had in a long time. He believed his prayers were being answered.

As the two men walked together, John discussed some of his plans with the captain. He told him that he wanted to build a foundry. He explained, "My trade requires good metal, which must be melted and formed. It takes a lot of heat to melt these metals to get the results I hope for. I can't explain, but let's say the fire may smell rather offensive. The people might frown on such orders emitting in the air."

The captain gave a simple nod, indicating he understood, and then said with a smile, "That, my friend, is the price of progress. Don't you think?"

On the edge of the budding town, they found just what they were looking for. A small rise led down to a nice flat spot. On this rise, John could build his foundry and in the lower land his blacksmith and silversmith shops. John knew he would need builders competent in their work to build what he needed. He would have to know about their skills before seeking their help.

Captain Raleigh smiled, as he could see all the ideas forming in his young friend's mind. He then said to John, "So may I ask what you're thinking?"

John pointed toward the hill. "I will build the foundry just there." He pointed in another direction and said, "Over there will be the barn for the smith shop, and over there ..." John suddenly realized that he was being played. He snapped his hands behind his back and turned to face the captain. "This will do nicely." A brief silence existed between the two men before they began to laugh heartily.

Later, the two men walked back toward town and headed for the tavern. Upon entering, they found a table. Captain Croshaw nodded at Abigail, and she called for the cook to prepare something special for her guests. Shortly thereafter, Abigail served them slices of roast pig and freshly baked bread.

John saw Raleigh slip Abigail a little extra money and inquired why he did such a thing.

Captain Raleigh explained, "It is a practice that some in English society do to get preferential treatment. We call it a tip in order to get the best service.

John smiled. "I very much doubt that Abigail would care much either way. After all, she is in love with a man the likes of my friend Henry."

No sooner were these words spoken than Henry appeared. He replied, "Did someone speak my name?"

John faked a coughed as he rose to his feet and quickly welcomed Henry. "Come, sit. I was just saying what a fine lady your Abigail is, and still, she loves a salty dog like you."

Henry tried to look offended as he replied, "Me thinks she has found in me the better qualities of a man." Then leaning forward so only they three could hear, he said, "I am quite fortunate. Am I not?"

Even Captain Croshaw tried to keep from choking at Henry's quick answer.

Henry grabbed a chair and joined his two compatriots. After he sat down, John told him of the outing that he enjoyed with the captain. After a time of pleasantries, John asked, "Captain, I would like to borrow Henry's services for a week or a bit longer if you can spare him. You see, I must return to the location of the shipwreck and my camp to fulfill a promise that I made to myself. While there, I must gather certain of my belongings. I will need these things before I can begin my work here. I seek permission from you to allow me to employ Henry's services to accompany me on this journey."

The captain admired the relationship of the two men. A friendship like theirs was special. Captain Raleigh replied, "It is obvious that you and Henry have a remarkable relationship born on seas of trouble. Together you have forged a lasting friendship. I had a friend like that once who died at sea from scurvy. I miss him and think of him often. We were very close." He leaned back in his chair before continuing. "Adversity and challenge drew you both together. Conflict secured your relationship." He raised his right eyebrow. "It would be my privilege to give him time to assist in your endeavor."

John was deep in thought as he offered, "Captain, I may never be able to replace a friend lost, but I offer myself as a friend to you."

The captain showed his approval with a smile.

Nathan stood at the shipmaster's counter. He kept a watch on all shipping as it entered into the harbor. Whenever a ship came in, he made his way to the harbor and the shipmaster to see what might have come in. Sometimes it was the pirate ship that entered the harbor. Other times, it was a British ship that the pirates, under order, left alone. Nathan was pleased with his circumstances. Already the contract he made with the pirates was paying off. The pirates were constantly hampering Dutch ships. What few ships had managed to escape were reluctant to leave New Amsterdam, fearing attack. The pirates had also raided the town.

The pirates had managed to deprive the settlers of New Amsterdam of long-awaited supplies, while at the same time keeping the town fearful.

The people of New Amsterdam needed supplies and materials. While the area around the settlement was plush with game and resources, they longed to have items from their homeland. Simple things like salt and gunpowder, along with lead for bullets were needed. Deprived of these things from abroad, they soon realized the only sources for these supplies were in Boston and Plymouth. Soon the residents of New Amsterdam sent men to Boston and Plymouth for the supplies and things they needed.

Nathan had convinced a mercantile to sell his business to him. Afterward, Nathan was more than willing to sell to those from New Amsterdam at a marked increase in price while keeping his prices cheaper than other merchants to residence of Boston. His actions were having an impact on Bostonians. Local merchants could not compete with his lower prices. The merchants knew Nathan had an advantage, but they lacked evidence to accuse him of any wrongdoing. Nathan was pleased that his plan was working so well. Now it was time to focus on his other endeavor. On that day, he would set in motion a plan that would impact a woman who remained distant and coy to him.

Nathan stood at the shipmaster's counter. A letter bearing his family stamp was waiting for him. Nathan turned away from everyone and slipped a small penknife beneath the wax seal, making sure that it did not break. Then, turning quickly to the counter, he demanded, "Who opened my letter?"

Those in attendance faced Nathan.

Looking squarely at the shipmaster, he charged, "I demand to know who opened this letter from my father."

Looking among the people, he showed them the evidence. "See, someone has opened the letter by not disturbing the seal." Nathan opened the letter and proclaimed, "Seeing that someone is so interested in my letter, I shall divulge its contents." He opened the letter and pretended to read. "Ah, my father sends his greetings from the king." He added, "My father is an advisor and trusted friend to His Majesty." He acted as though he read more, "I see that he has sent to me a sum of one hundred pounds." The letter said nothing of the sort, but it would have the effect Nathan wanted. He turned to the shipmaster. "Well, sir, where is my money?"

Everyone looked discerningly at the shipmaster. He opened the ship's bill of lading. There was nothing there. Addressing Nathan, he said, "I'm sorry, sir, but there is nothing listed in the ledger for you."

Nathan paraded around like a peacock acting angry and deprived. "I was depending on that money for my business. I see I shall have to take the matter up with the king." Before Nathan allowed another word to be uttered, he stormed out of the office.

A fiendish smile crept over Nathan's face. "That ought to get the people talking." Nathan was counting on the people to spread the word that he had direct connections to the king, and that was the effect. People began talking of the new merchant's relationship with the king. Before long, men doffed their hats to him. As if by magic, Nathan had suddenly become a man of importance.

At the same time, suspicion can create mistrust. A lie placed in just the right place can make a person seem more honorable. The next day Nathan waited till a good number of people had gathered at the shipmaster's office. Nathan entered, and as soon as people became aware that he was there, they parted for him, giving him direct access to the shipmaster. Nathan approached the shipmaster, thanking those who were there. He offered, "I will not take long." Then, turning to the shipmaster, he said, "I feel I have acted in haste. I offer my sincerest apologies to you, fine sir. I realize that it was not your fault that my father's money was not added to the lading. I am sure the fault rests in England with whomever saw to the manifest."

Turning back to those standing in the office, he said, "Our shipmaster is one of the finest men in the town. Forgive me for any concern I may have caused you to have in him." Nathan then nodded his head toward the shipmaster and backed away, bidding him, "Good day."

Nathan had managed to create suspicion and had just as easily quashed it. Once again, townsfolk spread the news through the town of the goodness of the honorable man named Nathan Porter and how he set the record straight concerning the shipmaster. The people told of Nathan's importance, kindness, understanding, and humility, none of which was true. Nathan congratulated himself on his resourcefulness.

His plans had a true purpose. He wanted to destroy George Abernathy and sew suspicion about Chastity Shepherd.

John and Henry shoved off the heavily laden longboat and into smooth waters. The early-morning sun was just starting to appear on the horizon. The tide was just beginning to rescind. There was a gentle lapping sound on the shore as tiny waves made their presence known. Sandpipers were running on the water's edge, looking for whatever morsel they could find. Gulls took to the air greeting the morning with their caw. The air was fresh and inviting.

John looked at Henry. "It's a perfect day for sailing."

The two men raised the sail. They had to shield their eyes from the bright sunlight. The light wind filled the canvas. John manned the rudder and sailed away from the shore till the boat was in sufficient depth to turn south. They remained in water no more than ten feet deep. The boat was held parallel to the coast.

Henry looked at the colorful coast and then back at the rising sun on the horizon. His voice broke the sounds of nature. "I never grow tired of this. There is something about the morning while on the ocean. Every day is different, but all have a beauty all their own. Many times I have been on the ocean fearful of the storms I have been in. I have rushed to the rail, relieved to see the first signs of land. There is nothing like being on the ocean. It is filled with mystery, excitement, and awe. What is best of all is when the journey is over, and you come home to someone who loves you."

John turned to his friend. "When you say you like coming home to someone you love, are you referring to Abigail? Are you in love with her?"

Henry smiled. "Enough to ask her to marry me. As soon as this trip is over, we plan to be married."

John returned the smile. He lifted his cap skyward and shouted, "Hoorah!"

Then Henry asked, "What of you, mate?"

John loved being called mate. It was a term that was stronger than a brother. It was not a word thrown about or shared casually. Only among the deepest relationships was it used, and it was meant in the most endearing fashion.

John answered, "After this trip, I will seek for her in earnest. I feel she is on American shores. I just don't know if she is in Plymouth or Boston. I dispatched letters to the family asking her whereabouts, but I can't wait any longer." Afterward, John paused, reflecting on what he would say next. "I dreamed of her last night, and she was calling out to me. There was fear in her voice, telling me that she was in danger."

Henry asked, "What do you think it means?"

John replied, "Chastity and I have always had this closeness. Once I dreamed that she came to my room in the night. She asked if I had room for her in my bed. I pulled back the covers, and she climbed in beside me. We just held each other all the night long. Later I shared this dream with her. She had a surprise for me. For on that same night, she had dreamed the same dream."

John looked to check on the sail and the position of the boat before adding, "I must go to her immediately. Even if I do not hear from my family, I will be heading north to see if she is there."

Henry thoughtfully replied, "'Tis a rare gift you share, and it is something I have never known."

John lowered his head. There was a loneliness that emitted from his words. In reply, he said, "I have been gone so very long. She has not heard from me. She may think me dead. Perhaps she has married and moved on. She may have been forced to marry."

Henry just listened. John looked to his friend. "I could not blame her if she did."

Henry replied, "Nonsense, man. You must believe—"

John shot back. "Believe what? That my peril was for my good? I question it all. My life under the blacksmith, the servitude with Captain Wise, and my being shipwrecked on this land kept me from her."

Henry slapped his hand onto John's shoulder. "And it woke you up."

John looked back and queried, "Woke me up?"

Henry had a sternness to his face. He explained, "You were a boy when you boarded the *Elizabeth Marie*. I recall the first time you wobbled at the movement of the ship beneath your feet, but in time, you found your footing. The hardships you endured more than anything molded you into the man you have become. The hardships you faced have caused you to find your footing." Henry's words struck a nerve with John. Henry continued. "Aye, John, you have changed. Oh, the character of the man is the same, but you have become savvier. In short order, you learned to put aside your naive notions and have developed a sharp eye."

John thought about this statement before asking for clarity, "What do you mean?"

Henry answered, "Do you trust Charles?"

John answered with little hesitancy, "Not really. I feel he must be watched. I need his talents, but I do not trust in him."

Henry smiled. "That is the man you have become. When you arrived on the *Elizabeth Marie*, you trusted everyone even when you were warned not to. You thought Captain Wise was honorable but soon realized he wasn't."

Henry adjusted the course a bit with the rudder and ordered John to fix the sail. Once corrections were made, he continued. "Your God has made you a better man. I know some of your Bible. Like Joseph of old, you have become a better, wiser man, and I have no doubt He has made your missy a better woman also."

John responded quickly to Henry's mention of Chastity. "I know she is true to me, but I fear someone may be attacking her by forcing himself on her. I pity the man if he has imposed himself physically on her."

Henry saw the concern on his friend's face. He reached over and placed his hand on his shoulder. "Then as soon as we return, quickly go to her."

During the journey, John shared what he had learned of the islands. From his inquiries, he found out that the name Currituck was the name used by the Indians for the outer shores. Already the English were calling the land the Outer Banks. Much farther south, the place of the ill-fated settlement known as Roanoke existed. The land where he had run aground was called Hatorask by the natives. Some of the English remarked that the waters near these islands were hard to navigate. Some ships had sunk during heavy storms, taking the lives of all the crew. Those who found out that John wrecked upon the shores called him the lucky one, but he knew it was God who protected.

It took three days for them to arrive at their destination. Pulling ashore, the land appeared desolate and undisturbed. Henry looked at John and asked, "Are you sure this is the place?"

John smiled. "Positive." John began showing Henry the sights of the island. He took him to the green meadow where he grazed Spirit. They crossed the island, and John showed him the water on the other side. Returning to the camp, he walked him over to the graves. The two markers were all that indicated that he had ever been there before. In reverence, the two men stood looking over the graves.

Henry spoke first. "It is an admirable thing you have done. I know how the man treated you."

John replied, "I may have had reason to hate the man but found forgiveness for him, especially when I understood the things he did."

After a while, John asked, "Help me with the stones?"

The two men removed the headstones and carried them to their final resting place. The writing on the stone was the same inscription as the wooden marker.

Henry commented, "What you made was excellent. I suspect it they would have lasted a long while."

John thought for a moment. "Perhaps, but they could not have withstood the storms or time. These men deserve to be honored in this way."

John also spoke of caring for their families. "I found the captain's ledgers, and I sent the money the sailors earned to their families along with a bit more."

Henry stated, "Most men would have been satisfied with the burial. Why did you send the money?"

In reverence, John replied, "Because I was once dead, and now I live. These men are dead, and their families deserved the right to know what happened to them. You know as well as I do that in short order, the families of these men will be turned out of their homes unless they receive some sort of pay. What I do isn't much, but it is all I can do for now."

The rest of the day was spent gathering items that had been buried in the sand. Small stashes of gold and silver were collected. After each item was collected, John quickly concealed the location by filling in the holes and then covering the place with limbs. When Henry asked why he did this, John replied, "To keep the place a mystery to adventurous treasure seekers."

That evening John cooked fresh fish and shrimp he had netted. He cooked these with vegetables he brought on the journey. The food was excellent.

Henry remarked, "I did not know you could cook."

John laughed. "Rica told me that I can't. He had to teach me how to cook over an open fire."

When they had had their fill, it was time to turn in. John walked over to the entrance to the dugout. "We will sleep here tonight." He reached for the hidden latch, which revealed a ladder leading downward. John led the way.

When Henry entered, he looked about. The fading sunlight revealed evidence of the captain's cabin. John lit a few candles before closing the entry. Henry stated, "And you did this all by yourself?"

John laughed. "Well, Spirit helped some."

Henry continued. "No one would ever know or believe it unless they saw it with their own eyes."

Come morning, the two men collected the remaining things John wanted to take back. From various places, John unearthed metals and clothing. Soon, they were busy loading the boat. It only took a few hours. John was not afraid to show Henry the location of the buried items. He had no intention of taking it all. He explained to Henry, "There are several places where I have money, precious metals, jewels, and more buried. I know that if I take it all, some will question me. If I take a little at a time or as I may have need, these things will last for years. I do not want to grow dependent on what is here. I want to make a way for me and my family to prosper and succeed through hard work."

Then John handed Henry a bag of Spanish gold. He explained, "I saved this for you even as I was building the dugout. I was alarmed how little the captain paid you when I read his ledger. I know your worth and how much more you could have demanded. I want you to use this to begin a life with Abigail. This will be my wedding gift for the two of you. I just ask one thing."

Henry asked, "What might that be?"

John showed an impish grin. "Name your first child after me."

Henry fell to the sand laughing. "Well," he said, "she might be the only girl around with the name of Jonathan."

Once again, John made sure the land was made to look like no one had been there. They loaded the two wooden markers into the boat. They saw to it that every opening and every location was concealed, knowing that nature would do the rest.

As they shoved off, John stated, "Someday I would love to build a house here."

Henry replied, "I can see why."

A day out from Virginia, John dropped anchor long enough to cast the two markers overboard. He watched them float away out to sea. Only the wind disrupted the moment. With respect, John stated, "I made those from the longboat. They should be set free on the ocean. If any should find them, it might lead them on a wild goose chase if they have a mind to find what remains of the *Elizabeth Marie* and crew.

The winds favored the return home. A few days later, John and Henry pulled into shore well below their destination. They would wait for nightfall before making the few remaining miles. As the sun began to set, they went back to sea to complete their journey. The two men sailed beyond the town and landed north of it. Just before the shore, they jumped into knee-deep water. They knew the heavy load on board would cause the boat to bottom out. With each wave that came in, they were able to pull the boat up onto the shore.

There was little time to rest. John needed to get the supplies to a safe location. John left Henry with the supplies, while he went back to get Spirit. John was still a little ways off when Spirit caught wind of him. Spirit let out a whinny and ran to the gate.

John greeted him. "Hello, my dear fellow. Are you ready for a little work?" He harnessed the horse to the travois and began the journey back to Henry.

John made several trips with Spirit during the night. Beforehand, John had prepared hiding places on his newly acquired property. With each load transported by Spirit, John reburied the precious items. It was close to midnight when John finally put Spirit in the stable. All was quiet. No one in the village was stirring this time of day. John rushed back to the boat to find Henry resting in it. As soon as John arrived, the two men cast off once more. To complete the secrecy of their trip, they would wait till morning to arrive back. Then they could be in full view of the townsfolk. None would be the wiser to what the two friends had been up to.

After arriving in Virginia, John rushed to his room to put on fresh clothes and make his way to the office to see how things were progressing with Charles.

As John entered into the room, Charles stood to his feet. "Welcome back, sir. How was the trip?"

John smiled. "It was good to be on the ocean again. Henry and I enjoyed the fishing and the time away." John hung his hat on a peg and removed his waistcoat. He looked at Charles. "I have a favor to ask."

Charles was surprised. "A favor?"

John replied, "Yes, for what I have to ask of you is beyond your agreed-upon responsibilities to me. My friend Henry is to be married. I ask that you might see to all the arrangements. I shall pay for everything."

Charles sat thoughtfully. "You have treated me with respect and honored me with confidence. It would be my pleasure to assist you in any way that I can."

John was pleased with his answer. Then Charles extended his hand toward John. In his hand was a letter. "The shipmaster delivered this yesterday."

It was too soon for John to receive any reply from his earlier correspondences. He took the letter and saw that it was from Pastor Elijah. John walked over to a chair and sat down. He did not know why, but he feared what might be written. He broke the seal, and with trembling fingers, he removed the letter from the envelope. John unfolded the letter, doing all he could to keep from shaking. He read:

Dear Brother John,

I write this hoping that this letter finds you. We have not heard from you in so long, and many fear that you might be dead. I hold to the hope that you are not only alive but prospering in Virginia. No one knows why we have not heard from you. I implore you to write and let us know your whereabouts and how you are doing.

I write to you with a concern for our dear sister, your betrothed, Chastity Shepherd. She is now in Boston. She was accompanied there by two from our church, Paul and Leah Stitch. I was able to secure Chastity a post as governess with a family. I have heard from Paul and have been informed that Chastity is in the care of George and Susan Abernathy. In the letter that I received from Brother Paul, he told me of another man named Nathan Porter. He told of his unscrupulous ways and how he made improper advances toward Chastity. This has troubled me greatly. Then last night I felt a great presence from the Spirit to write this letter to you.

My brother, I know that you are a servant to another, but I believe that you must somehow, someway find your way to Boston for Chastity's protection and care. It is with the upmost urgency that I write this. May God make the way for you.

In His Holy Name,
Elijah Brown

Charles watched as John wrinkled the letter with his fist. John knew in his own heart that Pastor was right. He looked over to Charles. "Please go get Henry for me."

Charles left immediately and without question. He knew something was wrong. John would not have asked for Henry unless there was good reason.

Charles arrived at Henry's cabin completely out of breath. He banged loudly on the door. A tired and red-eyed old sailor opened the door to see who would disturb his rest. Henry was still groggy from the long trip. Seeing Charles didn't help matters.

Charles was breathless but managed, "Come quick. Mr. Devine needs you."

The words shocked Henry. Henry bid Charles to wait and hurriedly dressed. Then the two men rushed back to the office. They entered and found John sitting, just staring at the wall. Henry rushed over to John and knelt down in front of him. "John, what's wrong?"

John continued to just stare into space. Exhaustion had overtaken him. The news had stunned him.

Henry removed the crumpled letter from his hand and read its contents. Looking back at his friend, he comforted him. "John, it will be all right." Henry tried to raise John, but he would not be moved. His hands trembled.

John was overcome with grief. Chastity was in trouble, and he had to get to her. Since arriving in Virginia, he'd worked hard to find order in all the chaos. Now, because of this letter, he pondered if he had done the right things. Adrenaline had driven him. The letter was like a swift kick in the gut. His mind and body had fought so hard to survive. He knew he had to rescue her, but his confidence was gone. He was exhausted and could not think clearly. He would not be moved till he had a clear course of action.

Slowly, John came to himself and looked to Henry. "I have to get to Boston immediately."

Henry took John's hand. "All right, but first you need to rest. Give it till morning at least, and then you can start. Tears began to fill John's eyes. He relented, and Henry helped him stand to his feet. John's heart was pounding. Looking to his friend, he stated, "I have endured so much in my life, and I would endure much more to protect her. Henry, I have to get there as quickly as I can."

Nathan held a drink in his hand. He was at the tavern meeting with some of the town men. Strong ale and rum were served, and drinks were being consumed freely at his expense. A few of the men were of importance, and some were also members of the church. Nathan watched the men drink.

When he thought they were feeling the effects of the drink, he announced, "My father tells me that the king is very pleased with the progress of this city. It is said the king remarks of the moral fiber of Plymouth and Boston. I too am glad that I have come to this city on a hill."

Men pounded the tables with the mugs in their hands, while some gave hurrahs.

Nathan continued. "His approval has settled things in my mind. I have decided to build a house here. I can't imagine not being a part of a place so respected."

Once again, the tavern was filled with approval.

Nathan began to stroll around the room. Looking about, he said, "Who do you think is the best builder in town?"

To a man, the answer was clear. "George Abernathy."

Nathan wrinkled his brow with a look of concern. "Is there not someone else?"

One of the men called out, "What's wrong with George?"

That was the question Nathan hoped to hear. He answered, "It's just that I question his character. Do you know that he has an unmarried woman living with him and his family?"

Immediately, some of the church men called back, "She has come from England to be governess to his children."

Nathan allowed a half-cocked smile to creep over his face. "Seems to me governesses are supposed to be old and strict, you know the kind. Such that can make a child cry just by looking at him."

The tavern filled with laughter.

Nathan lowered his head in mock concern. Then, lifting his head, he looked to the men, "I just think that it doesn't look right for a man to have a young single lady in his home."

The church men stood and prepared to leave the tavern. Among them was Paul Stitch. Before leaving, Paul stated, "You impugn the character of a noble and good man. You suggest unthinkable things against a respected woman." Then, pointing the finger at Nathan, Paul continued. "This libertine seeks to dishonor a man who is the best among us. Many of us owe a great deal to George Abernathy. The young lady he seeks to also dishonor is a fine girl betrothed to another." Then Paul walked over and slammed money on the bar. Turning back at the crowd, he stated, "This man has sewn an accusation that I will have no part of, and if you are wise, you will do the same."

Paul walked over to Nathan. "You, sir, are a serpent after the order of the one who beguiled Eve. Away with you, vile creature." Then, turning quickly, he and the other church men hurried from the tavern.

Nathan was resolute for a moment before chuckling and then laughing heartily. To the remaining lot, he said, "Seems to me that those men can't bear the truth. Now tell me, do I look like a serpent?"

A hearty laugh rose from those who remained. Nathan proclaimed, "Barkeep, another round for my friends." Nathan was pleased with himself, for he knew he had succeeded in sewing doubt. Suspicion would do the rest of his dirty work.

Paul rushed to go to the Abernathy home, but the moonless night made it hard to find his way. Many times he stumbled even after his eyes grew accustomed to the moonless night. He ran up the drive to the pitch-black house. Everyone was in bed. When he finally arrived, he began banging on the door. George was jarred awake at the alarm. He knew something was wrong. He rushed from his bed and down the stairs.

George flung open the door. He could barely make Paul out in the glowing light of the fireplace. George asked, "Brother, what be ye doing here this time of night?"

Paul exhaled. "I have to talk to you. There is trouble brewing in town. The devil himself is among us."

George beckoned Paul to come in. He lit a candle, and soon, the two men took seats at the table. Paul told what had occurred at the tavern.

George replied, "So it has come to this, has it? You said it well when you called Nathan Porter the devil. I am glad that I told the church leaders of this man's ways ahead of time, but that will not stop what others think. I cannot do anything tonight, but I shall send word to the brothers to meet with me on the morrow."

The conversation wasn't a long one. George asked Paul if he would care to spend the night. Paul thanked him, but refused, seeing as he had a wife and son waiting for his return home. It was only after Paul's departure that George sat once again at the table. He thought upon the things said to him.

Susan came down the stairs. Seeing George, she asked, "Who was that, my husband?"

George turned to face his wife and asked her to come over and sit with him. He pulled her over to his lap and lay his head on her breast. He spoke softly. "My love, we must pray. Evil has cast a dark shadow on our family and, more importantly, on Chastity."

The next evening the church leaders sat together to hear all that was said at the tavern. Paul and some of the others who were there could verify all that was said.

After the issue was thoroughly discussed, Deacon Bruce Barrett spoke up. "There is none here who has not seen for ourselves the honor of George and his family, and we have not seen anything but good from our dear sister. However, what Nathan Porter said has to be considered."

Bruce looked at George. "Why did you bring someone so young into your care?"

George was alarmed by the question, but he kept his temper. "I did not know the girl before she came to these shores. We were told by her pastor that she would be a good governess for our children, and may I say, she has proven herself to be all we hoped. The children love and adore her. Miss Shepherd has also become like a sister to my own wife and to some of your wives as well. Her virtue is undeniable."

Bruce then stated, "Brother, we are told from scripture that we must abstain from all appearances of evil. Surely, you can understand our concern."

George was thoughtful as he leaned forward. "So, Brother, art thou accusing me of some evil? Are you accusing me of having improper relations with my governess? Would you feel better is she was an old, grumpy woman?" The last question made the men laugh, which angered the deacon.

George continued. "God's Word tells us that we are not to take an accusation from one. There must be at least two." Surveying the room, he asked, "Who else wishes to accuse the woman?"

No one moved. Bruce saw the lack of response and charged, "I know some of you have offered suggestions to me. Would you have me point you out?"

After that, a few hands, mainly from younger men, began to rise. Bruce continued. "There is your evidence."

George's face reddened. He looked about the room and saw whose hands were raised. He stood and gave a great harrumph. He looked at the ones who raised their hands and called to them, "Stand up."

When the men were reluctant to do so, he shouted angrily, "I said, stand up, ye young, foolish cowards."

One by one, they stood. George walked over to each one and stared them in the eyes. He walked to the front of the gathering and turned to face those standing. "All of you who came to me to ask permission to court Miss Shepherd raise your hands."

All the young men raised their hands. George looked them over and commanded, "Sit down, you gutless lot. You are only making accusations because she is betrothed to another. You are too spineless to come to me, so you tend to gossip like women."

Many of the men laughed.

There remained two young men standing. George marched to within a few feet and fixed his attention on them. The men began to tremble.

George asked, "Have you come to this opinion on your own, or has someone poisoned your thoughts?" He looked at one man who had been at the tavern. "So how much did Mr. Porter offer you?"

The young man started to protest before being cut off by George.

"Answer the question," George demanded.

The man took his seat. There remained only one left standing, and all eyes were on him. He looked around, embarrassed. He began rocking back and forth before stating, "My wife thinks it's odd." Then he promptly sat back down.

Once again, the men laughed.

George walked before the others. He observed all who were there. "I think it deplorable that you would take the word of someone who is of such questionable character." George pointed a finger toward Paul and continued. "Ask Brother Paul there about this man and his actions aboard ship. Ask me how this man brazenly approached my governess in a most inappropriate way when she met my family for the first time or about the way he came to her cabin in the middle of the night. Maybe you find it easier to just blame a woman than look for the truth." Then George walked over to Bruce. "Tell me, Deacon, what is your real reason for your objection? No lies now, man—just the truth."

Bruce jumped to his feet. "Now see here, George ..."

George calmly stated, "Now this wouldn't have anything to do with an arrangement you made with Mr. Porter, would it?"

Bruce turned pale.

George once more turned and said, "Nathan Porter is ruining several of our merchants by undercutting his prices. Brother Bruce stands to lose all he has built here in Boston because of Nathan Porter ... So, did you make a deal with the devil at the expense of an innocent woman?"

Bruce simply sat down in silence.

George looked about the room. The men began to look at Bruce with disdain. George shouted, "Stop it, all of you. A moment ago some of you were just as accusative toward me and to her. The devil has succeeded in sewing doubt in your mind. There is no evidence of any wrong, but to save a few skins, you would hear an accusation. If it hadn't been Bruce, it would have been someone else. This devil of a man will not stop. We can ebb the attacks in our church, but we cannot change a village." George continued to walk about the room.

Next, Paul spoke. "Brother George is right. We must stand together or face the shame. Nathan Porter wants us to think he is honorable, when, in fact, he is scheming and shrewd. Chastity refused his advances when we were about to leave the ship. The man is up to something."

George bowed his head. He did not look at the men as he spoke. "Miss Shepherd has waited for her betrothed for more than two years. Both of them decided to come to this land as servants. Miss Shepherd has four more years of service to my family."

Bruce was not about to admit to any relationship with Nathan. Bruce regained his composure. He seized the opportunity to say, "These attacks against her will continue to grow. If not by Mr. Porter, then most assuredly by others. Given time, such suspicions will lead to greater accusations. I think Miss Shepherd should be told to marry or leave our community. What harm could come by her entertaining Mr. Porter? If she won't, then she should be forced to leave the community."

Paul jumped to his feet. He glared at Bruce. "How dare you. No, no, it mustn't be done. How can you think to turn her away like that? Nathan Porter will prey upon her more." Looking around at the rest of the men, Paul continued. "Would you satisfy yourselves by allowing a lie to force someone from us? You have daughters old enough to marry. Would you allow a lie to force them into marriage?" There was silence among the men.

Looking to Bruce, Paul stated, "You have brought shame and discord to our church. You took the devil's money and now have shamed us all. If you force Miss Shepherd from us, then my family and I will be gone also."

George added, "As will mine."

A few more added their commitment to leave with them.

Bruce sat wilted in his chair. George stood and was about to leave when Elder Titus Prior spoke. "These are sad, difficult times. We have enjoyed peace up until now. The men of this church have maintained honorability all along. Now this thing has been brought up." Elder Prior looked to George. "My brother and friend, you helped us settle on these shores and built our houses. Before these men, answer me this: have you any interest in this woman?"

George replied, "My only interest in her is for her care and well-being. All my love and attention is my wife's alone."

The elder then stated, "So what harm can there be in her marrying someone else?"

George was alarmed. "Would you have her break her promise? Does her betrothal mean nothing to you?"

Elder Prior answered, "I think only of the good of the church."

George pointed his finger toward the elder. "No, Brother, you only think of yourself. I will not have any part of this. I see now that you accept lies over truth. I have had enough." George grabbed his coat and hat and stormed from the hall. Several others followed.

John had all he dare carry in the longboat. He had just enough to sustain him. The longboat would have to endure the six hundred-mile trip up the coast, and John wanted to get there quickly. With the money he carried with him, he planned to buy back Chastity's service. He had the map and equipment to navigate the course. Henry and Charles had helped him with the preparations. The urgency he felt drove him like a madman. In many ways, he had thrown caution to the wind. He did not know the waters, but he didn't care. The woman he loved was on American soil, and she needed him. More than that, he needed her.

It was time to leave. John gave charge to his two friends. "Henry, if I do not return, all that I have is yours. Take good care of Spirit. I pray that you and Abigail have a wonderful life together. Charles, we have started a good work. Henry will oversee the operation, but it is up to you to keep it honorable."

Henry approached his friend. "John, the ocean this time of year can be difficult. I know you will want to get there as fast as possible. I urge you to put to shore or find a cove each night. Come back to us with your bride. We will be waiting for you. Abigail and I have decided to wait for your return to marry. May God watch over you as He has always done."

The men pushed the longboat out to into deeper water as a warm southerly wind blew. John rowed the boat far enough out to raise the canvas, and the wind did the rest. The boat responded and pushed forward. It was as though the ship knew it had to be somewhere and accepted the responsibility. With a wave of his hand, John bid his friends goodbye. John took hold of the rudder and sailed north. John whispered, "I'm coming, Chastity."

The southerly wind felt good. The sun was bright, and the water was cold. John squinted his eyes against the bright glare. He kept the boat parallel to the shore. He was taking a northeasterly course. There was no sign of life on the unclaimed land. Likewise, there was no sign of any ships on the horizon. John hoped that he might come across one that was taking the same route. He thought that he might join them to their final destination. It didn't matter. Regardless of whether one would come, he was determined to make it to Chastity.

John took readings and charted his course. He was traveling about twelve knots an hour. This was a good speed for the trip. John did not fool himself, because he knew the favorable winds could change without notice. He decided to take advantage of his good fortune and push onward as far and as fast as he could.

John sailed unto the nearly setting sun. He determined that he had traveled about seventy-five miles. If the prevailing winds continued, he would be there in a week. He spied an inlet and put in, making sure not to bottom out. He secured the boat by dropping anchor. The measurement beneath the boat was five feet. Even if this were high tide, he figured he was in a good enough depth. John stayed on board for the night and ate a little hardtack and salted pork. A smile crept over his face as he thought to himself, *Wish Rica was here. He probably knows how to make even this taste good.*

John was tired from the day of sailing. He wrapped himself in the wool blanket and lay back, looking at the stars. The clear, cloudless night allowed the stars of heaven to be displayed in all their glory. John saw a shooting star race across the sky. The Milky Way appeared so clear that it looked like a carriage could be driven on it.

John prayed, "The heavens declare the glory of God. Oh, Father, aid me on my journey and get me there in time. I must get to Chastity. Give me strength, Father. Give me strength." Soon, he fell fast asleep.

John was cold and shivering in the early morning mist. The clear skies of night were replaced by a heavy coastal fog. It was so thick that he could actually feel the weight of it. The wind had also changed. It now blew from the west. John thought, *There's a storm coming in.*

He straightened the boat and weighed anchor. He headed back out to open water. He knew sailing like this was dangerous, but he felt he had no choice. If a storm was coming, he had to make as much distance as he could. He raised the sail and made his way east and gradually north. He measured the depth of the water at about six marks. He surmised that as long as he kept this depth, he was a safe enough distance from the shore. He had learned from Henry that the shores of this land had a long underwater shelf. A small longboat could easily handle the shallow water of the coast.

He kept course with a compass, as the sun was not yet visible. He would plot his progress when the mist was burned off, which did not happen till nearly noonday. When it did clear away, John could finally see the shore. He was farther out than he intended to sail. The westward wind was blowing him farther out to sea. He corrected his course and took measurements against the sun. He had traveled nearly thirty miles. Looking back at the coastline, he could see numerous inlets and large bays. The land looked untouched by human hands. Overhead, the birds flew low. Their low flight was more indication that a storm was brewing.

By day's end, he had gone another fifty or sixty miles. Clouds had rolled in, and with them came the rain. John was being peppered with heavy drops. The temperature had dropped considerably, and the wind chilled him. His hands were numb. It didn't help that he had nothing to protect his hands from the rain and cold air. He tried to push himself farther, but Henry's words of warning resonated in his mind. John knew he had to be careful. It was time he put into a shore.

John sailed the boat up a small river. On both sides of the bank were trees to secure the boat and for shelter. He knew he had to get out of the elements. Once secured, John left the boat. His legs would not bend. His hands were numb. As a sailor, he'd seen men die from the elements. His immediate thought was to build a fire. Looking about, he decided that if any natives were near, they too would be taking shelter from the harsh weather. Then, speaking out loud, he said, "Well, if you're there, come and get me. I am much too cold to even care."

John found a strong tree he could lay brush and limbs against. He would build a simple lean-to. He made an opening facing the shore. He searched the foliage and found a little dry grass and pieces of bark and wood. He took out the flint, and with a knife, he struck the stone. Even the cold seemed to make the flint resistant to sparking. Added to that, the cold made his hands ache. It took several minutes for the grass to catch. Finally, a little smoke began to emit. John leaned down and gently blew at the base of the smoke. To his relief, the smoke turned to fire. John added more grass to the small flame, and soon he had a good fire. He put his hands over the hot flames, and his teeth began to chatter.

Shaking hands reached out to the flame. John could feel his body shiver uncontrollably. He added more wood to keep the fire going. The winds began picking up, and the flames whipped one way and then the other. The wind's direction was changing from west to northwest. The night air was turning much colder.

John slowly warmed. He left the fire to collect wood and brush for the lean-to. He leaned what he had collected toward the tree, creating a sort of teepee. He tied grass together and strapped the top of the lean-to, securing it to the tree so that it would not be blown apart by the wind.

When all was done, John prepared a hot broth from salted pork. He broke a hardtack biscuit into it. It took a while, but soon, the dried biscuit sucked up a large portion of the broth. John ate his fill. The hot broth warmed his insides. It was hard to relax, as he was ever fearful of the natives. He cleaned up quickly, grabbed his blanket, and climbed into the lean-to. He could easily reach the fire and added a little wood to it. This he would do throughout the night.

He was warm, dry, and bone weary. Even so, he only managed to doze for a little before waking up to put more wood on the fire. Throughout the night, he would wake, add wood to the fire, and sleep a little more. The night was anything but restful.

Morning came all too soon. He pulled himself from the warmth of the lean-to and began packing. He made more broth from the salt pork and hardtack. When he finished eating, he gathered his belongings and loaded the longboat. The weather was cold, and the northwest winds were blowing hard. The waters were choppy, but John was resolved to press on.

John decided to stay closer to shore as he continued his journey north by northeast. The little boat rose and fell with each wave. He knew he was not traveling as fast as before, which made him anxious. To overcome it, he kept his mind on Chastity. Pastor's letter stayed with him. John knew in his soul that Chastity was in harm's way. He was determined to make it no matter what. He tightened his grip on the till even though the cold caused his fingers to ache all the more. The waves grew as the winds increased. He carefully navigated each one, driving the boat toward the watery mountains. He felt he could make it. He had to … no matter what.

The weather was getting colder. John was used to the warm, southern routes of the Atlantic. John had no idea how harsh the North Atlantic could be. Soon, small waterdrops began to freeze wherever they found a place to settle. John could feel the cold stinging his unprotected hands. The ocean waters splashed up onto his face. Tiny skin cracks stung all the more because of the salt. His joints ached, but his heart pushed him forward. He pressed onward to reach his long-lost love. He could feel his joints tightening. Flexing his fingers was becoming harder to do. Whether he liked it or not, he was going to have to stop earlier than expected.

John sailed toward shore and entered an inlet. A short distance upstream he stopped and tied the boat to overhanging tree limbs. As he tried to leave the boat, he fell. He was cold and stiff. He lifted himself but felt dizzy and nearly toppled into the water. It was hard for him to keep his senses. His knees ached, and he could barely swallow. Once again, he realized that he had pushed himself more than he should have. He could not think on this now. He had to think about survival. He had to have a fire, but to his horror, everything was soaked. He knew that unless he got a fire started, he would not make it.

John walked around, flapping his arms about him. He began removing things from the boat. Movement helped some. Soon, his youthful joints responded to his heightened pulse. He wandered among some marsh grass, hoping to find enough of it dry to start a fire. He was about to pull up a handful when he spotted a duck sleeping in a well-covered nest. Ever so carefully, he reached for it. The unsuspecting bird awoke and rushed to escape, but John managed to grab a leg and hauled his prey into his arms. The young mallard had a dry nest. John gathered the dry grass and carried it to his camp. Thirty minutes later, John had a fire.

His hands trembled as warmth began to sting his fingers. He built a little larger fire than the night before. It had to be larger to dry the wet wood. He buried two limbs into the ground with the forks positioned straight up. He rested the fresh game on the forks, placing it directly over the fire. As it roasted, the grease from the bird dripped down, making the flames hiss and rise. John poured a bit of wine from a flask sparingly over the bird. The smell was wonderful. His mouth watered, and for the moment, his thoughts relaxed.

John build another lean-to. He hung his blanket near the fire to dry. He gathered as much wood as he could find. He needed rest, and that night, he would try and sleep. John lined the bottom of his lean-to with cattail stocks and dry grass. After a while, the heat drew small steam trails from the lean-to. Even the blanket emitted steam trails skyward. The rain had stopped, and the ground began to freeze. John noticed that with each step, the ground made a cracking sound. The sky was clearing. He knew it would get much colder overnight.

John tested the duck. He cut a leg and tasted it. It was delicious. He sliced off another portion and then another. He could hardly contain himself. Before long, he had eaten half. He took a deep drink from the flask. His stomach was full, and he was relaxed. He cleaned up after himself and prepared for sleep. He walked over to the blanket. It was dry and warm. He removed it from the line and wrapped himself in it. He walked back to the fire and added more wood. Then he crawled into the lean-to. Almost instantly, he fell fast into a deep sleep.

George sat at the table with Susan and Chastity. He was still fuming over the proceedings of the meeting with the men. His voice reflected his attitude. "It appears the devil has bought false witnesses from a couple of the men."

Susan replied, "From the church? I find this hard to believe."

George continued. "As did I. I never imagined someone could be bought off, especially from our small congregation, but tonight the guilty ones proved themselves. One in particular voiced the greatest objection. He is one of the elders."

Susan was stunned. "Who was it?"

George reluctantly replied, "One who stands to lose the most because of Mr. Porter's business. I will not mention his name, because I do not want to damage your opinion of him."

The three just stared at each other. Only the flickering flame from the fireplace exposed their thoughtful expressions.

From the silence, Chastity finally asked, "What is it that they want me to do?"

George turned his head away. "Either marry or leave. The outspoken elder stated that there were a number of eligible bachelors, and you should pick one."

Chastity calmly surmised, "Oh, so it isn't about loving someone or respecting one's betrothal. It's about marrying and having a family whether there is love or not? Tell me, George. What do you think?"

George got up and walked over to place his hand on the mantel. He stared into the fire, pondering the question. He did not look back at the two women. Instead, he spoke into the fire, "I think the deacon and those who have aligned themselves with the devil are wrong. Several others agreed with me. Those of us who left the meeting could hear the rest fighting among themselves. Everything you said is right. Me thinks that the only solution would be for us to move."

Chastity jumped up. "Oh no, I can't let that happen. It wouldn't be right. I'll go!"

Susan began to cry. Her whole world was collapsing about her. Her voice was urgent as she exclaimed, "But we haven't done anything wrong. Why would someone do this to us?"

George turned to the women once again. He walked over and placed his strong gentle hand on Chastity's shoulder and guided her to sit. He walked over to Susan and wrapped his arms around her. Afterward, he took his own seat. He replied, "I think it is time we put a fleece before God. We need to seek what is best for us and the situation at hand." Looking to his young governess, he asked, "Chastity, are you willing?"

Chastity thought a moment before responding. "What do you have in mind?"

George took Chastity's hand in one hand and Susan's in another. With a very humble tone, he continued. "Just this: we will pray for the Lord's will. That God brings Jonathan here immediately. If he does not show in a week, then we will consider the church's proposal. Only consider it, mind you."

Chastity turned pale. She could hardly breathe. She thought carefully about what George offered. This was truly a test of her faith. The biggest question was whether her faith was strong enough to trust God. Looking to Susan and George, she said, "I'm afraid."

George moved from the table to retrieve the family Bible. From its pages, he read from the book of James, chapter 2. He focused on the passage that read, "Faith without works is dead." Looking at Susan and Chastity, he spoke. "Early in this chapter it speaks of giving when it may cost what little you have, thus trusting God for your needs. I want you to hear this statement: faith requires strength, and there is strength in faith. When all this started with Nathan Porter, I was angry. One night I struggled to sleep. I came downstairs, and I read this passage. That is when I considered the relationship between faith and strength. The statement means that it takes faith to move forward, trusting in God with every step. The book of Hebrews, chapter eleven is filled with men and women who, by faith, followed God without knowing the outcome. David found faith to face the giant. Noah in building the ark. Abraham to obey God. It takes strength to walk in faith."

Chastity thought on these things. George's words were true. Faith requires strength. She replied, "So you are saying that if I have faith, God will see to my strength?"

George continued. "We had confidence in the Almighty to bring us to this land, didn't we? And we have been blessed, have we not? Now is the time for faith to follow the Lord. I know He can and will answer." George looked at Chastity like a loving father. He asked, "So are you with me?"

Chastity raised her eyes and smiled. "It seems to me we better get to praying."

The next day being Sunday, the family went to church. The ride was a somber one, except for Faith who continued to chatter about everything. When the family entered, they felt a coldness among the people. Joy had been replaced with suspicion, jealousy, and judgment. George led his family to their pew and directed the children to take their seats. George always sat with his family, and Susan sat next to him. Chastity sat between the four children, ever mindful of their behavior. She could feel the eyes of the congregation on her.

Then, just before the services were about to start, the doors opened, and a newcomer came through them. He was dressed like a peacock. He wore the latest fashion. He held a cane in his right hand and let the end of it tap the wooden floor as he made his way to the front. He meant to make many feel inferior to him. He was offered a seat by the same deacon who brought the false charges against Chastity. Before sitting down, he turned to look about at the congregation. He fixed his eyes on Chastity. She quietly gasped. It was Nathan Porter. He nodded his head toward her and then turned and took his seat.

If Nathan expected that the service would be like the Church of England, he was mistaken. The pastor entered the pulpit and announced the song to be sung. The people rose to their feet and sang. Today they did not sing as before. The music was still powerful enough to make Nathan squirm, but it lacked the joy Chastity had come to love. When it came time for the collection, Nathan put a good amount of money into the bag, making sure some saw his contribution.

Finally, it was time for the message. The pastor took his place behind the pulpit. He remained quiet for a moment. He then fixed his eyes on the deacon and on Nathan. The pastor announced his sermon. "Today I will preach a sermon titled, 'Do Not Accept False Accusations.'" His message was strong as he preached on the trial of Jesus. He told how two men were bought off to tell lies against the Lord. The pastor told how Jesus was so innocent and pure, and yet despised and rejected by men. He preached that through it all, Jesus endured the suffering and shame to pay the sin debt for all who would receive His blood and believe.

The message made the deacon uneasy. Nathan tried to smile in approval but hated the message. He wanted more than anything to shut the preacher up. The message made him despise the people. He thought, *Do these bewildered people really believe all this?* He couldn't wait for the service to end.

When it was done, the service had its affect. Several of the women, including Leah, came to embrace Chastity. Most let her know that they did not believe the accusations made against her. Many who had thought ill against her hid their faces and shamefully walked out. However, a few remained and lifted their noses as they passed by.

The pastor had taken his post at the door to thank the people for coming. Most stopped to thank the pastor for the word. When it was Nathan's time, he extended his hand toward the pastor and pretended he enjoyed the message. He said, "I appreciate all you had to say. I should consider being a member of your congregation."

Pastor replied, "That is, if you qualify, Mr. Porter."

Nathan did not like the answer but kept his composure. He dipped his head and walked from the church building. He overheard the deacon's defense, "What do you mean, if he qualifies?"

An evil grin crossed Nathan's face. He walked to the grassy area of the church and waited. He intended to speak with Chastity.

When George and the family came out, Nathan casually approached. Looking at George, he asked, "May I have a word with Miss Shepherd."

George was defensive. "What would you want to speak with her about?"

Nathan answered, "It would be a private matter, I assure you. Just a few minutes, if you don't mind."

George calmed himself. "I think my wife should be with her."

Nathan shuddered at his response. "I have no business with her. What I have to say is for Miss Shepherd. Please allow me a private moment."

Finally, George turned to Chastity. "He wishes to speak with you. Do you accept?"

Chastity smiled and answered, "Faith takes strength."

George smiled and turned to Nathan, "You may have a few minutes."

Nathan approached Chastity and asked her to walk a little way with him. When he was sure they were far enough from listening ears, he offered, "Chastity—"

She shot back. "Miss Shepherd, if you please."

Her tone startled him, but he managed to speak. "I know you must think me a terrible rogue for all I have done, but I assure you I only want what's best."

Once again, Chastity interjected. "Best? I very much doubt that. If it is, it would be only for you."

Nathan tried to keep his control. "You can save the town and the people. If you will agree to allow me to court you, then I will lessen the hold I have on the people. Marry me, and I shall make you the happiest woman in the world."

Chastity snapped back, "Happy? I am happy. You think you can come to this church and act all dignified? Mr. Porter, people can see through you. Oh, some have given in to you because they feel threatened by you." She started to walk away but stopped to look back for a moment. "I will not give you an answer today."

Nathan smiled. "Then let's say we give it a week?"

Chastity was completely surprised. She caught her breath before replying, "We shall see."

From seemingly out of nowhere, little Faith came walking up to Chastity. She raised her arms to be picked up. Chastity lifted her, and Faith wrapped her arms around her neck. Faith looked at Nathan Porter and said, "I don't wike you. You make people k-why."

John was nearing the Dutch town of New Amsterdam. This he felt was his biggest challenge. Tensions between the Dutch and the English were growing, and war loomed. John was warned that these waters were controlled by pirates. *Pirates.* The very thought of them made him shudder. He felt fortunate to have escaped their clutches when they attacked the *Elizabeth Marie*. He did not want to have to face them again. He anticipated danger the best he could. He hoped that if pirates were in the area, they would not take notice of a lone longboat in the night. Perhaps if he saw other boats, he could join them. He had to find a way to keep from drawing attention.

He put to shore some distance south of the city. About evening time, he saw several fishing boats heading out, dropping their nets behind them. He considered moving in among them. He watched them for several hours. Suddenly, a loud boom disrupted the serenity. From out at sea, a larger ship began firing at the boats. John watched the ship as it sailed in closer. The fishermen quickly gathered their nets and hurried back to shore. John's senses were on high alert. He watched as the ship sailed in closer. The ship wasn't Dutch or English. That could mean only one thing. "Pirates," he gasped.

John understood that the pirates were watching the coast, but he could not understand why they were keeping the fisherman from catching fish. While it was an interesting thought, it wasn't the most pressing issue. He had to find a way to get past the ship and her crew. John watched as the pirates took in sails and dropped anchor. Four longboats were dropped over the side, and the crew began to board them. Oars dipped into the water. John suspected the pirates were about to raid the city. If that were the case, he might have a chance. He made up his mind. He would wait till dark, row out to open water, and then sail past the town and hopefully from danger. It would be chancy, but he had no choice. He knew that there would only be a few crewmen left on board. Hopefully the raiding party would be too busy to worry about one longboat out to sea.

Come nightfall, John began rowing out to sea. His boat was but a mark on the ocean, and at this distance, he could be mistaken for a bird or even a large fish. More than anything, he hoped none of the pirates would be taking notice. He knew he could not raise the sail until he was sure he was at a safe distance. He would be easily seen. His plan was to go out about ten miles before risking it. Rain was beginning to fall again, and the wind was picking up. The good news was that the weather reduced visibility even though the clouds remained high.

John's muscles ached with every pull on the oars. The tide was going out, which made it a bit easier, but he rowed against choppy waters. John kept watching the pirate ship. Whatever they were doing, he did not care. He was more concerned about his own safety. Everything appeared to be quiet. When he was about five miles out, he heard the ringing of the ship's bell. He wasn't sure if the alarm was meant for him or something else, but he feared that he had been spotted. From that point, fear and adrenaline overtook him. He believed he had no time to lose. As fast as he could, he stowed the oars and raised the sail. He set a course for due north. If the pirates fired on him, he wanted to be a far enough distance from their cannon range. Still, he feared the depth of the water being so far out.

John was convinced that he had to get back to shore. The wind was working against him. If the alarm was because the pirates spotted him, there would soon be heightened activity on ship and shore. If they did decided to come after him, the prevailing storm would make it hard for the pirates to reach him. He hoped they would see him as too little prey for the effort. John struggled to keep a tack that would keep him a safe distance from the pirates and yet still on course to get him to the shore.

The ocean was becoming more violent. The winds and waves increased. If the weather was turning colder, John did not notice. Adrenaline took over. John kept making corrections to the sail to make sure it was set right. He was in danger, and he knew it. The elements, more than the pirates, were threatening his life now.

While John was concentrating on making corrections, he was surprised by a large wave that rolled the longboat dangerously to port. The waves were rising to greater mounds. At times, the waves were so high John lost sight of the shore. This was the most frightening thing he had ever experienced. The boat was at risk, and it could capsize in these conditions. He realized he may have chanced the elements once too often. John prepared for the worse. He picked up the bag with the money and tied it securely to his waist.

Another wave rocked the boat from behind, dumping large amounts of water into the hull. He could not bail out the water and handle the rudder at the same time. He was still a half mile from the shore when that which he dreaded happened. A wave caught him broadside. The boat remained afloat, but just barely. The water in the boat numbed his feet and legs.

He cried out, "Where are you, Father? Don't leave me. Get me to Chastity. Father, I need Thee. Father—"

Another great wave smashed the vessel from the side and tore the mast and sail away. John went overboard with it. John was underwater and partially tangled in the sail and rope. The water was colder than he could imagine. He was in a panic and grabbed at the water, fighting to get to the surface. Finally, with one hand, he managed to lay hold of the boat and pull himself above water. He gasped for air. He felt the freezing-cold deep in his chest. His fingers were numb, but he clung to the submerged haul.

John sobbed as he made one final cry, "Father, help me!"

Saturday had come. This had been a difficult week for all concerned. It seemed all in the church had one thought: *What will Chastity do?* George still had work, because many in town trusted his reputation over the word of a complete stranger. It was hard for Susan and him as they watched Chastity in all her grief. Together, they did all they could to comfort her. They spoke of faith and trusting God, hoping these words would give her strength. Sometimes they did. Sometimes they didn't.

Chastity mused, "I do have faith in God. It is the strength to have patience that is so hard."

Needless to say, the whole week was spent in prayer.

Chastity tried to hide her fears for the children's sake, but even they knew something was wrong. Little Faith would climb into Chastity's lap and ask, "Miss Tasty, what's wong?"

Chastity did her best to assure her everything was all right, but in the end, it was Faith who spoke clearly. "It da bad man, wight?"

Chastity would just smile, but in her mind, she asked, *What is God's answer?*

Each night Chastity prayed. She asked God about John. She prayed he would come and rescue her. Many nights she fell asleep on a tear-soaked pillow. Her sleep was anything but restful. The least little sound brought her to her senses. She stayed in the cabin against George and Susan's protests. Her argument was to protect their testimony.

One night she had just fallen asleep when the door flew open. She sat straight up, and in walked Nathan. His words seemed to his hiss from his throat, and she could swear there was fire in his eyes. He walked to the bed. "It's time you were coming with me. I am tired of waiting."

With that, he reached to grab her arm. Chastity immediately sat straight up and screamed into the silence. Chastity began to sob uncontrollably, for no one was there.

In town, Nathan tried to pose himself as a pious man, but people realized he was nothing but a charlatan. Nathan did not want a wife. He was in it for the conquest. For him, women were something to pursue and have for his satisfaction. Afterward, he didn't care what happened to her. So what if her name and reputation were soiled. He would simply convince the people that he was an upstanding man and the woman pursued him. It had worked in the past, and he saw no reason that it wouldn't work now. Nathan just thought about whatever it took to win the prize.

Chastity was Nathan's biggest challenge yet. She had proved to be most difficult. She resisted his charm, ignored his advances, and disdained his comments. Nathan thought that had they been in England, he would have found ways much easier to have her than going to church. There he could offer her things, and if nothing else, he could buy his way into her heart. He sneered as he admitted to himself that he wasn't really in love with her. Oh, he was taken with her beauty, but she was also smart and devoted to another. Maybe that is why he wanted her. It was as though he had to win. In many ways, he wanted to defeat her betrothed, whoever he was. Nathan thought of women he knew on the streets of London. Sooner or later, they would sacrifice their virtue for any man who promised something more, something better. Miss Shepherd had virtue. She was dedicated to God and devoted to her beloved. Like a spoiled child, Nathan would do whatever it took to break her bond with her betrothed and be his wife. After that, who cared?

One day after teaching was done and the kids were busy with chores, Chastity sat at the harpsichord and tried to play. She could not focus and became overly upset at every mistake she made. Susan came to her, took her by the hand, and brought her to the table. Two cups were poured with a malt beverage. Susan could feel her dear friend's fears. Chastity worked hard for the family, but it was out of love more than duty. Chastity was a part of this family and would never want to bring any shame or harm to them. She felt she had done both.

The silence was broken when Susan asked, "How do you think John will come?"

Chastity said, "Don't you mean *if* he comes?"

Susan grabbed her hand. "Stop that! We must believe that he will come. I pray that he will, and I believe God will provide the way. There had to be a reason for John not being able to communicate in the past.

We don't know his circumstances. His master may not be as caring as we hope we are."

Tears formed in Chastity's eyes. "You are the most loving and caring of all." She paused and thought for a moment before continuing. "I should not have let John come to America alone."

Susan again gripped her hand. "Then you might have suffered a similar fate. Have you thought of that?"

After a moment, Chastity replied, "But we would have been together."

Susan smiled. "True, but you would not be here to be a blessing to me or to my family."

Susan's warmth comforted Chastity. Chastity calmed enough to share the secret that had been between John and her alone. Looking into Susan's eyes, she stated, "I want to tell you something that some in the church may consider wrong about John and me. We have always known something about the other. We would tell each other our dreams and thoughts. We realized that the other had experienced the same thought or experience."

Susan smiled. "I see nothing wrong with that. I know God does draw people together, and He uses dreams at times to warn and show us the way."

Then Chastity hung her head before replying. "Monday night I dreamed that John was coming here, and the boat he sailed was capsized by a great wave. I saw him beneath the water struggling to reach the surface. I saw his finger reach the surface and hang on to the boat. I could feel the terrible, cold water soaking him. I watched as he was losing strength. I heard him call out to God to save him." Chastity sobbed as she finished. "Oh, Susan, I fear he is dead. What shall I do? What shall I do?"

Susan moved closer to put her arms about Chastity. She pulled her head to her shoulder and whispered, "I have something to tell you. George and I had our faith tested before we came here. When George's master heard that he was leaving for America, his master went to the magistrates to tell them we were part of the secret assembly of believers. His master would rather have George imprisoned and destroyed than lose him. It looked bad up to the day we were about to depart. As we were preparing to board the ship, a stranger came to us with a document. What I read was most unbelievable. The contents stated that after thorough examination, there was no substantial proof of the charge and no reason to detain us." Susan moved from the table to her bedroom. When she returned, she had the document in hand. She handed it to Chastity. Susan commented, "Look at who signed the paper."

The signature at the bottom read: "Elijah Brown, special envoy of Christopher, Earl of Sussex."

Hope rose in Chastity. She remarked, "Do you know who Elijah Brown is?"

Susan responded, "No, I have never met him before."

Chastity smiled before replying, "He is my pastor."

Evening came, and the tavern was filled with the usual crowd. In a dark corner, Nathan sat with Captain Jonas. Captain Jonas was most disagreeable and expressed it. "How much longer before this scheme of yours is exposed? It has been several weeks since a Dutch ship has attempted to come into New Amsterdam. Even my men are demanding that we sail out to sea to find ships laden with goods. The only thing we have fired upon are small boats of New Amsterdam villagers. Besides, colder weather is closing in, and me crew wants to go to warmer seas."

Nathan disliked the tone of the captain but concealed his displeasure by appearing to remain calm. Nathan attempted to reassure the restless captain by saying, "I need a few more weeks. Then our agreement will end. After that, you can do as you please."

Jonas just stared at Nathan, not knowing what to say.

Nathan placed both hands on the table and asked, "So then, what have you brought me?"

Captain Jonas answered, "Have you not been listening? There haven't been any ships coming into New Amsterdam. Our agreement is already over and done. Now pay me."

The demand was troublesome to Nathan. He needed the goods to advance his plan to take control and maintain the noose on the merchants of Boston. The least little slack could jeopardize everything. If he did not have the goods people needed, they would return to other merchants. No, this news was not good, and it could mess up everything. At the same time, Nathan could not afford to pay the pirates and proceed with his plans. Nathan needed to find a way to keep the pirates under his control for a little longer.

He carefully answered, "I have something for you and your crew. I recently received it from the king. He has awarded you commissions. The documents are in my position, which entitle you to the rank of captain in His Majesty's Navy." Nathan was lying. He had no such documents, but neither Captain Jonas nor anyone else would know this. Nathan continued. "All I have to do it toss them onto the fire, and you return to the status of pirate and shall be hunted by the king. So which do you prefer, Captain? British officer or pirate?"

Jonas shot back. "I want to see the papers."

Nathan gave a fake frown. "Ah, Captain, don't you trust me?"

Jonas was sharp in his reply. "Not in the least. I want to see the papers this time tomorrow, or I shall make you wish you never met me."

Nathan laughed. "Have no fear, Captain. I shall deliver."

Captain Jonas had one more question. "Where is the money?"

Nathan sternly replied, "In the past, you always had goods with you. The money I will pay for your services is hidden safely away. You will have to wait for it. That's all."

Captain Jonas was no fool. He sneered as he spoke. "Tells you how it is going to be. Tomorrow night me lads will be in town. If we receive our money, we will leave the town be. If not, we will ransack every bit of this sorry little place. You understand me, Mr. Porter? And know this, the first one we will come after is you."

Nathan understood. "I will have everything ready. Of that, you can be assured." Nathan rose to his feet. "There is another reason I did not bring the money with me. I am about to pay respects to a particular young lady, so I really must be going."

Captain Jonas sneered, "At this time of night? What kind of lady might this be?"

Nathan lifted his head as he thought of an answer and then replied, "The most difficult kind, I assure you."

Captain Jonas stood and emptied his cup. In disgust, he wiped his bearded lips with his sleeve. He looked at Nathan and then turned and left the tavern without saying another word.

Nathan waited a while longer before moving. When he did, he moved to the bar and placed the cost of drink upon it. He regained his composure and moved toward the door. Turning back to the crowd, he proclaimed, "Me friends, it looks like a wonderful night to keep company with a most eligible woman."

Some let out a chuckle. Nathan doffed his hat and quickly exited.

A solitary figure watched him leave. In his darkened corner, he'd had heard more than he was supposed to have heard. His piercing blue eyes seemed to illuminate in the darkness from the anger he felt deep within. He stood to his feet and laid down the cost of the beer on the table. He disliked Nathan Porter, and it was time to let him know.

Nathan made his way through the dark, carefully guiding the horse through the dark New England night. He finally arrived at the drive that led to George Abernathy's house. Tonight he would present himself respectfully to George and ask his permission to see Chastity. If need be, he would apologize for his ungentlemanly ways by going to her cabin unannounced. He was sure he could convince a simple-minded man like George that his ways were truly honorable.

Nathan climbed off the horse and tied him to a nearby tree. He would walk the rest of the way to the house. Just as Nathan turned to walk up the driveway, a strong hand gripped his shoulder and spun him around. Before Nathan could utter a single word, a hand clenched into a fist hit him squarely between the eyes.

Nathan fell to the earth and remained motionless. The lone figure drug the unconscious man to lean him against the same tree the horse was tied to. For a minute or so, the stranger looked at Mr. Nathan Porter before speaking. "I will take it from here." He then turned and moved toward the house where he saw a low glow of light in the window. He thought, *I think I will see this most eligible woman.*

The wind blew against the house. Tree limbs scratched at the outer walls. A single candle shed its light into the room.

Chastity sat at the table, twisting the ring John had given her around her finger. She whispered, "Where are you, my love?" She looked at Susan. "Maybe my faith isn't strong enough after all. Maybe this is God's answer." She folded her arms and laid her head on them. She began to sob once again, and Susan rushed to her to give comfort.

There was a knock at the door. Everyone suspected it was Nathan.

George sighed. "Seems the man wasted no time." George rose to his feet and walked over to open the door. When he did, there stood the stranger. The light revealed a tall man. He wore canvas cut from a sail like a cape about his broad shoulders. Ocean-blue eyes peered from the canvas hood. His blond hair was long, and he had a beard to match. Though a young man, his face showed lines made by the seas he had traveled. It was obvious he had traveled far.

Nothing was said between the two men until George invited, "Please come in. We have been expecting you."

The sailor walked toward the fire and reached his hands to warm them. Susan looked in his direction. She was puzzled. She was about to ask George who this man was, but he placed a finger to his lips.

Chastity remained still. The stranger untied the canvas robe and laid it over a chair. His clothes were soiled and badly wrinkled. He ran his hands through his hair and then turned to face the sobbing figure at the table.

Susan stood and walked over to look more closely at the tall, young stranger. She stopped a couple of feet short of him. She looked into his deep-blue eyes and smiled.

With a nod of his head, the sailor walked over and placed his hand on Chastity's shoulder. The touch was a familiar one to her. He called to her, "Chastity, my darling, I made it."

Chastity knew the voice. It was more than she could imagine. She lifted her head from the table and spun around to look at the shaggy, weather-beaten man. She stood to her feet, looking constantly into the ocean-blue eyes of the man she loved. She threw her arms around his neck and sobbed all the more. "John, my beloved, you came for me."

John smiled. "Aye, my love. I have."